THE UNDEAD CHRONICLES VOLUME 4

No Sanctuary

PATRICK J. O'BRIAN

FIDELI PUBLISHING, INC.

ISBN: 978-1-962402-60-6

Special thanks to Ron Meikle, Brad Wiemer,
Jobina Wiemer, Steve Couch,

Jeff Groves, Kelly Joe Watson, Dave Blackford,
Kendrick Shadoan, and John Herrick.

This book is dedicated to the memory of
Elisabeth Kathleen Couch, who was taken from this world too soon.

Other novels by
Patrick J. O'Brian include:

The Fallen

Reaper (Book 1 of the West Baden Murders Series)

The Brotherhood

Retribution (Book 2 of the West Baden Murders Series)

Stolen Time

Sins of the Father (Book 3 of the West Baden Murders Series)

Six Days

Dysfunction (Book 1 of the Terry Levine Detective Series)

The Sleeping Phoenix

Snowbound (Book 4 of the West Baden Murders Series)

Sawmill Road (Book 2 of the Terry Levine Detective Series)

Ghosts of West Baden (Book 5 of the West Baden Murders Series)

Red Rain (Book 3 of the Terry Levine Detective Series)

Sin Killer (Book 4 of the Terry Levine Detective Series)

The Doomsday Clock (Book 6 of the West Baden Murders Series)

Hallowed Grounds

The Undead Chronicles Volume 1: Home and Back Again

Uncertain Terms

The Undead Chronicles Volume 2: Darker Days

The Undead Chronicles Volume 3: Dead of Winter

Non-fiction works by Patrick J. O'Brian include:

Risen from the Ashes: The History of the West Baden Springs Hotel

Pluto in the Valley: The History of the French Lick Springs Hotel

Learn more about Patrick and his projects at:

www.pjobooks.com

Chapter 1

Friday August 26, The Previous Year

Brooke Palacio felt a sudden dread about the upcoming weekend, because her boyfriend unexpectedly coming home threw a monkey wrench in her plans.

An assignment at work had her traveling to a luxury resort to cover some upcoming events on the grounds, but her trip and her assignment were both a ruse. Brooke often posed as a reporter, usually under her own name, placing her in close proximity to famous and wealthy people. Adept as a reporter, and a mole for the CIA, she kept the two occupations separate in her mind, knowing her work for the government took precedence over all else.

She didn't particularly love her surname, because it brought about teasing as a child, and even now she envisioned being on the evening news, given an introduction by the news anchors.

"And here with a look at the weekend forecast is Brooke Palacio."

In reality, the surname originated overseas in Spain, where her great-grandfather was born. He migrated to the United States just before the first World War, finding love with a woman who helped him navigate the English language while he worked in a paper mill.

"This is the worst," her boyfriend said as he sat despondently on her living room sofa.

John Canfield worked as a coach for the only Major League Baseball team north of the United States, until two days prior when the head coach was fired, along with Canfield, the pitching coach, and the bench coach. For some reason, team management decided to hire a new coach, who wanted to bring his own people into the organization. Canfield became collateral damage, despite drawing interest from other organizations for management positions. He began coaching in the minor leagues after injuries hampered his abilities as a catcher, keeping him from reaching his full potential.

"You're going to get a new job," Brooke assured him. "A better one."

Canfield groaned, and while Brooke felt for him, she didn't particularly need her boyfriend sitting in her Chicago apartment the day before she headed one state over for an assignment the CIA deemed crucial.

"You've already gotten messages," she told him. "Most of them can't talk to you until the offseason."

"That's basically November," he lamented. "Then it's off to a new team, which means moving again."

Canfield kept a small house in a Buffalo suburb, which he rented while managing his organization's Triple-A affiliate the previous season. Seeing how Toronto was virtually a hop across the border, he kept the residence when he received a promotion to coach at the top tier.

"It's a rental, John," Brooke noted.

"I know. Glad I took your advice about renting."

When Brooke suggested he rent, her intention was to keep people from discovering where he lived through online property searches, but Canfield figured she meant not to put down roots.

Although her apartment contained modern furnishings, located near several Chicago airports, it lacked a personal feel. Canfield once asked why she didn't display family photos after making mention that her apartment didn't appear to be lived in. In truth, she spent very little time in her residence, or Chicago for that matter, because the CIA kept her on assignment much of the time.

Due to the nature of her job, she kept her relationship with Canfield casual. She required a partner with some clout, who allowed her to travel, but also had some connections she couldn't secure on her own. Purely by accident, she met Canfield while covering a sports fundraiser in Buffalo, which was her cover for a larger assignment. Brooke managed to report on the event, uncover crucial information about a government infrastructure hacking, and woo Canfield in the course of two days. Although athletes weren't part of her typical dating pool, she rather liked the former catcher, who was recently divorced.

Between his travels, and the fact that he made time for his two children from his previous marriage, Brooke figured he was nearly perfect for her cover, and for entry to some select groups. For the most part, Brooke dictated when they met, because she was often on assignment, or simply told him she was if she didn't want to rendezvous for a few days.

A few months short of forty years, Canfield sported a complete, brown beard that matched his full head of hair. He had recently gone from a hairstyle a bit too young for him, due to a lost bet with one of his players, to growing his hair to a conventional, short length. Although he remained in terrific condition, his body type was a bit stocky by baseball player standards because he was a catcher during his playing days. Possessing eyes of a caramel color, and a full face, Canfield appeared and conducted himself as the type of man capable of defending his partner.

Brooke required no protection, but she kept her training and abilities hidden, allowing Canfield to be himself.

"You're still getting paid, right?" she inquired.

"Yeah. They can't get out of that unless I breach the terms of the contract."

More than likely, the team didn't need to buy out his contract because he didn't make nearly as much as a head coach, so they didn't see a need to involve lawyers and agents.

"How long before you leave out?" he inquired, acting a bit needy by his own standards, though she understood losing his job certainly left a hole in his life.

And his bank account in a few months.

"I'm heading out tomorrow morning for a story at a resort."

"Sounds like a fluff piece," he noted, defending her talents by saying without words that such a story was beneath her.

Perhaps he wanted her to cancel the assignment and spend time healing his wounded ego.

"They can't all win me a Pulitzer," Brooke commented, though she had never nabbed any award beyond a few regional recognitions.

Canfield's phone dinged, indicating he had another text message. Since his release from the organization, his phone had provided him with well-wishes and a few indications that might become offers during the winter months.

"One of my former players," Canfield said without elaboration, sounding a bit despondent, though Brooke could tell he wasn't trying to drown her in his depression.

"Look, why don't you come with me on this assignment?" she asked, almost regretting her words the moment she said them, because the CIA made it clear that their assignments superseded all else.

"I don't want to interfere," Canfield objected.

Brooke had already laid the trap, and sprung it personally, so there was no retracting the offer.

"I won't be available every minute," she said, buying the freedom she required, "but there's lots to do, and you'll be able to relax."

"Relax, huh?" Canfield asked with a smirk.

"It's a small-town resort that thrives on convention business."

"Doesn't sound especially exciting."

Brooke walked over, using her right forefinger to rub the underside of his chin, seductively scratching his beard.

"After a hard day's work, I'm going to need to unwind," she said, slowly drawing a smile from her boyfriend of three years.

"That sounds promising."

Breaking away from him just as suddenly, Brooke crossed the room to check her own cell phone for updates. Finding none, she returned her gaze to Canfield, who suddenly appeared very interested in preoccupying his mind with some foreplay.

"We'll have time for that later," she promised.

Canfield proved a very well-trained lover, for which she couldn't take credit, but she questioned how many women he had bedded during his life, particularly his baseball days. Infidelity wasn't the demise of his marriage, but she didn't picture most athletes remaining monogamous during their heydays.

Brooke never prodded him too harshly about his sexual exploits, because she kept so much secret from him, including the fact that she sometimes slept with other men, and occasionally women, to complete her assignments. She remained extremely careful to avoid sexual diseases, and once considered a tubal ligation to prevent accidental pregnancy, but a lack of downtime prevented the procedure from taking place. Dating a father of two helped her avoid any talk of children before their biological clocks kept them from being effective parents. Canfield appeared committed to his son and daughter, visiting them whenever possible, and paying regular support, which might be jeopardized by his unemployed status.

"I hope you didn't unpack," Brooke said, turning to find Canfield unbuttoning his shirt. She shook her head. "I already said no to the naked games."

"I wasn't taking your comments at face value," he said, continuing to undo buttons between glances at her until she broke into a smile.

She walked over to him, planting a long overdue kiss on his lips, drawing a light moan from Canfield as his body grew less tense in her embrace.

"Don't get undressed," she said, breaking away once again. "We have a dinner reservation at Enrique's tonight."

"Seriously?" he asked.

"I'm buying."

"That's not what I meant."

Enrique's was a fine dining restaurant not far from the hubbub of downtown Chicago, within reasonable driving distance from her apartment. Typically, the couple went there to celebrate, but she needed to distract Canfield for his own good.

"Did you bring a tie?" she questioned.

"Don't I have like five of them in your closet?"

"Might as well call it your closet with everything you have in there," Brooke commented as she strolled into the bedroom to check her own attire.

Despite his part-time living arrangement at her apartment, Canfield had managed to equal her number of clothing items, as though dropping hints that they should make their partnership more permanent. Neither had made mention of the notion, though Brooke wouldn't be surprised if he popped the question at any given moment. She didn't expect a marriage proposal until Canfield landed another job, and she wasn't sure how marriage fit into her plans, or her career. Brooke kept her life practical, and free of attachments, but she wasn't getting any younger. A position that didn't involve lies and deception might prove more practical, though she felt her work meant something.

Canfield said he loved her first, and though she said it in return, Brooke didn't mean it the first time. Love wasn't something she grew up with, and Brooke wasn't entirely certain she knew how the emotion felt, but her relationship with Canfield felt right. She absolutely cared about him, or she wouldn't have risked her weekend assignment by inviting him.

He followed her into the bedroom, opening the second closet to rummage through his clothes in search of formal attire. Although Canfield tended to dress reasonably well wherever he traveled, he rarely donned a sport coat and tie. Plucking a different shirt from the closet, he held a few ties up to it, trying to figure out which combination worked best.

Brooke pointed to one of the ties in passing, and he returned the other tie to the closet.

"Do we really have to go out for dinner?" he questioned. "Delivery sounds perfectly acceptable."

"You just want to get in your comfy clothes and be lazy," Brooke called to him as she put a few dishes away in the kitchen. "I'm not letting that happen."

"I work my ass off," Canfield complained. "I feel like I've earned it."

He returned to the kitchen where they locked eyes from across the room.

"We're going out," Brooke said the final word. "We're celebrating the fact that a year from now you're going to be managing your own Major League team."

Canfield grinned as though he didn't believe her assessment.

"You've earned it, and that general manager was too chicken shit to promote you because he'd look stupid for not giving you the job sooner."

"Sounds like you've got it all figured out," Canfield said, taking a few steps closer to her. "I'm still not sold on celebrating the day after I was fired."

"You need it," Brooke said, placing a finger over his lips. "And if you don't finish dinner, you can't have dessert."

Canfield lit up like a firefly, turning around to check something in the bedroom.

"So, where is this place we're heading tomorrow, and are we driving?" he called.

"It's a resort south of Indianapolis," Brooke informed him. "We're taking a small plane out of Chicago in the morning, and flying directly to their local airport."

Brooke needed to update her reservation and inform the CIA that her boy-friend was accompanying her, since they hired the pilot and plane for her assignment. She wasn't sure her supervisors would approve, but Brooke could easily play it off as part of her cover.

"What kinds of things can we do at this place?"

"Oh, there's horseback riding, go-kart racing, bowling, spa stuff, and your favorite," Brooke said before pausing a few seconds. "Golf."

"Sounds fancy," Canfield commented from the bedroom. "Can't say I ever thought there was much south of Indianapolis, though."

"There isn't until you reach Louisville," Brooke commented.

A few minutes later, Canfield emerged from the bedroom, wearing the shirt and tie Brooke chose, along with tasteful slacks and a sport coat that finished his ensemble. She chose her dress the moment she decided to call the restaurant to place a reservation. With his schedule, she hadn't seen Canfield much since the spring, and she knew he needed a morale boost after such an unexpected blow. Managers being terminated through a regular season wasn't uncommon, but the remainder of the coaching staff typically remained the rest of the year to provide stability. Canfield kept a solid rapport with most of his players, which might have explained a need for his departure if management wasn't going to promote him.

"Full suit felt like a bit much," he said sweeping his hands up and down his torso, seeking approval from Brooke.

"You're fine."

"You always say that, and then you look like a million bucks compared to me with those designer dresses."

"They aren't designer dresses," she told him, like she had a dozen times previously.

He gave a cagy grin, accomplishing his goal of getting a rise from her.

Although he never addressed the issue directly with Brooke, Canfield har-bored a complex that he wasn't good enough for her. He often alluded to her beauty, possibly out of fear of losing her, but she caught him thoughtfully admir-ing her when doing so. Not overly jealous by nature, Canfield didn't particularly appreciate it when other men gave Brooke compliments or second glances in public, but he resisted acting on any impulses.

Unless her job deemed it necessary, Brooke never stepped out on Canfield, because she never found evidence that he slept with other women. Though the pair seldom saw one another throughout the year, their jobs kept them occupied, and they kept in regular communication. Just over a year into their relationship, the pair discussed being exclusive because they didn't have the time or energy to seek other partners.

"Give me a few minutes," Brooke said as she slipped past Canfield, closing the door behind her.

"Are you trying to surprise me?" he called through the closed door.

"I can't imagine how that would work," she retorted. "You've seen the goods."

Canfield chuckled.

When Brooke said she required a few minutes to change, she meant it. Her job made her exceptionally good at improvising on the fly, which sometimes included a swift change of clothing. She also hated wasting time because being efficient meant survival in the field, and the ability to accomplish more in her home life.

Nearly ten minutes later, she emerged from the bedroom, wearing an emerald dress with silver sequins in moderation along the upper portion of the garment. A necklace of white gold dangled from her neck, stopping just short of her chest, and her heels matched the color of her dress almost perfectly.

"Are you secretly a millionaire?" Canfield questioned when she stood before him, his eyes looking her up and down while his imagination likely undressed her.

"Says the professional baseball player."

"*Former* baseball player, and former coach, thank you."

"You're going to find work," Brooke said, grabbing her car keys from the countertop. "People will talk if I'm dating an unemployed homeless person."

"Wow," Canfield said with arched eyebrows. "So now I'm on the streets as well."

"You'll bounce back, and we both know it," Brooke said confidently, and they both knew she was kidding about the homeless comment.

As they prepared to head out for the evening, the couple had no idea they were about to enjoy their last fine dining experience.

Chapter 2

Saturday, August 27

Flying to the airport on the outskirts of French Lick, Indiana, didn't prove eventful on Saturday morning. Brooke's agency provided a small corporate jet for her to use, though not fancy enough for Canfield to question who covered the tab. When they landed, a rental car covered by the CIA awaited them, with the keys at the counter inside. Every aspect of Brooke's cover was secured by her employers, because they didn't want a soul knowing that an unassuming reporter worked for the government.

After requesting that Canfield drive them to the resort, Brooke checked her messages through a secured agency app on her phone, receiving an update.

CLARKE ARRIVING LATER TONIGHT. DELAYED BY MEETING WITH NADEAU.

Recently, Brooke's portfolio of work mostly included keeping tabs on associates of Jean Pierre Nadeau, because the FBI, and the CIA, received information that the man's personal and business practices had changed radically. While the government wasn't in the habit of monitoring business tycoons, Nadeau wasn't an American, despite many dealings in the United States. His net worth ranged between hundreds of millions and a few billion, depending on the day and the stock market.

Keeping tabs on Nadeau wouldn't prove difficult for the government, because he was a public figure. Instead, they chose to watch his associates and dealings because recently he wasn't spending money on philanthropic causes, posting on social media, or pushing the charge for a cleaner, greener planet.

"Brooke?" Canfield asked for the second or third time, bringing her back from the message to the green fields, tractors, and carports blurring past the car window.

"What is it?" she asked.

"You okay?"

"I'm fine."

"Thought I lost you there for a sec. I need to know where and when to turn."

Directing Canfield to continue driving north, Brooke turned up the volume on her phone so he could hear the directions. She didn't want to sync her phone to the car's Bluetooth, because Brooke knew better than to trust networks. Virtually every device possessed some kind of memory, and some harbored means to steal information.

Once again, she stole a glance at her phone's screen when a new message arrived.

CLARKE RESERVATION UNCHANGED.
TONIGHT AND TOMORROW NIGHT AT WEST BADEN SPRINGS.

"Everything okay?" Canfield inquired.

"Work stuff."

When the town of French Lick came into view, the couple saw a clean downtown, complete with murals painted on historic buildings. Casino money clearly helped maintain the area, and develop it based on the number of new gazebos and buildings with makeovers. Passing several local restaurants, a museum, and a central gazebo near a Denny's, they spotted the French Lick Springs Hotel on the left. Lengthy, and constructed from bricks painted a particular shade of yellow, the hotel stood six stories tall, complete with parking areas and a casino directly attached. Brooke didn't plan on gambling unless Rupert Clarke decided to try his hand at the slots or blackjack.

Clarke's delayed arrival provided Brooke more time to prepare for her spying activities. She imagined the man shared her distrust of technology, so she needed to set up audio and video surveillance that didn't rely on hacking into the resort's computers and servers. Fortunately, she knew he was staying in a suite at the West Baden Springs Hotel. She could inquire if any of the other suites were free, and if not, use her influence as a reporter to at least request a room on the same floor once she learned his room number.

"Interesting place," Canfield commented when their car crossed the invisible threshold that divided the towns of French Lick and West Baden Springs.

"I think 'quaint' might be the word you're looking for," Brooke commented as a few large buildings appeared ahead of them.

Either might have served as hotels in the past, but appeared to be welcoming centers, or something else in the present. Not until she glanced to her left, and spied a large yellow building with a red dome roof did she find her interest captured. Online photos failed to do the historic structure justice, and she almost failed to tell Canfield where to turn at a large arch painted the same color as the hotel.

She noticed Canfield ease up a bit as his grip on the steering wheel loosened, and he began to settle into vacation mode. He needed a distraction from his temporarily bleak life, and although Brooke required space enough to carry out her mission, she knew how to keep her boyfriend occupied. Canfield drove them under the right side of the arch, onto a red brick driveway that led to the hotel, and eventually wrapped around to the parking lot. As they passed the mammoth structure, Brooke stared upward, finding the yellow much the same color as the hotel in French Lick. Flowers and shrubs appeared trimmed to perfection, and the hotel felt remote from the two small towns and everyday life.

"I'm sure you see all kinds of places like this during your travels," she noted because Canfield paid more attention to his driving than their surroundings.

"You act like you never leave your apartment sometimes, Brooke," he commented. "And, no, I don't see places like this on the road because we get ushered inside by security teams and advised to obey curfews."

Although she felt bad that Canfield lost his job because of his affiliation with the manager, Brooke couldn't bear to coddle him much longer with his First World problems. He spent his adult years getting paid to play a game, and later, mold young men into slightly more mature versions of themselves. Meanwhile, she put her life on the line without fanfare, receiving government pay, and solving real problems. Brooke would never know how many lives she saved during her missions, because she *prevented* attacks and issues from ever happening.

"So, when do you start with interviews and research?" Canfield inquired.

"Interviews?"

"Aren't you reviewing the place?"

"Well, yeah, but there won't be many formal interviews. I may head to the library and see about the background information."

Brooke couldn't believe how adept she'd become at lying the past decade, because of her job.

Sadly, Canfield was about the closest thing to family remaining in her life. Brooke never had blood siblings, and her parents died when she was young. Their untimely ends opened certain doors for her that a conventional life wouldn't have permitted. Given opportunities to attend college, or trade school, Brooke wasn't sure what career she might have chosen if things had turned out differently.

In the back of the hotel, Brooke took notice of the valet station where several vehicles parked, their owners unloading luggage, or tipping the valets who fetched their rides. Canfield started to slow, but she looked at him with skeptical eyes.

"I don't make valet money," she said, "and we both have two good arms."

"Fine," Canfield replied, lightly stepping on the gas to head up a short hill to the standard parking lot.

A few minutes later, they grabbed their luggage from the car, made their way down the sidewalk to the hotel, and stepped through double sliding glass doors into a hallway built without corners.

Brooke looked to her right, then her left, seeing the hallway curve in either direction, meaning the dome hotel truly was round and the exterior wasn't simply an optical illusion. She asked a bellhop about the check-in desk, and he directed the couple through a set of double doors, already propped open, that led to a mammoth space flooded with natural light. Canfield stepped through first, his eyes immediately looking upward to the underside of a roof that possessed alternating skylights and traditional roofing materials in four-side shapes that weren't perfect rectangles due to the slope of the domed roof.

"Wow," he muttered, taking in the atrium bathed in natural light, with comfortable lobby furniture atop designer carpeting that took up most of the floor.

A small café occupied a portion of the atrium, and several people ate brunch, or drank coffee blends typically found in expensive shops, since the appropriate hour for spirits was a few hours away. Both Brooke and Canfield toted their wheeled luggage across the expanse of the room, which Brooke estimated spanned at least half of a football field.

Although Brooke still didn't know what floor, or exactly which suite Clarke reserved, she suspected a man of his means wanted the best accommodations. After reviewing a dossier provided to her by the agency, she learned that Clarke enjoyed his money, and liked to flaunt his wealth. She made small talk with the desk staff, learning that a few floors housed several types of suites, but the top floor contained the largest room. The sixth-floor suite contained several bedrooms, a kitchenette, a conference area, and a few amenities the other luxurious rooms did not. It cost nearly five figures per night, when available, because hotel ownership sometimes used it for meetings, or to impress VIP guests.

Canfield milled around the lobby area, taking in the stained-glass windows, original floor tiles, and some large frame photographs that showed the hotel in a state of decay some decades prior.

"Where is our room located?" she asked the receptionist.

"The hotel arranged for you to review one of the suites on the third floor. It has a hot tub, and-"

"Are there any rooms on the top floor?" Brooke inquired, keeping her voice down so Canfield didn't hear her trying to alter their accommodations.

Appearing puzzled, the receptionist checked her computer terminal, tilting her head slightly sideways at the results.

"We have two rooms, both facing outward," she informed Brooke, implying the view outside wasn't as beautiful as the inner rooms that overlooked the atrium.

"That would be great," Brooke said.

"You're sure?"

"Positive," Brooke replied as Canfield strolled her way, giving a look to the clerk that she wanted to keep the change of venue discreet.

A few seconds later, the young woman handed her a packet complete with map of the grounds, two keycards, and a paper that listed their room number on the sixth floor. She went through the map with them, indicating their room's location in relation to the elevators and ice machines. Because no one else was waiting behind the couple, she explained some of the activities on the grounds to them, including the spa, golf, horseback riding, and tours.

Canfield waited until they were approaching the elevator with their luggage, to speak about their room.

"You're reviewing this place and they put us in the center of the top floor?" he questioned with an arched eyebrow.

"I requested a standard room," Brooke lied. "It'll give me a feel for a typical stay, and it saved a few dollars."

"You need to work for a better publication. You're better than standard room rates."

A few seconds later, the elevator door opened, granting them access as they pulled their luggage in behind them.

"You talk as though you read my articles," Brooke chided him.

"They're on my tablet, so I read them between games when I had a job."

Brooke gave him a quizzical stare.

"You really read my stuff?" she asked as the elevator car ascended.

"I believe I've said so in the past."

"I thought you were just saying that to appease me."

"When have I ever lied to you?" Canfield asked, taken aback.

"Never, that I'm aware of."

Now he gave her a rather sour stare.

"I'm to the point in my life that I don't want to play games. I may not have employment at the moment, but I'll get back on my feet, and I want you to be part of my life going forward. If that ever changes, I'm not going to screw around. I'll tell you I'm unhappy, and we'll end it, but I don't see that happening, because I think we still have things to learn about one another."

Brooke suspected her boyfriend didn't know the half of it. In truth, she wasn't sure how to respond to such honesty, because her life choices prevented her from being forthcoming.

Fortunately, the elevator gave a ding, and the door slid open, revealing a small lobby and two directional choices. For the moment, Brooke felt spared from responding to his heartfelt words, wishing she were capable of being so open.

"Feel free to respond," Canfield said about halfway to their room as they each pulled their suitcases with them.

"If you're asking if I've been with someone else, the answer is no," Brooke told a partial fib, stopping to address Canfield directly. "I don't want to be with anyone else, and I'm happy with the way things are between us."

Although Brooke had slept with other people during the course of her duties, she didn't consider her actions a betrayal, because she didn't lust after another man. Relief washed across Canfield's face at her words, possibly because he required assurances in his current state.

Brooke took a few seconds to admire the mix of contemporary and vintage replicas in the grand hotel. Much of the carpet, and the décor, was created with gold, olive green, beige, and red colorations, giving each piece a regal feel. Light fixtures mounted to the walls looked Victorian, and again, the hallway continued in one unbreaking circle.

A few minutes later, they walked into their room, left their luggage near the door, and sighed collective relief that the weekend was their own, minus any work on Brooke's part.

Canfield walked to the window, finding it stared outside, which overlooked portions of the hotel, more so than the large garden, outdoor pool, or the brick path.

"Not much of a view," he commented.

"Again, typical stay," Brooke reminded him.

Canfield grunted, possibly thinking she deserved better, never suspecting she gave up a luxurious suite. She had learned that he didn't expect people to know him in public, though an occasional studious fan knew him from his now former team, or from his minor league playing days. He never declined to give an autograph, and Brooke always giggled at his expense when she saw his old baseball cards, because he had no facial hair and a baby face in those days.

Part of the reason she felt she couldn't ever wed Canfield was the fact that he didn't know the true her, and he deserved transparency before entering such a commitment.

Her phone vibrated, indicating she needed to communicate with her liaison at work. Brooke had never met the person she knew as Taylor in person, and truly knew nothing about him or her. Because the content of the work messages was so straightforward, Brooke couldn't discern any clues from the wording.

"I need to go set a few things up," she told Canfield, who nodded.

"I'll check out the grounds and stretch my legs in a few."

Brooke exited the room with her keycard, walking down to one of the rest spots, which the hotel considered small lobby areas. Typically adorned with a few chairs and a floral centerpiece atop a small table, they passed for lobbies, she supposed. Brooke took a seat, pulling out her phone for a look at the most recent message.

CLARKE LEASING TOP FLOOR SUITE FOR TWO NIGHTS.

Without feeling smug, a wave of relief washed over Brooke for guessing correctly about the suite.

She considered it odd the man wanted to stay into Monday, but the information allowed her to extend her own stay and create an excuse for Canfield to stay with her. She didn't think he would mind, considering he didn't exactly have baseball teams knocking down his door during the regular season. During the winter, she suspected he might field numerous offers, because he was ready to manage a team on a larger stage, and players loved and respected him.

Only twice had she visited his home near Buffalo, discovering he kept memorabilia from high school, college, and his brief minor league career. More telling, he also kept notes and keepsakes from players he had coached, thanking him and showing their appreciation. In a world where everything was done in text messages and emails, such gestures felt rare.

Brooke didn't know much about Rupert Clarke, because he wasn't a public figure like Nadeau. He owned several businesses, and therefore, numerous factories, in Canada and the United States. She knew her employers didn't waste time, money, or energy on false leads, so something about Clarke caught their attention. She didn't possess details, likely because they didn't know exactly what to have her observe. The fact that Nadeau had gone radio silent across social media, and the news couldn't pinpoint his location or activities worried them.

She agreed with their analysis.

Her phone chimed again with another message.

ADDITIONAL INFORMATION FORTHCOMING TONIGHT OR TOMORROW MORNING.

Brooke read the message, deciding to respond, though it wasn't necessary.

THANKS, TAYLOR.

Brooke seldom replied, because she never received responses with any personality in return. She felt almost certain her contact knew almost everything about her, and she possessed only a name and a phone app in return.

Giving an audible sigh, she decided to explore the hotel, and the grounds, before meeting up with Canfield again.

***

Two Days Later

Brooke felt like a failure on Monday morning, both to her government and the people who paid her salary.

As expected, Clarke kept a tight lid on his electronic devices, but worse, he seemed reluctant to use them, much like his associate Nadeau. Brooke had managed to secretly set up a miniature camera and microphone in the small lobby just outside his suite. The lobby could easily hold a half dozen tables and appropriate seating if necessary, but only a few small tables with fresh flowers occupied the space at the moment. Brooke made certain to remove her devices from the vase on Sunday morning before fresh flowers were delivered, and on this morning, she simply moved them to the underside of one of the tables while pretending to check her phone and drop it on the floor.

Clarke arrived with a younger woman who was not his wife on Saturday evening, and mostly kept to himself except to eat and enjoy the hot tub at one point. Brooke conducted several brief interviews to make her stay appear legitimate to Canfield and the hotel staff, but she learned facts that she could have easily researched online.

When she stepped downstairs that morning, Brooke knew her checkout time was shortly before lunch, meaning mere hours remained to discover anything useful about Clarke. The informational packet arrived through her phone app on Sunday, providing little additional information about Clarke, or his affiliation with Nadeau. She knew the man's factories were altering some production lines, which didn't sound entirely out of the ordinary.

Her phone acted as the means to watch and listen whenever her devices detected movement or noise in front of the suite, much like wireless home security systems. She had yet to catch anything meaningful from Clarke whenever he stepped outside of the suite, though he seemed to have a good time with his companion.

Brooke could relate, having given herself to Canfield each night during their stay. She had spent time with him, including dinner on Sunday evening after he went on a horseback riding tour in the afternoon. She kidded him about being from Texas, and riding horses being second nature to him, which he denied, saying he hadn't been on a horse since his teenage years.

Taking a break from fretting about her lack of progress, Brooke took the elevator to the ground floor, walking around until she ended up inside a library just off the main lobby. Filler books occupied the shelves within, likely to prevent theft, and a community computer was available for guests to check emails, or surf the web. She paid the room little attention, finding the lighting too low, and the dark wallpaper and heavy wood accents rather depressing. Instead, she walked to the window, where she found her boyfriend seated in one of the outdoor veranda chairs, enjoying the last morning before they headed back to Illinois.

Pensively staring ahead towards the sunken garden, Canfield drew on an expensive cigar he purchased at one of the local shops. Brooke had gotten him to give up chewing tobacco, at least in her presence, and she wasn't about to dampen his weekend by denying him one guilty pleasure.

Deciding to leave him to his thoughts, she found an exit in a different area of the hotel, stepping outside to enjoy the morning air before the heat and humidity left the area unbearable. Green shrubs and colorful flowers planted by the grounds crew swayed gently in the morning breeze, creating a sense of calm for the guests isolated from big city life. If not for her assignment, Brooke might have fallen prey to such tranquility, but tragic days in history often started in much the same way.

Brooke's phone indicated she had a message just before she considered stepping off the sidewalk and heading into the garden.

NADEAU ALLIES ARE ALL TRAVELING TO VARIOUS DESTINATIONS RIGHT NOW. SOMETHING BIG IS ABOUT TO HAPPEN.

Brooke's mind immediately went to dark days in her country's history where bombs exploded, planes were hijacked, and towers fell to the ground. She couldn't fathom Nadeau orchestrating such a mammoth attack without someone, somewhere, knowing something more than the travel plans of his associates.

She decided to inquire, because Taylor never spouted random messages to her, and this sounded borderline nervous.

DO YOU HAVE INSTRUCTIONS OR OPTIONS FOR ME?

Brooke turned around, prepared to head inside in case she needed to tail Clarke, or subdue him to search for additional evidence.

STAY CLOSE TO CLARKE IN CASE HE TRIES TO LEAVE. SEE IF YOU CAN FIGURE OUT WHERE HE'S GOING NEXT.

Knowing she needed to return to the sixth floor to keep an eye on Clarke, Brooke began to question her surveillance equipment. Neither Clarke, nor his companion, had stepped outside the room all morning. She recalled them receiving room service and the staff bringing the cart directly inside their room. Brooke questioned why the man needed a suite for a mere two people, beginning to think he spent the weekend constructing something nefarious, rather than catering to his ego.

She walked into her room, finding Canfield had left the television on one of the local stations. Brooke walked over to her suitcase, unzipping it to find zip ties, a syringe that could inject toxin with the push of a button, and her handgun, complete with suppressor. Brooke didn't know the extent of what methods she might need to subdue Clarke with the threat level basically in the red. Wearing blue jeans and a green button-up shirt for comfortable travel, and now to conceal the tools of her trade, Brooke was about to step outside her room when breaking news caught her attention on the television.

Glued to the television for the next five minutes, she watched as footage displayed an explosion in a Michigan factory where car components were manufactured. By all accounts, the damage appeared minimal, and most workers suffered from what the reporters termed smoke inhalation. Many were being transported to the hospital, and speculation from eyewitnesses indicated the act might be that of terrorists, rather than an accident.

"Shit," Brooke muttered, pulling out her phone.

As she did so, a message appeared, indicating Taylor saw the same footage.

IT'S HAPPENING.
LANSING AND LITTLE ROCK SO FAR.

Brooke contemplated her next move.

If Nadeau's friends and business partners were all mobile, why would Clarke remain in rural Indiana? Either he wasn't in the loop, or he had an objective to complete before leaving for whatever safe haven awaited him. She was about to step outside the room when the news reported an incident of similar nature in Little Rock, and another in Portland, Oregon. She decided she wasn't going to wait any longer, and as she stepped into the hallway, she didn't hear a sound. More than likely, the few remaining hotel guests were staring at televisions, or attempting to check out.

She passed a room with a cart outside and a cleaning lady inside, holding a sheet she had pulled off the bed, while her eyes remained fixed on the television.

"And we have reports of similar incidents in Bakersfield, Knoxville, and Atlanta," a female reporter's voice echoed into the hallway.

With the cleaning lady transfixed on the news, Brooke looked over the cart for any kind of keycard that might gain her access to the suite. She suspected that staff members likely kept the master cards on their person, meaning Brooke might need to subdue or outwit the hotel staff to obtain a card. Fortunately, she found a keycard magnetically adhered to the underside of a metal shelf on one end of the cart, and she plucked the plastic device free before heading directly to Clarke's room.

An older couple walked past her as she made her way down the hall, and Brooke felt thankful she hadn't reached for her pistol yet. Part of her questioned whether she dared blow her cover in plain view of hotel security cameras, but

Taylor had never led her astray with bad information, and this threat appeared valid, and spreading like wildfire.

Standing outside the main door to the suite, Brooke drew a deep breath, placed the card inside the slot, and opened the door inward, prepared to reach for her firearm if necessary.

Instead, she peered inside, finding the conference room area directly in front of her with the small kitchen off to the right. Daring not stand in the open doorway for very long, she stepped inside, flipping the security latch and letting the door close against the device, so it didn't secure. Standing perfectly still a moment, Brooke heard voices farther within the suite. She stepped forward, finding additional rooms to either side, but the discussion emanated from a bedroom at the end of the hallway.

Quietly stepping towards the room, Brooke listened for evidence in their discussion, but the couple spoke conversationally. For a moment she thought perhaps she misread everything about her messages from Taylor, and the breaking news. For all she knew, Clarke traveled to a remote resort simply to meet with his mistress, unaware that the world he knew might crumble around him.

"It's already started," she heard a male voice say in a low grumble, sounding tense. "I thought we had another hour."

"Between all of the time zones, it'll be a wonder if they all go off during the same day," the mistress added.

"Lucky for us, we'll be driving while everyone else scrambles for flights. In a matter of days, the world will be crippled without cell phones or power."

"And we'll be there to help it rebuild."

Brooke heard the sound of a noisy smooch, and she nearly shuddered in revolt, but instead she reached behind her and pulled the suppressed weapon to a ready position.

As she sidestepped into the threshold of the doorway, taking aim at the surprised couple, she spied a woman younger than her, and a man with thinning hair who clearly cared more about himself than his family several states away. Clarke started to say something, perhaps ready to bargain for his life, but she aimed at the center of his forehead. The slug hit home, causing blood to spurt as his head snapped back and his body crumpled to the ground.

"No, please," the woman pleaded, but Brooke had heard enough of their conversation to validate what she already knew.

Atop the bed sat a small tote, virtually a cross between a briefcase and a suitcase, with two gas masks lying on it. Beside it, she spied a vial with some kind of white substance sealed inside, almost assuredly about to be released on the populous of Orange County, or a larger city down the road. Vacationers barely knew about the terrorist acts occurring across the country, possibly the world, and Clarke intended to make them casualties.

Brooke wanted answers, but she couldn't bring this woman to justice because she didn't have arrest powers in this instance. The time for juries and trials had clearly reached an end, so Brooke exercised her only realistic option, pulling the trigger a second time and ending the woman's life with a round to the forehead. Based on what she saw and heard, Brooke wasn't about to leave the duo alive one extra second because she didn't want them bringing harm to innocent people. She hoped the box before her, or perhaps their luggage, contained the answers she required, because she didn't have any legal backing at this point.

If what the dead couple discussed was true, the world was about to be hurled back to the Dark Ages, and her actions wouldn't matter.

About to step forward and examine the contents of their belongings, Brooke saw a shadow block some of the light behind her. Whirling around with her firearm, she found Canfield standing there with a bewildered look crossing his face.

"What have you done?" he asked, his shock readily apparent.

Chapter 3

The Adirondacks, Present Day

Dan Metzger began packing the essentials he required for a flight to Virginia with family members and a few trusted friends. Unfortunately, some of his luggage came in human form, and Adam Hewitt wasn't going quietly. The man knew the location of the resort where Metzger and his family had stayed the winter months, and he disliked all of them, making him a threat. Something in his blood spared him from growing gravely ill and passing away, only to reanimate like the virtually brainless, predatory dead roaming the snow-covered state of New York.

Nearing the end of March, the past few days had brought a warm front from the west, melting enough of the snow that Metzger believed he could drive everyone to the airport where he left a perfectly good plane in the fall. Hope alone wouldn't start the plane, so he required fuel that wasn't broken down over the cold, winter months. Driving to Buffalo from the Adirondacks was a risky venture, so Metzger considered alternative options over the cold months.

A fire crackled in the fireplaces of each occupied cabin because the warm front did little to combat the lingering winter air.

"That airport runway needs to be clear," Scott Timmons told him while watching Metzger pack inside Metzger's cabin.

"I'm aware of that. The last snow wasn't too bad, so most of it should be melted."

"And you're sure you want to go through with this?"

"We've been over this a hundred times, Scott. The military is going to come looking for me and Bryce. We don't want to be here when they arrive."

"But you're okay with leaving your brother's in-laws and three young adults here to fend for themselves?"

"They'll get by. And they'll have fewer mouths to feed."

Metzger looked up, sensing disapproval in some form from his older friend.

"I know you don't like this plan, but I'm not going to hand me, or you, or my brother over to the military on a silver platter."

"Your plan has a lot of 'ifs' in it. Just being in the same state as the consolidated military is enough to make me nervous."

"We won't be there long. We arrange delivery of Hewitt to them, which gives them the means for the vaccine they need, and then we meet up with this CIA person so we can hunt down Nadeau."

"I'm not sure why you're so intent on finding him."

"As long as he's out there, we're always in danger."

"You're countering your own logic. By handing the military Hewitt, you're giving them the means to defend against another chemical attack."

"What if there's another strain, Scott? Or he got his hands on abandoned weaponry we don't know about? I'm more concerned about why they're spending so much time searching for my brother and me, instead of knocking down his door."

Timmons tightened his lips, likely seeing the logic in Metzger's statement.

"There's more risk than reward by staying here," Metzger added. "I know it's a paradise compared to what awaits us out there, but we stand to lose everything, and put other people in danger."

"I trust you," Timmons said. "Always have, always will. I know why you kept Hewitt alive after everything he's done, but I'm just worried because a *lot* of things can go haywire during this flight."

Metzger looked over the duffel bag he packed with a few clothes, weapons, and ammunition, seeing no other alternative except returning to Virginia. His friends there found a welcoming community, which gave him a base of operations, and somewhere to meet this former CIA operative. If what she said held any validity, the group might locate Nadeau in less than a week.

Morning sunlight pierced the nearby trees for the first time in nearly a month after clouds and snow dominated the Adirondacks. Metzger felt optimistic about getting to the plane and flying south to see his friends. He wasn't sure everyone else in his group agreed, because his plan involved moving parts, but they needed to avoid the military, yet appease that same entity that threatened their freedom.

Metzger had looked over local and state maps the past few days, since learning about the woman who possessed information about Nadeau. He didn't see a need to backtrack all the way to Buffalo if there were closer airports that might harbor a variety of planes. Their best hope was Burlington, Vermont, which wasn't far from them, though it required finding a bridge to cross Lake Champlain. Albany sat almost directly south of their location, but it was farther away, and likely besieged by the undead.

Every part of Metzger's plan hinged on the group locating a plane capable of holding his friends and family. Beyond that, they required a cleared runway, adequate fuel, and functional components within the plane. He knew Timmons could fly virtually any aircraft they might encounter, but Metzger didn't want to linger and get his party caught in a sudden winter storm, or miss the opportunity to speak with the government operative.

"I'm not sure everyone is onboard with your plan," Timmons commented as Metzger zipped the pack in his hands.

"This shouldn't be a surprise to anyone. We all knew staying here beyond winter was a dangerous move, and our hand has been forced. The military almost captured my brother twice, and it's just a matter of time before someone drives up here or parachutes in to try again."

Timmons referred to Isabella, his sister-in-law, who wasn't thrilled about the idea of leaving her parents with the young adults who tried to take over the resort in hostile fashion at the start of winter. Although they had since become a solid part of their very small community at the mountain getaway, Isabella worried about other forces wanting the resort for themselves. Few places in the world had electricity, hot water, and running appliances, so the group remained vigilant, turning off the lights every night so they didn't provide a beacon to travelers. They also kept the area clear of the undead, and did their best to keep footprints and tire tracks from leading back to the lodge.

"Your brother is a tough dude, but he'll have his hands full convincing her to go," Timmons said, shaking his head.

"He's had two days to convince her. If she stays here with Nathan, the military would use them as leverage to get me and Bryce in their clutches."

"You're ready to go, I see," the Navy pilot said, nodding toward the packed duffel bag.

"The sooner, the better, but I need to see if our prisoner is going to be problematic."

"Don't let him get in your head, son. He's been playing way too nice since you brought him back here."

"He's the other reason we can't come back here. He'll tell that general everything he knows because he hates us so much."

"Lucky for you, I've been looking forward to canned beans and sleeping bags in the wilderness this whole time."

Metzger flashed a grin, knowing his friend's deadpan humor by now.

"I'm sorry about all of this."

"Look, I knew what I was signing up for. Even if my former employers won't make Nadeau their top priority, you've got the right idea. We find him, figure out what he's up to, and go from there."

"I know it sounds stupid, even to me sometimes, but I just want to know why, Scott. There might never be a history book about all of this, but I just have a need for answers."

"You're not alone. Everyone on the base always wanted revenge against the people who killed their loved ones, but the brass never put out feelers. Not with aircraft, anyway."

"That's wrong in so many ways."

"Agreed. I know you've got things to attend to, so I'm going to grab a few things for the road."

Metzger watched his friend exit the cabin, took a deep breath, and prepared to confront Adam Hewitt for the first time that day. He kept his encounters with the man brief, mainly because he wanted to kill Hewitt with every fiber of his being, but the mass murderer possessed the same gift as Metzger and his brother.

His blood carried the means to fend off the infection from a zombie bite, or the original substance that decimated most of the world's population.

Metzger wished he had done more than graze the man with a bloody sword the first time they battled, but now Hewitt provided him with leverage to keep the government off his back. They wanted a human guinea pig with immunity to the disease, and Hewitt was a saving grace that might satisfy their need for a vaccine.

Since the beginning of the apocalypse, Metzger had struggled with the concept of taking a human life until he encountered Hewitt. Because they couldn't radically transform a cabin into a secured jail cell, the group cuffed Hewitt's hands and bound his feet with rope, chaining him to a steel rail along one wall. Strangely enough, their prisoner acted as though he looked forward to being on the military base, as though three square meals and protection all day long were a given. Metzger knew being under the care of the military meant being watched constantly, and given no real freedoms. During his time on the base, he was constantly followed by guards until Isabella and some friends manufactured his escape.

Even worse, he knew food and supply shortages would hit the base much like they had everywhere else on the planet. He didn't see how the military could maintain their numbers, and loyalty, if they kept listening to orders from politicians tucked safely away in bunkers.

Feeling prepared for the upcoming adventure, Metzger found his body tingling with the prospect of tracking Nadeau again. Part of him seared with anger that the people with the world's last remaining technology stopped tracking the man after one reconnaissance trip, but Metzger supposed his mandate stemmed from his own making.

Drawing a deep breath, he decided to speak with his prisoner, hoping his brother made headway with his in-laws, who likely didn't want their family heading into new dangers.

***

Bryce Metzger said little as his wife explained their new situation to his in-laws, Harold and Phyllis Padgett. After having a discussion with his wife about the hazards of remaining at the mountain lodge, he offered to let her stay with their son while he traveled with his brother. She wouldn't have it, particularly after spending months waiting for his ship to dock in Norfolk, not knowing day after day if he would survive the high seas once the apocalypse began.

"You need to promise me we'll come back here when we can," she said during their discussion, to which Bryce nodded without saying a word.

Standing inside the main building of the resort, where a kitchen, a laundry room, the old reservation desk and lobby, and a few small bedrooms were surrounded by glass walls, Bryce let his wife explain the situation to her parents. They seemed to understand, and they all knew the military might find them at any given moment. Bryce talked to fellow officers at sea, telling stories about growing up near Buffalo, and the beautiful resort his in-laws managed. If the military brass began interviewing those officers, someone might remember details, prompting the military to scour the Adirondacks for Bryce and the special qualities of his blood.

Holding his son close at the moment, he understood the mental anguish Isabella experienced, having to leave her aging parents behind with three young adults who were acquaintances at best. The apocalypse cost Bryce his parents, who were reaching their retirement years, ready to kick back and enjoy grandchildren. Instead, their bodies rested in a charred stack with any number of strangers behind a school, with no grave markers, or testimonial to their living years.

From his experiences overseas during his military service, Bryce knew life wasn't fair. He saw poverty, violence, and people near death, prior to the end of the modern world. That fateful day the previous August exacerbated the cruelty of some people, leaving only a handful of kind-hearted survivors and the military to combat their evils. Unfortunately, Bryce's former employers appeared preoccupied with creating a vaccine and keeping their military family together.

Out of respect, the three young adults left Isabella to speak with her parents, and to carry out a few chores. They had learned the hard way that they needed to earn their keep at the resort, because they weren't capable of maintaining the property themselves when appliances and solar panels began to fail. Harold taught them how to replace items when they went bad, and how to use tools to repair the cabins. Phyllis showed them how to catch and clean wild game before cooking it, in addition to helping decipher what types of lures to use in which local waters.

Everything from bass, trout, and land-locked salmon could be found in the area, along with pike and muskies. Anxious to contribute and atone for past errors in judgment, the youngsters often brought home several large fish that fed the group for a night or two.

"Do you have to leave *today*?" Phyllis asked her daughter as both parents appeared slightly stunned that their last remaining family members were heading back to a different sort of danger.

"It's a time-sensitive thing," Bryce interjected when he found Isabella searching for the right words.

"Isn't it always with you military guys?" Harold retorted. "You and your brother want to find the man who did all of this, and for what?"

"In case the attack in August was just the first wave," Bryce answered, quelling his anger before it surfaced.

Harold and Phyllis hadn't seen the true destruction the apocalypse brought upon the world. Harold sampled it the few times he went to remote cabins and abandoned stores, dodging a few of the undead, or shooting them when necessary. He never faced scores of them, or looked into the glazed eyes of someone he knew before they transformed into a ravenous monster.

"You don't have to drag them along with you," Harold continued, and Bryce realized his father-in-law simply vented his frustrations because he didn't know how else to cope with his family departing the safety of the resort.

"Dad, we have to go," Isabella stated softly. "If we stay, the military will find us, and they'll use us as bargaining chips to get to Bryce and Dan."

"I know," Harold conceded with a sigh. "We have a good thing going here."

"We will again," Isabella promised. "Dan's friends have a safe place in Virginia where we're all going to stay."

"I still think you should put a bullet in that other kid," Harold stated. "He's a loose cannon, and he knows too much about us."

Bryce harbored mixed feelings about Hewitt.

"If he serves their purpose, the military won't let him out of their sight. They let Dan slip away, and they won't make that mistake again."

Kneeling down to Nathan's level, Bryce addressed his son directly.

"Let's go pack our things, so Mom can have a few minutes with your grandparents."

Nathan nodded somberly. Although he didn't understand the rationale, Nathan knew they were leaving the beautiful wooded area and his maternal grandparents.

As he stepped outside, Bryce came across the three youngsters he reluctantly entrusted to keep his in-laws safe.

"You three take care of them, you hear?" he said, receiving sheepish looks and nods. "We'll be back here when we can."

"You're taking Adam with you?" Amber Rinehart inquired.

Bryce didn't think she had any concern left for her former boyfriend, but her question likely came from worries about her safety.

"We're going to deliver him to the government."

"Good. He deserves a lot worse."

"We'll keep this place going," her brother, Ronnie, promised the Navy officer.

"I know you will. You three have redeemed yourselves these past few months."

Bryce led his son to their cabin, prepared to pack lightly, because belongings always felt temporary in the new world.

***

Metzger stepped into the cabin where the group held Hewitt captive, finding it completely dark, except for the fire within the fireplace used to battle the cool temperatures. He located Hewitt near a corner, still chained and confined to a railing along the wall.

"Would it kill you to give me a book to read?" the man complained.

"It's dark in here," Metzger replied. "I don't want you straining your eyes."

"Look, I'll comply with whatever you want, but give me something to occupy my time. I can't just sleep all the time."

"Please?"

"Please."

"No," Metzger answered. "Lucky for you, we're about to head south to your new home."

"I'm thrilled," Hewitt said with no inflection in his voice.

Hewitt rattled the chains momentarily, shifting his weight in an attempt to get comfortable along the cold wooden floor.

"I'll just be thrilled to be rid of you," Metzger said.

"I'm sure you'll continue your noble quest to find that Nadeau guy. If the government can't find him, you're just spinning your wheels. You should enjoy life a little and enjoy the finer things. Maybe take over a resort."

Hewitt's last comment, made to anger Metzger, succeeded, but Metzger refused to let his emotions show. His prisoner had stacked roughly two dozen people like firewood behind a resort down the mountain after murdering them for their food and comfortable living quarters. Twice, Metzger bested him in combat, the first time believing he had ended the man's life by cutting him with a sword that had just been used to down the undead.

Hearing the door open behind him, Metzger turned to find his girlfriend, Jillian Varitek, stepping inside.

"Oh, look, it's your adoring girlfriend come to check on you," Hewitt said, feigning admiration.

"You can go fuck yourself," Jillian addressed Hewitt directly, before turning her attention to Metzger. "We're almost ready."

"I'm so excited to see my new home," Hewitt said, interjecting himself into the conversation.

"We'll see if you make it all the way to Virginia."

"You need me," Hewitt said confidently.

"If we need to jettison some weight along the way, guess who goes first?" Jillian asked, providing a fake pleasant smile for Hewitt's benefit before exiting the cabin.

"I like her," Hewitt admitted. "It's a shame I'm going to kill everyone in your family once I'm done at the base."

"They won't let you go."

"They won't? Either they'll come up with a cure, or I'll get bored and escape."

"Come after me, and it'll be the last thing you do."

"I wouldn't come after you," Hewitt said, narrowing his eyes, growing intensely serious at last. "I would take out everyone you care about, then disappear, so you can feel that pain gnawing at your soul for the rest of your life."

"You don't deserve to live," Metzger said, shaking his head as he refused to let Hewitt's words affect his mindset.

"Kill me. I dare you."

Metzger said nothing, though his blood began to boil. Perhaps Hewitt wasn't worth the trouble, but he needed to free his family from the burden of being tracked down by the government. If the military hadn't yet learned of the Adirondack resort, he might spare Harold and Phyllis the burden of being invaded.

"You care too much about your brother to let him get captured."

Drawing a deep breath, Metzger stared intently at his prisoner.

"I have ears," Hewitt said, attempting to explain how he knew so much about the business of those around him. "I also have little else to do in this cage."

"You're going to go peacefully with us to Virginia, or you're going to get thrown out of a moving plane. The choice is yours."

"I'll play nice," Hewitt said adamantly. "But mark my words, you and me aren't finished yet."

"If you know what's good for you, we are."

"When I leave that base, there isn't a man or woman alive who will keep me from finding you. You're predictable. Weak."

"You leave that base, I will end you," Metzger promised. "I won't have you killing more people."

In response, Hewitt gave a knowing grin, barely visible through the light, and Metzger indeed suspected he might have to confront Hewitt again one day.

Chapter 4

What would have been a reasonable drive of two hours before the apocalypse, took most of the daylight hours for Metzger and his current group. After riding in the pickup truck that provided a crew cab for everyone except Hewitt, the group eventually found a company van capable of seating over a dozen people. Half a tank of fuel came as a pleasant surprise for the group, but only after they dealt with the three undead souls left inside.

Being more humane than he cared to, Metzger kept Hewitt in the back of the van, and his brother kept a gun grasped in his right hand in case the man tried to escape or attack them. Being handcuffed, Hewitt could hardly mount an assault, even if he wanted to, but he appeared content to travel peacefully to his next destination.

Isabella and Jillian studied a local map of Burlington, discovering the Burlington International Airport might serve their needs. Rather large, the airport sat along the northeast edge of the city, meaning the group might need to navigate through a sea of the undead. Their time might have been cut significantly if the group had gone to one of the towns with docks facing Lake Champlain and located a functional boat. Even with a fueled, capable vessel, the group would have faced numerous dangers, not limited to just heavy winds and frigid temperatures. They weren't going to put Nathan, or their prize, in danger, because any number of issues might occur in the middle of a lake.

Metzger personally felt a bit rusty after dealing with the three mindless creatures in the van they requisitioned, discovering his conditioning wasn't as fine-tuned after a winter of limited activity. Granted, he went out for collection runs, chopped wood, stacked the wood, and did some fishing, but such activities paled when compared to cutting off zombie appendages.

"I'm not looking forward to exploring this airport," Timmons admitted when they reached the western edge of Burlington, after crossing the waterway that divided New York and Vermont.

"What do you expect to find?" Metzger asked.

"Airliners. We'll be lucky to find another small plane."

"We have to try," Bryce said. "We might save a day or two compared to driving to Buffalo."

After tearful goodbyes between Isabella and her parents, along with Nathan, the group couldn't go back, or waste time reaching their destination. Weather, the undead, and other factors conspired to keep them from heading south, so they *needed* to locate a plane, and quickly.

When they reached the edge of the small city, Isabella attempted to navigate them through the normally scenic landscape. She attempted to keep them on highways as much as possible, to make for an easier route, because the group didn't possess a local map. They didn't come across a welcome center, or any tourist buildings, and no one wanted to waste time searching for maps or supplies. Returning to Virginia kept them all on edge, excited to see other friends, and hunt for Nadeau, coupled with the prospect of landing so close to the military that sought them.

"We good on gas?" Metzger asked Timmons, who assumed driving duties after they found the van.

"We'll be fine if we don't take any detours."

Because the van traveled slowly much of the time, it didn't burn through much fuel. Metzger began to question whether they needed to find lodging for the night, or if the airport was within reach. Now in Vermont, they reached the edge of Burlington, finding sights familiar in virtually any town or city. The undead staggered around the roads and sidewalks, weaving around stalled vehicles that remained covered in snow. As for the dead, they moved stiffly, as though their muscles hadn't thawed from being directly exposed to the winter elements.

"Everyone keep your eyes peeled," Bryce said, seated across from his brother.

Despite the extended time reaching the city of Burlington, the group experienced few issues during their trek, and Metzger began to wonder if a disaster awaited them within the city, or at the airport. His mind kept wandering to Virginia and seeing his old friends once again, but also the most effective way to deliver Hewitt to the military. After entertaining several plans, he decided on one in particular, because it put no one in his group in jeopardy of being captured.

Jillian cautiously stepped to the back of the van, relieving Bryce from guard duties as she took his seat, already holding a semi-automatic pistol. Metzger looked to Hewitt, who appeared to be sleeping, but he considered that the man might be pretending to rest so he could eavesdrop. Metzger didn't much care, because he never planned on seeing Hewitt again, despite what the killer believed.

"We're going to see Colby," Metzger said to his girlfriend.

"I know," Jillian answered with an even tone.

"He's going to want to tag along when we go after Nadeau."

"What are you getting at, exactly?"

"Bryce and his family are staying in the village once we arrive," Metzger replied. "That's an option, you know."

Jillian provided a disapproving stare in response.

"You'd rather have Colby along than me?"

"I'm weighing the options, Jillian. I can't have distractions, and I'm not convinced you and Colby can occupy the same space. Besides, I want you safe."

"You're not going anywhere without me," she said after a moment of thought.

"I wish you two would just put a bullet in my skull," Hewitt said without opening his eyes, his body slumped against the window in the rear seat.

"Just because you're incapable of human emotions doesn't mean you should be sickened by them," Jillian commented.

"Emotions will get you two killed, and I'll still be roaming the Earth, taking whatever I want."

"You have an inflated opinion of your future," Metzger said.

Metzger refused to take his eyes off the man for more than a second or two, because Hewitt tended to pick people off when they least expected it. Inside the van, it proved impossible to chain or handcuff Hewitt to anything without opening a window or placing him on the floor. In a pinch, Metzger didn't want to scramble to free Hewitt, or put himself in close proximity to the man to unlock handcuffs.

He heard Isabella directing Timmons along the roads, and he felt the van swerving to avoid the undead, or vehicles, occasionally. Glancing out the windows, Metzger found the city looked like most urban areas, though the snow appeared a bit thicker along the roads in the area. Thus far, the van hadn't gotten bogged down, though the rate of travel slowed significantly sometimes when Timmons ascended a hill, or avoided larger banks of snow.

Passing a museum, followed by large brick buildings that appeared to be part of a campus, the group collectively felt their stomachs tighten as they drew closer to the airport. As dusk approached, Metzger thought back to the small towns and cities he saw as a child with snow on the ground and holiday lights strung up in the downtown areas. Whenever significant snowfall struck the area, he and Bryce went outside for snowball fights, and to build a snow fort that drew neighborhood kids, providing parents with much-needed breaks. While Burlington still possessed much of its charm, the winter weather making it appear like a postcard, no working lights existed to guide them to their destination.

Jillian patted Metzger on the knee before standing to move forward in the van.

"Don't forget that shooting him is still an option."

"I wish," Metzger muttered.

He glanced out the window once more while Timmons drove them through the University of Burlington campus, maneuvering the van around several objects in the road. Metzger recalled the city harbored several universities, and only when he spied a sign beside a building did he realize which campus they were visiting momentarily.

Several zombies were lying in the snow, barely visible above the melting substance. A few groped upward, unable to free themselves from the slushy precipitation due to lack of strength, or because they remained frozen like the soil beneath them. Metzger heard a few of their throaty growls, sounding like sickly cougars, and something thumped against the side of the van, which he imagined was a zombie straying too close to the moving vehicle.

Several stood in place, feet frozen to the ground, with arms flailing like the tube man advertising gimmicks that car dealerships once used in their lots. Some stood mostly still, as though their limbs remained overtaken by the cold temperatures, snow perched atop their shoulders. Others remained partially buried in the snow, some not moving at all. Perhaps they died, having never been infected, or the elements destroyed their physical forms so badly that they no longer functioned. Metzger kept a mental inventory of the various dead he saw in their natural settings, but he couldn't rationalize what kept them mobile in the first place.

Bryce returned, holding a firearm in his right hand, ready to give his brother a break from guard duty.

"Timmons wants you up there."

"Okay," Metzger said before making his way up the narrow center aisle of the van, which felt more like a small bus the way the seats were laid out to either side.

He reached the front, finding his friend and his sister-in-law occupying the front seats.

"What's up?"

"There's more snow than we bargained for," Timmons said. "Taking off would be difficult, if not impossible."

"What are you saying?"

"I'm suggesting we take a look at the airport, but we need to find a place to settle in for the night. Maybe a residence with a fireplace?"

"I'll get everyone to watch for somewhere useful. Are we close?"

"Getting there," Isabella answered. "We're hoping more snow will melt by morning. If not, we're going to have to pray we find a snowplow that still works."

Based on personal experience, most vehicles still fired up, even after the cold snaps through the winter months. He doubted to expect such good fortune the following winter, meaning he needed to formulate a plan for permanent residence, or different methods of travel, in the coming months. Without another word, he turned around, finding Jillian seated beside a window on the driver's side of the van.

"I heard," she told him. "I'll start looking for chimneys."

"Thank you."

Metzger sat beside his nephew, pointing out the window.

"Can you watch for any houses that have fireplaces?" he asked, trying to make it a game.

"Chimneys, right?" Nathan asked, having helped them stake out certain buildings and items the few times they dared remove him from complete safety for supply runs.

Isabella didn't much appreciate her son leaving the safety of the resort, but Metzger and his brother both thought the boy required acclimation to hazards in case he ever needed to defend himself. In Metzger's experience, kids believed they were ready to confront the dead, and even said as much, but pale eyes, gnashing teeth, and rotted skin tended to freeze them in terror instead. Like anyone else, Metzger felt a sense of shock the first time he put down the undead, as though he was committing murder.

Over time, the experience numbed him altogether, and he simply viewed cutting them down as a survival technique.

Campus appeared cluttered with the undead, and looming buildings, providing them little cover or quality shelter. Beyond that, they discovered a business district, comprised of hotels, restaurants, oil change stations, and old insurance buildings.

"This doesn't help," Jillian stated. "This whole place is a danger zone."

"I don't see any chimneys," Nathan added.

"You probably won't, buddy," Metzger said, patting his shoulder. "But keep looking."

Metzger returned to the front of the van once more.

"We're getting close, aren't we?"

"We're running out of daylight," Timmons said. "We'll be lucky to get a glance at this place before we have to locate housing."

Metzger didn't like the idea of driving with headlights once daylight abandoned the group. Other survivors, or the military, might take notice and follow them to whatever lodging they found for the night.

A few minutes later, the van approached the airport, and Metzger found most of the fencing surrounding the area intact. With the sky turning a hazy purple, visibility spanned only so far, and he spotted more snow and undead along the grounds than he anticipated. He moved up beside Timmons and Isabella in the front, trying to get a better view of the airport as Timmons located a gate that had long since been removed, permitting them easy access to the property.

As they pulled inside a secondary gate, also removed by tools, or a large vehicle, Metzger glanced toward one of the hangars, thinking he saw a small light of some sort quickly disappear.

"Did anyone see that?"

"See what?" Timmons asked.

"I thought I saw a light over there."

Timmons shrugged, and Metzger wondered if he simply caught a reflection from any number of metal objects in the distance. With the sun setting, it felt unlikely any natural rays struck the shiny surfaces, but he didn't grow alarmed until Timmons noticed another disturbing issue.

"Oh, shit," the pilot muttered. "We need to get out of here *now*."

"What?" Isabella questioned, prompting Timmons to point directly ahead at the landing strip.

Metzger stared out the windshield, finding the concrete nearly plowed in an area large enough for a plane to land or take off, causing his spine to tingle in apprehension. Someone most likely located an airport snowplow and cleared off the runway, and the distant light suddenly made sense to him. Metzger figured someone was flying in, because it appeared at least one person remained at the airport. Timmons likely drew the same conclusion, because the moment he found enough space to turn the van completely around, he did just that, striking a zombie in the process. Most of the undead in the area had headed toward the hangars, close to the area Metzger spotted the light.

"Flip off the lights and get us to a residential area," Metzger suggested more than demanded.

"Already on it," Timmons replied, reaching for the headlight controls.

Behind them, halfway across the airport, a pair of headlights from another vehicle suddenly appeared, switching to the bright setting to illuminate the van as it departed the airport.

"Fuck," Metzger muttered, praying the military hadn't somehow found them as Timmons stepped on the gas to depart the airport hurriedly.

Chapter 5

As darkness overtook the community of Maplewood, a small group met inside one of the houses to discuss their current situation. Most everyone else inside the gates had gone to a spring dinner hosted by Robert and Nancy McAllister.

"We need to come clean about all of this," Luke Johnson said as the group sat near the roaring fireplace inside the living room.

"We've said about as much as we can to the McAllisters without compromising our situation," Gracine Tucker noted.

Luke had sent his adopted daughter, Samantha, off to play with some neighbor children. He, Gracine, Colby Sutton, and Sean Sutton occupied the living room of the cabin where Gracine and her current boyfriend resided with another family. Mike Mullins and Brooke Palacio, who recently came across some of the group members, sat nearby, brought into the community under the guise that they were simply passing through.

In order to keep the community elders distracted, Father Paul McNulty and Sister Rosa Alonso went to the dinner function, despite knowing the truth. They sided with the group, because Brooke provided proof she was within striking distance of Nadeau, and once the group spoke of their experiences with the military, she balked at the idea of continuing to the military base. Had they not volunteered the services of Timmons, she might have struggled the remainder of the way to Norfolk, but the idea of locating Nadeau precisely appealed to her.

"We haven't heard from your friends," Brooke noted, growing concerned about letting people know her secret and not moving forward. "It's best we don't spill the beans until we know they're safe and heading this way."

"Dan will contact us," Sutton said assuredly. "He said the moment the weather breaks, they'd locate a plane and get back here."

"Our hosts aren't going to remain gracious much longer," Luke said. "We all know how they feel about guests."

Typically, guests only stayed a night or two, before being sent down the road, or they were initiated into the community if they had a skill or belongings that benefited the residents.

"This is more important than us staying here," Sutton said.

"Speak for yourself," Luke said, a deep look of concern crossing his face. "You don't have a youngster to look after. And if you all take off, that doesn't bode well for me and Samantha."

"I told you bringing him into this was a mistake," Sutton said to Gracine.

"Luke is one of us," Gracine assured him. "He deserves to know. And he has an obligation to keep that little girl safe."

"All of this hinges on your friend making it here," Sean said to his father before turning his attention to Brooke. "How long are you prepared to wait?"

"Depends on the generosity of my hosts," she answered.

"We're well enough to make it to the base, if need be," Mullins said from a nearby chair. "We were on death's doorstep when you found us."

Sutton appeared agitated, possibly because he hated being confined within walls.

"Give Dan a little more time," he insisted. "He'll find a way here."

Brooke liked what she heard about their friend, but she dared not wait much longer for a low-key flight. Going to the military was always a sketchy move at best, especially if what her current company told her proved truthful. If the military didn't put much effort into finding Nadeau, they had little reason to assist her. Based on Nadeau's extensive planning, she suspected he possessed food and supplies enough to last for years, and likely a small force of mercenaries to protect him.

Heading into his base or fortress alone would certainly be a suicide mission if Brooke were to attempt such a move by herself. Her only hope of entering such a place might lie in deception, acting like a member of Nadeau's camp, to avoid being shot on sight. She knew the last two possible hiding spots for Nadeau, and based on their locations, she suspected they might be former bunkers used by the military for securing politicians and world leaders.

She knew the government often catered to the rich and powerful, providing another reason for her not to readily trust the military if their every move hinged on political approval.

"I'm still confused about the overall plan," Luke confessed. "If our leadership here isn't going to allow Brooke or Mike to stay, how do we convince them to protect the other half of our group?"

"Because they'll be staying in our place," Sutton answered. "Some of us are going to escort Brooke while those of us watching kids stay behind."

"Who exactly?"

"We aren't forcing anyone to go," Gracine answered. "You stay here with Samantha, and Dan's brother and sister-in-law will stay here with their boy."

"And what about Reggie?" Luke inquired with a raised eyebrow, speaking of Gracine's current love interest. "He approves of *you* going?"

"We haven't discussed it yet."

"This should be good," Luke said sarcastically. "Robert barely trusts us since we've been sneaking around like this, and you're going to alienate Reggie, too?"

"Whose side are you on?" Gracine asked, raising her voice.

"We decided to stay here for a reason," Luke stated. "This divides us, and our purpose."

Sutton shook his head with a low growl.

"And here I thought you were changing."

"I have," Luke assured him, "but if things go sideways, you may not have a home to return to."

"That sounds like a threat," Sean said.

"It's not. I'm just pointing out the fact that we've had to earn trust at this place, and now that hangs by a thread."

Brooke cleared her throat.

"*None* of you need to come with me. This is going to be a surveillance mission."

"Do you really think Nadeau won't have top security in and around his compound?" Sutton asked rhetorically. "He gets wind of you on his turf, there won't be any escape."

"I don't necessarily have to get close to his base to know if he's there," Brooke commented. "Once we locate him, the military can take action."

Sutton grunted doubtfully.

"What do you propose?" Brooke questioned. "We conduct a frontal assault?"

"We could get the numbers," Sutton replied. "People would line up for a chance to put a bullet in his skull."

"And then what?" Luke questioned. "We risk lives, and our future, for revenge?"

"He has answers," Brooke answered. "I want information, because he surprised the world once, and I don't want to see that happen again."

"Was any part of the world safe from this?" Sean asked her.

"No. The few areas not originally affected were contaminated later. We're our own worst enemy when we scramble to see family members and bring the plague with us."

"A few flights with infected people would spread the sickness," Sutton reasoned aloud.

"If you were CIA, wouldn't your people have been in touch with the military?" Luke asked. "It seems like you're uncertain about a lot of things."

"I was a field agent," Brooke explained, not feeling the least bit agitated about them questioning her occupation. "Things take a while to trickle down to us, and just like everywhere else, our people caught on quickly that there wasn't going to be a tomorrow for a lot of folks."

"Did they skin out?" Sutton inquired.

"I think a lot of them did. My agency contact stayed with me until communications began to fail."

"Is the military keeping the sat phone service operational?" Sutton asked.

"I believe they are. It's the most reliable method of reaching one another, given how everything else began to fail."

Mullins stepped to a window, moving a curtain for a look outside.

"Some of them are starting to leave the dinner," he reported.

"Might be time for us to end this little soiree," Brooke said before turning her attention to Sutton. "Keep me posted about your friend's travels."

"If I hear from him, you'll be the first to know."

***

A few at a time, the group left the house, and Sutton exited with Gracine, mainly so he could ask her a few questions.

"Does it seem like Luke is falling back into his old patterns?" he asked her directly once they were halfway across the community grounds.

"He seems a bit skittish, if that's what you mean."

"He's acting like these walls are the most important thing in the world."

"Well, he does have a daughter to protect," Gracine noted, looking to Sutton directly. "You should know a little something about that."

Sutton stopped, and she paused beside him.

"I just thought he was over being scared of everything. Having walls and a fence doesn't mean we're secure."

"Not everyone shares your sense of survival," Gracine reminded him.

Sutton looked toward some of the residents filing out of the main house after enjoying a meal that few survivors experienced during the apocalypse.

"They don't know how good they have it," he muttered.

"We've earned their trust," Gracine said, believing her own words. "Luke is right when he says we could lose everything."

"McAllister and his wife should trust us, but I'm not entirely sure I trust *them*."

"Why?"

"He's probed several times about Dan and his brother, Gracine. He knows about their value to the military, and I'm worried he'll sell us out. It's also the reason I wish you'd stay here when we search for Nadeau."

"I've seen too much not to tag along, Colby. I want to see it for myself when you ram a pistol through his teeth."

"I don't like the idea of leaving Sean here with Luke and Dan's family. A lot can happen in a few days."

"It's riskier on the road."

"We keep getting the group back together just to go our separate ways again and again."

"Sounds like someone is developing attachments," Gracine noted.

"Speaking of attachments, your man isn't going to like you traveling with me."

"He'll get over it," Gracine assured him, her mind wandering to a time when she believed she and Sutton might pursue a real relationship.

His son's death proved too much, and he began shutting out everyone in his life, including his only remaining son, for a time. Sutton had already dodged a few questions and comments during this conversation, meaning little about the man had changed over time.

Several lanterns lit the way around the community, allowing a few kids to run outside, despite the darkness of night. Resources other than food began to grow limited, and the military likely scoured the same areas as the community. Sutton realized this, saying as much to Gracine during previous conversations.

"McAllister would be a fool to bargain with the military," Sutton said. "They don't have anything to offer us."

"Protection?"

"I doubt it. They're spread thin, trying to stay alive just like us. And they didn't exactly welcome us with open arms."

From the corner of her eye, Gracine spied Mitchell exiting one of the houses down the road, and before she could say a word, Sutton turned and walked the other way. She wanted to believe Sutton thought primarily about keeping their current secret from him, but she suspected he was afraid of experiencing attachment. He often tended to keep discussions brief, finding different reasons to bow out early each time.

Putting her best face forward, Gracine smiled when she pretended to notice Mitchell in the small crowd ahead. She approached him, hoping he hadn't seen Sutton walking away, because she didn't need more questions, or guilt, complicating her life.

***

Luke met up with Allison Deckard during the return stroll to his own living quarters. Like him, she lived a lonely existence within the walls of Maplewood

45

as a homosexual without a partner. Unlike Luke, Allison remained behind the community walls almost from the beginning because her parents knew Robert McAllister.

"We missed you at dinner," she said.

"I had a few things to take care of," Luke said, trying to avoid telling a complete fib.

"None of the others from your group were there, either," Allison noted, causing Luke to panic internally that someone noticed *all* of their clan hadn't attended dinner.

"I thought most of them were going," Luke lied outright. "You sure you didn't overlook them?"

"Pretty sure," Allison said, "but I was busy looking at Misty Atwell most of the time."

"Got you a little girl crush?" Luke asked, happy to change the subject.

Although barely an adult, Allison typically acted mature for her age, like most young adults in the apocalypse. He believed she once said she was twenty, but he couldn't recall for certain.

"She'd never notice me," Allison said. "She's into half the boys her age."

"I hope you don't mean in their beds."

"Nah. Hard to get anything like that done around here. I just meant I'm not her type."

Luke enjoyed talking with Allison during their brief interactions, because he felt as though he helped her come to terms with being gay, and ignoring what some people believed. Her experiences hadn't been particularly negative thus far, and he wanted to make certain no one inside the community bullied her. She had come out to her family, and him, but he wasn't sure if she had mustered the courage to tell anyone else.

"I found that coming forward opened up a new world for me," Luke confessed.

"How so?"

"Sure, I had people who turned their backs on me, and some of them never looked at me the same again, but I found a whole new set of friends, and a community full of acceptance when I came out."

"I'm glad for you," Allison said, "but your community probably wasn't less than a hundred people in total."

"Maybe there's someone else in here who's just like you, waiting and watching, when the two of you could be together."

Allison gave him a doubtful smirk.

"I think you're just saying that because you found Kevin."

Allison spoke of Kevin Gebbert, a younger gay man Luke discovered through a mutual friend who lived in their community. Like Allison, he remained inside the walls due to a family connection, carrying a bit of a wild side with him. People termed him flamboyantly gay, and he conducted his daily life fearlessly without a care of what they thought or believed.

"I can't say Kevin is anything more than a friend," Luke confessed, being straightforward. "He's a bit too immature for me."

Luke's last partner, Albert, was certainly the more mature and conventional of the pair, and Luke considered taming Kevin at some point, but Samantha remained his focus at the moment.

"I know you two have been talking," Allison said as they continued to walk.

"He's a bit lost," Luke responded. "I don't think he's found an identity, or a purpose, especially trapped in these walls."

"His family lets him do his own thing. They always have. He's the equivalent of a spoiled rich kid."

"Maybe he needs some better mentors in his life. A little time outside these walls would put things in perspective in a hurry."

"Maybe," Allison said thoughtfully as her voice trailed off.

"What is it?" Luke asked, ceasing his walk momentarily.

"Just a word of warning, everything Kevin does is very self-serving."

Having taken notice of that behavior from Kevin, Luke considered it part of the immaturity, despite the younger man being in his mid-twenties.

"I appreciate you telling me that," Luke said, drawing an apprehensive look from Allison as though she hadn't covered every detail on the subject of Kevin. "Is there something else?"

Samantha came running their way, yelling for Luke with her arms spread apart for a hug.

"Daddy!"

Luke knelt down, pulling her into an embrace for several seconds.

"Did you have a good time with your friends?"

"Yeah!"

When he looked up, Allison had moved along, leaving him to ponder what direction their conversation was about to take. He returned his attention to Samantha, using his best fun, fatherly voice.

"I heard Miss Patty found some ingredients for ice-cream, and she was going to let some people sample it tonight. Want to see if there's any left?"

"Yeah!"

Samantha spoke more often as her comfort level around Luke grew stronger. Devastated by the untimely deaths of her parents due to the undead, she remained a shell of her young self for months until he defended her life against a child predator and saved her.

Shortly after that she began referring to Luke as her father.

Taking her by the hand, he led her down the road to a house where a kind older woman occasionally made frozen dairy treats for the community when they found her the ingredients. Made in the style of the Amish, it wouldn't be the best Samantha ever tasted, but Luke doubted she remembered much about ice-cream from the store.

He hoped to return to such care-free days eventually, but for now he would settle for the safety of the gated community.

Chapter 6

The Next Morning

No one in Metzger's current group slept particularly well during the night. While the vehicle that flooded them with bright lights at the airport didn't follow their van, everyone knew the van wouldn't be difficult to track. Even in melting snow, only one set of tire tracks appeared throughout the city streets, leaving interested parties a virtual breadcrumb trail to follow.

After finding a house that suited their needs, a few of them cleared the residence while Timmons found an area down the street to hide their vehicle. Throughout the early morning hours, they took turns keeping vigil, and monitoring Hewitt, while a fire kept them warm. A few supplies remained inside the residence, which kept them from eating what food they brought. No one felt particularly hungry, but after an hour or two, they felt certain it hadn't been the military at the airport, or they would've been hunted down and captured.

Dawn came early for Metzger, and he stepped outside to look and listen for dangers, finding the morning air warmer than usual, and crisp. Perhaps masked by the melting snow, the air did not reek of death and decay.

When they returned to the airport, Timmons parked the van some distance from the area, and Metzger took his brother to the top of a nearby building to look ahead with binoculars. Five stories in height, the building barely allowed the naked eye a look inside the airport, but with binoculars, they were able to see the plowed path was now melted enough that patches of concrete poked through the glazed surface.

Upon taking a turn with the binoculars, Metzger noticed several downed planes, as though inexperienced pilots had attempted landings and failed, or other circumstances caused the planes to miss the landing strip. His hopes of finding a decent plane intact dwindled, and searching for a suitable aircraft wouldn't be easy with the undead now milling around after their wintery incarceration appeared to reach an end.

"Ideas?" Bryce asked.

"It appears our fellow airport enthusiasts are gone."

"Indeed. Looking for a plane won't be easy with the dead everywhere."

"The hangars are probably unlocked," Metzger reasoned aloud. "We'll drive around and look for prospects. If we find something promising, I'll jump out and defend Scott while he looks it over."

Bryce appeared concerned.

"They might have laid a trap."

"Doubtful. I think they were doing the same thing as us, whoever they were."

Metzger observed the dead staggering around the area momentarily, finding more of the snow melted within the airport, much like the local streets. They didn't congregate in one area, meaning no human activity had recently caught their attention. Looking through the binoculars, he saw several sets of tire tracks, and a few vehicles left behind, as though everyone had jumped aboard a plane when it departed.

"I think they all boarded a plane and got out of there," he informed his brother.

"It could be a trick."

"If it is, I doubt it's the military. They could have easily tracked us last night if they wanted to."

"Maybe they didn't know it was us."

Like everyone, the military suffered limitations during the apocalypse, but he imagined they would shake down anyone who might lead them to the brothers.

"I'm pretty sure they'll be visiting Harold and Phyllis at some point," Metzger thought aloud. "Let's hope they don't think we're dumb enough to return to Virginia."

"We're definitely smarter than *that*," Bryce commented sarcastically.

A few minutes later, the brothers returned to the van, climbing in to find all eyes looking to them anxiously.

"It looks clear," Bryce announced. "We still need to watch our backs in there."

Timmons drove them through the downed fences, immediately drawing attention from the undead. Wasting no time, the pilot navigated the van toward the hangars, and everyone waited with bated breath because some of the doors were open, or collapsed in a few cases, meaning others had scoured the airport before them.

"I'm going to have to look at these up close," Timmons reminded everyone as he drew close to the first hangar.

"I've got your back," Metzger assured him. "Jillian and Bryce can help."

"And I can keep an eye on our guest," Isabella said, nodding at Hewitt who simply rested in one of the rear seats, not volunteering for anything.

"Ready?" the pilot asked, his left hand already poised at the driver's side door handle.

Metzger looked to his brother and Jillian, who both nodded affirmatively.

"Yeah," he answered as they all opened the van doors closest to them, leaping out to secure their way out of Vermont.

Wearing duck boots instead of the cowboy boots he preferred, Timmons stayed low, making his way quietly along the nearest hangar. Metzger kept his head on a swivel, observing his friend and the dead between quick glances. A few of the undead, still stiff from their unintended deep freeze, attempted to maneuver towards the trespassers, but their legs barely moved. Jillian and Bryce were able to put them out of their misery using large knives, permitting Metzger to move closer to Timmons.

"Any luck?" he asked his friend.

"One's too big, and the other is dismantled," Timmons grumbled in response.

"There're plenty more hangars," Metzger said, finding a livelier member of the undead rounding the corner ahead of Timmons.

Drawing the short sword he typically kept with him from its sheath, he eyeballed the woman ahead of him, who appeared dressed for a business trip she never took. Blood streaked her face, and her right eye appeared to be missing, at least in part, as though a bird or scavenger had eaten at it after her untimely passing. Using her one remaining eye, she stared, unblinking, at Metzger as a source of food.

Returning to the moment, his practical nature took over, and he made a clean slice through her skull, dropping her and the upper portion of her head to the concrete below. Except for the banks created by a plow the previous evening, snow remained only in patches throughout the airport. The section cleared by the strangers the previous evening provided a clean runway without debris or the undead littering the path.

Timmons moved to the next hangar, finding the three front doors closed, which prompted him to look for a regular entrance. Along the closer side, the pilot located a conventional door before reaching for the knob.

"Knock first," Metzger warned, drawing an acknowledging nod from Timmons, who tested the doorknob anyway.

"Locked," he reported before giving the door a few quick raps on the metal door.

In response, he immediately received a growl from the other side, and then another, before at least one member of the undead thumped against the door.

"Is it worth the trouble?" Metzger asked, staring at the door.

"Nothing inside has been touched by the living," Timmons replied. "Might be our best bet."

Metzger gave a quick sigh, readying his sword as he approached the door.

"Go ahead and check the next hangar," he suggested, prompting Timmons to give a quick, informal salute before moving onward.

Examining the door momentarily, Metzger couldn't find an easy way to work around the lock, so he put his back to it and gave a mule kick, failing to move the door. Trying twice more, he broke the area close to the doorknob, permitting the door to swing inward as he whirled to see what awaited him. Taking a few steps back, Metzger realized his brother and Jillian had taken his side, and Timmons remained undefended as he continued searching.

"Bryce, find the captain. He went ahead to check more hangars."

Without a word, his brother followed the same path Timmons took, and Metzger saw two members of the undead battling to see which one could squeeze through the door first. Not accomplishing their goal at all, the two became wedged in the doorway, allowing Jillian to stab each of them in succession through their skulls. They fell, impeding the path for additional undead, so Metzger used his knuckles to rap the door several more times, hearing nothing in return.

Jillian readied a flashlight before he could fish out the small light he kept in his pocket, shining it inside for them to have a look.

Keeping his sword at the ready, Metzger allowed his girlfriend to step inside first, illuminating the large hangar for the both of them. No other noises reached his ears, though the stench from the undead nearly overwhelmed him because the walls had contained their carcasses for months. After looking for danger along the concrete floor, and finding none, Metzger looked up a bit to examine the stored aircraft.

Finding four in total, he saw two that didn't hold seven passengers, one that probably could, and a small corporate jet of some sort. He couldn't readily identify planes like Timmons, but he knew enough to determine their suitability.

"Will any of these work for us?" Jillian asked.

"I think so," he said, finding all of them completely intact from an exterior view. "I wonder if those two tried to hole up in here to avoid the dead."

"I'm surprised two dead heads kept people out of here," Jillian said.

"Path of least resistance," Metzger surmised. "Let's get the captain and see what he thinks."

Both of them stepped outside, finding a few of the local denizens staggering towards the van. Isabella might have dealt with them, but they lingered outside of the exit door she would likely use, making it dangerous to grant them even momentary access. Besides, she was the one person left who could hold a gun on Hewitt.

"I've got this," Jillian assured Metzger, allowing him to locate his brother and Timmons while she eliminated the threat.

Metzger didn't have to travel far before spotting Timmons, who examined a small plane inside the next hangar. Shaking his head, the pilot didn't seem to have words to match the obvious disappointment he felt.

"This place is picked over," Timmons muttered.

"You're only in the third hangar we've seen," Metzger said, deciding to prolong telling his friend the potential good news.

"All of these planes have issues, Dan," the captain continued. "They're either partially dismantled, or they won't carry all of us."

"What did you find?" Bryce asked when he turned from the hangar to his brother.

"A couple of dead, and four aircraft that look to be fully intact."

"Why didn't you lead with that?" Timmons asked a bit testily.

"One of the rare joys in life for me is hearing you bitch about everything under the sun," Metzger confessed a half-truth.

Timmons groaned, following him back to the hangar with the four aircraft. A glance at the van revealed Jillian had handled the undead with ease because their bodies lay at her feet, and the knife she held glistened with dripping blood.

When the pilot laid eyes on the aircraft, all grumpiness left his face as he broke out in a genuine smile. Bypassing the two small planes Metzger deemed too small to carry their party, the Navy man examined the remaining two aircraft with more scrutiny.

"Can you fly them?" Bryce asked, knowing all too well that civilian aircraft were like apples and oranges when compared to most military planes.

"The jet could be a little tricky," Timmons admitted, eyeing it more closely, "but I think I could get a feel for it. Then there's still the matter of fuel."

"And the plane?" Bryce inquired.

"Piece of cake," Timmons replied. "That's a Piper Seneca. We could use regular gas if necessary, and we could squeeze in there."

"Wouldn't be comfortable," Bryce said after taking a closer look at the interior.

"I believe I implied that," Timmons retorted.

Turning around, the pilot opened the hangar door on the far end, indicating he preferred the small jet over the plane.

"I need the lighting to look these over," he said. "Give me ten minutes of peace from the infected and I'll let you know our better bet."

Metzger and his brother exited the hangar, prepared to scour the area for pulseless threats when a sound reached Metzger's ears. At first, he thought he was hearing some kind of animal noise, because insects certainly weren't flying about, but it sounded like a buzzing sound, low in register. He looked to his left, where the noise originated, realizing the sound of an aircraft buzzed in the sky, possibly drawing close to their location. One look at his brother indicated Bryce reached the same conclusion, so Metzger turned to Timmons.

"We may not have ten minutes, Scott!"

***

Sutton wandered around the neighborhood with his dog, Buster, the next morning, anxiously awaiting word from Metzger about their impending travel. He had kept the phone charged through a car charger, using one of the vehicles the group kept near the grounds for scavenging trips. Several people knew he possessed the phone, and he didn't advertise the fact because he knew people might desperately try calling their loved ones, despite the fact that normal cell phone service died a week or so after the apocalypse began.

One of the few animals living within the walls of Maplewood, Buster became adored by the local children, soaking up the attention. On this particular morning, however, virtually no one stepped outside to enjoy the warm front passing through Virginia. The state enjoyed warmer weather than states to the north, despite being closer to the ocean. Even so, Sutton wore his plain green jacket that looked like a cross between military surplus and trendy winter wear.

Sutton wasn't entirely certain how the dynamic of replacing Brooke and Mullins in the community with Metzger's immediate family would work, but he felt compelled to make certain they remained safe. When the time came, he wanted to propose a temporary exchange of residents, because he wasn't certain any of them would choose to stay at Maplewood going forward. Luke seemed interested, because he wanted to keep Samantha safe, but the others showed signs of wanting to move forward. Maplewood offered fireplaces, and security, but Sutton knew his former group was capable of creating a similar situation.

Gracine remained a wildcard, but Sutton would learn more about her intentions based on whether she wanted to hunt down Nadeau, or stay safe at Maplewood.

While Buster sniffed around the grounds, Sutton detected someone approaching him from behind. Turning, he felt a bit surprised that Brooke sought him out, and the expression she wore indicated she had business on her mind.

"How are you this fine morning?" he inquired, continuing to stroll behind his canine.

"I've been better," she replied.

"Something in particular?"

"No. I just wanted to let you know that I'm leaving for the military base if your friend doesn't reach out soon."

Sutton paused his walk to look directly at Brooke.

"What kind of deadline are we talking about?"

"Tomorrow morning. I know the military isn't my best option, but I need transport and able personnel."

"Both of which we can provide," Sutton assured her.

"If your pilot can't get a plane here, I don't have much faith in him crossing state lines."

"State lines, huh?" Sutton asked, realizing Brooke hadn't been forthcoming with details.

Buster trotted up to Brooke, asking to be petted or scratched, and she obliged, rubbing the underside of his jaw with her fingertips.

Sutton took a moment to look at the trees surrounding the gated community, spying a few of the towers where lookouts could strategically see through the trees to spot trouble for up to a mile in any direction. At the moment, only one was manned, meaning there might be a shift change at the other, or no one scheduled to keep watch. He didn't particularly love the setup, because even if the sentries spied trouble, they lacked adequate methods to alert everyone in the village. That, coupled with the fact that only a few people carried firearms, left them at a disadvantage virtually all the time.

"You know I'm not going to say much until you live up to your end of the bargain," Brooke said once a nearby shrub caught Buster's attention and he went to mark his territory.

"When they're in the air, Dan will call me," Sutton promised. "That's the deal."

"After that, it should be a matter of hours before we're on our way to finding Nadeau."

"Could it really be that easy?"

"Locating him, possibly," Brooke said. "Based on the infrastructure he set up to protect him, getting to him won't be nearly as easy."

"I'm sure we can be persuasive if we find some of his people."

"I was thinking some trickery and stealth might get us further."

"Those aren't exactly my strengths," Sutton confessed.

"If you care about those around you, you'll follow my lead. Being a hothead is a good way to get us all killed."

Sutton grunted, but internally, he recalled the time he failed to act in time to save Jillian's father. While their original group seemed destined to split up when they did, leaving with Jillian so angry at him didn't sit well with Sutton. A loner out of necessity in the beginning of the apocalypse, he grew to like being around other survivors, though he never confessed his thoughts on the matter. Although a random asshole in the woods killed one of his sons, Sutton blamed Nadeau for creating the circumstances that put his sons in danger in the first place.

"I want Nadeau dead," he said flatly.

"We all do," Brooke said, "but before that happens, we need some facts from him. This entire world is in danger if he whips up another batch of the chemical he used. And something tells me he created a serum before he unleashed it across the globe. If that's the case, we need it to prevent any further outbreaks."

"How far do you think his network reaches?"

"At first, I thought he had hundreds of followers, which I found hard to fathom."

"How so?"

"Don't you think at least one person out of hundreds would leak his plot to the FBI, or the CIA?"

"Maybe he had moles there, too."

"I wouldn't doubt it, but even moles couldn't stop the spread of information once it reached the right ears."

Buster returned to the duo, cocked his head, and left again when they didn't pay him enough attention.

"Maybe someone spoke up, but the government didn't take it seriously," Sutton suggested.

"That's possible," Brooke said, "but I grew to believe his network was vast, and secretive, reaching into the thousands worldwide."

"How did you figure that out?"

"I've been to nearly a dozen of his outposts to get this far," she answered.

"How did you get his people to talk?" Sutton questioned with a furrowed eyebrow.

"I didn't ask nicely, if that's what you mean."

Sutton felt a bit intrigued, and frightened of Brooke simultaneously.

"We're not a year into this," he said. "You work quickly."

"I had some help, even before I met Mullins."

Chapter 7

August, The Previous Year

Canfield stood just inside the suite, eyes wide, mouth agape.

Brooke, believing she had carried out her objective in secret, whirled to face him with the gun in her right hand.

Instead of aiming it at him, she stepped forward and reached for his hand, but Canfield recoiled, and she felt certain he was about to flee the room, but a hurt, mournful expression crossed his face.

"What have you done?" he asked a second time. "I...I followed you up the stairs because I didn't know what you were doing."

Passing by him, Brooke shut the suite's main door to ensure no curious hotel guests, or housekeeping, stepped inside for a peek.

"John, there are a *lot* of things I haven't told you about my life," she said, setting the firearm on a table beside her, taking her hands and cupping his face, refusing to let him back away. "I don't have time to explain everything right now, but I need you to trust me."

His face, especially his darting eyes, didn't speak volumes of trust to her. She felt reasonably certain shock might be setting in after he witnessed two people being shot dead.

"John, do you trust me?"

He put his hands up to grab her wrists and Brooke wondered momentarily if he might create a new dilemma by trying to subdue her. Instead, he gently clutched both of her wrists and focused on her gaze.

"I've been watching the world fall apart on the news," he said. "I don't think a lot can surprise me right now." He paused a moment to choose his words. "Even so, I hope you have a good reason for gunning two people down like some trained assassin."

"Come with me," she urged, walking into the bedroom where the two corpses remained on the floor, and the tote remained unzipped and open atop the bed.

Canfield followed her to the door, a bit squeamish about entering the room where two bodies stared back at him with blank eyes when he glanced in their direction. Brooke still wasn't certain that he hadn't simply said what she wanted to hear, buying time so he could dash from the suite when the right moment arrived.

Brooke held up the gas masks for his benefit, one in each hand.

"Do normal guests bring these along?" she asked him.

"Maybe they were anti-government types," he said almost sheepishly.

"I work for the government," Brooke revealed. "Our government doesn't gas its citizens."

"All this time, your job as a reporter was a façade?" Canfield asked, bewildered.

"We call it a cover in my line of work," Brooke said, carefully setting the unopened vial aside before examining the contents of the tote.

"What is that?" her boyfriend inquired, pointing at the vial.

"I'm not sure. It can't be good, though."

Canfield put an arm against the doorway to support his weight, appearing overwhelmed by the news that terrorists were attacking a variety of cities, and his girlfriend of several years wasn't the person he thought he knew.

Finding no clothing inside the tote except for a microfiber cloth used to cover some items, Brooke removed the cloth, finding three more vials inside. Secured by a plastic harness with padded sides, the vials appeared perfectly safe and intact, except for one small problem.

One of them was already emptied of its contents, and the cap securely replaced.

"Oh, shit," she muttered, failing to see Canfield retreat from the doorway, taking a seat at the table in the other room momentarily.

Brooke dared touch the bottom of the tote to see if the vial had leaked, but there was no wetness, and the cap was already replaced on the glass tube. The deceased pair had already struck somewhere, and she blamed herself for not keeping a better eye on Clarke. Of course, his companion might have dumped the vial somewhere without him, and either way, Brooke assumed anything around her might be contaminated.

Quickly searching both of the bodies for further information or evidence, she found a few papers on Clarke's body. They appeared to be instructions, but the man had also written some information by hand along the bottom of one page. She placed the papers inside of the tote for safe keeping.

When she looked up, Canfield had returned to the doorway, but now he held the gun on her.

"John, we really don't have time for this," she said calmly, taking a step in his direction.

"You murdered two people!" he cried, his flush face on the verge of tears as the life he knew crashed down around him.

"John," she said, trying to reassure him as she took another step forward, causing him to flinch the gun a bit and take a step back.

She noticed he knew enough to make certain the safety was off, which impressed her. Canfield had never mentioned using firearms, and she had never risked looking knowledgeable by taking him to a gun range. Because he was from Texas, she assumed he knew at least some firearms basics.

"I have to call the police," he said.

Brooke felt her device vibrate from a pocket, but she didn't dare look down, or she risked losing Canfield's trust forever.

"You have to trust me, John. These two just poisoned a water supply, a food supply, or maybe something worse. They're part of what you're seeing on the news."

"How can I trust you? Our relationship was built on lies!"

"Not all of it," Brooke said, feeling a bit hurt that he spoke the words. "If I didn't care about you, I wouldn't have brought you here. You've had a rough week."

"You think?" he asked, exasperated. "I lose my job, my girlfriend is an assassin, and now the entire world is getting attacked by terrorists."

Brooke decided Canfield wasn't going to shoot her, so she pulled the electronic device from her pocket to read the latest message from Taylor.

NADEAU HAS LAUNCHED A CHEMICAL AGENT.
POSSIBLY A CONTAGEON. GET TO SAFETY.

"John, we have to get somewhere safe."

"I'm not safe with you."

"How can you say that? You're acting like I kill people indiscriminately. These two were about to kill *thousands*, John."

Brooke grabbed the gas masks, holding them up to support her argument.

Putting them on the bed, she took another step toward Canfield, and this time he didn't shrink back, allowing her to gently take the gun from his shaking right hand.

"You're here because I want you here," she said, cupping his bearded cheeks once again. "I didn't know any of this was going to happen."

"What now?" he asked, his voice much quieter than usual as he waited for her to take the lead.

"I'm not sure," Brooke answered. "These two poisoned something, so we don't drink water that's not from a bottle, or eat food that isn't from a can. And we keep these gas masks handy."

She took one last look at the bodies before handing the gas masks to Canfield and hefting the tote from the bed, prepared to find a safe resting place for the remaining vials.

"Let's get out of here," she said, prompting Canfield to follow her.

Brooke knew she would need to check the room more thoroughly for additional paperwork and hidden items before the police were alerted, so she placed a sign on the exterior doorknob to indicate no linens were necessary. Hoping the sign kept housekeeping from entering the room, she exited with Canfield, needing to solidify his trust once again during the coming hours.

***

Several hours later, Canfield remained glued to the television, because the news continued to stream horrific news and unexplained phenomena. Particularly in urban areas, people weren't safe because contaminants floated through the air, and people who breathed them became gravely ill in a short period of time.

"Anything new?" Brooke asked when she walked in from the bathroom after splashing some water on her face.

Following the events in the suite, the couple returned to their room, and Canfield hadn't set foot outside as the media informed them of the horrors awaiting them. Brooke went to the suite once more, let herself inside, and discovered a few more paper files and a thumb drive, all hidden behind a desk and secured with clear tape. She grabbed them, cleaned the room of all fingerprints that she and her boyfriend might have left, and made her way discreetly downstairs.

Being a Monday, the hotel wasn't packed, particularly as a number of people checked out before worldwide explosions provided panic in every corner of the globe.

"You weren't lying," Canfield admitted soberly, his eyes still fixed on the television. "What the hell do we do now?"

"We wait. The hotel isn't going to kick us out with a pandemic out there." She paused, considering something important. "Have you reached out to your family?"

"Why?"

"They need to stay indoors, John. And away from the cities."

"I've been texting my brother and my ex-wife. Sounds like they're staying put. Guess I need to check in with my folks and my sister."

"Go ahead," Brooke urged him. "I'll see if I can get any updates from my sources."

Canfield took up his phone and keycard before heading into the hallway. Brooke seized the opportunity to check in with Taylor, who had been eerily silent the past hour.

WHAT'S THE NEWS?

She waited a moment before receiving a response.

GROWING PANIC AROUND HERE.
HOSPITALS ARE ALREADY FLOODED.
THOUSANDS SICK FROM BREATHING THE CHEMICAL AGENT.

Brooke didn't learn anything particularly new from the message, but the pandemic remained in an infant stage. She feared the death toll would grow, and such events were always followed by reactions from the public. If people dared step outside, they would purchase consumables, or loot retail stores, and wipe out supply. Looting and plundering would tax the already overworked public safety personnel.

In her mind, she already envisioned the National Guard occupying cities, and empty streets as everyone stayed indoors for their own safety. If the person behind these attacks turned out to be Nadeau, she felt the man earned her respect, even as a mass murderer. Simultaneously, or almost simultaneously, detonating hundreds or thousands of chemical packs to explode across the globe was no easy feat.

Thinking ahead, Brooke decided she wanted to get some supplies before more people fell in line with her predictions. She had noticed a drug store and a local grocery store between West Baden and French Lick, and they certainly carried canned goods and bottled water. Whether the world fell apart, or she simply needed to cover her tracks for ending the lives of Clarke and his traveling companion, Brooke required supplies. She was about to take up her keycard and car keys when Canfield walked through the door.

"What's up?" he asked, seeing her reaching for the rental car keys.

"It might be wise for us to get some supplies in case things get really bad. Did you reach your family?"

"Everyone is holing up," Canfield reported. "They want me to come down there."

"That probably isn't happening for a while, John. At least not until we know what we're dealing with out there."

"I know, and I told them that," he said with obvious disappointment.

"Is anyone else here?" Brooke inquired, picking up the car keys from the table.

"A few employees milling around. It looked like a few people were getting ready to check out."

"I would book another night, but we can't chance it."

"There are cameras everywhere in this place," Canfield noted as they stepped into the hallway.

"It's unlikely they saw me, because I kept my head down when I went to the sixth floor," Brooke said, "but they undoubtedly got some good footage of you following me."

"I'm going to get framed for murder," Canfield lamented.

"You're not getting framed," Brooke chastised him with a look that a parent might give a child in the wrong.

"You know what I mean," Canfield said, openly concerned. "The cops are going to take one look at the video and assume I'm the guilty party."

"That's sexist," Brooke said, stopping in the hallway.

"I'm not sexist," he protested with his hands in the air. "*They're* sexist!"

"The cops who exist only in your mind at this point are pinning this murder on you because you're a man?"

"Something like that?" Canfield answered the question with a diminishing voice, wincing as though he expected to be struck in the face.

Brooke started walking down the hall, and Canfield quickly caught up.

"I think the cops are going to be way too busy to worry about us after the doomsday scenario Nadeau cooked up," she stated.

"Too busy to solve a murder?"

"Yes."

"And who's Nadeau?"

Brooke explained her true mission to him as they found an elevator and rode down to the ground floor, where literally no people could be found until they approached the valet counter on their way out of the hotel. Two young men stood there, and both appeared on edge about something. At first, she wondered if the world events were plaguing them, but she considered the possibility the staff knew about the two bodies in the suite.

"Hello," Canfield said cordially with a nod, and the two valets returned courteous nods, saying nothing.

Stepping outside, the couple found no vehicles parked along the drop-off area, and a glance up the hill revealed a nearly empty parking lot.

"Not good," Canfield murmured as they ascended the sidewalk to the main parking lot atop a small hill.

Streets in the two small, adjoining towns were virtually barren, which meant people were likely hunkered down, either watching their televisions, or possibly ill from whatever action Clarke took before his untimely death.

Brooke walked into the local grocery store with Canfield, and sent him to grab a short list of items while she grabbed essentials for the road. Daring not linger at the hotel much longer, she knew they were going to need food, fluids, and possibly even toilet paper for the road. She also picked up a few red gas cans in case fuel became scarce in her future travels. A nagging feeling that this event was so much worse than 9/11 and past pandemics stuck with her. Her agency's leadership didn't conduct surveillance without just cause, and she wondered if they were spread too thin to monitor Nadeau's inner circle more closely.

When she found Canfield, he was in a back corner of the store, crouched down while talking to someone who wore a nametag, and appeared to work in the deli. The young man's skin appeared ashen in tone, and he was sweating profusely.

"What happened?" she asked.

"He took an early lunch," Canfield said. "Said he's been feeling sick ever since."

"My coworkers called me an ambulance," the man said weakly, "but I haven't seen anyone in a few minutes."

"Can I get you something?" Canfield offered.

"Water," the employee replied. "My insides feel like they're burning up."

Walking over to a nearby cooler, Canfield grabbed a water, twisted the cap off, and handed it to the young man. The employee drank it hastily about halfway before he stopped with a cough, as though his body rejected any further hydration.

Brooke provided Canfield with a look that indicated they needed to get moving, because she suspected Clarke and his companion might have poisoned items within the store. The store made sense, because it could infect locals and tourists alike, helping spread whatever contamination sent people to hospitals in droves. She noticed Canfield carrying a few snacks and bottled drinks in addition to the items she requested. Reluctantly, he stood, taking her side while carrying the items in both arms like a newborn.

"Make sure none of those have punctures, or have been opened," she warned, looking down at the items that could be poisoned by a needle, or sealed a second time.

"Shit," Canfield said, understanding what she implied immediately.

A woman dressed like a manager appeared from the back, tending to the employee with a phone in her hand.

"The ambulance is coming," she told him, "but they're backed up at least an hour with everything that's been happening on the news."

Brooke noticed Canfield staring with empathy, unable to imagine the cornucopia of tormented thoughts passing through his mind.

"We need to get moving, John."

Nodding numbly, Canfield carried their goods behind Brooke.

An eerie feeling overtook both Brooke and her boyfriend as they reluctantly left the employee, because no other employee had come through the store. Canfield set the bottled drinks down, opting for a 24-pack of water, pulling it from the middle of a nearby stack after moving a few other packs aside.

Barely finding an employee to ring up their items, the couple tried to avoid appearing nervous as they panned the store for hazards, or additional people.

"I'm so sorry," the cashier had said when she emerged from the back.

Brooke wasn't certain what kept their employees, or if virtually everyone quit at once, but she felt at that very moment, as though she bore witness to the calm before the storm. She helped the older woman behind the register bag the groceries, prepared to make a dash for their rental car when she decided to ask a question first.

"Where is everyone?"

"Under the weather," the woman answered. "The manager brought in breakfast, and a few of them started feeling bad. Must've been some kind of food poisoning."

"Probably," Brooke said, putting forth a calm front. "Hope everyone gets to feeling better."

"Thank you. The rest of us have been glued to the television all day. Have you seen what's been happening?"

"We have."

"I'm glad we're in a small town," the woman said as she scanned items with little more than a glance. "Things like that don't tend to reach us down here."

Canfield released a knowing sigh, but the woman didn't appear to notice. Brooke realized she, and her employers, didn't truly know the extent of Nadeau's reach. Without knowing, they couldn't possibly combat his plans, and fear would soon overtake the public.

Canfield stared at the woman, knowing the same truth, and Brooke had to tap him on the arm before he compromised them.

"They're sick," he said, waiting until they crossed the parking lot to their car.

One of only a dozen vehicles in the lot, it served as a reminder that something dire overtook the tourist towns, most assuredly propelled by Clarke. Perhaps he tapped into a smaller water supply, or several, to infect the town. Not knowing the details infuriated Brooke, and she now wished she had kept Clarke or his companion alive for interrogation. At the time, she dared not risk one of them infecting her, shooting her, or calling for help.

"We need to get our stuff and get moving," she said, assuming the driver's seat.

"Where?"

"Anywhere but these sleepy towns. If housekeeping *does* find those bodies, we'll be stuck there when the cops start interviewing everyone."

Even so, Brooke left several items in her room that she required before they headed to their next destination.

A few minutes later, Brooke pulled the car into the parking lot, which appeared to hold a few less vehicles than before, if that was even possible. Leaving their supplies in the car, she and Canfield walked down the hill to the valet area. Making her proud, Canfield took notice of the black sedan parked just outside the entrance doors, and Brooke recognized it as a police vehicle. Unable to determine whether it belonged to the sheriff's department, or the state police, she didn't much care, because the vehicle's presence indicated at least one officer, or detective, had come to the hotel.

"I'm taking the back way to the room," Brooke told Canfield quietly as they walked through the sliding entrance doors. She spied a detective walking across the hotel's grand atrium, meeting a man who appeared to be the manager. "Keep them distracted if you can, and I'll meet you at the car."

"How am I supposed to distract them?"

"You're from Texas. Aren't you people conversational?"

Canfield rolled his eyes.

"I'll think of something. Do you want me to handle the checkout?"

"If you can. Meet me outside when you're done."

Brooke avoided the main lobby where hotel staff waited to check guests in or out, using the service elevator not far from the valet desk. She pressed the button, waiting a moment for the elevator car to descend. As she stepped inside, Brooke caught a glimpse of a man wearing a suit from the corner of her eye. He called to her with an authoritative tone, but she slipped her keycard into the slot, allowing her to choose a floor as she pretended not to hear the detective. A bulge along his right side indicated a firearm, and as he called to her, he had been reaching for what she assumed were his police credentials.

Holding her breath, she waited for the doors the doors to close, wishing she had chosen the stairs instead. When the doors closed before the man could get a hand in the way to stop them, Brooke breathed a sigh of relief.

She would take the stairs on the way down, she decided.

***

Canfield approached the lobby desk, internally struggling to keep from acting strangely in front of the hotel staff and the detective who stopped to question them. Wearing a suit, the young investigator stood beside the hotel manager, who appeared ready to take him somewhere. Everyone eyeballed Canfield when he strolled into the lobby, and he wondered just how much the investigators knew. Possibly summoned about discovered bodies, Canfield hoped the detectives were there about shots fired instead, and they hadn't been on the top floor yet.

Either way, Brooke needed to hurry, and he began to think checking out wasn't such a great idea, but turning around and leaving left him appearing guilty.

Although he fought to subdue his Texas accent and lingo for years following his departure from his home state, Canfield decided now was the time to fall into natural habits.

"Good mornin'," he said, approaching the desk with a young woman standing behind it.

She glanced at the manager, as though to ask whether she should carry out her normal duties, and the manager nodded approval. A few minutes passed with a tenseness in the air as the manager said he would take the detective upstairs. Canfield fought to keep his composure, hoping Brooke got what she needed, and quickly, because confirmed deaths meant a full team of investigators swarming the hotel and asking questions.

Canfield didn't make small talk, and the hotel clerk didn't speak about the weather, or the fact that cities across the world were being bombed with particulate chemicals. She appeared uneasy, as though worried about family, or something wrong at the hotel. Canfield decided inquiring might make him suspicious, and he simply wanted to escape the property with Brooke before speaking to his family members. He wasn't certain he could stay with her any longer, particularly if she was on the run, or planned to track down more terrorists. Canfield had two children to worry about, and if the world was ending, he wanted to be with family members he trusted.

Canfield's brother and sister both worked in careers that kept them outdoors, meaning they knew how to hunt and fish. Canfield no longer had roots in Buffalo, and nowhere else that meant much to him, so he needed to head south.

"You're all set," the hotel employee said, bringing him back to the present as she handed him the receipt, forcing a smile. "Hope you enjoyed your stay."

"I did," Canfield lied, thinking his life took a terrible turn when he lost his source of income.

Now he had aided and abetted in two murders, and the end of the world might be upon him. Picking up the pace as he crossed the atrium, Canfield simply wanted to get outside before anyone with authority crossed his path. He figured that examining the bodies would take any cops on scene at least several minutes, so he took a deep breath when he crossed the sliding glass doors one last time. Fresh air felt good on his face, and Brooke already had the rental car coming down the hill toward him. She stopped just in time for him to slide into the passenger's seat before accelerating.

"Where to now?" he asked.

"I need to review those documents," she answered. "Let's get somewhere that we can watch the news and I figure out what these people are up to."

Canfield couldn't argue with her logic. He would stay in contact with his family and formulate a plan, because he needed to lay low at best, and protect himself from deadly chemical agents at worst. For now, survival meant staying with Brooke, because she clearly knew more about this attack than the media, or any average cop.

Chapter 8

The Present

Although the sun's rays struck the ground, the sky remained spattered with clouds, making it difficult for Metzger to determine the location of the aircraft flying near the airport. He determined that the advantage belonged to his group, because the people in the plane wouldn't be able to see details along the ground.

He turned to his brother.

"Park the van off to the side and leave a few doors open so it looks abandoned."

"What about Hewitt?"

"Keep him in line." Metzger turned to Jillian. "Can you help with that?"

"On it."

Ushering Isabella and Nathan into the hangar where Timmons continued to examine the two possible flight options, Metzger began to close one of the overhead doors when his ears detected a welcome sound.

"It's passing us," Timmons said, barely looking up from the small jet in the hangar corner.

"Could it be turning for an approach?" Metzger asked.

"Of course it could, but they're swinging awfully wide for that."

Metzger let his friend continue to work, stepping outside with Isabella and Nathan behind him as his brother and Jillian finished relocating the van. Bryce took his side momentarily, and Jillian closed the van doors after hearing the sound of the overhead plane diminishing.

"Where's Hewitt?" Metzger inquired.

"In the van," Jillian answered. "Still sleeping."

"That's all he does."

"Should we be worried?" Bryce asked, looking skyward.

"Not unless that plane turns around."

Metzger walked over to the van, opening one of the doors to begin gathering their belongings. The others chipped in, helping him stack their bags and weapons near the hangar so they could move quickly once Timmons determined their best method of travel.

Ten minutes later, the passing plane faded from their minds as no overhead sounds could be heard. Timmons stepped from the hangar, dusting off his hands as he looked to everyone in the group.

"Both should fly," he reported. "The jet is a bit low on fuel, but it'll allow us to communicate easier, and we would get there quicker."

"Does it have enough fuel to make Virginia?" Bryce questioned.

Timmons gave a skeptical look as he held his hand flat before wavering it to indicate an iffy proposition.

"We need to think beyond Virginia," Metzger noted. "We need a plane that'll get us there and wherever we need to take this CIA person."

"Then we take the Piper," Timmons decided. "It'll be tight, and technically, we'll be over the weight limit, but it shouldn't be a problem."

"We can't afford to dawdle," Metzger said. "Is there anything I can do to help?"

"Have your brother watch our prisoner. If you and Jillian could find me some fuel to top this off, that would help."

Bryce heard what the captain said, and didn't particularly like being circumvented around in conversation. Metzger knew the two Navy men were accustomed to falling in line and obeying regulations and ranks, so he typically took charge of most situations personally to avoid conflicts. As the member of their group who'd survived amongst the dead the longest, his words mattered to the others. Even Bryce and Timmons tended to listen to his advice, and Metzger didn't attempt to be an alpha male. He listened to the others, and often soaked in their words and stories, but at the end of the day he possessed an uncanny knowledge of the undead that continued to grow.

Although his brother said nothing, the lieutenant commander huffed a bit before heading for the van where Hewitt continued to lazily accept his fate. Isabella and Nathan followed him, permitting Timmons to continue inspecting the plane he chose for the next phase of their journey.

Metzger knew regular fuel could sustain the plane, but if they hoped to use the Piper for several trips, he wanted to locate fuel specifically made for the aircraft. Without power, the fuel pumps couldn't function, and he doubted he could get lucky a second time and locate a fuel truck like he had in Virginia.

"What are we looking for?" Jillian asked as they made their way toward the airport's structures, stabbing a zombie in the skull along the way.

"A fuel truck would be ideal, but a generator to run the pumps would work."

"Most generators we've found are dry, Dan."

"True. In a pinch, we syphon gas from a car."

Metzger noticed Jillian's body language, which indicated she wasn't pleased about something. Around the time he decided to leave the resort, which provided the group with safety, food, and warmth, she acted slightly withdrawn.

"What's wrong?" he inquired as they walked along a taxiing area, not far from the central hub.

A few undead trapped behind glass took notice, and pawed at the already smeared, dirty windows. Metzger felt a sense of déjà vu after finding the same scene at several airports where people went to escape, finding only their demise instead. He and Jillian stopped in front of the window where the dead acted like moving mannequins, displaying tattered, soiled clothing.

"You never asked," Jillian replied, looking him in the eye with disappointment.

"Asked about what?" Metzger responded, though he felt certain he knew the answer.

"We had a good thing going up there, Dan. Food, water, shelter."

"You know who I am, Jillian. From the day we met I've made no bones about the fact that I'm going to find the person, or people, responsible for all of this."

Jillian said nothing, appearing exasperated for a moment.

"People depend on you, Dan."

"You're an adult, Jillian. You could've stayed, and I would have come back to you."

"You know I'm committed to you. To us."

"Is this about confronting Colby again?" Metzger asked, wondering why this conversation hadn't occurred sooner.

"This is about us surviving and making a life at some point."

Metzger considered her words momentarily as a few of the undead rounded a corner behind his girlfriend.

"Right now, that life is little more than a fantasy. We don't know that Nadeau is done. And like it or not, no one out there is safe until they develop a vaccine, which requires me or my brother to cooperate with the military."

"Another decision you're willing to make without me?"

"Excuse me," Metzger said, stepping past Jillian to slice through the skulls of the two undead drawing dangerously close.

Metzger took the time to wipe the blood from his blade across the clothing of the downed undead before returning to Jillian.

"Where is this coming from?" he asked. "You and I want the same things, but there are people out there who need help."

"Help you aren't obligated to provide, Dan. The military didn't exactly treat you like royalty once they discovered you were useful to them."

"I don't want to run and hide, looking over my shoulder all the time. They tracked down Bryce twice already. I want a life where we don't live in fear from terrorist attacks, or the military finding us. This is all means to an end, Jillian."

"This is all *so* dangerous. You received the gift of finding your family. Most people don't get that opportunity these days."

Metzger realized she wasn't being selfish, or thinking of her own safety, but rather his well-being. He cupped her chin, providing a knowing grin.

"I love you," he said. "Whatever happens, good or bad, I want you by my side."

"You said it," Jillian whispered, a tear running down her cheek.

"I've said it before," Metzger said, not understanding the magnitude of his declaration.

"I know, but the way you said it was different, like you believe we have a future together."

"That's the reason I'm doing this," he said emphatically. "Our window of opportunity to live halfway normal lives is closing. We're going to run out of food and fuel, and life will be tough enough without having to deal with outside threats. It's the reason I want some of these issues eliminated. And that includes Nadeau and his people."

Metzger gently cupped both of her hands.

"I'm doing this to protect the family I have left. And that includes you."

Jillian wiped the moisture from her right eye.

"Maybe I should stop talking so much and find us some fuel," she said, sniffling a bit.

"We'll find it," Metzger said confidently, looking ahead of them to see a few disabled vehicles and more undead wandering around the airport's exterior.

He provided Jillian with a quick kiss on the cheek and they trudged forward to deal with the slow-moving threat.

***

Timmons continued to examine the plane when he heard the van's engine roar to life from the side of the hangar. Curious, and a bit paranoid about Hewitt after the man assaulted him on more than one occasion, the pilot stepped from the hangar's interior to see Bryce driving the vehicle to its original parking spot.

"Why did you do that?" Timmons questioned when the lieutenant commander stepped from the van.

"Did I need your permission?" Bryce asked testily.

"No," the pilot answered firmly.

Bryce stepped forward, leaving his wife and son beside the van, and Hewitt presumably inside. Before speaking, he used the key fob to lock the vehicle, ensuring Hewitt couldn't simply open a door and attempt to flee without them hearing several distinct noises first.

"Just because you can fly us somewhere doesn't automatically mean you're in charge."

"I leave the decisions to your brother."

Timmons tested a few bolts inside a panel, finding them sufficiently tight.

"Like when he just ordered me to keep an eye on Hewitt? Oh, wait, that was you."

"Would you rather I asked you and your son to battle the dead while searching for fuel?" Timmons countered.

"I'd rather you just do your pilot thing and leave the survival stuff to us."

"Where is this coming from?" Timmons inquired with an arched eyebrow, still holding the socket wrench in one hand as his arm draped over the motor housing. "If I didn't know better, I'd say you want me gone completely."

"Out here, rank doesn't count for much, Captain."

Timmons chuckled, giving a cagy grin.

"I outrank you in the Navy, and in life, kid."

"I don't know what Dan sees in you, for the life of me."

"Do I detect a hint of jealousy?" Timmons asked, deciding to push Bryce's buttons. "You're acting like I'm some kind of bad influence."

"Dan doesn't need another father. Our parents were damn fine people."

"I believe that, based on how both of your turned out."

Timmons set down the socket wrench and closed the compartment door before turning to Bryce.

"I don't know where this animosity is coming from, but I'm not trying to be your boss, or Dan's dad. Just trying to do my part to get us from one safe port to the next."

"It was awful convenient that you were right there when Dan was about to escape the base."

"It's a shame that you weren't there to protect him after he went through hell to reach you."

Isabella stepped forward from the van, causing both men to look her way.

"You two can stop this bickering. Everyone got along all winter, and you two choose now to air your grievances?"

Timmons felt bad about some of the exchange, but he wasn't about to allow Bryce to smear his actions when he looked after the younger Metzger for the better part of two months at the base.

"We're all in the same boat," Isabella noted. "If the consolidated military finds us, we're screwed."

About to agree with her comment, Timmons heard a distant noise that caused him to pause, looking skyward. The others heard the sound of a plane as well, and Timmons felt certain the aircraft had circled around for some reason and now wanted a better look, or to land dangerously close to the group.

He turned to Bryce when he realized the plane appeared to be lining up for a landing.

"Get that van out of sight and don't let Hewitt make a sound."

Bryce didn't immediately move, standing firm to make a point.

"Please," Timmons added, prompting the younger man to take his wife and son over to the van to keep them all from being spotted by the pilot and any passengers above.

Taking a look upward, the Navy captain felt certain he had approximately one minute before anyone above could spot activity on the ground. He closed the hangar doors from the inside, emerging to scour the area for any of his travel companions.

He spotted Bryce moving the van between hangars, keeping his family outside of the van. The slightly tinted windows didn't allow for him to monitor Hewitt, but Timmons needed to find cover because he knew for certain the plane was going to attempt a landing. Giving a cursory glance in the other direction, the pilot didn't see Metzger or Jillian, assuming they understood the situation and found cover. When he looked upward again, Timmons spotted the single-propeller plane making a turn to line up for its landing. He patted the sidearm holstered at his side in case he required its service, preparing to find cover until the plane landed.

Hearing the crunch of some remaining snow behind him, Timmons spun too late to properly defend himself against an incoming attack.

***

When Metzger heard the plane returning to the airspace above their location, he touched Jillian's hand, immediately alerting her that they needed to move.

He wanted to find somewhere safe to keep them from being spotted by anyone in the plane, but not too far from his family and Timmons in case they required assistance. Anyone from members of the military to someone searching for family members might be landing beside them within moments. They might avoid contact altogether, or end up in a shootout that risked their travel plans.

"Fuel truck," Jillian said, spotting the object they sought, nudging Metzger lightly. "We can hide behind it and see if it runs."

Metzger didn't love the suggestion, because the location of the fuel truck placed them farther from their companions, but the plane became visible in the distance.

"We don't have time to get back to them," he thought aloud. "Fuel truck it is."

Tucked behind a school bus, a disabled plane, and a dedicated snowplow, the fuel truck couldn't have been spotted by the group, given the route they used to enter the airport. Metzger glanced upward every few seconds during their dash to the collection of vehicles, finally seeing the plane come into view. He and Jillian weren't in danger of being spotted by the pilot unless they darted into the middle of the airport and flailed their arms. The vehicles covered their movements once they reached the snowplow, and the remaining undead now stared blankly at the sky, curious about the sound breaking the silence at the airport.

Metzger quietly opened the driver's side door to the fuel truck, trying to avoid luring the undead to their position. He didn't see keys in the ignition, but a quick search under the seat, then the overhead visor, revealed their hiding spot. Sliding them into a pocket for safekeeping, he waited with Jillian between the disabled plane and the snowplow, watching the plane descend for an attempted landing.

"Could it be the military?" Jillian asked as they hunkered down beside the snowplow, continuing to look skyward.

"Only if their fleet is depleted, or they're trying to pull a fast one."

"What do you mean?"

"That thing is worse than most of the planes we've been in," he said as the plane sputtered briefly, as though making his point.

"Maybe he's just low on fuel," Jillian suggested.

Metzger grunted quietly, considering her notion plausible.

"Speaking of," he said, beginning to maneuver around the truck, opening the driver's side door again.

"They're about to land, Dan."

"We may need a quick getaway," Metzger retorted. "No better time than now to see if this will start, before they can hear us."

Jillian shook her head negatively.

"The dead can hear us."

"I'll be quick," Metzger promised, turning the key and discovering the truck was hesitant to start as the engine attempted to turn over a few times, each cycle sounding meeker than the last.

Metzger tried once more, but the second try sounded even worse. He jumped down from the truck as the plane began to touch down at the end of the runway.

"If there's good news to be had," he said, "I think the truck just needs a jump and we'll be set."

"Sure," Jillian said. "If the military doesn't pile out of that plane and capture all of us."

"We'll be fine," Metzger said, feeling reasonably confident, "so long as everyone stays out of sight."

***

Timmons whirled too late as two undead emerged from behind the hangar, remaining much more silent than usual for some reason. Caught off balance, he tumbled backwards as one of the zombies landed directly on top of him, pinning his left arm to the ground. Forced to use his right forearm to fend off the zombie's snapping teeth, which made a grating sound when they gnashed, he watched helplessly as the second member of the dead dropped to his knees in an attempt to bite at his throat.

Attempting to wriggle free, Timmons barely moved more than a few inches because of their combined weight. Wearing a winter coat made from a material similar to canvas or fire hose, he shrugged his left shoulder so the second zombie, a female wearing hiking gear, bit into the fleshy area between his collar bone and shoulder, rather than the flesh along his throat or cheek.

Timmons yowled in pain, catching a glance of the plane coming in for its landing from an upside-down position. Although he didn't think the teeth of the undead could pierce the winter jacket, the zombie's jaw acted like a clamp that didn't let up, or feel pain. He didn't particularly care about being spotted by the plane's passengers because his mind switched to survival mode. Continuing to squirm while jaws snapped at him, he considered letting his right hand reach for the gun at his side, or the knife sheathed along the small of his back. Either move likely spelled his demise, so he continued to hold the zombie atop him at bay while raising his left elbow enough to clock his other attacker in the head.

Hearing new footsteps crunch to his right side, Timmons dared not look as they drew to a stop. The next few seconds felt like an eternity until he heard a knife plunge into the head of the zombie pinning him down, followed by a blade entering the eye socket of the attacker on his left shoulder. Feeling his body relax, partly because his strength was sapped, Timmons went limp, simply lying on the ground a few seconds to collect himself.

"Come on," he heard Bryce say, seeing his fellow Navy man offer a hand as the noise from the plane drew closer.

Timmons accepted the help, and both men scurried behind some nearby crates left beside the hangar.

Taking a moment to evaluate his injuries, Timmons saw no puncture marks through the rugged winter jacket. His shoulder still hurt, however, as though some large hand had reached down to pinch his trapezius muscle, and hadn't let up.

"Why did you hesitate?" Timmons asked when they were out of sight. "Did you think about letting me die?"

"No," Bryce answered emphatically, his face indicating he told the truth. "My knife was stuck."

"Took you long enough," Timmons commented.

"I was following *your* orders and watching Hewitt, Captain. You can't have it both ways."

As Bryce spoke the words, the plane drew closer to them after touching down and slowing along the runway. From what little bit Timmons heard and observed, he guessed the pilot possessed a fair amount of skill and experience flying a plane. At this point, he tried to catch his breath after dealing with the two zombies, but Bryce stared at the plane stonily, as though he expected something evil to emerge from the aircraft.

"What happened to you out there?" Timmons asked, softening his tone a bit when he realized Bryce had never provided details about his travels while the military searched for him.

"I came to realize they don't really care about us."

"They gathered your families while you were at sea, and kept them safe."

"Let me guess," Bryce said, turning to the pilot while the plane taxied in their direction. "Those families are now expected to contribute and help wash clothes, or grow food, or clean the base."

"That doesn't sound much different than what we all did for your in-laws."

Bryce grunted.

"We'll continue this later."

Both men watched as a single pilot emerged from the old Cessna, with no passengers. Colored red with a white stripe from front to back, the plane displayed some blemishes, possibly even bullet holes, from what Timmons could discern. He remained in cover with Bryce as they observed the pilot open a door behind him, removing a backpack and a sidearm before closing the door. When the man turned in their direction, Timmons gauged him to be younger than either Metzger brother, with a determined look etched in his face.

"Do we let him pass?" Timmons whispered to Bryce, feeling reasonably certain the younger man might simply leave the airport in search of what brought him there.

"No," the lieutenant commander said, pulling his sidearm from its holster and emerging from behind the crates to train it on the unsuspecting young pilot. "Stop right there."

Whirling to face the voice barking orders, the young man raised both of his hands, each holding items, as Timmons slowly rose beside Bryce.

"I didn't want to land here," the man said. "My plane was low on fuel, and I realized I couldn't make it to the next airport."

"Where are you heading?" Timmons asked.

Bryce stepped forward, keeping the gun pointed at the young man, snatching the backpack and firearm without a word. He began patting down the man's clothing, and Timmons wondered if his fellow service member thought the man might be another Marine or soldier sent to track down the lieutenant commander. He didn't know much about the details, because Bryce told only his wife and brother about his time on the road, but Timmons knew something scarred Bryce along the way.

"Morrisville-Stowe," the man answered. "We have a settlement nearby. Look, I don't want any trouble. You can have the plane."

"Why did you leave the settlement?" Bryce questioned, finding nothing worth retrieving from the man's clothing.

Hesitating a few seconds, the pilot apparently decided cooperation might gain him trust, and freedom, instead of holding out.

"We had friends near Syracuse," he said. "I was transporting five or six at a time to our settlement."

"What's so special about this settlement?" Bryce asked, relentless with his mistrust of the young man.

"I'm not telling you that," the pilot answered, showing his first signs of defiance. "And I won't tell you the location."

"I'm betting you will," Bryce said, taking an offensive position as though he might strike the pilot.

Isabella and Nathan approached, and Timmons saw the van behind them. He hoped Hewitt didn't attempt an escape, because he might pull it off with everyone distracted. The sight of his wife and child did little to settle Bryce's temperament, and without Metzger nearby, Timmons decided to act with the hope of settling the lieutenant commander. He drew near Bryce's right ear so no one else heard his words.

"If you're worried about him being sent by them, check the plane, and check his bag," Timmons suggested. "He'd have a radio, or a tracking device, wouldn't he?"

Bryce looked at him with a hint of shock, as though he didn't expect Timmons to know the details about the previous men sent to locate Bryce, or his brother. He blinked several times, as though realizing his paranoia might cause him to harm an innocent survivor. Now he looked directly at the pilot, still training his gun on the man.

"Open your bag and show me what's inside."

Momentarily, the man balked, his face indicating he didn't particularly want to comply.

"Just show him, so we can get you on your way, kid," Timmons said casually, trying to alleviate the tension.

When the pilot continued his reluctance, Bryce shook the gun in his hand slightly, continuing to aim it at the traveler.

"You're making me think you're one of them," the lieutenant commander stammered, not acting his calm and collected self.

"One of who?" the man asked, exasperated.

Before another word was spoken, a fuel truck pulled up beside the group, adding to the pilot's anxiety, but providing a welcome sight to the others when Metzger and Jillian stepped down from the cab.

"What's this?" Metzger questioned.

"Your brother thinks this guy was sent to track us," Timmons said calmly, because Bryce wasn't lowering the firearm.

"That's a possibility," Metzger agreed.

"I wasn't sent by anyone," the young man virtually pleaded. "I swear, I'm trying to get back to my group."

"We can relate," Metzger said. "I'm guessing my brother asked you to show us your belongings for confirmation. Can you do that for me?"

Again, the man hesitated. Finally, he tossed the bag to Metzger, and Timmons walked over to the plane, opening the doors before searching behind and under the seating.

"I think you can lower that," Metzger said to his brother, referring to the gun.

Isabella walked over to her husband, gently pushing his arms down, keeping the gun from being pointed at anyone.

Metzger went through the bag, finding another firearm, a small notebook, and some medications. They appeared to be antibiotics, and other pills used for more specific ailments. Such items weren't easy to come by in the apocalypse, explaining the man's reluctance. Even now he eyeballed Metzger with trepidation that his medications might be stolen by the people who greeted him so rudely at the end of the runway.

"I don't see anything that threatens us," Timmons reported as he closed the plane's hatches.

"Me either," Metzger said, zipping the bag shut and tossing it to the relieved pilot. "I apologize for our paranoia," he said, addressing the man directly. "We have some people trying to track us, and we can't afford to take chances."

"I can relate," the young man said with a nod. "After that last trip, I think I'm done with the plane if you want to take it. She was on fumes when I landed."

"I think we can handle that problem," Metzger said, thumbing towards the fuel truck behind him. "You got a vehicle?"

"I did at the other airport."

"We might be able to help with that."

"Much obliged," the man said. "I'm due for some good luck."

Metzger nodded politely.

"Give us a few minutes, and we'll have a van for you. It's in good shape, but also a bit low on fuel."

Metzger tugged his brother by the arm, leading him over to the van.

"You okay?"

"I will be," Bryce said. "It's just hard to trust anyone after what they did to Molly."

"I get it, big brother. We grab Hewitt and we head back to Virginia for the exchange. After that, our worries should be behind us."

"Until we find Nadeau."

"Until we find Nadeau," Metzger agreed with a grin, tapping his brother on the arm to show solidarity.

Chapter 9

An unusual sensation overtook Sutton because he felt nervous about several things at once. Typically well-prepared by nature, he hated having to rely on others to come through, but he needed to hear from Metzger before he moved forward with their plan. Once he knew they were in the air, he planned on revealing the details of the past several days to Robert and Nancy McAllister, because taking Hewitt to the military base depended on their cooperation.

Sutton considered his life much simpler before joining up with Metzger and his group, but at this point he wouldn't trade the experience. Finding his one surviving son made the leap of faith worthwhile, and he rather enjoyed protecting the others, at least until they were separated and a questionable decision led to the death of Jillian's father.

He paced the community's shrinking yard with the sat phone in his pocket, awaiting Metzger's call. Walkable areas dwindled as the residents brought in more items that took up space, such as firewood, storage sheds, and a few spare vehicles in case they needed to evacuate quickly. If the yards were an interior space, Sutton would call them a fire hazard because they felt so cluttered.

Uncertain of how the inevitable discussion with the community leaders might go, Sutton felt a bit concerned that people he had traveled with weren't all thrilled about the plan. Twice already, the group had been together and split into segments. Once again, they would be reunited, but someone needed to make certain Hewitt was delivered to the military, and others would work with the CIA operative to locate Nadeau. He and Metzger agreed on the best course of action, but without McAllister and his wife onboard, the group might experience delays in their plan, or have to leave the community for good.

Sutton's experience at keeping secrets served him well, but he didn't like endangering others he cared about. He understood that Luke wanted to stay in the community at all costs to keep Samantha safe, but hiding behind brick walls only kept residents safe for so long. Another group always wanted what safe people possessed, and outside threats like Nadeau could always strike again.

When the sat phone in his pocket rang, Sutton scrambled to grab it and answer it before anyone noticed he was carrying a phone with him. He nearly fumbled it a few times after pulling it into the open, but he pressed a button to answer it, finding no one in his vicinity to take notice of him talking on a phone, or eavesdropping.

"Hello?" he answered the phone with subdued volume, feeling strange talking on a phone after nearly eight months of the apocalypse.

"It's Dan," a familiar voice said from the other end.

"I'm glad to hear your voice."

Sutton ducked behind a house, since he couldn't exactly hop over the wall, or exit through the secured front gate.

"Something wrong?" Metzger inquired.

"Our CIA person is growing impatient."

"We're on our way, Colby."

Sutton could hear his friend clearly, but the hum of a plane in flight filled the background.

"I'll get things in motion on my end. You'll either be welcome, or the rest of us may get kicked out of here."

"Maybe you should let Gracine do the talking," Metzger said, half-joking by his tone, because Sutton wasn't always the most patient person in conversations.

"I've got it handled. Believe it or not, these people like me."

Metzger chuckled, though not in a condescending way.

"We should be there within a few hours. I could use a signal to help us land closer to your village."

"I'm pretty sure I can honor that request once we hear your plane."

"Good."

"Is everyone okay on your end?"

"Yeah," Metzger answered. "We all made it."

"Same here. And we have a few more allies I think you'll like."

"Glad to hear *someone* likes us. With luck, we'll see you in a few hours, Colby."

"Safe travels, Dan."

Sutton severed the connection by hitting the phone's red button, only to look up and see Father Paul standing a few feet from him.

"Sounds like it's about time you have that talk with Robert," the priest stated.

Sutton and Father Paul had bonded over the winter, often hunting together. While Sutton shot deer in a kill box the community designed, the priest often covered him, watching for any strangers or undead. He wasn't Sutton's only hunting partner by any means, but he didn't converse with the other people nearly as much. Father Paul and Sister Rosa knew of the plan to bring Metzger and the others to the community to meet with Brooke. They had been brainstorming a safe way to deliver Hewitt to the military without wasting precious time as well.

"I'm not sure how this is going to go, Paul," Sutton addressed his friend without placing the title ahead of his name. Sometimes he simply used his name, much like a traditional friend, and not a Catholic priest. "I could be putting some of us at risk."

"I think I can help facilitate the discussion," Father Paul offered.

"I don't want to put you in the middle of this."

"You trusted me and Rosa enough to tell us your secret early on, so trust me to help with this." Father Paul provided a knowing smile. "Besides, I'm already in the middle."

"Alright," Sutton agreed. "Let's go see what our fate will be."

***

"What?" Robert McAllister yelled at the top of his lungs after Sutton explained the past few days, along with the plan to deliver Hewitt and possibly bring new residents into Maplewood. "You're just now telling me this?"

"We didn't want to bring it to you until we knew everything would work out," Sutton replied.

"But you managed to hide the fact that our new houseguest is former CIA," McAllister spat, making Sutton regret his decision about providing virtually every detail of the past few days.

Both he and Father Paul stood in the man's living room, which appeared far more elaborate than any other living room in the community. Decorated with mounted hunting trophies, including some from overseas, porcelain vases more than a century old, and artwork that looked far too pricy for Sutton's taste, the room almost appeared overstuffed. Sutton knew McAllister liked to put on a show for prospective residents, and even his neighbors, because the man had always enjoyed money and power. The apocalypse somehow permitted him to continue his lifestyle, because he nabbed Maplewood for himself and controlled who came and went, once he convinced a few capable people to protect his new village.

"Did you know about this?" McAllister asked the priest, turning a fiery gaze upon the man of the cloth.

"I did," Father Paul answered truthfully. "There wasn't any point telling you until we were sure they were coming."

"Strangers," McAllister said angrily. "You're asking me to bring new strangers inside my gates."

"Strangers to you," Sutton said, "but some of the most trustworthy people I've ever met."

"Colby, we have rules for a reason," McAllister said, beginning to calm down a bit.

He never crossed Sutton too harshly, because he knew the man was far more capable than other Maplewood residents.

"Your rules, which are not entirely defined by the way," Sutton said flatly. "Which means you can give my friends sanctuary while some of us hunt down the man who put us in this predicament."

McAllister appeared far from convinced.

"You're putting a lot of faith in the word of this CIA operative. Wouldn't the rest of the government have hunted this man to the ends of the Earth?"

"Our elected officials are hunkered down in bunkers, leaving the rest of us out here to fend for ourselves. I put more faith in her than I would any messages they might send."

"And this group includes your two friends who have immunity to the infection?"

Sutton heard a discernibly sharp tone to McAllister's inquiry, because the man had made mention previously that he believed the Metzger brothers should surrender to the military. McAllister hadn't been turned away at the gates of a military base, so he likely considered them benevolent and trustworthy. Sutton experienced their cold nature firsthand, and Metzger was treated like a prisoner, despite his cooperation with their requests.

"I feel like the less I tell you, the better," Sutton said.

"I'll take that as a 'yes.'"

McAllister paced his living room floor momentarily before returning his gaze toward Sutton.

"If I take these people in, I'd be harboring fugitives. The Navy base isn't that far from here, you know."

"They're not all fugitives," Sutton said, growing irritated at the community's unofficial mayor. "And I'm not asking for all of them to stay. Most of them will be heading out with me to find the man responsible for the apocalypse."

"So, you would leave this community undefended while you go on some wild goose chase?"

Sutton audibly sighed through his nose, his blood pressure and temperature rising.

Taking notice, Father Paul stepped in before anything rash was spoken.

"Robert, considering everything Colby has done for this community, both with his initial donation, and his continued hunting, I think he's earned our trust."

"How long will you be gone?" McAllister addressed Sutton as though he hadn't heard the priest's comment.

"As long as it takes," Sutton replied, feeling slightly calmer, deciding not to provide any more facts than necessary. "Could be a few days, or a few weeks."

"Who is going on this wild goose chase with you?"

"Only a few of us," Sutton promised. "I'm trusting you to watch over these new guests, and my son."

McAllister raised an eyebrow.

"You're leaving Sean here?"

"Of course I am. I'm not going to endanger him, and I plan on coming back."

McAllister appeared genuinely relieved that Sutton meant the words he spoke. He exhaled calmly, looking Sutton in the eye.

"This community is built on trust. In the future, please include me in any discussions of bringing in new people long-term. I can smooth this over with the council, but going forward, we need to know about such things to bring them to a vote."

Sutton had lived in the community long enough to know that the village council bowed to McAllister's every wish, so the words rang hollow in his mind.

"I'm sorry, Robert, and yes, I'll be forthcoming in the future."

"Very good. I'm sure you have some packing to do, and I'll tell the council to make arrangements for our new guests once you give me a headcount of who's leaving."

"I will," Sutton said with a nod, turning with Father Paul to head outside.

Once the two exited the residence, Father Paul turned to Sutton.

"Don't trust what he said in there."

"I don't."

***

Gracine found herself alone with her boyfriend, Reggie Mitchell, in the house she occupied with him most of the time. Their housemates had left for chores already, and Gracine told Mitchell about her decision to head out with Sutton and a few others in search of Nadeau.

"So, you're choosing *him*, is that it?" Mitchell asked angrily, openly upset about her decision.

"Fuck no," Gracine fired back. "This is about finishing what I've started with my friends."

Mitchell paced the floor momentarily, weighing something over in his mind.

"You think you're going to find him in some cabin somewhere, and it'll be just as simple as walking up to him and putting a bullet in his head? The man took out better than ninety percent of the world population in one fell swoop, Gracine."

"All the more reason to go after him."

"Don't you think there are more qualified people doing the same thing?"

"They don't have the answers, or they aren't really looking, Reggie," Gracine said.

"And you just happened to come across the one person in the world who can find him? Come on."

Mitchell's tone indicated his intense skepticism.

"We didn't sit on our asses when terrorists took down the Twin Towers, did we? Someone *that* evil can't be allowed to go on, Reggie."

"Is this you talking? Or Colby?"

"You know better than to ask me that."

Mitchell approached her, attempting to put his hands on her cheeks, but Gracine wasn't about to let him off the hook. She backed up, shaking her head at him.

"You are more than welcome to come along," she said, "if you think you'll miss me that much."

"I have commitments here."

"To what? I thought you were committed to me, Reginald."

"There are people here who depend on the security I provide. And you may be gone for weeks, maybe months."

Gracine stared at him, beginning to think she didn't really know him at all.

"This may be over in a matter of days if we locate Nadeau. We have a plane, a pilot, and everything we need."

"'We'. Meaning you and Colby."

"And a few others, which could include you."

Growing agitated, Mitchell paced back and forth a few times.

"I'm not going," he finally stated. "I trust you, and I'll wait for you to come back. But I can't go."

"Maybe you shouldn't wait," Gracine said, putting her emotions aside. "I know you don't trust me with Colby, but I'm going to be a rock out there. Who knows, maybe I won't make it back at all, but I'm not going to betray your trust."

Mitchell said nothing, touching her hand briefly before turning away. Gracine waited a few seconds, deciding there wasn't anything left to be said between them until she returned. Taking a deep breath, she sighed as she exited the house.

***

After nearly four hours of waiting, and growing more impatient by the minute, Brooke indicated her desire to move on without assistance when the ringing of Sutton's sat phone indicated her backup had arrived. A few words over the phone, and a flare fired within a few miles of the community indicated where Timmons needed to land. Metzger was able to guide him close enough to see the flare in the first place, based on instructions from Sutton, and the Piper Seneca came to a gentle stop along a stretch of road clear of vehicles and the dead.

Metzger exited the plane after his friends, towing Hewitt along with him. A pickup truck and a van pulled up to the plane, several minutes later, visible nearly a mile out without the hubbub of traffic and pollution to deaden the senses. Although he felt reasonably certain his allies were in the vehicles, he kept a hand on his sidearm just the same. A wave of relief washed over him when he saw Sutton emerge from the driver's seat of the truck, knowing his friend wouldn't let anything harmful near the group.

Along with Sutton, Luke and Samantha stepped from the truck, and a dark-haired woman stepped from the van beside Mullins. An older man also emerged from the sliding door of the van, studying the plane's passengers with the narrow eyes of a predatory bird. Gracine appeared from the other side of the vehicle, along with a taller man who appeared military in nature, wielding a rifle of some kind. Metzger assumed he was there to guard the older man, who likely controlled the Maplewood community, and Sutton talked about briefly.

Jillian stood beside Metzger, and he wasn't certain how she was going to act around Sutton, because she never fully explained her thoughts to him. If they were both going to accompany him in close quarters for hours on end, he suspected they were destined to find out. For a moment, as though captured in a photograph, everyone stared at one another without saying a word. At long last, the older man stepped forward, speaking to Bryce directly.

"I can only assume you're the man I've heard so much about from my new residents."

Bryce shook his hand, appearing a bit reluctant as he shifted his head to one side.

"My brother is probably a bit more famous than me," Bryce admitted.

"So sorry," McAllister said before properly introducing himself and shaking hands with everyone who walked off the plane, except for Hewitt. "Robert McAllister."

"I appreciate your willingness to house some of our people while the rest of us travel onward," Metzger said, stepping forward.

"My pleasure. Colby told me of your plans. I can't say I agree with any of it, but I wish you luck."

"The man, and his underlings, are literally the reason my parents are gone," Metzger said. "I feel like I have a right to some answers, and the pleasure of putting a bullet between his eyes."

Sutton stepped forward.

"Robert, my friends have been through a lot, and traveled some miles to reach us. Perhaps we should get to the safety of Maplewood before we talk."

"Agreed," McAllister said.

"The dead will be heading this way after hearing the plane and seeing that flare," Timmons noted.

"We need to get going," Brooke said, prompting Mullins to introduce her formally to everyone.

"This is Brooke, the CIA operative I told you about," he said, addressing Metzger in particular.

"It's afternoon," McAllister said. "Come back and finalize your plans, get a bite to eat, and spend one more night if you need to. If your terrorist has eluded detection this long, he's either dead, or he's not going anywhere."

"I'm going to need a few particular weapons," Sutton said to McAllister.

"Whatever you need, Colby. Let's get behind our walls so you can get organized before heading out."

A few undead appeared in the distance, blindly following the sound of the plane that no longer reached their ears, or the flare that drew their attention before fizzling out.

Taking stock of their situation by looking into the fields in either direction, the armed man looked to McAllister as though asking whether he needed to act. McAllister quickly shook his head negatively before ushering everyone into the vehicles.

"Let's head back before blood starts flying."

Metzger looked to his friends, giving a nod as most eyes landed on him.

"We can't get anything done out here," he reasoned aloud. "We get to safety, go over the plan, and return to the plane."

With that, everyone headed to the van, or the pickup truck, prepared to rest at least a few minutes, an hour perhaps, before moving on to their next destination. Metzger turned and looked at the plane, instinctively believing some kind of intervention would keep their plan from going smoothly. He didn't blame his karma, but something, or someone, always interfered with his objectives.

Metzger didn't want to be the next person who tried thwarting his plans of locating Nadeau and dealing with the man permanently, because that person would not receive mercy.

Chapter 10

Numerous discussions soon took place within a small building designed to serve as a community center, set closer to the front gates where open land had been available. Sometimes the building served as a church, or an area for council meetings, but right now Sutton spoke with his son in one of the two smaller rooms toward the rear.

"Dad, I want to go with you," Sean Sutton stated as Buster took the younger man's side.

"I need you to stay here," Sutton said emphatically.

"Then *you* stay, too."

"I need to see this through, Sean."

His son sighed, shaking his head.

"You spent forever looking for me and Jake. And now you're risking your own life for this? If something happens to you, I want to be there. I don't have family here."

"You have Buster," Sutton offered. "I won't have him fly with us, because he'd probably hate it, and I need you to stay for a reason."

"And that is?"

Sutton drew close to ensure only his son heard his words.

"I want you and Buster to protect the priest and the sister, and what few friends we have here. That includes the people who just arrived. I also want you to keep an eye on McAllister. He plays his moves close to the chest, and I don't trust him right now."

"And if he gets too far out of line?"

"You may have to get drastic."

"What does that mean exactly?" Sean asked, the confusion written on his face.

"It means this community may need some new leadership, and that would require a coup."

Sean stared at his father momentarily, but nothing in his expression indicated he disagreed with the notion.

"I'm not sure we have the numbers," he said flatly.

"You've been more social around here than me," Sutton said. "Without raising suspicion, get a feel for who's fed up and might be ready for a change."

"How will I know when it's time to act?" Sean questioned. "If it comes to that."

"You'll know, son. McAllister seems to think my friend and his brother should be marched to the military base. That *cannot* happen. I'll protect Dan, and you make sure his brother is treated as a guest at this place. Understood?"

Sean took a deep breath, looking his father in the eye.

"Understood."

Sutton quickly pulled his son into a rare hug.

"You take care of yourself, first and foremost, but do right by our allies."

Choosing his words carefully, Sutton considered himself a person with few true friends, and most of them died when the apocalypse began. Nowadays, he aligned himself with people based on their beliefs, but the few he trusted implicitly, Sutton deemed friends.

He hoped as Dan Metzger discussed the immediate future with Robert and Nancy McAllister in the next room that his friend didn't reveal too many details.

***

"I'm trying to make certain I'm grasping the entire setup here," McAllister said as Metzger, Bryce, Gracine, Mike Mullins, and Brooke stood beside him.

"Gracine and Colby are coming with me," Metzger stated for the second time. "I'm asking you two keep my brother and his family under your protection while we're gone."

"And you're going with them, to show them the way," McAllister said, looking to Brooke.

"Yes."

McAllister turned his attention to Mullins.

"And you're staying here to deliver this prisoner to the military base."

"Yes," Mullins answered.

What Metzger hadn't told McAllister was that he wanted Mullins to deliver Hewitt because he trusted the man, and because part of the deal he struck with General McCall was for the doctors within the base to give Mullins a full medical examination, which included a cancer screening. He knew the man dealt with cancer once before, and admitted he hadn't been feeling quite right the past month.

"Any particular reason you're entrusting the prisoner delivery to just one man?" Nancy McAllister inquired.

"Because I trust him, and he's dealt with people like Hewitt before," Metzger answered calmly. "Mike knows what to do."

"We aren't used to having strangers dumped on our doorstep," McAllister said, his gaze entering the other room. "But I trust Colby. He and Gracine have been invaluable to our community this winter."

"We don't plan on being at this very long," Metzger said. "If we're lucky, we'll bring back supplies, or information that might help everyone going forward."

"You really know who ended the world?" the older man asked, looking to Brooke.

"I do. And I've narrowed down his hiding place to two bunkers."

McAllister smirked, appearing skeptical.

"A man like that isn't going to let you waltz into his lair and take him down."

"Bunkers aren't impenetrable," Brooke assured McAllister. "I've been after this man since last fall, and I've been gathering information about every aspect of his plan. The reason we're all here right now, the reason we've all lost loved ones, is because of a very deliberate act on his part."

Metzger noticed she had struggled to speak the last part of her sentence, as though someone near and dear to her succumbed to the primitive nature of the planet's remaining inhabitants.

"I didn't mean to offend," McAllister apologized rather stiffly. "It would be a shame to put forth so much effort and risk if it gets innocent people killed."

"That's our choice," Metzger argued.

"And not necessarily the best," McAllister countered. "If something happens to you, from my understanding, it may take longer to develop a vaccine."

Metzger smirked, shaking his head.

"I plan on making the return trip, believe me. And don't put too much faith in the military, Mr. McAllister. They're only interested in keeping their own people alive, and listening to politicians who speak to them from secure bunkers."

Metzger looked around, wondering where Timmons had gone. It wasn't like the pilot to stray too far, though a hot meal and some rest might be enough to tempt the Navy captain away from village politics.

Jillian remained outside with Isabella and Nathan, receiving a tour from Sean Sutton and a few of the other residents. Metzger worried about her, and his family, finding it hard to trust these new people, despite Sutton integrating with them over the winter. He also disliked the notion of leaving his brother behind, but he wasn't going to risk Bryce's health, or leave his nephew without a father if their plan went awry. Despite the military mistreating him, or at least misleading him, Metzger knew he or Bryce needed to provide them with blood samples eventually for any vaccine hopes to remain.

Personally, Metzger felt impressed by the habitation level within the community. While they didn't have power, the residents were able to chop wood and hunt to keep warm and fed. Sutton had told him about using bait for hunting, and how he sacrificed his box truck to get the group inside the walls. He also indicated that McAllister proved extremely cautious about letting new people through the front gates. Sutton also noted that the man wasn't thrilled about learning that some of his people were leaving, only to be replaced by strangers.

"I'm sorry we brought all of this to your doorstep," he said to McAllister. "I would appreciate it if you could keep my family safe. We'll bring back what information and supplies we can."

"Both would be appreciated," McAllister replied. "We managed to get some quarters together for you and your people."

"We'll be heading out at dawn."

"Where to?" McAllister inquired.

"I'm not sure, exactly," Metzger answered honestly, noticing that Brooke had moved on to speak with someone else. "Our informant hasn't seen fit to provide us with a location. Everything has been moving pretty quickly."

"Sounds like you'll find out in the morning," Bryce said.

Metzger glanced at Brooke across the room as Sutton weaved through the sea of people in an attempt to exit the building.

"Sounds like," he said without returning his gaze to his conversational partners.

***

Sutton stepped outside, spying Jillian talking with Luke and Samantha after receiving a brief tour of the gated community. Both sucked in nervous breaths, hesitating, and for Sutton's part, he considered turning around and walking away, but he didn't want to be rude. Twice already, Jillian had accosted him with slaps across the face, blaming him for the death of her father.

She excused herself from Luke and his adopted daughter, deciding to approach Sutton, who simply stood in front of the community center building, uncertain of whether to say something or duck. When they drew within a few feet of one another, both stopped and stood awkwardly a moment until they both spoke the same words simultaneously.

"I'm sorry-"

Each chuckling, they fumbled with their hands and feet momentarily before doing the same exact thing.

"You go-"

Sutton waited patiently without speaking this time until Jillian provided a grin mixed with sorrow and the stark reminder of what created tension between them.

"I'm sorry," she began, and Sutton started to utter the same intentions, but she held up a hand. "Please let me finish. This has been hard enough as it is."

Jillian hesitated as a few community residents walked past them, giving her and the other new strangers quizzical stares.

"I was angry after what happened to my father," she continued. "For the longest time I wanted to blame you, because I needed to direct my anger somewhere, and you were a convenient target. All winter I had time to think, and talk with Dan, and I realize now that you would *never* have done anything like that on purpose. You were just trying to survive and get back to us, and things went sideways."

Sutton digested the words before responding.

"When I met those men, I had the option of joining them, or dying if I refused," he said. "I feel completely certain they would have killed me and taken my stuff, and eventually found your father's town anyway. What I'm sorry about is that I didn't act sooner, because I've played that day in my mind a thousand times and wondered what might have been if I followed my own advice and shot them before they had the chance to act on their words."

"I'm focused on what lies ahead," Jillian said. "Dan needs to see this through, and I want to be there for him."

"We all need to see this through," Sutton said. "We've all lost people thanks to this Nadeau character."

Sutton hesitated briefly before asking his next question.

"What about the pilot? How's he working out?"

"You really don't trust him, do you?" Jillian asked, finally smiling while shaking her head. "I can tell you this. He's loyal to Dan, almost to the point that he would step over the rest of us to save him."

"Trust doesn't come easy for me, and my instincts are usually right."

"Scott contributed at the lodge," Jillian added. "He went on runs with Dan to the nearby towns, and he saved Nathan once."

"Only a heartless asshole wouldn't save a kid," Sutton noted.

"I'm not telling you to lower your guard, but don't ruin this for Dan. Timmons is the closest thing he has to a father figure since his parents were killed."

"Dan doesn't need to look up to anyone. He's already the best of us."

Sutton spoke the truth without a filter, and Jillian tilted her head.

"What?" Sutton asked.

"You might be human after all, Colby."

"Don't be telling people I have a soft side," Sutton said, suppressing a grin.

"I won't," Jillian promised. "And for the record, I'm glad you found your son, and I'm sorry about your younger boy."

"Thanks. This world isn't fair to anyone, and there isn't much we can do about it."

"Finding Nadeau might prevent any future attacks, at least."

"I don't know how the man could make it much worse than this."

"His network is too intricate to be formed *after* the apocalypse began," Jillian stated. "There's no telling if he had more attacks planned, or if there's a cure, or how far his reach goes. Until we locate the man, we'll never know."

"I don't trust the military," Sutton growled. "Their lack of progress has me even more skeptical."

Jillian sighed through her nostrils, appearing concerned.

"I'm both nervous and excited about the prospect of finding Nadeau," she admitted. "There's no way he'll be living like a hermit, off in some cabin by himself."

"He'll probably have his loyal followers with him. But that's why you have me."

Father Paul reluctantly approached the pair, and Sutton introduced him to Jillian, who apparently found the timing right to excuse herself and return to the others.

"How can I help you, Padre?" Sutton asked his friend.

"I came to wish you well on your adventure, Colby."

"I appreciate it."

Sutton looked around, finding no one else within earshot.

"I have a favor to ask."

"Name it," Father Paul replied.

"I know you're a man of the cloth, but please keep an eye on my friends and make sure McAllister keeps his word."

"You think he may contact the military?"

"I'm not sure what his intentions are," Sutton answered honestly, "but I don't fully trust him right now."

"I'll watch over them," the priest promised.

Sutton looked at his friend with additional concern.

"What's troubling you, Colby?"

"Don't let McAllister push you around, Paul."

"I'm not sure I catch your meaning."

"He treats you like the hired help half the time, instead of showing you the respect that he should."

"The man saved Sister Rosa and I from a dire situation, my friend."

"You've more than repaid that debt. Your words should mean more than anything *he* has to say."

Father Paul smirked.

"If I didn't know better, I'd say I've converted you."

"Let's not go that far, Father."

"I appreciate your concern, but McAllister likes to put on a good show."

"I know your profession doesn't allow you to speak ill of others, but God doesn't mind you spouting some truth about some of our neighbors, Father."

"That would be in poor taste, Colby. And not very Christian of me."

Sutton took in a deep breath, feeling prepared for some rest before the group hit the road in the morning.

"If I can just say one more thing, Paul, there's going to come a time when you'll have to act to save your friends. You can't just sit back and expect the Lord to work out everything for you."

"I don't," Father Paul responded. "And I never have."

"Good," Sutton said, giving his friend a quick hug. "When I get back here, I expect you to be running this place."

Father Paul gave a chuckle.

"That might be pushing it. But I will keep an eye on your extended family."

"Thank you."

As the priest walked away, Sutton mentally scrolled the list of things to do before morning. He needed weapons, some clothes, and at least a little food and water for the journey. A party of six people were heading to wherever Brooke told them, and he required supplies enough to equip each of them.

He felt like a kid the night before Christmas, because Nadeau might finally be within reach, and Sutton had a chance to be part of something that the military and the government literally blundered all along. If the government somehow chose to ignore, or cooperate with Nadeau, Sutton would feel justified about his previous stances regarding the chosen elite. He wanted to put a bullet between Nadeau's eyes, but he also wanted answers like everyone else.

Uncharacteristically, Sutton said a little prayer that nothing went wrong with their departure in the morning.

***

Metzger spent the latter portion of his evening with his family, uncertain of what the future held for any of them. He walked the grounds with Bryce and Isabella, as Nathan found some kids within the community who invited him over to play. Gracine took Samantha with Nathan and promised to watch over both children to alleviate concerns.

"I spoke with Colby," Metzger told his brother and sister-in-law. "We're going to leave one of the sat phones with you because I don't know how long we're going to be gone."

"I heard someone say a matter of days," Isabella said, concern scrawled across her face.

"That's *if* everything goes to plan, and we all know that *never* happens."

"I wonder how she has it narrowed down to two locations and not one," Bryce thought aloud. "I guess we know from experience that Nadeau's safehouses were stepping stones to more information, and eventually, Nadeau himself."

Isabella folded her arms as the evening air grew chilly from a passing breeze.

"Is six of you enough for this mission?" she asked.

"I hope so," Metzger answered. "If not, we'll just have to make sure we survive to bring back whatever information we learn."

"You've got to make it back," Isabella urged. "I already have an uneasy feeling about this place, so the sooner we leave, the better."

"Colby says you can trust the priest and the nun," Metzger told them. "You'll have Colby's son and Luke here as well."

"You sure it's a good idea bringing Jillian with you?" Bryce asked.

"It's not," Metzger assured him. "She insists on coming, and for some reason she's been worried about me doing anything dangerous lately."

Bryce and Isabella exchanged knowing glances. Although they hadn't said anything about it, both had observed Jillian's recent change in behavior.

"What?"

"Are you two planning a family?" Isabella asked.

"In these conditions?" Metzger asked incredulously. "No way!"

He caught their meaning, and he tried to remember the times he and Jillian were romantically intertwined. They had been cautious, using protection each time, but a pregnancy might explain her change in mood, and her outlook on the future.

"There's no way," he said, shaking his head. "We've been careful."

"It's probably nothing," Bryce said with a shrug, trying to play off his wife's open suspicions. "You need to focus on Nadeau and worry about the other stuff later."

"If there's any chance you two are having a child, you can't let her near Nadeau," Isabella said. "You probably shouldn't let her go at all."

"There's no changing her mind," Metzger said, thinking about her determination to tag along. "Bringing it up would only make things worse, so I'll just have to keep her out of danger."

With such a dangerous seed planted in his mind, Metzger felt a bit numb, contemplating the notion of being a father in such a dangerous world. Perhaps Jillian simply wanted to keep him safe, and away from a task that ultimately might lead to answers, but a hollow satisfaction. If Jillian remained with him, Metzger could keep her safe. He didn't entirely trust the leadership of the Maplewood community, but he required a centralized location where his group could stay together, and Mullins could deliver Hewitt to the Navy base.

"How the hell do you two keep from freaking out about Nathan in this world?" he asked.

"Well, it hasn't exactly gone to plan," Bryce answered first. "When you become a parent, nothing else matters except protecting your child."

"And you left the safety of the base," Metzger said, looking to Isabella.

"I saw the writing on the wall, Dan. Being trapped behind those walls wasn't what I wanted for Nathan. And I knew you could protect us out there."

"You did fine yourself, you know."

Isabella gave an appreciative nod.

He was about to continue the conversation about future children when Timmons came bursting out a front door a few houses down. He was carrying some of his belongings, including his winter boots and his jacket, appearing to be hurried. Metzger started toward his friend when he saw an angry man who likely lived in the community wildly swing the front door open in pursuit. He wore steamed up eyeglasses, and held a shotgun in his hands, despite a woman desperately tugging on his right arm as she followed him through the door.

"Oh, shit," Metzger muttered, picking up his pace as Timmons came to a stop and several villagers gathered round or stepped out from their houses for a look.

Metzger quickly put himself between Timmons and the angry man.

"What the hell happened?" he asked his friend as the other man took two more steps and stopped while Metzger switched his glances between them.

"I'll tell you what happened," the man stammered. "This son-of-a-bitch slept with my wife!"

"She said she wasn't committed," Timmons said quickly, realizing a lot of eyes were looking his way.

"Bullshit!" the man screamed, taking another step forward.

Metzger held up both hands, attempting to diplomatically settle the argument.

"I'm sorry for the misunderstanding, mister."

"There was no misunderstanding," the man answered with a scowl.

"Samuel!" McAllister called from a few houses down, bringing a cooler head to the heated conversation. "What's the meaning of this?"

"One of these new people put the moves on my wife and I caught them in bed," the man answered.

"Is this true, Karen?" McAllister inquired upon turning his attention to the man's wife.

"Yes, I lied to get this man in bed," Karen said, pointing to Timmons. "Samuel hasn't been a real man to me in years."

"You fucking bitch," Samuel said, turning to face his wife, shotgun still grasped in his hands.

"That's Samuel and Karen Brown," Gracine said quietly, stepping up to Metzger. "Their marriage isn't what you would call conventional."

"I can tell," Metzger replied.

"She's always talking down to him," Gracine said before taking a step away.

McAllister drew closer, unafraid to put himself in the center of the situation, similar to what Metzger had done.

"Samuel, you're not supposed to have weapons," he said, drawing the attention of the irate man.

"She cheated on me," Brown said, his voice beginning to crack while a range of emotions crossed his face.

While he continued to hold the shotgun, no one knew what to expect.

"You're a damn fool," Karen said, chiding him. "When a real man came along, I knew exactly how to get satisfaction after all these years."

"Karen, you're not helping," McAllister said in a subdued voice.

Metzger looked to Timmons, who appeared genuinely stunned and remorseful for having forced a wedge between a married couple.

"Give me the gun," McAllister encouraged the mentally shattered man, and for a few seconds it appeared that Brown would comply.

Had an audience not gathered and made a public spectacle of the event, Brown might have cooperated, or even tried to reason with his wife, but Metzger sensed that someone was due to be injured, or killed. He kept a close watch on Brown, and even tried inching closer when it appeared the man wasn't going to hand over the weapon. Monitoring everything around him, even in his devastated frame of mind, Brown took notice of Metzger's movements.

"Don't," he warned.

Metzger decided to try a different tactic instead, stopping where he stood.

"Samuel, I don't know you at all, but I can tell you that life these days is more precious than ever."

"What would you know about it?" Brown asked angrily, beginning to point the gun more upward than into the crowd, or at the ground.

"I know that using that gun in any way will effectively end your life, and I don't want to see that for you."

"You don't even know me."

"That's true, but the fact that you haven't used the shotgun tells me you're a good person. You've probably put up with more than your fair share of shit over the years, and maybe this is where things turn around for you. But it can't happen while you're holding that gun so close to these folks."

Brown's hands shook, and Metzger couldn't tell if the man shivered with anger, or he contemplated the consequences of actions he hadn't yet taken. Timmons began to step forward, but Metzger put a hand up, holding his friend back so the pilot couldn't possibly complicate the situation. He also needed to keep Timmons safe, because without him, they couldn't take Brooke very far, and she would likely turn her attention to the military.

"Samuel, hand me the gun," McAllister said, virtually stepping in front of Metzger to ensure he wasn't outshined in this crucial moment.

Brown held the gun lengthwise in both hands, staring at it momentarily. At least his wife found sense enough to avoiding taunting him, simply staring at him with contempt as though he had somehow wronged her. Metzger didn't know the details of their courtship or marriage, but he sensed there wasn't any going back for them, regardless of how this situation ended.

Metzger felt his heart continue to race as Brown simply stared at the firearm, ignoring McAllister's words. Deciding he was going to get shot, or bring an end to the standoff, Metzger stepped forward, beside McAllister, and addressed the distraught man again.

"Samuel, you're the most important person in my life at this very moment," he stated. "You determine what happens to me and the rest of these people, and I don't want to see you hurt anyone, or hurt yourself."

Brown soaked in the words, sucked in a deep breath, and looked to Metzger with a combination of sorrow and regret in his eyes. Metzger thought for certain he had pushed the man to the brink of blowing his head off, but Brown turned the shotgun barrel upward before offering up the weapon to Metzger.

McAllister stepped forward to intercept the shotgun and Brown gave him a look that bordered on disdain for less than a second. Despite this, he let the community leader take the weapon and nodded appreciation to Metzger.

"You did the right thing," Metzger said.

"Did I?" Brown asked, his eyes glazed because he appeared on the verge of tears.

"You were always weak," Karen called as someone began leading her away.

"That's enough!" Metzger called instinctively, attempting to stand up for the man he might have just saved from suicide.

McAllister brought the henchman from the makeshift airfield back to the area to lead Brown somewhere. Metzger felt reasonably certain the community didn't have any sort of jail, but he supposed some kind of restraints, or a locked room might suffice.

"You did well, there," McAllister said somewhat flatly to Metzger.

"I was a teacher, so I'm used to conflict resolution. I'm just glad no one got hurt."

"That's been boiling for a while," McAllister admitted. "Sorry it was your friend who triggered Karen's desires."

"Me, too," Timmons said, standing back a few feet after having replaced all of his clothing. "I swear to God she told me she didn't have a husband or a boyfriend."

Metzger looked back to his friend before returning his attention to McAllister.

"I'm so sorry for this," he said. "We'll be out of your hair in the morning."

McAllister gave an airy wave, as though it was water under the bridge.

"Think nothing of it. We'll help you with whatever you need in the meantime."

When the community leader walked away, Metzger turned his attention to Timmons, not bothering to disguise his anger.

"We're here less than half a day and you almost get yourself killed over a one-night stand? What the *fuck*, Scott?"

"I promise I asked all the right questions," Timmons said, his face desperate for Metzger to believe him.

Metzger simply shook his head.

"We can't afford to screw this up when we're so close to finding Nadeau."

"I know," Timmons said emphatically. "I swear, she came on to me, and told me all the right things. And, if I'm being honest, Dan, it's been a *long* time since I-"

"I get the gist, Scott. You're forgiven, but promise me you'll be a saint the rest of the night."

Timmons held up his hands.

"I swear."

Metzger groaned, wondering what else could go wrong before they departed the community in the morning. He knew Sutton harbored reservations about McAllister, but the man hadn't proven to be dangerous in Metzger's eyes. He seemed like a man determined to protect his people and keep order in the community he started. Metzger hoped Luke and a handful of others he barely knew would be enough to protect his family and integrate them into the village.

Looking up to the starry sky, he hoped the weather remained calm, dry, and comfortable during their takeoff and flight. Despite his escalated adrenaline during the odd domestic disturbance, Metzger felt dead tired, wondering if he could sleep peacefully through the night once he found his temporary quarters.

He intended to find out momentarily.

Chapter 11

Metzger met the other five members of his group in the center of Maplewood the next morning, prepared to head out shortly. Useful daylight remained an hour away, but everyone had what clothing, food, and weapons they required in backpacks or duffel bags. The morning air remained cold enough for Metzger to see his breath, though he didn't feel particularly cold in the spring weather.

"We have everything we need," Sutton informed him, thumbing towards a gray van parked just outside the front gate for their use.

"Hey, everyone," Metzger said, drawing them into a circle along with him. "This is the last chance if any of you want to opt out of this trip. I wouldn't fault any of you, seeing as the circumstances have changed a little bit over these past few months."

"Nothing has changed in my mind," Sutton answered. "This prick took my son from me."

"I've lost everyone because of this," Jillian stated. "I'm in."

Timmons shrugged.

"You know I'm in."

"I've been looking forward to this for a long time," Gracine chimed in.

Brooke had nothing to say as her work since the beginning of the apocalypse centered around bringing down Nadeau. Metzger didn't know many details except that she had visited many of the safehouses to gather information about the man who caused the collapse of civilization.

"Let's start loading up," Metzger said before motioning for Timmons to join him aside from the others.

"What's up?" the pilot asked.

"I'm going to ask McAllister about the distraught husband from last night."

Timmons looked at him with a confused expression.

"What about him?"

"Just to make sure he's going to be alright. And to make sure what happened last night doesn't jeopardize my family staying here."

"The guy had a loaded shotgun aimed at me," Timmons said as though Metzger required a reminder of the events.

"After you bedded his wife."

"We didn't get that far," Timmons said, holding up his hands defensively.

"The implication is the same, Scott. We arrived here, and the first thing you did was try and get your rocks off."

"I *didn't* go looking, Dan. She came to me."

Metzger knew his friend wasn't going to pass up an opportunity for a sexual rendezvous after a winter of solitude. He couldn't judge too harshly, since he spent most evenings with Jillian lying beside him in bed.

"Even so, it doesn't make us look good. I just need to smooth things over before we leave."

"Wait," Timmons said as Metzger was about to find McAllister. "You weren't asking if one of us wanted to back out because you wanted to bring that husband along, right?"

"No. This whole thing is dangerous, and I didn't want anyone to feel obligated."

"Except me."

"Yes, except you, because you're the only one who can fly."

"But you're getting close," Timmons promised with a smirk.

Metzger grinned in return.

"Look, I'm going to talk to McAllister a minute, and I'll be right there."

"Don't do anything stupid," Timmons uttered a warning he had never spoken to his friend previously.

"You know I won't," Metzger said before approaching the community leader, who hadn't strayed far from the group all morning.

Approaching the man, he shook his hand.

"I appreciate everything you're doing for us, Robert."

"You're quite welcome."

"Before we head out, I was wondering what you were going to do about Mr. Brown after yesterday."

McAllister sighed a bit before smiling.

"We're going to give him a few days to cool his heels before moving forward. I've been told that Karen has never been kind to him, so we need to make certain we don't have any more public outbursts."

Metzger found the wording a bit odd, unless McAllister worried more about public perception than keeping the peace in his town.

"Understood. He just seemed lost yesterday."

"I appreciate your concern, but we'll see to it that he gets what he needs."

Giving a nod, Metzger returned to his group, prepared to set his own supplies inside the van and head to the Piper Seneca a few miles down the road.

"You're not always going to get the answers you want," Timmons said, reading the situation perfectly, helping Metzger place his backpack in the back of the van. "And you can't redeem everyone."

"I just feel bad for him," Metzger said. "Clearly his wife doesn't give a shit about their marriage, and treats the guy like dirt, but he shouldn't be locked away and forgotten."

"I'm probably not the best person to give life advice, but the last thing we need on this trip is your brain focused on marital problems."

Metzger conceded the notion, nodding.

"You're right. The most important thing right now is finding Nadeau."

"Look, I'm sorry I created that mess," Timmons apologized sincerely. "I didn't mean to make us look bad."

"You were duped, doing something any of us would've done in your shoes. We can set things right when we get back."

Once Metzger got his equipment loaded, he joined the others who had good-byes to say, giving Bryce, Isabella, and Nathan each a hug. Sutton said farewell to his son and Buster, though no hugs were issued on his part. Gracine said goodbye to her boyfriend, and Metzger looked to Sutton, who stared at the couple with a rather neutral expression. Metzger felt certain Gracine only cohabitated with the man because Sutton made himself unavailable. Being a detached person by nature, Sutton had gone through an emotional crisis when he lost his youngest son, though he never openly displayed his grief.

Brooke spoke briefly with Mullins, giving him a quick kiss on the cheek and a hug before she returned to the traveling group. Metzger didn't know what the two had endured on the road, but she appeared beholden to the former cop from the beginning. Considering Mullins was about to escort Hewitt to the military base by himself, he would share danger equal to that of the travelers, and Metzger made certain Mullins knew what Hewitt had done in New York.

Once they completed their goodbyes, the group returned to the borrowed van, which community members would retrieve later. Metzger assumed the front passenger's seat beside Timmons, who insisted on driving for unknown reasons. The pilot remained quiet during the short drive to the plane, and Metzger detected an earthy odor.

"Are you wearing cologne?" he asked his friend.

"It's from last night," Timmons answered. "The stuff I found over the winter."

"You dog," Metzger said, prodding the pilot. "You came to town looking for a chance to score."

"Hey, I was trying to make a good first impression and not smell like the dead."

Metzger grunted lightly with satisfaction that he guessed correctly, despite what Timmons said.

When they arrived at the plane, they found it completely intact with a handful of undead stumbling around the area. Metzger casually walked to the back of the van, opening the rear doors for access to his pack. He grabbed the sword from his pack and began taking out a few of the staggering assailants while Timmons opened compartments and conducted a preflight check of the mechanical components.

"Didn't you just fly in this yesterday?" Brooke inquired as though the check was redundant in her estimation.

"It's been out here all night," Metzger said, cleaning slicing through the skull of male zombie covered in moist mud. "Anyone could've come along and stolen something, or tinkered with the plane."

"It would be a shame to crash just minutes after we take off," Timmons chimed in, overhearing their discussion. "Cutting a fuel line, or tampering with the wings would cut our trip short."

"I know," Brooke admitted, her frustration showing. "I'm just ready to find Nadeau."

"Speaking of which," Metzger said as he wiped the blade of his sword against the clothing of a downed undead member, "where are we going exactly?"

Brooke looked to him unhappily, because she knew he wasn't going to like what she said next.

"I've narrowed his location down to two possible bunkers."

"Bunkers?" Metzger asked with a furrowed eyebrow.

"Yes, bunkers. He apparently purchased several decommissioned bunkers from our own government and made them his own."

Metzger groaned.

"And where are these bunkers?"

"That's where the bad news gets worse," Brooke informed him. "One is in Wyoming, and the other one is located in New Mexico."

Considering the two bunkers were located only two states apart was a silver lining, but both were several thousand miles from Virginia.

"Please tell me you're leaning towards one of them," Sutton said, grabbing his gear from the back of the van.

"Unfortunately, both were the final destination listed in some of the safehouses I ransacked," Brooke answered.

"And you're certain they're the only two possibilities that exist?" Sutton asked skeptically, throwing the strap for his sniper rifle over his shoulder for ease of toting.

"Nothing is certain," Brooke replied, but I've been through a number of these places and no other possibilities materialized."

Everyone stopped what they were doing and looked at her with skepticism.

"It took me a *lot* of safehouses to get to those, so I feel confident we'll find Nadeau in one of these. He wanted his followers to find him and protect him."

"Maybe one safehouse is for Nadeau, and another for his family," Jillian said, reasoning aloud why the man provided two locations.

"And maybe they're just another stop that will have us hopping to other locations," Sutton said.

"I don't think so," Brooke said, standing her ground. "I discovered proof that both locations are former government bunkers."

Gracine appeared somewhat confused at the statement.

"You mean the government just abandons these things?"

"Or sells them," Sutton said.

"So, our government might have sold Nadeau the very thing he's using to stay warm and safe while the rest of us fight for our lives out here?" Gracine questioned.

"It's not unreasonable," Timmons said, still checking the plane for any issues. "I flew a cargo mission one time where they removed items from an old bunker."

"For relocation or disposal?" Metzger asked.

"That was never made clear. Truth be told, I didn't much care because we throw away a *lot* of outdated supplies in the military."

"Less talking, more inspecting," Metzger chided his friend.

"I haven't heard a destination yet," Timmons said, his blue eyes never leaving his work on the plane.

"Historically speaking, whichever one I pick turns out wrong," Metzger said to Brooke.

"My luck isn't much better," she replied. "How about we flip a coin, or a rock, or something?"

"How about we go to New Mexico first, because it's warmer," Timmons suggested as he closed a hatch on the plane.

Everyone looked to one another with gentle shrugs, knowing they had to start somewhere.

Metzger already knew at least a few stops would be required for fuel, which wasn't easy to obtain. Not every airport was going to have fuel trucks readily available, so they would have to syphon fuel at some point and hope it hadn't gone bad over the winter. Timmons possessed flight charts that covered the areas they had flown to recently, but he would need additional charts to make his way west. Electronic means proved hit and miss after the apocalypse, and he wanted to be prepared for anything.

"Ready when you are," Metzger said to Timmons, who appeared to be done with his inspection.

"We're ready. Let's bring this fucker to justice."

Everyone put the last of their belongings into the plane, and Metzger looked in the direction of the community kind enough to host his family. He hoped to complete his self-imposed assignment quickly, to ensure he and his family could return to whatever a normal existence in the apocalypse might be.

***

Within a few hours, Mike Mullins was provided with a truck, a revolver containing six bullets, his old knife, and a prisoner to escort to Naval Station Norfolk. McAllister personally escorted him to the front gate and asked if Mullins planned on coming back.

"I hope to," he replied. "It may take a few days."

Hewitt stood beside the truck loaned to Mullins by the community, though Mullins felt the people of Maplewood had amassed a few dozen vehicles for their use, and didn't loan out the better ones.

"You going to remove these?" Hewitt asked Mullins once McAllister returned inside, having his people close the gate behind him.

Hewitt referred to the handcuffs still clasping his wrists, holding them up and jingling them for Mullins' benefit.

"Hardly."

Because the old Chevy S-10 was a crew cab truck, Mullins assumed one of the back seats, buckling himself in before sternly suggesting Hewitt drive them toward the base. He possessed the key to the handcuffs, but wasn't about to give Hewitt any form of freedom until they reached the base.

"My pleasure," the arrogant man replied. "I'm looking forward to three square meals and protection."

"It'll be harder for you to indiscriminately murder people at the base."

Hewitt chuckled as he started the truck and directed them to the closest roadway.

"I killed because I needed to survive," Hewitt explained. "The more people you have around, the more food and ammunition goes to waste."

"Waste?"

"Don't give me that bullshit about people being a resource, and working together can restore the world we knew."

"No," Mullins said somberly. "We'll never see supermarkets, processed foods, and the internet again."

Mullins knew the military enjoyed such benefits on a limited scale, but only portions of the country could be reopened, and even that required clearing the dead and manufacturing power.

"Take a right up here," he said.

Hewitt followed directions, taking the next few local turns until they were on a highway, heading in the direction of the base.

"What's your reason for doing this?" Hewitt inquired.

"For doing what?"

"Being my escort while your friends fly off to bigger and better things."

"I'm not sure they're going to find much of anything," Mullins answered, seeing leafless trees and open fields along the highway.

It seemed no matter which state he visited, the scenery looked much the same. Nature didn't cease its seasonal cycles, but highways and interstates remained cluttered with disabled vehicles. Mullins wondered if the dead skin flakes from the undead created the sepia backdrop he noticed in urban areas, or something else left the world looking drab.

"If you must know, the agreement is for me to get a full physical from the military doctors."

"Physical?" Hewitt asked, turning halfway around to get a glimpse of Mullins.

"More specifically, a cancer screening."

"Ah," Hewitt said, continuing to drive, weaving around a few of the undead and some stalled cars.

"You don't seem like quite the asshole they said you were," Mullins commented.

"I'm friendly enough if you don't get in my way," Hewitt responded. "If we both leave this base at some point, I'd probably kill you so I don't have to compete with you for supplies."

"Noted," Mullins said, not taking the man's words lightly.

He continued to keep his right hand on the firearm, though he suspected Hewitt genuinely wanted to find safety within the walls of the military installation.

For his part, Mullins supposed he sought something similar. A few days of hot meals, and perhaps a hot shower would be nice, he thought, but he mostly required truth. During the trip to South Carolina with his friend Brad Weir, he felt certain aches that he affiliated with his previous bout with cancer. A general fatigue overtook his body that wasn't associated with malnourishment or being physically taxed. He didn't want to have cancer again, but he also didn't want to live with uncertainty. When Metzger made him the offer, and confirmed it with the general in charge of the joint military, Mullins agreed.

Craning his neck to see a bit more clearly, Mullins saw a group of the undead along the highway ahead of the S-10. As though they were picketing, the zombies formed a line across the road, mostly standing still as though waiting for something to grab their attention. Hewitt noticed a moment later, and began to slow the truck because the dead weren't separating, even as they turned to see the truck heading at them.

"They're tied together," Mullins noted aloud.

"Shouldn't be a problem," Hewitt said before his foot pressed down on the accelerator.

Mullins noticed why the zombies weren't able to move very well, but he couldn't possibly warn Hewitt in time that each of them had spikes pointing upward from the punctures in their feet.

"No!" he screamed as Hewitt plowed the truck into the row, immediately puncturing the front tires as the truck stopped awkwardly, jerking both men forward.

"What the hell was that?" Hewitt questioned aloud, his face appearing dumbfounded.

"Someone hammered spikes through their feet so they'd be a natural spike strip."

"Like cops use to stop cars?"

"Yeah, like that," Mullins said as the undead, now free of their bonds, began surrounding the truck.

A few lost limbs during the collision, dragging an extra arm behind them as they moaned and pawed at the glass of the truck.

"How the hell are we going to deal with them?" Mullins questioned, trying to imagine how to open one of the doors without getting bitten immediately.

"What's this 'we' stuff? You've got all the weapons."

"And you drove us straight into a trap," Mullins noted. "Someone didn't put this here as a practical joke. They either want our stuff, or they want to kill us."

"We don't have stuff."

"Exactly. We'd better get to steppin', or you can drive this thing with two blown tires as far as it'll take us."

Hewitt looked at the undead surrounding the truck, covered in blood with their busted appendages, and decided to hit the accelerator.

Chapter 12

Aside from further damaging the tires and rims on the truck, Hewitt ran into the initial herd of zombies, getting muscle tissue and blood wrapped in the grill. Mullins wasn't certain if the engine died first, or the truck's ability to maneuver in any direction seized up with the shattered rims. He was bumped around as the truck began to shudder involuntarily, and he could clearly see that Hewitt hadn't hit the brakes. Regardless, the two men were going to be walking for some time, and Mullins knew the area vehicles were either disabled, or out of gas.

He didn't allow himself to trust Hewitt, either. Although the man expressed nothing except an interest to reach the base and be safe and secure, Mullins knew he had murdered more than two dozen people in the Adirondack region of New York. Metzger wouldn't exaggerate the truth about something so dire, and Mullins had dealt with types like Hewitt during his years as a cop. Back then, people were restrained by laws and consequences, or more people would have killed indiscriminately before the apocalypse.

When the two men stepped from the truck, they found no dead in their immediate vicinity. An increasing number pursued the truck at a slow pace, but most of them remained a few hundred yards behind the disabled vehicle. Hewitt turned to face Mullins, holding up his handcuffed hands with an expression that asked if Mullins was cruel enough to let him remain defenseless. Shaking his head negatively, the former cop refused to give the man any advantages over him in the wide-open lands of Virginia.

Mullins reached in for the small survival pack the residents of the village provided. It included a few cans and packets of food, a flashlight, a lighter, and a few other useful trinkets. He remembered how the highway became a tunnel that continued beneath the surface of the water, west of the military base. He questioned how many years the tunnel would remain safe from collapse and other natural disasters without workers to inspect and repair it routinely.

"Who set that trap back there?" Hewitt questioned when Mullins shouldered the pack and neared the prisoner.

"How should I know?"

"Is it a warning from the military?"

"The military has guns, and they don't stray this far from the base."

Hewitt began walking east when Mullins ushered him by waving the revolver in that direction.

"Six shots isn't going to protect us against a crazy group."

"Maybe you can join them if they're like-minded crazies."

"I'm done explaining myself to you."

"Then maybe you can shut your trap before you alert the locals to our presence," Mullins stated.

"Maybe I don't want to," Hewitt said, causing Mullins to groan aloud.

"You barely said a word the entire time we were at Maplewood, and now you want to be a chatterbox."

"I didn't particularly want to walk."

Mullins kept a sharp eye on his surroundings, maintaining a safe distance from Hewitt in case the man decided to make his own way, despite his shackles.

Based on his previous visit to the base, he knew the military didn't need to set up traps in the road. He couldn't imagine who else might want to keep travelers away from the area, because all roads led to the base once they reached the west side of the tunnel.

One silver lining in the area proved to be a minimal number of the undead. The military continually cleared the area surrounding Norfolk and the base, which thinned the numbers significantly. While more undead migrated from surrounding states, hundreds fell into the Virginia waterways over time, either sinking, being devoured by marine life, or floating out to deeper waters.

Constructed to keep shipping lanes moving along the water, several bridge tunnels allowed traffic to continue beneath the tributaries that led to the Atlantic Ocean. The highways often went several hundred yards out, across the water until they descended slightly into tunnels beneath the watery surface. As they drew closer to the first such tunnel, Mullins reached into his backpack to locate the flashlight, but he glanced up, discovering he might not require the device to see in the tunnel.

"That's weird," he muttered.

"What is?"

"I don't remember the lights working in here the last time."

Solar panels on either end of the tunnel system powered lights leading up to the tunnels, and incrementally inside. He wasn't sure if they always worked independently of the grid, or someone made the effort to reconfigure the system following the apocalypse. With the military almost assuredly scouring for food and supplies like everyone else, it certainly benefitted them to have the tunnel bridges providing light to keep their personnel safe.

Even so, Mullins never saw evidence of their people working outside of the base and the city of Norfolk. Standing at the tunnel entrance, he spotted a few vehicles along the righthand side of the road inside. He remained still a moment, listening for undead, or living people who might have created the spike strip behind him.

"You're not getting cold feet now, are you?" Hewitt questioned.

"It's either this, or swim across the channel," Mullins replied. "I'm not sure you're up for swimming with handcuffs on, and I'd like to make sure we aren't walking into a trap."

"You already sprung the trap," a female voice said from somewhere inside the tunnel, causing both Mullins and Hewitt to stiffen.

"We aren't looking for trouble," Mullins said after a few seconds, his heartrate beginning to elevate because he felt certain he was about to be surrounded.

"Neither am I," the woman responded, "which is why I didn't want vehicles racing through my current residence."

"You can come out," Hewitt said. "There are only two of us."

"I know. I've been watching you two jibber-jabber the last half mile."

"Look, whether you come out or not, we simply want to pass through this tunnel."

"I'm not going to stop you," the woman said.

Mullins looked to Hewitt, who showed indifference about their next move. Keeping his hand perched atop the revolver holstered at his side, Mullins led the way, looking cautiously around the tunnel as he stepped inside. His eyes required some time to adjust to the lower light, and he couldn't necessarily pinpoint the woman's location based on her voice, because it echoed within the tunnel whenever she spoke.

Prepared to duck at any given moment, Mullins stayed low and crept into the tunnel entrance, knowing full well the woman, and any unseen associates, had already spotted him.

"Why does the tall one have handcuffs on?" she inquired, still not revealing her location.

"He can be a handful," Mullins answered vaguely on purpose.

He didn't want to give anyone a reason to open fire on them, and stating that Hewitt murdered more than two dozen people seemed reason enough. Giving away their motives for heading to the military base also didn't help his cause.

"You're clearly heading to the base," the woman stated, causing Mullins to keep his head on a swivel, searching for her location. "They patrol the city regularly. You won't make it far before you're intercepted."

"We're expected," Mullins answered.

"I wish you luck."

"I'd feel a little better if we formally introduced ourselves."

"I see you're armed. I'm not defenseless."

"We don't mean you any harm," Mullins said. "My name is Michael."

"Rose. If you don't mind, I'd like to skip any shaking of hands. I'm not very trusting after what's happened to some of my friends."

Mullins and Hewitt both stepped forward, prepared to cross the treacherous tunnel that typically posed a different kind of threat. Neither spoke a word, and about a minute later, they passed the first stalled car when the sound of a cough echoed through the tunnel. Mullins looked to Hewitt for reassurance that he had heard the sound correctly, because the cough did not sound feminine to him, and his unsavory travel companion appeared to share his notion.

"Let's get moving," Mullins said just above a whisper, suspecting Rose had at least one other person living with her in the tunnel bridge.

He dared not trust her, and if she lured them inside with a full crew at her disposal, the two men stood little chance against armed survivors with the advantage of knowing the bridge's hiding spots. Adding to his growing trepidation, the lights within the tunnel flickered several times. If they went out altogether, Mullins would be blind within the tunnel, leaving him vulnerable if any attackers possessed flashlights or night vision equipment.

Taking a quick glance around, Mullins noticed the tunnel walls were a glossy eggshell brick, and the ceiling appeared to have a sheen as well when the lights were working to illuminate everything nearby. Two lanes existed for traffic that no longer flowed, and a pedestrian walkway hugged one of the walls. Mullins thought he saw the occasional access door along the side, wondering if it simply led to the other tunnel that once brought traffic back from the Hampton Roads area. Because the skin flakes from the dead, and dust particles didn't readily enter the tunnel bridge, it looked rather clean.

Picking up his pace, Mullins found that Hewitt appeared equally worried, jogging along just behind him. No gunfire erupted, and they heard no more voices by the time they reached what he believed was the middle of the tunnel. So long as the lighting remained functional, he felt good about their chances of reaching the other side of the bridge that dove beneath the channel.

Suddenly, however, he heard the sound of a heavy vehicle coming from the other side. His ears detected more than one, meaning a convoy, indicating military personnel were heading away from the base.

"Shit," he muttered. "The military."

"Isn't that who we're looking for?" Hewitt asked with a perplexed expression.

"Yeah, but not out here. They're looking for supplies and parts, not trying to pick up survivors. We need to get to cover until they pass."

Hewitt followed him over to a tall Ford truck that received a lift kit treatment at some point. They ducked behind the front and rear tires on the opposite side respectively before anyone in the convoy spotted them.

Mullins detected two civilian vehicles and three transport vehicles that looked sparsely occupied the one time he dared take an extended glance. He guessed they were saving the space in the hopes that their supply run was fruitful.

The few faces he took in appeared weary, as though the soldiers or sailors on the mission weren't happy about their prospects.

He imagined being confined to a military base instead of exploring the seven seas, or fighting for their country abroad, grew stale. Working for food and very basic shelter didn't appeal to him, and he suspected the men and women at the installation remained there only to keep their families safe. If Mullins didn't get double-crossed by the military, or murdered by Hewitt along the way, he didn't plan on staying at the base for very long.

"I thought you trusted these people," Hewitt scoffed once the possible danger passed the two men and they stood once again.

"I barely trust them more than I do you. The deal in place is for me to deliver you to the base. Grunts aren't going to give two shits about either of us, so I'm not going to engage them."

"This is sounding like less of a good deal for me."

"Nothing has changed. They *need* you. They *don't* need me."

"Why do I need you?" Hewitt questioned.

"Because I'm the passcode that keeps us from getting shot the second we step in Norfolk."

Hewitt gave a strange combination of smirk and sneer, which left Mullins uneasy. He didn't like the feeling of having no one left in his life to trust on the road. After fulfilling a promise to accompany his friend to South Carolina, Mullins was left to build trust with people he barely knew.

Fortunately, he possessed good instincts, and years as a cop taught him to judge people quickly for what they were. He decided he was going to make it to Norfolk with Hewitt, or be forced to shoot the man along the way.

***

Closer to noon, the Piper Seneca crossed the eastern side of the Tennessee border, and Metzger began examining charts for potential landing spots. Timmons indicated they had ample fuel for the time being, but wanted to locate somewhere safe to land where the group could top off their reserves and rest for a few minutes. The journey from Virginia to New Mexico was virtually a straight shot west, with a bit of a southern incline along the Atlas.

"Thoughts on private airports?" Metzger asked his friend.

Timmons groaned, but stole a glance at the flight chart Metzger held across his lap.

"They're hit and miss on fuel, but I don't expect to get lucky enough to find another fuel truck anywhere we go."

"So, that's a 'yes'?"

Timmons noticed the dozen or so airports Metzger had located in the Knoxville area.

"It looks isolated," he said to himself, more than his passengers. "If we don't locate fuel there, we can hop over to another airport."

Both Metzger and Timmons wore headsets to dull the noise of the engine, allowing them to communicate clearly. The two spare headsets were shared behind them by Brooke and Sutton as Gracine and Jillian attempted to get some rest with earplugs in place.

"What should we expect from this place?" Metzger asked, turning to Brooke.

"I'm not entirely sure," she answered. "I only have coordinates."

"Don't these usually have concealed blast doors of some sort?" Sutton asked.

Brooke gave a slight chuckle.

"A few are like that, but some are housed beneath everyday businesses. There might be a hotel, or a restaurant, sitting on top of the bunker. It depends on the make and model."

"How the hell would Nadeau get his hands on a bunker?" Sutton inquired.

"He has wealth," Brooke answered. "He might have purchased an older bunker from the government, using a political contact. Bunkers have been around since the Cold War, and like anything else, they get antiquated over time."

Metzger hated the idea of Nadeau securing his own safety by obtaining a bunker through some political favor, or handing the government a lump sum of cash before murdering millions of innocent people. Not a day passed that he didn't think of his personal struggles, heading from the Cincinnati area to his home state, only to find his parents had perished at the hands of Nadeau's associates. While many survivors took the apocalypse personally, he had better reason to seek revenge.

"What's that place called?" Timmons inquired about the private airport on the flight chart.

"Skyranch Airport," Metzger answered. "It's close to water, and a highway by the looks of the Atlas."

"So, there's hope for fuel."

"Well, it shouldn't be packed with the dead, and there are probably a few planes there we can syphon from."

"Off the subject, Captain Timmons," Sutton said after a few seconds.

"You can call me Scott."

"Dan told me you prefer your formal title," Sutton said with mild confusion.

"Dan is an asshole sometimes," Timmons answered, causing his friend to snicker beside him. "Anyway, what's on your mind, Mr. Sutton?"

"Colby. And I owe you an apology."

"For what?" Timmons asked with surprise since the two had only met once, and momentarily at that.

"When we left the base last year, I warned Dan to keep his eye on you. It sounds like you've been a big help, and I'm sorry I doubted you."

"Well, being cautious is a good thing in this world," Timmons stated. "You have nothing to be sorry about, but I appreciate you saying that."

"Why do you dislike being called by your title?" Brooke inquired.

"It's a life I chose to leave behind," Timmons answered. "Out here, I don't like people knowing I worked for the military, or that I can fly, unless it needs to be said."

"I can relate," Brooke said.

Metzger turned to look directly at her.

"If I may pry, what exactly is your intention when we find Nadeau?"

"I feel like it's similar to your own, except I want to extract information from him first. Painfully."

"That's pretty close," Metzger admitted. "I have a very personal stake in seeing him pay."

Everyone remained quiet a moment.

"How did he pull it off?" Sutton finally asked Brooke.

"I honestly don't know," she answered. "Well, I have some idea. He had so many trucks planted in factories and populated areas, that my people couldn't comprehend how it slipped past government intelligence."

"Were you part of some brain trust?" Sutton inquired.

"No. Nothing like that. I worked in the field."

"Then how did you get on Nadeau's trail?" Metzger asked.

"It's a long story."

"We've got time."

Brooke drew a breath and exhaled through her nose.

"Well, no one else is going to hear it, so here goes."

Chapter 13

Early September, The Previous Year

Brooke and Canfield left Indiana shortly after purchasing some supplies, which turned out to be a smart move on Brooke's part. The days following the explosions resulted in panic across the nation, if not the world. People frantically looted stores, committed crimes at an all-time high without consequences, and watched the numbers of the living drop in record numbers as the undead became the majority.

Deciding to do right by her boyfriend, Brooke charted a course that eventually took them to Texas to reunite him with his family.

Eventually.

On the road, she found more time to study the documents found at the hotel, discovering a few safehouse locations that appeared to lead to the man responsible for the attacks. She also found two documents made of thicker paper, something like a diploma, or legal document, that had some kind of silver coating in one corner that appeared holographic in nature. Certainly distinguishable, it likely provided proof that the recipient had pledged allegiance to Nadeau, deserving shelter and hospitality in the new world.

Stopping at a convenience store shortly after crossing the state border into Kentucky the day after they left the resort, Brooke and Canfield caught their first glimpses of the undead on the television. Urban areas were hit much harder by the terrorist event, and breaking news covered virtually every cable and satellite network. Police and National Guard personnel attempted to incapacitate the dead, learning quickly that only trauma to the head downed them permanently. At first, footage appeared blurry, or shot by handheld cameras, as though the authorities weren't letting reporters near the danger zones. Perhaps the channels attempted to edit out some of the more disturbing footage, but eventually they relented because the internet had already allowed hundreds of user videos to be uploaded.

"This is fucked up," Canfield muttered as Brooke placed a few items on the counter, wondering how much longer her credit cards and phone would work.

She almost had to pry the clerk's eyes away from the television mounted above them to purchase her items. A Pakistani man who likely owned the store, he almost assuredly had weapons within his reach, whether legal or not. He didn't appear overly concerned, as though the event would end swiftly once the government got a foothold on the disease that killed people before reviving them in a less capable state.

Fortunately, she hadn't lost contact with Taylor from her workplace, though it sounded like government employees weren't exempt from the growing nationwide panic.

"We need to get moving," she said, touching Canfield on the arm before exiting through the glass door.

Almost immediately, traffic along highways and interstates proved nightmarish with gridlock, accidents, and virtually every conceivable type of stoppage occurring at once. Brooke had navigated for her boyfriend, taking county roads and avoiding the major thruways. Her mind constantly churned over their survival, taking weapons, food, ammunition, and fuel into consideration. Brooke had never trained herself for life in an apocalypse because time simply didn't permit in her occupation. She had contacted Taylor about getting some kind of supply drop, but she hadn't received a reply regarding that particular request.

As they crossed the parking lot to the rental car she now intended to keep, Brooke noticed three white men heading towards the front door. One of them appeared ashen and sweaty, as though he suffered from an affliction. With flu season being months away, Brooke suspected he might have inhaled the poisonous substance shortly after Nadeau's bombs exploded, or been bitten by one of the infected. She noticed at least one of the men had a gun tucked in his pants along the small of his back, and for some reason, Canfield took notice as well.

"Are they going to rob the place?" he questioned, stopping and staring.

"It's not our concern, John."

"Not our concern? Where I'm from, we stand up for what's right."

Both of them heard shouting from within the store, followed by gunfire a few seconds later. Two more shots followed the first, and a few cries of pain filled the air.

"What I'm doing is more important than all of this," Brooke said. "If we locate Nadeau, we have a chance of getting answers. Maybe a cure."

Canfield continued to look at the store, as though wanting to help the owner, or see what happened. Brooke decided to change tactics, sometimes forgetting that Canfield wasn't as hardened as her to the world, or the recent developments.

"I don't want anything to happen to you," she said, gently cupping his cheek with her right hand. "I need you."

She didn't expect the billionaire to give up answers after he pulled off such an elaborate plot, but she needed to sell Canfield on her plan.

He stared at the store momentarily, and when no one emerged, Canfield accepted that the world wasn't going to be the same going forward. When they started to turn for their rental car, the front door burst open with a jingling bell and a thud as the door struck the exterior building frame. Both whirled, finding one of the men stumbling outside, his hand clasped over a bloody wound on his abdomen. He reached forward, as though pleading for assistance, trying to speak words that failed to emerge, before the store owner callously walked up behind him, kicked him to the ground, and shot him in the back of the skull. With the situation resolved, Brooke and Canfield made their way to the vehicle, making certain the man didn't make any aggressive moves toward them.

Barely glancing at the pair, the uninjured clerk tucked his gun away, and began dealing with the mess of the bodies, as though he feared the scene might detract from his business. Brooke wondered why the man didn't get that the world was ending around him. Perhaps he simply wanted to go down with his figurative ship, knowing he couldn't send money to his loved ones, or return to his homeland. Brooke didn't always understand the human psyche, especially in such unfamiliar surroundings, so she focused on the mission at hand.

A small city named Henderson just ahead of them in Kentucky offered a number of businesses, and possible lodging. Brooke knew the grid wasn't going to last much longer, so she wanted to reach out to her contacts and receive any final information and orders before proceeding. Based on what she knew, cell phones were on borrowed time, credit cards would be useless when the internet crashed, and eventually the dead would far outnumber the living.

"Isn't heading into a town what we're trying to avoid?" Canfield asked as he drove south, following her directions.

Still visibly shaken by the convenience store encounter, he hadn't accepted the future Brooke fully anticipated. She knew what items to grab, and what would be scarce very soon, but their car could only hold so much inventory. Driving anything larger meant draining fuel reserves all the more quickly in a world where fuel was about to become highly sought.

"The urban areas will be overrun first," Brooke said. "This city isn't that big."

"Sounds like it's big enough to have a hospital. Isn't that where a lot of the trouble started when the sick went for medical attention?"

Brooke didn't answer as a message from Taylor came across her electronic device.

I'M DROPPING A CARE PACKAGE FOR YOU IN SEBREE, TN WITHIN THE NEXT 24 HOURS.

Taking a look at the map, Brooke realized it wasn't very far to Sebree, but at the pace she and Canfield were making, the care package would likely arrive before them.

DETAILS COMING LATER.
INSTRUCTIONS AND INFO INCLUDED IN PACKAGE.

"Instructions?" Brooke wondered aloud, drawing a confused look from Canfield.

A green sign along the side of the road indicated they were a few miles from reaching Henderson. Canfield turned to ask Brooke something when a man staggered into the road less than three car lengths in front of them.

"Look out!" Brooke shouted, causing Canfield to slam on the brakes just short of the man, who turned away from the vehicle.

Fortunately, they hadn't been traveling at a high rate of speed since the road wasn't very smooth, and they came across the occasional stopped vehicle.

Being reactionary, Canfield stepped out of the driver's side to yell at the oblivious pedestrian, but Brooke already suspected they might be encountering their first member of the undead.

"John!" she yelled at him from her seat before throwing open the passenger side door. "Don't touch him!"

Canfield turned to look at her, and the noise prompted the staggering corpse to turn and look at them with its mouth partially agape, teeth showing, as it made a throaty growl. It looked very much like them, with pale, speckled skin, and a walk that didn't appear natural. Its cloudy eyes possessed an unusual powder blue tint that appeared to be illuminated from within, immediately informing Brooke the man wasn't among the living.

"Oh, shit," Canfield said, stepping back a few paces since he possessed no weapons. "It looks alive. But those eyes."

His voice tapered off as he spoke the last sentence, indicating he felt the news was correct in assessing that the dead were rising.

Brooke pulled her sidearm from the door's storage slot, hesitating momentarily to study the zombie as it took a liking to Canfield, focusing its attention solely on him. From what they had seen on the news, the coverage seemed spot-on as the zombie appeared driven, but primitive as it simply pursued Canfield with no regard for its surroundings.

"Please shoot it," Canfield asked as he walked in reverse momentarily before picking up speed to put some distance between himself and the zombie.

"Just a second," Brooke said, already holding her firearm, but studying the fresh, walking corpse for signs of a bite mark.

Seeing none, she wondered if this unlucky individual had breathed in the toxic chemical that killed thousands before reanimating them.

"Shoot it *now*, please," Canfield said again, more emphatically this time, on the verge of pleading with his girlfriend.

Bad knees from years of catching in baseball kept him from being able to run proficiently, and sometimes they stiffened up at random times. Brooke wasn't going to put him in peril, but she wanted an understanding of how the undead functioned before they encountered more of them. In the urban areas, their effectiveness appeared to come in great numbers, so the couple needed to avoid a swarm of the undead at all costs.

Canfield steered wide of the car to avoid bringing the potential assailant near Brooke, but now he made his way around the car because both sides of the road had shallow ditches and foliage that presented a tripping hazard. Brooke saw the unrelenting zombie never deviate from its pursuit of Canfield, and she began to understand that they functioned on rudimentary levels of existence.

"Hey!" she yelled at the zombie, causing its head to snap in her direction and change focus immediately.

It had barely taken a step towards her when she fired a bullet into the center of its skull, causing it to fall to the ground like a deflated blow-up decoration.

"Thank you," Canfield said between heavy breaths. "Why did you wait so long?"

"I needed to know what makes them tick. We're certain to encounter a *lot* more of them. And soon."

"That's not comforting."

"We need more weapons. And we need to get you up to speed on using them."

"I'm a decent shot," Canfield said a bit defensively. "I *am* from Texas."

Brooke gave him a knowing smile.

"Even so, we're going to want more than just guns. If this plays out the way I think, we'll have our pick of houses and stores to explore."

"Now we're breaking and entering?"

"John, you're delusional if you think things will ever be the same again. It's going to take everything we have just to survive this, and we need to hope there isn't more of that shit in the air. Or there isn't a second wave coming."

"I just can't believe our government isn't capable of fixing this."

"A lot of them are in bunkers for their own safety. That isn't a good sign for the rest of us."

"Fuck," Canfield said, hanging his head.

Brooke walked over and gave him a reassuring hug.

"We're going to get through this. Let's get to the next town and see what's there."

When Canfield left her embrace, he walked over to the corpse, standing above it momentarily as the only thing moving was its hair in the breeze. He knelt down beside it, patting the blue jean pockets until he found a wallet along the back. At first, Brooke wondered if he was trying to search for money that was about to be useless to every worldly resident still living, but he pulled out the driver's license to examine it.

"I know what you're thinking," he said, "but the guy had a name. Somewhere, his family might be wondering where he went."

Brooke realized her boyfriend was going to be a bit slower about coming around to the gravity of their situation, and just how many times this exact same situation might happen. She had to be patient with him, but she also needed to make him capable of defending himself. He didn't have her training, but Canfield possessed above average strength, and the advantage of having been a professional athlete.

"Maybe it's best to leave the ID with the body, in case they find him," Brooke suggested.

"I will," Canfield replied. "I just wanted to see the name and remember that he was flesh and blood before he turned into *this*."

Canfield replaced the license in the billfold and placed it in the pocket where he found it. He rose slowly and turned to Brooke with a bit more determination in his face.

"I'm good," he assured her. "Let's go see what Henderson has to offer."

***

Buildings of limestone and brick lined the main drag in Henderson, giving Brooke the impression that a hometown festival or farmers market might fit in perfectly in the small city. Picturesque, the streets made for brochure material, a website tourism page, or even a vintage painting during any season. Unfortunately, the streets appeared mostly barren except for a few cars, and a few people hurriedly trying to get to safety.

"The town that dreaded sundown," Canfield commented, slowly driving down the road, allowing Brooke to observe their surroundings.

"There are a few stores," Brooke commented, taking notice of the usual businesses.

Insurance agencies, antique stores, a few banks, and an optometrist's office lined the first few blocks. Brooke noticed a few people peering from the large picture windows at the passing vehicle, as though she and Canfield were violating a city curfew by daring to drive in broad daylight. Perhaps the local residents followed the advice given by the government and medical experts on the news. Brooke assumed a miniscule chance of the dust-like toxin might linger in the air, or on the ground, but she doubted Henderson, Kentucky was directly targeted by Nadeau.

"This doesn't look promising," Canfield commented as they started into a new city block.

"We need to see if we can find a place to hole up, John. This may be the last time we get to stay somewhere with power."

"It's going to get that bad?"

"If the problem isn't corrected soon, and it likely won't be, the grid will collapse."

Both of them continued to look for anything of use along the downtown area, and Canfield pulled into a parking spot surrounded by lots of other empty spots.

"What is it?" Brooke asked.

"There's a baseball card shop here," he answered, prompting her to begin chastising him before he finished his sentence. "And next door is a sporting goods store. They might have guns or ammo."

Brooke decided to humor him by stepping into the baseball card shop with him first. The owner appeared to be busily boxing up some items from his display case and the wall. A few squares appeared in the wall where posters or frames once hung, darker than the surrounding paint. Hundreds of sporting cards remained inside the glass cases, priced individually, while boxes of less rare cards sat atop the cases for perusing.

"Closing shop?" Canfield inquired.

"You know how these things go," the older man replied. "They tell us to stay home so the criminals can loot and pillage the streets. I'm just grabbing the important stuff."

Canfield looked around like a kid, taking in the baseball history through the cards and memorabilia on the walls.

"Anything in particular you're looking for?" the owner asked.

"We were just passing through and I thought I'd see what you had," Canfield answered. "Any minor league stuff?"

"Mostly common cards in the boxes. I sell them for a dime each. Got a few stars in the display cases."

"John here played in the minors," Brooke informed the owner, attempting to put Canfield on the spot.

She knew he was going to fiddle around until the topic came up, so she decided to expedite the inevitable. In truth, she wanted to see if her lover was as humble as he acted in other venues. He seldom brought up the subject, so she often did so on his behalf. He *loved* talking about his profession, though not so much about his career because he didn't truly succeed until he became one of the youngest minor league managers ever in baseball.

Fans never felt as enthusiastic about managers and coaches, despite the tireless, thankless hours the men and women put into their profession.

"Is that so?" the owner asked with an arched eyebrow.

"Toronto," Canfield said. "I manage, managed, for their organization after my playing career came to an end."

He tilted his head slightly when he changed his meaning to the past tense mid-sentence.

"They had a rough season this year," the shop owner commented.

"He was collateral damage," Brooke said, siding with Canfield.

"You won't be out of work long, once this pandemic comes to an end," the older man said with an assuring nod.

"I'll land on my feet," Canfield said neutrally before giving Brooke a mischievous smirk. "It would really blow your mind if I told you what my girlfriend did for a living."

"Oh?"

Brooke walked up and clasped him by the arm before Canfield could reveal information that might compromise her assignment.

"We really should be going."

"Best of luck," Canfield said to the older man.

"Same to you two," the man answered with a smile as he started packing a few more items. "Godspeed."

Brooke stepped outside with Canfield before addressing him.

"You can't be doing that," she said.

"Doing what? Putting you on the spot like you do with me all the time?"

"You like the attention," she pressed.

"Sometimes. But a lot of the time I just want to feel normal. And now, even that's being stolen from me."

"Sorry," Brooke apologized, feeling genuinely terrible for ruining his experience inside the sports card shop.

"It's not you," Canfield said. "It's this," he added, holding out his arms, looking around the nearly vacated city.

A moment later, they stepped inside the sporting goods store, finding the shelves rather hit and miss with inventory, like a clearance sale after the holiday season. Brooke headed straight for the firearms section while Canfield deviated, looking as though he conjured up an idea of his own for weaponry.

"Do you have any firearms left?" Brooke asked a salesman nearing middle-age, seeing numerous empty slots behind the glass counter.

He appeared as though he might have done some hunting on the side. Not particularly handsome, the man looked comfortable working around firearms and goods used in the outdoors.

"A few. Mostly shotguns, and a few handguns. We've had quite a run with everything on the news the past few days."

"Two shotguns, and two of those," Brooke said, pointing to two nine-millimeter pistols.

"You even know what those are?" the clerk asked.

"Yes. Ruger EC9s. I'm a little surprised you have any left."

Brooke's training included knowledge and proficiency in firearms, much like that of a police officer. She was trained to disarm adversaries as needed and use their weapons to defend herself.

Although the clerk appeared impressed that she knew her firearms, he still hesitated.

"There's the matter of the background check."

"Perhaps this will help speed things up," Brooke said, pulling out her government identification before slapping it atop the glass case. "I'll also need as much ammunition as I'm allowed to purchase."

"We don't have a limit," the man stated. "You planning to hole up and defend your homestead?"

"Not exactly."

A few minutes into the background check, Brooke noticed Canfield coming her way with a cart full of items. He had chosen a machete, several knives that appeared surprisingly adequate, and two baseball bats with a number of baseballs. She looked over the items before making eye contact with him. He appeared rather proud of himself and his selections.

"The baseballs were a bonus," he admitted. "I can use the bats to bash in their heads."

He said the last part loud enough that it drew the attention of the clerk.

"We do a Halloween thing every year with fake zombie heads," Canfield quickly said to the clerk, who dismissed the notion and went back to work.

"You're off to a good start, but we might want some canteens, and camping supplies, too," Brooke told him. "And see if they have any prepackaged food, please."

"Okay."

Canfield appeared to have gained an understanding of their impending situation as he took the cart to a different area of the store. Brooke had no qualms about maxing out her credit cards, if necessary, because she suspected in a matter of days that banks, credit cards, phones, and electronic devices would be useless. Henderson didn't appear heavily impacted by the attacks just yet, but once urban areas were overtaken by the undead, everything would filter outward, creating gridlock, more deaths, and the end of society as the world knew it.

After close to an hour, mostly because the store appeared short-staffed, the couple checked out with as many supplies as their car could hold. A teenager, or in her early twenties, the clerk didn't appear surprised at their bulk purchase.

"It's been a busy few days," the young woman commented, finally glancing at their items.

"Where is everyone?" Canfield inquired, making small talk, or possibly gathering information on Brooke's behalf.

"The mayor asked everyone to stay home unless absolutely necessary. I think a lot of people are staying with family, or gathering supplies."

"Why?"

"My dad says it's the end of the world."

Brooke spoke so only Canfield could hear her words.

"He may be right."

Canfield asked the girl where the area hotels were located, and she pointed them in the right direction. He thanked her, likely thinking of how good a hot shower would feel for the last time. Brooke could tell that he wasn't comfortable having insider knowledge of how civilization was crumbling when so many remained oblivious.

A few minutes later, Brooke handed items to Canfield so he could place them in the trunk, or the back seat, depending on how nearby they wanted certain weapons. A few cars passed them in the street, and in one car, Brooke noticed a family of four wearing surgical masks to keep particulates from entering their lungs. She doubted it would help against the minute dust Nadeau had created and dispersed in major metropolitans.

"This is depressing," Canfield said as he closed the trunk once they were finished.

Brooke was about to respond when they heard a man's scream in the alley behind the baseball card shop. Canfield grabbed one of the bats from the back seat and followed Brooke as they dashed around the building, finding the store owner being pursued by a female who had recently turned. She wore a stained white blouse and a powder blue skirt as though she died during her lunch break from the bank, or perhaps a legal office. Her jaws snapped at the store owner, but he used a sizable box to keep her at bay.

"I don't want to hurt her," the man said with panic in his voice.

"She's dead," Canfield said the words before Brooke could come up with a better way to inform the man.

He looked bewildered, almost dropping the box as his face registered shock.

Canfield took up the bat and walked around the woman where he could use a right-handed stance to swing away.

"The head," Brooke reminded him.

"What are you doing?" the man asked with shock and terror.

"I'm about to swing away. Duck on the count of three."

Canfield counted, and swung, creating a thud when the bat connected with the woman's skull, sending her to the ground, and leaving the tip of the bat covered in blood.

Absolutely dumbfounded, the shop owner stared at the body momentarily before his face met Canfield's with an expression of sheer horror.

"What have you done?"

"Have you not been watching the news?" Canfield countered. "These people are dead, and they are *returning to life*."

"You killed her."

"I did no such thing."

Brooke took Canfield's side, ushering him away from the older man who clearly did not understand, or believe, what the media said about the effects of the terrorist attack.

"I'm calling the police!" the man shouted as they walked away from the scene.

"Go ahead!" Canfield called back. "Tell them how I just saved your life!"

Brooke cupped his arm, trying to reassure him.

"Ungrateful prick," Canfield commented.

"You did the right thing, but people aren't going to understand what they're seeing at first, John. And that's why a lot of them are going to die."

"Shit," Canfield said, stopping short of their rental car.

"What is it?" Brooke inquired, concerned he was injured by the zombie.

"Does this mean we don't get to stay in a hotel?"

Brooke flashed a reassuring smile.

"The cops are going to be too busy to look for us. We'll find one somewhere."

Chapter 14

"What the fuck is this?" Timmons asked, interrupting Brooke's recollection of her travels leading up to Maplewood.

Ahead of them, at what Metzger termed an airport from what paperwork he possessed, was a grass landing strip squeezed between a road and a waterway. Looking more closely, Skyranch was actually surrounded by water, with a short access road that bridged the airport to the local road. With winter barely behind them, and the grass likely untended by human hands for more than seven months, he began to question if Timmons could land smoothly.

"Sorry," Metzger said to his friend. "The maps don't exactly tell if the strip is pavement or natural terrain."

"They put it here for a reason," Timmons surmised. "Let's hope they have what we need."

Metzger turned briefly to see everyone awake and alert, their eyes looking out whatever windows they could to see what had their pilot upset. The river beside the grassy strip appeared brown, as though spring mud still ran thick through the water, threatening a potentially soggy landing. Metzger felt his body tense as Timmons lined up the Piper Seneca for their approach. He hoped he hadn't steered his friend wrong, and potentially stranded the entire party on such an isolated airfield. Finding a vehicle might prove difficult if they couldn't fuel up, or take off from the cozy airport.

He visualized the plane landing on a soft, muddy surface, with the rear tires embedding themselves in the mud. From there, the plane hurled forward, tail over propeller, causing a mix of broken ribs and fractured skulls among the passengers. Metzger quickly shook the image from his mind, knowing Timmons possessed a masterful touch during takeoffs and landings. As though realizing his mind was rifling through some dark scenarios, Timmons spoke to him casually while pulling levers and pushing buttons to adjust the speed and flaps.

"One of these times, you need to land a plane."

"I'm not ready," Metzger answered, despite Timmons coaching him for hours each time they took flight.

"You're ready. It's not rocket science."

As the plane drew closer to the ground, Metzger saw just how much water surrounded the small airport, and he grew concerned that a watery spring might have left the landing strip soft. With numerous hangars on the grounds, he imagined the owners maintained the airport, and kept it smooth, but they likely perished, or moved on, with the advent of the apocalypse. He tried to keep negative thoughts from entering his mind, but as Timmons brought the plane closer to touchdown, Metzger felt his body tense more than usual.

"You need to relax," Timmons told him as the plane's rear wheels touched down, followed by the single front tire, barely felt by any of the passengers.

"Sorry. I was just concerned that I found you a hazardous landing spot."

"You kill the dead, I land planes. We've each got our thing, son."

When the plane rolled to a stop near the office and the hangars, each passenger exited the vehicle with stiff legs and backs, ready to explore the area. Beside them, the sound of moving water from the river reached their ears, overpowering any other nearby noise.

"You okay?" Jillian asked Metzger as they walked toward one of the hangars in search of fuel, supplies, or another plane if they couldn't fuel the Piper Seneca.

"I'm good," he answered.

"When the captain notices you acting weird, something is wrong."

Metzger stopped short of a hangar, turning to her.

"I feel like the world is on my shoulders, trying to keep everyone safe."

"We aren't kids, Dan. We chose to tag along because we care about you, and about finding Nadeau. You aren't obligated to protect us every waking second."

"I'm also worried about failing. There are so many things that could go wrong. And we're taking this woman's word on where to find him."

"A woman we barely know," Jillian noted.

"But she has documents similar to the ones we found in Nadeau's safehouses. Except our trail went cold."

"He has a reason for keeping his followers around," Jillian reasoned as Metzger looked at the hangar, trying to locate the best entry point.

He banged on the white, metal door to see if any surprises awaited them inside. Hearing nothing, he walked to the side, finding the regular entrance door unlocked, with one plane and some tools inside. One look at the aircraft informed him the plane had been partially dismantled at some point, possibly for parts.

"Nothing useful," he said to Jillian. "Let's check some of the other buildings while Scott locates his flight charts."

***

Sutton walked with Gracine on the other side of the airport, which technically had only one runway for incoming and outgoing planes, making it rather small by comparison. They approached the hangar closest to the office, which Timmons appeared to be entering.

"That was noble of you to eat crow," Gracine said.

"Eat crow?"

"When you apologized to the pilot."

"He had all winter to pull a fast one, and he didn't, but that doesn't mean I trust him completely."

"You don't trust anyone, Colby. That's your problem."

"It's kept me alive this long."

"I think anger has kept you alive this long."

"What's that supposed to mean?"

"Nothing."

Sutton felt a bit confused by her comment, but he ignored Gracine's words long enough to examine the hangar for an entry point.

Before he could go around the side of the metal building, he heard a throaty growl that didn't sound like it came from within any of the buildings. He looked to Gracine, noticing that she heard it as well because she reached for the knife at her side.

Making their way around the hangar, the pair heard the river wash past the airport, along with more primitive noises of the undead. It wasn't until they saw the river with their own eyes that they discovered its majestic power, which delivered a few undead to their location as several others floated past. Two of the zombies had made their way to the shallow water beside the airport, gaining their footing and trudging toward the plane they either heard or noticed from the water.

Both of them struggled against the current, even in the water that barely reached their knees. Sutton and Gracine stopped short of the water, simply observing their hungry adversaries a moment.

"They'll wash away with a push," Sutton said, moving his hand away from his sheathed knife.

"So they can be someone else's problem?" Gracine chastised him. "They could wash up somewhere and kill someone."

She stepped forward, challenging the water before pulling her knife from its sheath and stabbing the closer straggler in the skull. The second attempted to take a step closer to her, but a surge in the current caught its one planted foot and tripped it, allowing the current to take it downstream.

Both of them watched it momentarily as it reached back for them, growling in defiance as the spring current took it to whatever shore awaited it.

"You're like them sometimes," Gracine said to Sutton.

"How's that?"

"You're just existing day to day."

"Why are you on my case today?"

"I've been on your case a lot longer than that, Colby. When you discovered Jacob had died, you shut down completely."

Sutton simply stared at her, remembering the pain that overtook his mind and body that fateful day.

"I wanted to be there for you, and you shut me out. Even when we reached Maplewood, you shut me out. Why the fuck are you so afraid to love someone?"

"Do we have to talk about this right now?"

"We may be confronting Nadeau in a matter of days. There might not be another time to air our grievances, Colby."

Sutton felt uneasy, and uncomfortable, because he didn't like talking about his emotions under any circumstances. He kept an invisible wall between himself and others, never wanting to talk about subject matters that didn't ensure his survival or complete whatever objective he set for himself. His face flushed, and he wanted nothing more than to walk away from Gracine, but he respected her enough that he stood before her.

"We were getting somewhere in our relationship before you got that bad news," Gracine said. "You can't stay emotionally crippled forever."

"You're with Reggie now," Sutton commented, using his only available defense.

"You know why," Gracine said, cocking her head to one side to show her displeasure. "Why the fuck are you fighting this?"

"This isn't the time for this talk."

"It's never the time. And you don't have to be an island every minute of every day."

Both of them stood in silence momentarily, neither willing to change their stance.

"This business of finding Nadeau needs to be our priority, Gracine. If we aren't focused, we won't survive to see Maplewood again."

"And if we do, then what?"

"If we get to a point where we aren't constantly in danger, and settled somewhere, that changes things," Sutton admitted.

"Okay," Gracine said. "Let's find what we need in the meantime."

***

Timmons walked inside the main office by simply turning a doorknob. He found the usual array of equipment and paperwork, such as flight logs, lying around. Some of the flight charts were strewn across a large, round table, and he flipped through a few of them, not finding any that displayed territories southwest of their location.

A bit surprised by how contemporary the office appeared, Timmons had seen private airports that looked like they needed a makeover from decades of the same wood panel walls and stained yellow ceilings. Based on the sheltered patio outside, and the newer furnishings within, he surmised the owners took pride in the airport and maintained it regularly.

"Can I help?" Brooke asked, walking into the office behind him.

"I need flight charts that cover the areas west of us. They should have some that cover both of our potential locations."

"Tell me where to look."

"Storage. They tend to keep older charts in storage when the updated charts arrive."

Brooke walked over to a closet, using her knuckles to rap the wooden door before turning the doorknob. Timmons walked toward the closet, noticing the daylight streaming through several windows didn't illuminate the storage area very well.

"Flashlight?" Timmons offered, drawing closer to the former government operative.

"You know what you're looking for. I can hold the door for you."

Timmons stepped into the room, finding the charts organized by boxes with dates on them, like tax returns from previous years, making his search easier. He held the flashlight between his teeth while he carefully rummaged through the various paperwork used to plot courses.

"I really need to create my own library of these things," he said after removing the flashlight from his mouth.

"Why don't you?"

"Lack of storage, mainly. We haven't exactly settled into any one place for long."

"I'm guessing you care for these people," Brooke said as Timmons found one of the flight charts he desired, pulling it from the box.

"A few of them, yes. The others I don't know very well. Why are you asking?"

Timmons continued to dig, finding the other chart among others that covered the Midwest and bordering states. He hesitated, deciding to grab several other charts that bordered both areas, just in case their travels took the group elsewhere. The charts were folded multiple times, like posters from magazines during his childhood, making them easy to carry.

"When we arrive, they'll only slow me down," Brooke stated. "It's much safer for all of you to stay with the plane."

Timmons stood, exiting the room with charts in hand, giving her a quizzical stare.

"You make it sound like I'm wasting everyone's time by flying anyone except you out west."

"I'm just saying, if you care about them, they shouldn't come."

Now the pilot stood erect, sizing up the government agent, seeing that she meant her words.

"I have little doubt you're good at your job, missy, but no one should travel alone in this world. These people have a stake in finding Nadeau as well."

"Exactly," Brooke countered. "They have emotions, and emotions get people killed."

"And what is your plan? You're going to go strolling up to Nadeau and whatever protective force he has around him and open fire?"

"I can infiltrate, and play a role."

"You're doing a terrible job of blending in right now, with talk of abandoning my friends."

"It's safer if they don't make the final part of the journey."

Timmons knew how much confronting Nadeau meant to Metzger, and to the others. Everyone lost someone, or something important to them, when the world ended.

"Safer for who? I can't believe I'm hearing this."

Brooke appeared as though she regretted speaking the words, and Timmons could tell she lost something along the way as well.

"Your man," he said. "He didn't make it, did he?"

"You don't see him here, do you?"

Timmons almost pressed her for the rest of the story, but time constraints wouldn't allow her to tell it properly.

"Look," he said, being sympathetic. "We never had this conversation. I can't speak for the others, but count yourself lucky to have Dan and Jillian by your side."

"This is something I can, and should, do by myself," Brooke said as a tear ran down her face.

She quickly brushed it aside, as though showing emotion was a display of weakness.

"We're all here because we believe in the same things," Timmons assured her. "I left a perfectly good military base to join these folks."

"Why would you do that?" Brooke asked him, as though he were insane for giving up guaranteed meals and safety.

Timmons set down the flight charts momentarily, pacing the floor.

"Two reasons," he finally said. "One, I came to realize the people I worked for weren't being entirely truthful about a number of things."

"And the second?"

"That kid out there."

"Dan?"

"He doesn't know it yet, but he's going to do great things in this world."

"How could you possibly know that?"

"He's a leader. I sensed it the first time we met, and he's done right by us every step of the way. He's willing to see this Nadeau business through to the end, and I'm willing to risk everything to help him. Right now, that means helping you. So, we never had any talk about keeping people safe, because we're in this together. These folks are tougher than you could imagine, and they're smart."

Brooke contemplated his words momentarily.

"We have to play this smart," she finally said. "We have to assume they'll see us coming miles away."

"We're onboard with whatever needs to be done. I dare say we're all patriots who don't like outsiders fucking with our country."

"Says the guy who bailed on the military."

Timmons shrugged.

"We all play the hand we're dealt."

"Was putting the moves on a married woman part of that hand?"

"*That* was completely her fault for deceiving me," Timmons said, holding up his forefinger for emphasis.

She gave him a knowing smile, and he knew she was pushing his buttons, having fun at his expense.

"You are devious," he said.

"I've had a lifetime full of bad men," she revealed. "It took the apocalypse to finally meet a few good ones."

"I feel like you're messing with me again."

"I'm not," Brooke stated. "Sorry I've got some trust issues, but I really don't want to see any of us get hurt."

"Then guide us," Timmons said. "You're the expert, so we'll follow your lead."

"I just have this feeling that, even if we find him, we'll get more bad news. Or not the answers we want to hear."

"You probably think I'm a traitor to my country, seeing as you're going through all of this, but another reason I left my post is because I discovered the people I believed in were lying to all of us. Our so-called leadership is hiding out, just like Nadeau, trying to call the shots."

"I'm aware of their status," Brooke said, not hiding her disgust. "A lot of my people left their posts as well when things turned bad. I don't fault people for wanting to get to safety, or find their loved ones."

Timmons collected the charts, ready to head outside and see if anyone located supplies or fuel for the remainder of their journey.

"I don't hold out much hope for us finding Nadeau at either location," he admitted as they stepped outside, finding everyone else returning from the various hangars and outbuildings.

"Why not?" Brooke questioned.

"We're basically eight months into this thing, and he could've easily moved on, been killed, or never been at one of these safehouses."

"He wanted his followers to find him, Captain. I think he wanted a layer of protection, and the ability to strike again."

"Strike at what? There's probably ten zombies to every one of us. I'd say he won the war."

Meeting up beside the plane, the group members exchanged glances, a few holding minor finds from the property.

"Looks like we're syphoning fuel," Metzger reported. "Or we can grab a different plane. A few had full tanks."

"I'm surprised more of the owners didn't get over here and escape," Gracine commented.

"Maybe they're dead," Timmons said. "Or they had better accommodations locally."

As everyone stood silently a moment, the sound of flowing water could be heard, which felt unusual to the pilot who had landed in well over a hundred airports during his military tenure.

"Did you find what we needed?" Sutton asked.

Timmons held up the folded charts as proof.

"We should be able to reach another airport with fuel, or a new plane," Timmons said, "but we'll be cutting it close to dusk."

"Darkness shouldn't be a deterrent," Sutton stated.

"We have coordinates," Brooke noted. "We don't necessarily know what we're looking for until we get there. The bunker could be in a town, or isolated, and we don't want to stumble into a trap, or give Nadeau forewarning."

"Agreed," Metzger said. "We need to play this smart. One of the easiest things for them to spot would be a plane."

"Let's get these hangars open so I can have a look at our options," Timmons said.

"We've got the old suction hose if none of them are to your liking."

"We'll work it out."

Timmons observed as everyone opened the various hangar doors, displaying the various planes within, as though an auction were about to begin. He walked around the various hangars, seeing a variety of planes, none of which appeared to be a major upgrade in speed or passenger room. Several vacant spots in the hangars were likely created when survivors helped themselves to the small jets and newer planes they located early in the apocalypse.

"Looks like we're syphoning fuel," he said after his visual inspection. "Maybe the next airport will have an upgrade for us."

Metzger went through the Piper Seneca until he located the short section of garden hose the group often carried to syphon fuel from vehicles. A few gas cans with varying quantities of fuel also aided them, allowing for easier transportation of the syphoned product. Everyone knew they were going to spend the better part of an hour or two transferring the fuel, even if all of them worked simultaneously.

Because there wasn't equipment enough for him to help, Sutton waited his turn off to the side, and Timmons approached him while everyone else remained occupied syphoning fuel.

"I know you're not the trusting type, so I'm here to tell you I'm not sure about that one," the pilot remarked, nodding towards Brooke.

Sutton stared ahead, not even blinking as the spring waters raged behind them.

"I could've told you that," Sutton replied without taking his eyes off the group. "She's using us, and I'll be damned if I let her bring harm to anyone except Nadeau."

Chapter 15

Early the next morning, Bryce stepped outside after a fitful night's sleep to sample the morning air. He spied two Maplewood residents doing morning chores outside one of the houses. One of them noticed him, giving a cursory wave, and the other, an older woman, simply stared at him a few seconds before returning to her work. From what he could tell, they were tilling a small garden area with hand tools, because the Virginia climate practically guaranteed no frost would claim their crops.

Hearing a noise behind one of the houses that sounded like the slam of a tailgate, or a vehicle door being shut, Bryce decided to see if any friendly faces were up at the break of dawn. He stepped around the corner, finding an older pickup truck near the front gate, and a man wearing dark clothes, sporting a rifle in his right hand as he examined the gear in the truck bed. Possessing only a fringe of red hair, and a thick beard that matched the color, he appeared to be the man Sutton referred to as Father Paul. Bryce had only caught a glimpse of some of the residents the previous evening, and introductions flew by, but he knew to remember Father Paul and Sister Rosa by name and sight.

"You the priest?" Bryce asked as he approached the man.

Father Paul turned to face him, wearing a smile as he rested the rifle against the truck.

"You must be the Navy brother I've heard so much about."

Bryce returned a smile, shaking the priest's hand.

"Not sure there's much to tell about me. I was at sea when the world fell apart."

"I was waiting for my neighbor to wake up before I went hunting, but if you have time, you're welcome to take his place."

"I'm not sure my aim is good enough for hunting."

Father Paul provided a knowing smile.

"I can handle the shooting. We always bring a partner to watch our backs in case any dead come along."

Bryce nodded.

"*Those*, I can handle."

"I'm Father Paul McNulty, by the way."

"Bryce Metzger."

Nodding toward the truck bed, the priest appeared set for the hunting trip.

"Do you need to tell your family where you're going?"

Bryce arched an eyebrow.

"You know of my family?"

"Colby filled us in about your brother and his group. He sounds like quite the adventurer."

"That's one way of putting it."

"I hope to formally meet him someday."

"Hopefully when they return from their search."

Father Paul appeared concerned.

"I pray that no harm comes to them. And I hope they find some answers."

"Me, too," Bryce said solemnly, wishing he could assist his brother.

Metzger insisted he stay behind and watch over Isabella and Nathan, because Maplewood wasn't a guaranteed safe haven, and the military wasn't done searching for either brother.

"I'll let my wife and son sleep in a bit," he informed the priest. "I'm assuming we'll be there a few hours?"

"Usually less, depending on my aim," Father Paul said with a shrug. "Then again, I'm usually the spotter."

A few minutes later, the two men watched from inside the truck as one of the villagers opened the gate, permitting them to leave, and Father Paul drove the truck with knowledge of their destination.

"What happens when you hunt the local deer population to extinction?" Bryce questioned.

"We try to limit the hunting to once or twice a week," the priest answered. "We've been fortunate to have other food sources available."

"Colby expressed some reservations about your community," Bryce said forwardly, since he was told he could trust the priest.

"McAllister had power before the apocalypse," Father Paul explained. "I suppose he likes being in control, but he does look after his people."

"What exactly is the problem, then?"

"For starters, he's beginning to realize his mortality. And I think he's seeing some of his power slip away because outsiders hold more value to a community that's been running low on resources."

"Outsiders?" Bryce asked.

"People like Colby and your brother's friends. We've mostly been sheltered behind walls while they've been out there battling the dead. They brought us resources at a time when the community was hurting."

Bryce peered outside the window momentarily, seeing spring on the horizon as trees presented their buds, the sky took on a baby blue coloration, and the grass grew greener. Every so often he spied a zombie walking through one of the open fields, and they appeared oblivious to everything around them.

"You mentioned McAllister had power before the world fell," he said. "Did you know him back then?"

"He attended my church. Every so often he likes to remind me that I'm alive because he came into the city to take Sister Rosa and I under his wing."

"You don't sound like his biggest fan."

"It's not in my nature to speak ill of people, but I will tell the truth."

Bryce noticed the priest provided him with an ambiguous response.

"Do you know your brother's friends very well?"

"I've only met them briefly," Bryce admitted. "Dan fought tooth and nail to find me at the base, and then we got separated again."

"There's something to be said for stability," Father Paul said.

"What do you mean?"

"I just meant that we're all clamoring for shelter, food, and warmth like we had before. Having people around me, behind walls, is nice, but having family must mean the world."

"It puts things in perspective, yes."

Father Paul continued to drive, looking down the road.

"Do you worry about your brother going after Nadeau?" he inquired without breaking his gaze.

"Of course I do."

"I find it curious that the military isn't going after the man. Seems there are a lot of questions Nadeau could answer."

"I agree, but the military remains loyal to leadership determined to keep power in a social climate that no longer functions."

"Ain't we a pair?" Father Paul said, looking to Bryce with a smirk and an arched eyebrow, and the Navy man caught his meaning.

A few miles down the road, both men noticed a car off the side of the road, its front bumper buried at least a foot into a large tree. For all intents and purposes, the car wouldn't ever run again, and as Father Paul slowed when they neared the vehicle, he eyeballed the wreck suspiciously.

"This is new," he said, indicating the car hadn't been there previously, like so many other vehicles simply left near roadways.

"There's still smoke coming from the engine," Bryce noted.

Their truck slowed to a stop, and both men stepped out cautiously, approaching the car as they peered into the various windows. They found no one inside, but the driver's side door swung open. Tall, untended grass and weeds obscured their view further into the field, but both men heard a noise that sounded like someone eating sloppily, without proper chewing techniques. Bryce noticed several empty bottles in the car that once contained Vodka and other potent forms of alcohol.

Peering inside the vehicle, Bryce noticed droplets of blood covering the steering wheel, and fresh blood on the driver's seat. He wondered if the accident caused the bleeding, or an attack began in the vehicle, spilling out to the vast outdoors.

Father Paul had already taken a few steps beyond the car, and Bryce took his side as a look of horror crossed the priest's face. His lower jaw twitched involuntarily as the man of faith couldn't break his stare from the grisly scene before him.

Like a toddler eating spaghetti o's without a concern of messes or etiquette, a member of the undead used its hands and mouth to reach into the stomach area of a recent victim, devouring bloody intestines. Standing like statues, both men observed some involuntary movements from the victim, who hadn't yet died, but felt nothing because his body went into shock. Even from several feet away, Bryce could smell alcohol, knowing the young man made some poor decisions, likely based on emotional trauma suffered during his life.

Bryce finally turned, returning to the truck where he opened the passenger side door, then the glove compartment door, grabbing a small revolver tucked inside. He walked past the car, feeling a bit numb inside, because everyone struggled with depression and loss in the apocalypse. Most leaned on friends to help them cope, but some people didn't have friends, or a community, in the new world.

"Do you know him?" Bryce asked when he reached the priest's side a second time.

"Never met him."

Now the victim convulsed and blood sputtered from his mouth during a half-cough, causing Father Paul to turn away as blood flew upward, landing on the victim's face in droplets. Bryce lifted his arm, aiming the revolver for only a second before pulling the trigger and striking the zombie squarely in the skull, dropping it beside the victim. He took a few steps forward, beginning to take aim at the dying man when the priest rushed to his side.

"Wait," Father Paul pleaded softly.

"He's suffering, Padre."

"Last rites," the priest said with compassion in his eyes. "I can make it quick."

"You better, for his sake."

Reaching into his coat, the holy man pulled out a small Bible with at least twenty different small ribbons of various colors, acting as bookmarks. He adeptly flipped to the page marked by a red ribbon and found the necessary paragraph in seconds. For the next minute, Father Paul spoke under his breath, making the sign of the cross twice with his right hand, and finally turned to Bryce with little more than a nod.

Bryce took one last look at the victim, his intestines splayed across his body, and onto the ground, blood covering portions of his body, and no chance of recovering. He didn't know what drove the young man to such poor decisions, nor would he ever in all likelihood, but he slowly shook his head, raised the firearm, and shot the gravely injured man in the forehead, ending his life.

He turned, walking to the car to see if anything useful remained inside. Taking the keys from the ignition, Bryce opened the trunk, finding a few firearms, and a backpack full of survival food. He removed both, set them down, and began rummaging through the car, even beneath the seats.

"You act as though you've done this sort of thing before," Father Paul commented as he stumbled over to the car, his mind still hazy from the bloody scene.

"I haven't, honestly," Bryce said. "I've been stuck at sea, or a military base, through much of the apocalypse."

"Sorry I'm not being very pragmatic. You would think I'd be accustomed to this after one of my best friends nearly took a bite out of me in the early days of the pandemic."

Bryce pulled a box of ammunition out from under the passenger's seat, finding a candy bar and a bottle of pain reliever in short order.

"We all adjust differently," he said. "I'm not trying to be cold, but we have to help the living, Father. We're the best resource God left on this planet. Well, *some* of us are, anyway."

"Should we bury the body?" the priest asked.

"We don't have a shovel, or the time. I'm not trying to be callous, but nature will take its course."

He saw that his words didn't comfort the priest at all.

"Look, we didn't put that kid behind the wheel of a car after he downed all that booze."

"This world," Father Paul said, burying his face in his hands momentarily with exasperation. "I'm not sure how we keep going."

"Look at it as going back to basics, only the dead are the predators now."

Nodding, the priest appeared to understand Bryce's statement as he put out a hand to steady himself on the disabled car.

"Sorry," Father Paul said after a moment. "I'm supposed to be a good host, and here I am having a breakdown."

"You're fine," Bryce said. "We all have moments of uncertainty these days."

Distant growls and hisses caused both men to look up as nearly a dozen undead emerged from the wooded area beyond the former crop fields.

"Guess this area isn't as cleared as we thought," Father Paul thought aloud. "They must've heard the shots."

"That was quick," Bryce noted.

"Unfortunately, there isn't much else to distract them. We should get moving before they start migrating toward the community."

"We aren't going to deal with them?"

"They'll follow us. If they get too close, we can put them down while we hunt."

Bryce nodded, leading the way to the truck. He wondered about the residents at the village, and how Isabella and Nathan were fitting in.

***

By the time daylight pierced the various trees surrounding the Maplewood community, Isabella stood outside, watching her son play with some of the local children. Seeing Nathan be a kid once again brightened her spirit as he ran through the neighborhood playing tag. Making adult friends proved a bit more difficult for her because only a few people appeared to be awake and inside the walls at the moment. Most of them carried out chores, walking around carrying items, or tending to the small garden.

"You must be Isabella," a man with blond hair said, silently approaching her and catching her off-guard.

"I'm sorry," she said, not knowing him.

"Luke Johnson," the man said, shaking her hand. "I was part of Dan's group."

"Oh," she said, registering her surprise. "Are you the one who adopted the little girl?"

Isabella felt terrible because she couldn't recall a better detail to put forth regarding her knowledge of the man.

"That's her," he said, pointing to Samantha, who chased one of the boys behind one of the houses.

"She's adorable."

"Thank you. Has your stay been good so far?"

"We're a bit jetlagged, but otherwise good. Say, have you seen my husband? He's the one who looks a lot like Dan."

"Can't say that I have. He might be helping someone with their chores."

Isabella showed her confusion.

"Not all chores are done in here. Some take place down the road."

"Oh."

"I'm actually looking for someone myself."

"Who's that?"

"A young man named Kevin. He's kind of a handful, and I haven't seen him since last night."

"I'm guessing people don't go missing around here very often?"

"No. Most of them are scared to step outside these walls. I thought he was one of them."

Isabella gave him a knowing smile.

"Can't say I've had a lot of experience with the dead personally."

"Same here."

A few silent seconds passed between them.

"How is it here?" Isabella inquired.

"It's secure, which is more than we had out there. We took Dan to the military base, and when they turned us away, things got a little crazy for a while."

"I'm sorry about that, Luke. If it's any consolation, the base was far from perfect."

"Perfection is going to be hard to find these days."

Isabella thought back to the resort where she stayed with her parents during the winter months. Everyone there had to work, but they had electricity, food, and warmth. She hoped her parents continued to thrive after she left to stay by her husband's side. Dan basically insisted none of them tag along while he searched for Nadeau, causing Isabella to wonder if they should have simply stayed safe in the Adirondacks. She knew as well as anyone that the military might track her family down and come looking for Bryce just the same.

"Are we safe here?" she asked Luke.

"Of course. We've got the walls, and guns."

"No, I mean are my husband and son safe here? I heard that some of the people here know about Bryce and Dan's immunity to whatever caused the dead to return."

"Oh," Luke said with a sigh. "I'm afraid that came out during some supper talk."

"The one thing that keeps the government pursuing my husband and my brother-in-law slipped out to strangers?"

"They aren't complete strangers," Luke admitted. "And no one meant any harm. Truth be told, that's why I wanted to find Kevin. He's one of those people who uses information to his advantage."

"You're making me feel worse about staying here by the minute."

"Sorry. Kevin is also scared of his own shadow, so I can't see him acting on the information, if he even knows it."

Isabella shook her head.

"It doesn't sound like very much stays secret around here."

She decided to remain vigilant during her stay at Maplewood. Even if she needed to find a way to access weapons, or make alliances, she wouldn't let the government simply come and imprison her husband the way they did his brother.

Until the residents provided reasons for Isabella to trust them, she would not.

Hearing a clanking noise in the distance, she and Luke both turned to see the main gate opening for a pickup truck.

A moment later, the man she knew as Father Paul emerged from the driver's seat, and Bryce opened the passenger door, smiling immediately when he saw his wife.

"Any luck?" she asked, approaching the truck as he removed a hunting rifle from the back.

"Got one," he answered. "Sorry I didn't tell you, but I figured you could use the sleep."

"No problem. Nathan is making friends."

She saw a buck in the back of the truck, shot through the neck.

"Some nice shooting," she commented.

"The priest shot him," Bryce said. "Said he was aiming for the chest."

"*Lucky* shot, then."

Bryce pulled a plastic ammunition box from the back of the truck, appearing perplexed when he turned to his wife.

"What's wrong?" he inquired.

"Ask me later," she answered, putting forth a forced grin.

"Alright," he said. "I'm going to mingle a bit and help with the deer."

Isabella nodded.

"Yeah. I think I'm going to get to know some of our new neighbors as well."

Walking away from her husband, Isabella planned to discover just how many people knew Bryce's secret, and if any of them planned to profit from selling out Maplewood's newest residents.

Chapter 16

"If that's not it, I don't know what is," Metzger commented from the secondary pilot's seat in the Piper Seneca.

"There's nothing else here," Brooke added. "It *has* to be the spot."

Upon request, Timmons kept his distance from the coordinates, making it difficult for the pilot and his passengers to see details below. This particular area of New Mexico displayed a desert landscape with sparse green patches, dust, and occasional tumbleweeds. Several dilapidated buildings, more like shacks, formed a tiny town of sorts. They appeared bland, as though wind and the elements had chipped away at their paint over the years. Sitting near the center of the smaller buildings, a white building with red trim, like something from traditional Mexico, looked less weathered, but not in pristine condition.

Each of them took turns peering through binoculars Sutton pulled from his pack.

"This could be a bunker?" Gracine questioned.

"Bunkers work because they're hidden," Sutton answered. "Sometimes in plain sight."

Along the way, the group made one other stop along the western edge of Oklahoma to top off their fuel, finding a functioning fuel truck that cut their time on the ground significantly. They also spent the night near the airport, finding a house with propane, and minimal undead nearby, so they could cook and rest in peace.

Now, edging towards mid-afternoon, they circled the area the coordinates almost assuredly led them to.

"It looks abandoned," Jillian commented when her turn with the binoculars arrived.

"How far out do we need to land?" Timmons asked, turning to Brooke, who wore one of the supplemental headsets.

"Down there looks nice," she said, pointing to what appeared to be an open field some distance from the ruins.

"That's a few miles out," Timmons noted.

"I know."

"It's likely they've heard us already," Sutton said. "Do we really want to give them time to escape?"

"They haven't heard us if they're inside," Brooke answered. "We land, we walk closer, and you look for heat signatures through your scope."

She referred to the thermal scope attached to one of Sutton's rifles, which he managed to maintain, despite giving most of his worldly belongings to the residents of Maplewood as the price of admission.

Timmons managed to set the plane down with ease, because literally nothing except level ground surrounded the ruins for miles. Everyone maintained their direction compared to the coordinates, and all six began removing weapons from the plane.

"I'm not sure all of us should go," Brooke said, looking specifically at Timmons as she threw a pack over her right shoulder.

"There's no way I'm staying here alone," he responded. "People who stay behind in the movies always get killed."

"I agree all six of us can't go barging in there," Metzger said. "We can decide how to split up for safety when we get closer."

Because so little obscured their path, the group members took notice of the village within a mile of their destination. Sutton stopped, holding up his rifle for a look, reporting that he saw no movement whatsoever.

"Every other place has some kind of greeter or sentry," Brooke said. "This doesn't feel right."

"Nadeau wouldn't have people come here for nothing, would he?" Timmons asked no one in particular.

"It could've been overrun," Jillian said.

"By what?" Sutton questioned, corkscrewing his face as he looked around at the vast nothingness.

Metzger contemplated what type of trap awaited them, because the area felt eerily quiet. He wondered if the outbuildings held video and sound equipment, alerting occupants to the fact that trespassers neared the primary lair. He didn't like leading his friends into danger, but he hadn't come all this way to back down. Prepared to lay down his own life, even if the others weren't, he marched forward, followed by his weary travelers.

When they drew another half mile closer, everyone stopped so Sutton could observe the village once more through his thermal scope.

"Nothing," he reported.

Exchanging uneasy glances, the group members pushed forward.

"What do you make of this?" Metzger asked Brooke.

"I'm not sure. You've seen the satellite stations. There's always one devoted follower with some paperwork. This is different, but it doesn't feel right. I expected dogs, guards, cameras, *something* around the place."

"Nadeau is too careful not to have protection in place."

"Even if this isn't his bunker, we need to see if there's more information inside."

"Agreed."

By the time the group reached the outskirts of the ruins, the entire group felt nervous about stepping near the presumed bunker. Breaking into pairs to begin inspecting the outbuildings, Metzger took Jillian with him, noticing the buildings possessed no visible power sources, with most of their windows smashed, or hanging on by a thread of caulk. Due to the lack of undead, he drew his father's old .357 from his side, opting for a firearm instead of his sword.

"Look for any hidden compartments or rooms," he told Jillian as they stepped through the main entrance, which no longer had a functioning door.

Instead, the door remained just inside the building, propped against a wall. Metzger noticed dust on the floors with no footprints anywhere. Carefully, and quietly, they checked the small residence, finding only a round kitchen table with three legs, and a few chairs that didn't match. No electrical components remained, and Metzger only noticed a few outlets throughout the building.

"This place screams abandoned," Jillian commented.

"Then why would Nadeau bring anyone here?"

"We're taking Brooke's word on this, Dan. Perhaps she's wrong. Or worse."

"She has no reason to lead us into a trap."

"I'm not saying she is. Maybe Nadeau laid a trap, and we're about to spring it."

"We'll know shortly."

Metzger walked outside, waiting for the others near the main building, which appeared to have more paint left on its exterior, and less damage than the outbuildings. Within a few minutes, the others joined them, reporting similar results about the other buildings.

"Alright," Brooke said. "We're looking for a bunker entrance, and if it wasn't in one of these buildings, it almost has to be inside the restaurant, or whatever it is. We're looking for a solid door, steel perhaps, or a basement."

Exercising more caution than ever, the group members watched as Sutton opened the heavy single entrance door, leading the way inside. There, they found a heavy wooden counter that still held a cash register, and a cooler with a clear door, still displaying some soda pop inside. Custom wooden tables and chairs lined the inside of the old restaurant, and it appeared as though the place had been abandoned suddenly, on a whim, with no regard for the contents.

"What the fuck?" Sutton questioned aloud. "Who builds a restaurant out here?"

"There were some small towns down the road," Metzger said. "Maybe some grand plan never played out for the owners."

"Or Nadeau bought them out," Gracine quipped.

Some of the garish yellow and orange colors still lined the walls and signage, barely dimmed by inactivity that accompanied the apocalypse. Because the front entrance remained closed, Metzger didn't notice dust along the floor in the restaurant. A thin layer lined the countertop, causing him to wonder if the place closed well before the previous August, or the entire tiny village was a façade created by Nadeau and his people.

"This place isn't that big," Brooke said. "Let's split into pairs and look for what we came to find."

Metzger walked with Jillian once again, taking a hallway that led into the kitchen area while the others checked the dining area, and the management offices respectively.

"There's nothing here," Jillian said, not disguising her surprise. "No cameras." She paused. "Just nothing."

"It's beginning to look like we're heading north in a while."

When the pair walked into the kitchen, they saw industrial stovetops, prep tables, and a number of utensils. Because natural daylight didn't follow them into the windowless room, Metzger pulled a flashlight from his pocket, using it to illuminate the room while Jillian did the same. Several pans still hung from ceiling hooks, indicating the kitchen once functioned, and the items inside the building weren't simply props. Metzger examined the walls, moving several hanging items in search of a door frame, or some sort of locking mechanism. He cursed under his breath, because the flashlight hindered his search, and he began to think the entire trip was an exercise in futility.

"There's a latch back here to the walk-in freezer," Jillian informed him a few seconds later.

Taking her side, he watched as she pulled the latch, revealing a dark abyss ahead of them that the flashlight beams helped illuminate.

"It's just a walk-in," she muttered softly.

"There are shelves everywhere in here," Metzger said, finding a few cardboard produce containers on some of the shelves.

Fortunately, any perishable goods were removed, or a horrific smell would surely have greeted the couple.

Metzger found a few utensils nearby, wedging them beneath the freezer door to ensure they didn't get stuck inside. Upon standing, he immediately lit various portions of the freezer area with his flashlight. To his left, a few chrome wire shelves faced glass doors, providing kitchen help easy access to their goods without having to enter the freezer when the restaurant existed. The back wall, and the wall to his right had more permanent shelving, assembled and stable, but certainly easy enough to move.

He began by pulling down the shelving to the right, because there was more of it, finding nothing except smooth, insulated walls. Giving a sigh, he walked to the narrower wall along the back, attempting to pull the shelving away from the wall, only to discover it was attached in multiple places.

"Why?" he questioned aloud.

"'Why' what?" Jillian asked, taking his side.

"There's no reason for them to permanently attach this stuff to the wall. It couldn't have held anything very heavy in the first place."

He reached behind it, using his flashlight to guide his right hand as he felt along the wall, feeling certain he felt a thin seam of indentation that might indicate a door swinging away from the walk-in freezer. A further examination of the shelving revealed that it was segmented, particularly where the door might open, as though that specific portion of the shelves swung in with the door.

"There might be some kind of switch or something to open this door," he told Jillian.

"But there's no power."

"No power that we can see," he noted. "There has to be a way to access that door, because nothing looks disturbed."

"Maybe no one has made it out here," Jillian suggested.

Metzger considered the lack of footprints in the outbuildings, wondering if the continual winds regularly stirred dust and dirt outside. He couldn't imagine Nadeau's intended path led to this spot with a hidden door, and no indications of previous human activity inside. He wondered why Brooke lacked additional information, and why this spot didn't have a designated greeter like the other safehouses. A feeling of something about the place being off plagued him, and he felt more uneasy with each passing minute.

Before he could address his concerns with his girlfriend, the others caught up with them, having checked their respective areas.

"Have you found anything?" Brooke inquired.

"Yeah," he answered, refusing to outwardly reveal his find until he posed a question. "There really aren't any instructions about what to do when we get here?"

"They didn't exactly leave printouts lying around, specifically because of people like us who found them. Some of the information rested with the sentries left at the safehouses, in their minds."

"And I'm guessing they weren't incredibly cooperative?" Sutton asked.

"Some of them didn't survive," Brooke said almost defiantly. "I didn't go in guns-a-blazing, but each encounter with these people provided challenges."

"I may have found your door," Metzger revealed, ready to proceed. "My problem is I have no idea how to open it."

"Where?" Brooke asked, and Metzger pointed out the area.

"There's a seam around the door, and the shelving appears attached to it."

Brooke felt along both, agreeing with his assessment.

"There's probably some kind of switch or keypad, separate from the door," she said. "It may not look like it, but this place has power."

Everyone began searching the room, pulling on random objects, and opening drawers. Metzger walked over to the area where the door was located, touching and pulling on parts of the chrome wire, and the brackets holding them in place. On the third shelf from the door, he felt a bump along one of the brackets, and tapped it with his thumb softly several times to test it. Realizing it was a button, he pushed it inward, hearing a beep from the hidden door as a green light went off above the door that previously blended in with the wall. Excited about the find, he approached the door, which hadn't unlocked, much less opened, and discovered the pale outline of another recessed light about six inches from the green light. A small rectangular area that looked like an LED screen occupied the space between the two circles.

"Shit," he muttered. "There's another hidden access point in here."

"Where did you find that one?" Timmons asked first.

He showed everyone where he located the button, hidden from plain view because it was small, and blended in with the bracket.

"They didn't make it easy," Gracine muttered.

"We have to scour this place," Sutton said. "It could be on the floor, or under some cabinets for all we know."

Once again, all six members of the party separated to different areas, this time being even more thorough about checking every corner, crevice, and underside they found. After about five minutes with no luck, the green light above the door made a beep and went back to blending in with the wall once more. Everyone took a cursory glance before returning to their search.

"This whole thing seems odd," Sutton commented. "If he wanted his people safe, you'd think he would bring out the welcome wagon."

"Maybe he knows we're here and we *aren't* welcome," Gracine commented.

"I didn't see any cameras," Brooke said. "No one would possibly go through this unless they knew there was a bunker here, so he's probably making his people work for it. Besides, it would be a full-time job to monitor this area, or have a guard patrol the grounds."

Metzger went through a corner of the kitchen he felt someone else had already covered when he noticed Gracine lying on the floor, and scooting under the kitchen sink. Timmons handed her a flashlight, and a few seconds later she called out.

"Found it!"

"Let Dan press his button, first," Brooke instructed, attempting to make certain they didn't screw up some kind of necessary sequence.

Metzger returned to the shelving, found the button, and pressed it. Once again, the circle above the door lit up green, and Brooke nodded for Gracine to push the button she had located beneath the sink. A few seconds later, Metzger watched the second circle turn green, though the screen between them remained the same coloration as the bland wall that encircled the kitchen. He heard a pop reminiscent of a lock unlatching, followed by a slight hissing sound as the hydraulics controlling the hidden door allowed it to open into a new, completely dark area.

A stale odor flooded into the kitchen, as though the group had opened a crypt, undisturbed for decades.

"What the hell *is* that?" Gracine questioned.

"It doesn't smell like the dead," Metzger answered. "Just musty as fuck."

Timmons remained at the original door, as though making certain it didn't close on the group. Metzger shined a light ahead, discovering they currently stood in a steel foyer of sorts, because another steel door was centered ahead of them. Metzger turned to Timmons before approaching the door.

"At least one of us needs to stand outside that original door just in case this is some kind of trap."

Timmons nodded, taking a step back.

"Don't make me come in there and save you."

Metzger knew his friend was kidding, but he didn't feel confident about entering the next portion of the bunker. As he drew near the steel door, he noticed a porthole window centered closer to the top, although the shape was square instead of round. He brushed off a layer of dust before attempting to shine his light through the thick glass.

"See anything?" Sutton asked.

"No. It's like the glass refracts any light, but I think I can see some light on the other side. Maybe."

Unlike the previous entrance, this door possessed a handle, like the helm on a ship, only constructed from metal. Metzger touched one of its eight handles, finding it cool to the touch.

"Everyone ready?" he asked, receiving affirmative nods when he looked into the eyes of those around him.

He waited until Timmons took a step back before grasping handles with each of his hands and turning the device counterclockwise. He heard a click, followed by a heavy clank, and the door swung away from Metzger, into the following area.

Keeping his flashlight defensively in front of him, cupped in his left hand, Metzger settled his right hand atop the holstered .357 Magnum. He stepped into the next area, his flashlight beam illuminating more metal walls along the sides and nearly fifty feet ahead. As he moved forward, a few overhead lights turned on, likely set to activate when sensing motion.

"This place is thick," Jillian muttered just above a whisper. "Like a bank vault."

"That's the idea," Sutton said.

Centered in the wall directly ahead of them, a door with another rectangular window and large, turning knob awaited them.

"Well, no time like the present," Sutton said, taking several steps toward the next door, anxious as always to see what awaited them on the other side.

Metzger began falling in line behind his friend, Jillian by his side, when they heard another loud click, followed by a clank, and the door before them slowly opened. Immediately, the dim room provided just enough lighting to illuminate the grayish hands reaching through the opening greedily. Metzger whirled, finding the door behind them beginning to close, equally slowly, as Brooke made a dash to exit the way the group had come in before it slammed shut. Timmons looked at him with bewilderment, unsure of how to proceed until Metzger held up an open palm, instructing his friend to remain safely on the other side.

For emphasis, he shook the same hand slowly, extending it slightly towards the pilot.

Timmons shook his head with concern, his expression displaying his dismay as Brooke managed to squeeze past him before the door closed and both were lost from view. Knowing at least one friend remained safe, Metzger turned to confront a new threat that poured through the door, one after another, endangering everyone in the small, steel, impenetrable room. Although the lighting remained on within the room, it flickered, and barely illuminated the dangerous undead coming at them.

All four members of the group took a few steps back, each holding at least one weapon in their hands.

"We need to pick them off as they come through the door," Metzger thought aloud, holstering his revolver and plucking the sword from the small pack he wore on his back. "No guns unless we get overrun."

At least half a dozen undead had already passed the threshold, eyeing the four survivors with insatiable hunger as they lurched forward.

Metzger took a step forward before turning to the others.

"I'll take out as many as I can with the sword."

"Not alone," Jillian said, touching his arm.

"I'm not alone. I have you three backing me up. I'll take the lead since I'm supposed to be immune."

"Let's get down to it," Sutton said. "Sorry I sprung the trap."

"It was going to get sprung, regardless," Metzger told him. "Let's foil their plan."

Metzger went from holding his sword defensively in front of him to lifting it and aggressively moving forward to dispatch the latest threat.

Chapter 17

"What are you doing, missy?" Timmons asked when the steel door slammed shut, preventing him from assisting Metzger and the others.

"We have our own problems, flyboy," Brooke answered, drawing a befuddled look from the pilot.

"We aren't the ones trapped in there with the dead, and you just abandoned them."

Brooke looked up, literally above and beyond Timmons, prompting him to turn and see a timer counting down between the two dim circles that were once green lights granting access to the metal deathtrap.

It had started at thirty minutes with a descending countdown in red LED lights like a digital clock.

"We need to try those buttons again," Timmons insisted, his body numb because he felt powerless to help his friends.

"I'm positive it won't do any good, but we can try," Brooke agreed.

Each of them walked to the area where the two buttons were found. Timmons located the one Metzger had pressed, and used his thumb to press it inward.

"Pressed!" he yelled as the first green light illuminated and a single beep sounded throughout the room.

He heard a second beep, indicating Brooke had followed through, and saw the second light turn green, but the door remained closed.

"No!" he screamed, thrusting his shoulder against the shelving attached to the door, not moving it a fraction of a millimeter.

He followed that by smacking the shelving several times with his hands, bloodying both sides of each hand as the unforgiving chrome wire slit his skin.

"Save your strength," Brooke said, stepping into the walk-in area with a purpose. "We're going to have company soon."

"How do you know *that*?" Timmons asked with surprise in his blue eyes.

She projected a calm he couldn't possibly feel at the moment, despite his training as a pilot preparing him for the worst kinds of pressure.

"We can't be the first people to stumble on this place. Someone has to come in and clean up the bodies, and it's likely whatever we tripped alerted those people immediately."

"What about Dan and the others?"

"I think they can handle themselves. We have to make sure this compound is secure when that timer finishes its countdown."

Timmons realized Metzger asked him to stay behind for a reason, possibly to monitor Brooke, but mainly to ensure the entire group didn't get trapped inside the bunker. So long as the lighting inside held up, he imagined Metzger and the others could fend off the incoming undead. He still couldn't wrap his mind around why someone would set up a trap within the bunker, much less purposely lead people directly to it.

"This is a trap, right?" he asked Brooke.

"What do you mean?"

"This place didn't get overrun, or have some kind of meltdown, right?"

"There's a fucking timer above your head, with self-locking doors behind you. There isn't anything accidental about this place."

"Why? Why would he lure people out here?"

"My guess is this is their dump site for troublemakers like me, or people he no longer trusts. And, as much as I would love to stand here and discuss the possible logistics of this place with you, we probably need to get ready to defend ourselves."

"How are you so sure someone's coming?"

"The few seconds I was in that room, I saw that it was clean. No bodies, no fecal matter, no skeletons. Someone comes along and cleans that room when the dead finish off their victims."

Timmons felt genuinely surprised and impressed at her intuition.

"You picked up on that in just a few seconds?"

"I observed during those few seconds. The deductions came afterwards."

Brooke started out of the kitchen, into the main portion of the abandoned restaurant. She looked around at the walls and ceiling, likely searching for security cameras. Timmons personally saw none, meaning any caretakers of the property simply waited for an alert when the trap within the vault was sprung.

"What can I do to help?" Timmons asked.

"I'm looking for a good spot to hide so I can ambush them when they arrive."

"I can help with that," the pilot volunteered, feeling left out.

Brooke let out a chuckle.

"What?" he asked incredulously.

"You'll just shred your hands punching that shelving. Save your hands for flying us out of here and leave the mercenary types to me."

"Ain't you a little spitfire," Timmons commented. "I have a firearm. I can back you up."

"Please don't," Brooke said, her tone just above condescending. "If you want to help, see if you can find a way to override, or short out those vault doors."

"Fine," Timmons groaned, assuming she wanted to keep him safe to he could fly the survivors to safety.

He returned to the kitchen area, staring at the timer above the first door. 00:26:32.

He felt terrible that he couldn't help the others fight the dead, but determined to assist them however he could from the outside.

With that in mind, the pilot began visualizing the wires behind the wall that went from the buttons to the display above the door. If he could find the power source, he might be able to disconnect it long enough to reset the entire setup. He worried about making the situation worse, possibly leaving the doors locked without means to open them, or cutting power to the lights. His primary concern was whether or not the four people trapped within four solid steel walls could survive until the timer reached zero.

***

Blood droplets stained the steel walls after Metzger decapitated the first six undead without any assistance. He didn't feel too winded, but the line of zombies waiting to enter the room appeared to have no end. Opening fire might cause ricocheting bullets to strike one of the four survivors, and he didn't want his friends getting up close and personal to stab the undead with knives.

"You need a break?" Sutton asked.

"No," Metzger answered. "If I can kill enough of these, we need to try stacking them in front of the door to create a kill zone."

He stepped forward, using the blade's sharp tip to stab the next in line in the center of the forehead. Most of the undead appeared significantly decayed, as though many were placed there months earlier, or fate dealt them a terrible hand at the start of the apocalypse. Taking the time to further examine them would certainly prove hazardous, so he made certain none of his friends had walked up behind him before swinging at the head of the next zombie in line. He watched the top portion of its head fly through the air like a frisbee as the body toppled to the floor. Behind it, four others had already managed to make their way through the door, and Metzger didn't know how he could possibly blockade the door if the line of attackers didn't slow or cease.

Taking a few steps back, he found the others taking his side.

"We have to attack them all at once and let the bodies stack up at the door," he said.

Everyone already held knives in their dominant hands, knowing the danger of using firearms.

"We're with you," Jillian said confidently.

"Let Colby and I get up front," Metzger said. "We don't want to be slashing each other, so he and I will take them down and you two can back us up in case any stragglers get through."

Metzger attempted to get on the right side of the growing stack of unmoving undead while Sutton assumed the left side. Metzger didn't realize a widening pool of blood emerged from the stabbed dead, and slipped badly enough that he toppled to the ground, allowing a few of the attackers emerging from the open doorway to set their sights on him and fall to their knees as they attempted to bite any part of his body they could reach.

Having kept hold of his sword, he was about to unleash it in a wild frenzy to avoid being bitten, but Jillian stepped forward and kept her balance by stepping on the dead, and not the blood. She stabbed each of them in succession in their skulls, allowing Metzger to scramble to his feet, though his blue jeans felt moist from the blood that soaked into them.

"You good?" Jillian asked with concern in her eyes.

"Yeah," he answered quickly. "I can handle the next wave."

He looked to Sutton, who stood his ground on the opposite side of the growing mound of flesh and bone.

"What do you have in mind?"

"Let's try and stab them at the door," Metzger replied. "Kill a few more out here, to add to the stack, then we pile them at the door."

"Wait!" Gracine said before she realized she was distracting her two friends closest to the danger zone.

She pointed at the door, prompting Sutton and Metzger to each cut down another member of the undead before returning their attention to her.

"Why don't you two drag some of those bodies toward the door while Jillian and I cover you?"

"It can get crowded quick over here," Sutton noted.

"Work smarter, not harder," Jillian said, stepping forward, and around her boyfriend, to stab a zombie through the left eye socket as it took a swipe at Metzger.

Gracine stepped past Sutton and pushed a female zombie back before driving a knife into the side of its skull. Sutton and Metzger each grabbed a fallen zombie by the arm, dragging them respectively close to the door, clogging the entrance for the remaining attackers. Metzger heard the echoes of throaty growls, not knowing if half a dozen remained, or hundreds.

"Did that fucking bitch betray us?" Gracine asked, waiting for Sutton to drag another body up to the door before thrusting her knife forward and downing another threat.

"I don't think so," Metzger said, believing his words deep down. "We didn't see anyone, but someone keeps this place clean and resets this hell hole."

"She could force your boy to fly her anywhere she wants," Sutton pointed out, grunting as he grabbed another arm, heaving this particular body atop the growing stack.

"She won't," Metzger assured him. "And Scott wouldn't leave us."

"You mean he wouldn't leave *you*," Gracine corrected with a bit of attitude in her tone.

"That's not true," Metzger said, using his sword to stab into the forehead of a zombie attempting to squeeze past the door, falling instead atop the blockade.

He and Sutton pulled a few more bodies into place, keeping the incoming horde at bay for the moment, providing the group with a break. Almost overwhelmed by the foul odor of coagulated blood reaching fresh air for the first time, Metzger took a step back a put his forearm across his nostrils.

"It's a little true," Jillian said, agreeing with Gracine's assessment.

"I promise you he's up there right now trying to figure out a way to get us out of here."

Everyone looked up as the lights inside the room began to flicker.

"He'd better hurry," Gracine commented with concern, "or we're going to be fighting these things in the dark."

***

Timmons had checked every conceivable corner and crevice in the kitchen area, finding no breaker box or any indication of wiring anywhere. He suspected the bunker was built, for good reason, with no possible way for intruders on the surface to sabotage any portion of the safe haven below. Of course, he also began to realize the entire bunker had been converted into a death trap of some sort to eliminate unsuspecting travelers, or enemies of Nadeau.

It occurred to Timmons that the main portion of the restaurant had no power, as the group had tried several light switches during their walk-through of the building. None of the machines functioned, and he didn't see a breaker box while walking through the office area, or the patron seating. Perhaps the topside was powered from below, where people could presumably seek safety if they navigated their way through the swarm of undead. He also considered the possibility that a power source could be activated in one of the exterior buildings, or behind the restaurant.

Heading through the main portions of the building, he didn't see Brooke, though he didn't dwell on her location, figuring she might be thinking along the same lines. Light streaming through a stained glass window caught his attention, and the pilot thought back to a time he was stationed in Texas. Working at a joint base in San Antonio, he and his fellow pilots had many an enjoyable evening on the town. One such night took place in a restaurant that looked similar to this one, with empty beer mugs lining the table, and outlandish stories being shared. This wasn't a night for picking up women, but bonding over an elite brotherhood. One of the four pilots from that evening died in a crash during a training exercise before the apocalypse. He hadn't seen any of the others in years, causing him to wonder if they found safety in one of the secured bases across the nation.

Shaking his head clear, Timmons moved along, prepared to keep his current colleagues alive.

When he stepped outside, he noticed the wind had picked up, blowing dust directly in his face as he squinted to avoid being pelted. He also put his right arm up, trying to determine the best way around the restaurant. Considering the group had already searched the outbuildings, Timmons decided to start behind the main structure, doubting he would find a power source in the open, but determined to try, just the same.

"Let's go to New Mexico first," he muttered, raising his voice an octave, chastising himself as he walked around the side of the restaurant. "It'll be warmer."

Once he rounded the side, the pilot found that the structure protected him from the wind, but he nearly stepped into a major hazard. He put his arm down just in time to look down, finding a gaping hole dug a few feet in front of him.

"What the hell?" he questioned aloud, finding a hole the size of a small crater dug behind the restaurant with a nearby payloader.

Mounds of dirt surrounded the hole, and as he looked inside, a thin layer of dirt covered most of the details, but he saw a few random hands, feet, and faces piercing the soil. He didn't know if these were victims of the trap inside, some of the undead killed during their use as murderous weapons, or a combination of the two.

He stared only a moment before the sound of a powerful engine pierced the wind, prompting Timmons to carefully return to the building for cover. If his friends survived in the reverse panic room, he needed to ensure they weren't gunned down while trying to leave its confines. Reaching behind him, Timmons pulled the semi-automatic from his lower back where it had remained safely tucked in his belt. Bringing it to a ready position, he quietly approached the front corner of the restaurant for a look at the new arrivals.

A large black, diesel truck pulled to the center of the outbuildings, coming to a stop before someone shut off its loud engine. Doing his best to avoid detection, Timmons peered around the corner in quick intervals, taking notice that two people exited the truck. A man slightly larger in stature than himself had been driving, and what appeared to be a woman exited the passenger side. Both walked toward the restaurant with determination in their strides, and he wondered if Brooke was prepared to deal with two adversaries. The man carried a shotgun, while the woman carried a rifle, possibly an AR-15.

He began to wonder if Brooke remained on the grounds, because he didn't see her during his last walk-through of the main building.

Although Timmons didn't feel confident about his aim if he found himself in a shootout, he wasn't about to let Metzger and the others be gunned down while trapped in the confines of the shelter. He stepped around the corner, moving forward in a crouched walk until he reached the front door. Hesitating slightly, he heard sounds of a struggle inside, figuring Brooke had stuck around after all. Sucking in a deep breath, Timmons held his sidearm in a ready position and entered the structure, finding her kicking the man several times in succession, each one hitting him higher after she started around his abdomen.

"Stop her!" Brooke shouted. "She went for the bunker!"

Timmons noticed the shotgun lying on the ground, and he briefly wondered how Brooke managed to knock it from the man's grip. He scooped it up as he glided through the room, prepared to stop the woman at any cost from harming the four souls trapped inside the secured room.

It wasn't clear to him if the woman went ahead of the man in the first place, or darted for the kitchen area after Brooke attacked them in the restaurant's greeting area. He approached the corner, figuring there wasn't any way for her to override the timer, so he put away his sidearm and aimed the shotgun ahead of him.

He checked the trigger guard, switching the safety toggle to the off position, and ducked as he rounded the corner out of instinct.

Fortunately, the round that rang out from the kitchen sailed over his head, and Timmons fired the shotgun blindly, using the split-second it provided him to observe the woman ducking for cover to his left. Everything happened so quickly, he barely found time to feel nervous about his life nearly ending. He sucked in a few cautious breaths, feeling woefully unprepared to stalk someone who possessed cover and tactical advantage.

Images of the kitchen ran through his mind, and he tried recalling any hiding spots where the woman might wait to ambush him. Several metal tables and countertops provided adequate cover to the left, and Timmons dared not rush in there. So long as she couldn't open the door, the woman posed no threat to Metzger and the others, meaning Timmons didn't have to risk his well-being at this exact moment. Instead, he crouched low enough to view the timer directly ahead of him above the sealed door inside the walk-in cooler.

00:11:36.

"Fuck this," he muttered, doing an about-face and returning to the room where Brooke continued to battle a larger, stronger adversary.

Timmons entered the room as the man managed to catch one of Brooke's martial arts kicks, yanking her in quickly and clutching her by the throat. About to counter the move before her throat was crushed, Brooke caught a glimpse of Timmons aiming the shotgun at her adversary as her eyes widened.

"Oh, shit," she muttered before using her knees to provide some distance between her and the man who meant her harm.

As Brooke extended her legs to propel her body away from her assailant, Timmons aimed at the man's closest knee before pulling the shotgun's trigger. He watched as flesh and blood spurted from their new adversary's knee and upper leg, dropping him to the floor as he yowled in agony. He let out several curse words directed at Timmons, and Brooke simply stepped on his injured appendage, adding to his pain.

"The woman?" she asked, directing her attention to the pilot.

"She's holed up in the kitchen," he reported.

Brooke drew a knife from the sheath along her right side, poising to end the first intruder's life, but Timmons stepped forward.

"We need information."

"Not really," Brooke responded, implying they had all the information necessary already.

Timmons turned his attention to the man who continued to moan and groan, clutching the shattered remains of his knee.

"Are you going to be the one to tell us what we want to know?" Timmons asked him directly. "Or do we let you bleed out and give your partner first dibs?"

Still grasping his bloody knee, the man looked up with pain etched in his face, fighting not to wince and show weakness as he spoke his next words to the military man.

"Fuck you."

Timmons shrugged.

"Don't say I didn't give you a chance," he said, turning toward the kitchen as he heard one final scream and the sound of a knife plunging into a body part that ended the man's life.

A thud followed the man's final exhale, but Timmons didn't turn around. He felt determined to prevent the woman from harming the man he considered a son, and see if he could open the secured door somehow.

"You can't just walk in there," Brooke said, running to catch up to him.

"Watch me."

She physically stepped in front of him, letting an understanding sigh escape her mouth. Timmons stopped in his tracks, rather than walk into her.

"You were right," she admitted. "We want her alive, if at all possible."

"I don't want her killing anyone," Timmons added firmly.

"I agree, but a shootout isn't going to end well for anyone."

"You're suddenly all about negotiation?"

Brooke provided a sour expression in return.

"No one wants to die. Even the fanatics working for Nadeau."

Without another word, she turned and walked to the threshold of the kitchen, not close enough to make herself a target.

"You have nowhere to go," she yelled into the room.

"I can take a few of you with me!" the woman yelled in return.

Brooke lowered her head, shaking it momentarily at how stubborn Nadeau's followers could be.

"I want information," she said. "If you cooperate, and no harm comes to my friends in there, you can walk out of here without a scratch."

Timmons showed his displeasure when Brooke turned to him, because he didn't want future threats, including Nadeau's people warning him about the group gunning for him. In return, Brooke provided an expression, and a gesture with her hands, that indicated she was simply speaking the words that might sway the woman into cooperating.

"Here's what's going to happen," Brooke spoke into the kitchen, addressing the woman. "In minutes, you're going to be outnumbered and we're going to either shoot you, or capture you and torture you until you tell us what we need. You can avoid all of that by cooperating."

Timmons noticed Brooke glancing at the time.

00:08:21.

"This offer expires in thirty seconds in case you're thinking about waiting and attempting to harm our friends inside."

"They're already dead," the woman replied, still hidden behind some of the kitchen furnishings. "When that timer reaches zero, my job is to clean up the mess."

"Can you open that door now?" Timmons demanded more than asked.

"No. It's automated."

A tense pause filled the air between them and the mystery woman.

"Is Mark dead?" she finally inquired.

"He is," Brooke answered, obviously assuming she spoke about her armed companion. "But you don't have to die, too."

Several seconds of silence passed. Timmons looked to the timer, which continued its descent to zero.

"She's stalling, isn't she?" he asked so only Brooke could hear.

"I think so. She may also have the means to hurt the others."

Timmons envisioned electrified walls, or some sort of flamethrower device being called upon to incinerate the living and dead alike. He felt as though they had covered every square inch of the kitchen, finding the two buttons that gained them access to the bunker.

"What's it going to be?" Brooke inquired of the woman, partly to assess the situation.

A few seconds passed before the answer came.

"I'm not interested in dying."

Timmons looked at Brooke skeptically when nothing happened for a few seconds, followed by a few more. He began to question if she merely stalled for time, or actively worked at something to kill everyone in the building if she couldn't survive the trap she helped Nadeau maintain.

"You have thirty seconds to come out of there, or we're coming in," Brooke informed the stranger.

She looked to Timmons.

"We need some kind of shield. A chair, trash can lid, *something*."

Both of them scoured the area for anything useful in a frontal attack. Timmons didn't spy anything useful, much less recall anything from his first pass through the building, so he stepped outside to see if the diesel truck held additional weapons, or makeshift shielding.

He neared the truck within a few seconds, and as he reached for the front passenger side door, Timmons heard a noise from inside. With the window rolled down halfway, he was able to use the step attached to the truck to hoist himself up for a level view into the vehicle. As soon as he did, however, a large rottweiler charged him from within, its face striking the window as it attempted to snap at him. Timmons fell backwards to the ground, his heart pounding while the canine continued barking and snarling at him.

"These people are insane," he muttered while scrambling to get his footing.

As he ran inside the restaurant, the throaty sounds of the dog barking followed him until the door closed. His ears detected muffled shouting from the kitchen area, so he shook his head and marched directly to the doorway that separated the cooking area from the rest of the building, finding Brooke on the verge of charging inside.

"What did you find?" she asked, turning to face Timmons at the last second.

"A guard dog that wanted my face for lunch. What's with the yelling?"

"This bitch won't come out, and I'm sure she's working on something that might kill all of us."

"I'm not opposed to shooting her."

"Neither am I, but we're both targets the second we go in there."

Timmons drew a deep breath, still disconcerted by the dog nearly biting him. He turned to Brooke, who appeared ready to provide him with a nod to rush the kitchen area, but a female war cry interrupted them. The scream grew closer, and Brooke noticed a split-second before Timmons that the woman had rushed around the corner, aiming the rifle in their direction, still charging them.

Brooke pushed Timmons away from the gun's intended destination before using her pistol to fire twice at the woman, even as several rounds flew her way. Timmons kept his footing, able to see the brief skirmish unfold, even as a round grazed Brooke in the left shoulder. He managed to swing his head the other way, watching blood spurt from the woman's chest as Brooke's two rounds hit home, ending the woman's life within seconds.

"Fuck," he muttered once the gunfire ceased. "We're never going to get any of them to talk."

"They're fanatics," Brooke said, ignoring the bloody area atop her shoulder to step forward and check the woman for a pulse.

Finding none, she turned to Timmons.

"They're loyal to Nadeau," she said. "I've never had luck getting information out of them."

"It's probably easier when they aren't armed."

"That's true," she said with a sigh, rising from the body.

Both looked ahead to the timer.

00:03:42.

"Any chance we can get Fido out of the truck to see if there's any information?" she asked.

"Not without bodily harm, I'm afraid."

"I really don't want to kill a dog," Brooke said before checking her sidearm.

"You okay?" Timmons asked, trying to get a better look at her shoulder.

"I'll be fine. It went through."

"More like 'across,'" he noted, seeing a tiny semicircle across the top of her shoulder.

For Timmons, waiting the next three minutes felt like an eternity. His mind filled with horrific scenarios, and he closed his eyes, saying a brief prayer that Metzger and the others survived the trap. Either way, he wanted to see Nadeau and his regime come to an end, because the man acted like a tyrant, taking human life without a second thought.

Brooke examined the area, trying to determine if the woman attempted some kind of additional harm, or another trap, before deciding to charge her adversaries. Timmons questioned the verbal exchange between Brooke and the deceased woman, wondering if the former CIA operative somehow provoked the attack. She didn't seem keen on taking prisoners and questioning them, as though they somehow compromised her plan, or slowed her progress.

"Find anything?" Timmons asked while she continued to scour the kitchen area.

"Nothing we hadn't spotted before. Let's hope that door pops open when the timer counts down, and they don't spray poison gas, or incinerate the room."

Timmons felt his body shudder. He hadn't even considered a secondary trap to ensure no survivors emerged from the steel room.

"Would they do that?"

"It's Nadeau," Brooke replied. "You've seen what kind of fucked up things the man does."

When the counter reached the zero mark a few seconds later, the click of the lock, followed by a hydraulic hiss, reached the pilot's ears. Seconds passed, feeling like an eternity, and he finally took a cautious walk toward the door, wondering if his allies, or the insatiable dead, would cross the threshold.

He feared the worst when he saw the first two people stagger into the kitchen, seeing them absolutely covered in blood. Timmons quickly realized they were Sutton and Gracine, barely recognizable with their clothes stained so badly. He was about to inquire about Metzger when Jillian stepped through the doorway, followed by the young man. They, too, were coated with moist crimson after battling the undead inside the confines of the metal room.

"You all okay?" he asked, receiving slow nods in return.

Sutton looked ahead, spying the body of the woman in the kitchen.

"Looks like you had your own issues."

"We did," Timmons admitted. "The cleanup crew showed up, but they're both dead."

"Guess that means we won't be getting answers from them," Sutton said sourly.

Brooke walked over to the group.

"They're following Nadeau with blind allegiance," she said. "They aren't going to sell him out. The captain and I did what we had to."

Timmons wasn't necessarily thrilled that she included him in the slayings. He wanted to interrogate at least one of them, but they forced Brooke's hand in the end.

Sutton looked to the pilot, and Timmons remained neutral, not saying a word, or indicating his feelings either way.

"In good news, we have transportation back to the plane," Brooke noted.

"Except it comes with a vicious guard dog," Timmons added.

Another timer, set for one hour this time, began counting down above the hidden access door. Metzger assumed the doors remained open for the cleanup crew to remove any bodies and clear the mess, resetting the trap for the next unsuspecting victims. Loud music blared from within the room behind the vault where he had nearly lost his life, causing the remaining undead who fought and clawed to get past the door to turn around and return to their original lair.

Metzger stepped to the door for a look, deciding not to step inside, because he understood the efficiency of Nadeau's plan.

After checking the bodies, the group found no additional clues, and no keys for the truck. Metzger devised a plan to open one of the rear crew cab doors while standing in the truck bed to let the dog free while everyone else waited on the other side, ready to clamor inside. His plan worked, except once the rottweiler jumped outside the truck, it kept jumping and snapping at Metzger. He managed to shut the door, keeping his friends safe and maintaining a safe height, before the canine could think to jump inside and attack his friends.

"You good?" Sutton called back from the driver's seat.

Because of Sutton, the group couldn't simply shoot the guard dog. Even though they didn't know how the animal would react, Sutton continually remained protective of animals, especially dogs.

"Ready," Metzger responded.

Alone in the truck bed, Metzger watched the restaurant and its surrounding outbuildings diminish in size as the group pulled away. After a few dozen paces, the dog realized it wouldn't catch the truck, giving up the chase to search the area for its former masters. Metzger felt bad in virtually every regard, because two people died needlessly serving Nadeau, and the dog was now homeless, destined to become feral to survive. The only accomplishment the trip provided was disrupting the murderous cycle of the bunker, at least temporarily.

Driving to the plane took far less time than their walk to the restaurant, but Metzger heard upset cries from within the truck when they neared the Piper Seneca. As the truck began to slow, he stood, focusing his attention on the plane.

His heart sank when he saw major damage to the plane, making it impossible to fly without extensive repairs. Numerous dents covered the plane, and both propellers displayed damage, including portions of their structures being bent in various directions. Both engine covers remained open, and Metzger could readily see that wires ripped from their housings, and engine components damaged. Apparently, the cleanup crew decided to make certain no one escaped New Mexico in case they failed to eliminate the group. Likely hearing, or seeing, the plane during its approach, they must have observed a group too large for them to efficiently eliminate. Their goal, above all else, was to protect Nadeau and the path he laid out for his followers. A sledge hammer was left near the front of the plane, as though a visual message for anyone left alive to find it.

Everyone slowly emerged from the truck once it rolled to a stop near the plane.

"Well, this fuckin' sucks," Timmons muttered.

"Is there any chance of fixing it?" Gracine inquired.

"No," the pilot answered. "I can do light maintenance, but nothing like this. This is a complete overhaul that requires tools we don't have."

"What now?" Jillian asked.

"We scavenge everything we can from the plane," Metzger stated. "Our next objective is directly north of us, albeit a few states away. We'll drive or walk to the next available airport and hope for the best."

"These bastards are something else," Sutton groaned. "I can't wait to shoot a few of them in painful places."

"I agree," Brooke said, walking toward the disabled plane. "After what I've seen here, it's unlikely we can talk sense into any of them."

Metzger shrugged as all eyes fell to him. He felt ready to see what awaited them in Wyoming, though he suspected Nadeau wasn't quite the adversary he first envisioned, or anticipated.

If anything, the man felt more dangerous than ever, because he possessed an unknown number of loyal followers who would die for him and his cause.

Such dedication made all of them dangerous.

And deadly.

He looked to Brooke as she removed a few of her belongings from the plane, wondering exactly what extremes she carried out to gather information about Nadeau's network.

Chapter 18

Mid-September, The Previous Year

Brooke followed instructions from Taylor to pick up a care package that included some rations, an extra sidearm, ammunition, and a few gadgets that made her feel like a female James Bond.

One was a protective garment, and the other looked like a charm bracelet, that apparently fired toxic darts, capable of rendering a person unconscious within seconds. Instructions were included, but she didn't have time to read them immediately because she and Canfield neared the first safehouse she deciphered from Rupert Clarke's luggage in Indiana. Unlike later installations, this particular safehouse wouldn't be found unless someone possessed the means to follow latitude and longitude coordinates. Brooke supposed Nadeau's most trusted followers prepared for such challenges well before the apocalypse.

During their travels, the human experience grew bleaker with each town they entered. Fewer survivors lined the streets, and most people avoided them, which Brooke preferred. One silver lining she discovered was the growing number of undead providing practice for Canfield when it came to swinging his bat.

He used pine tar and whatever useful adhesives he found to glue small, jagged rocks, scrap metal pieces, and even arrow heads to the end of the bat to help penetrate the skulls of the undead. Trial and error helped them learn that virtually *any* loud noise attracted the undead to the source of the sound. Because of this, they avoided using firearms when possible, traveling through towns only out of necessity. Brooke didn't sleep particularly well most evenings, because she often expected nomads, or the undead, to find them.

Most plans in the apocalypse never worked out in a timely fashion, because issues always managed to impede progress. On the day before Brooke expected to arrive at the safehouse, she and Canfield passed through a town so small it didn't even have a sign to declare where travelers had arrived. A gas station, a small restaurant, and an inn that closed before the end of the world lined the main drag, along with a few houses with adequate space between them.

A van on the opposite side of the road from most of the buildings had crashed directly into a utility pole. An older model, the van had two rear doors, and the one with the handle appeared open by a few inches. Brooke approached the passenger side, while Canfield drew a sidearm in case an aggressive person remained inside the disabled vehicle.

After walking for part of the day, the couple would have preferred to find a functioning vehicle, but they also checked on a regular basis for supplies. Finding the front seat clear, they walked to the back, opening the door to discover a variety of retail goods, mostly clothing, awaiting them. Most of the clothing held little interest for Brooke because they were mostly men's items, and sporting goods. Canfield filed through a few of the sports jerseys, finding an old baseball jersey in the mix that appeared to fit him. Brooke waited patiently a moment until he started rifling through a second tier of jerseys.

"What?" he questioned. "I smell like a wet dog."

"We've barely been within shouting distance of a living person in days."

Canfield's face lit up when he snagged a baseball cap from behind the stack of tops and shorts. He pulled out a white baseball cap with a blue "T" centered above the brim.

"This was our team's short-lived alternate color scheme for training camp a few years ago."

"I'm always amazed at the things that get you excited, John," she said, immediately realizing she robbed him of momentary joy when the smile ran from his face.

"Sorry."

"No," she said. "I'm sorry. I promise I'm not trying to be a total bitch."

Brooke felt compelled to say something more, or reassure Canfield with physical contact, but a throaty growl disturbed their brief conversation.

"Looks like we disturbed the locals," Canfield said, turning to see three members of the undead heading their way from various directions.

He set the cap on the van's bumper, looking to Brooke.

"Don't want it to get dirty. It's white."

"It's going to get dirty, John. You're delaying the inevitable."

Canfield studied the end of the bat, which had some dried blood and tissue stuck in the various sharp components. He stepped forward as a male zombie staggered near him, wearing business casual, already stained by weeks of the various activities the undead carried out in their limited mental capacity. Canfield did a hop and a short skip toward the cold adversary as he wound the bat behind him for a solid swing. He unleashed a smooth uppercut at its skull, barely giving it time to emit another hiss before a croak emerged from its mouth. It collapsed to the ground as he pried the bat free.

"Not a drop on you," Brooke informed him when she examined him from head to toe, placing the cap at an awkward angle on his head, drawing a thin smile. "Besides, there's probably a dozen of them in there."

"Nope," he said. "Just the one."

She observed him taking practice swings on the other two undead, impressed at his improvement in dealing with the primitive adversaries. Her mind shifted, however, to how alone she felt in the apocalypse as the few people she once knew dwindled to only Canfield and Taylor. Canfield lost contact with his family less than two weeks after bombs went off by the hundreds worldwide, and Brooke hadn't heard from Taylor in two days. Their means of communication wasn't in jeopardy, considering their devices used satellites that were still operational, but Taylor had expressed concerns about a workplace shortage with everyone leaving their posts.

Until he received word from his ex-wife that she and their two children made it to his family's property in Texas, Canfield remained in a slight bout of depression. He received the news one day before cell phone towers began to fail in their area. Although he didn't speak long with her on the phone, he learned that she opted to travel to his parents' ranch because it provided far more safety for the kids. Beyond that, he didn't receive much news, except that his folks and siblings were all safe as well. His spirits improved significantly after the call, and he found new determination to survive and make his way south.

A few hours later, dusk threatened to leave them out in the cold, but they found a car with a few supplies, including some alcohol. Canfield drove while Brooke navigated, taking them to the outskirts of Elkton, Kentucky, near the co-ordinates. Neither wanted to stay in a town, because towns attracted drifters and the types of people willing to kill for supplies. Brooke didn't particularly want to approach the safehouse until daylight, so they began scouring both sides of the road they traveled.

"Something that doesn't scream danger," Brooke said to herself as she found a few houses with vehicles parked in their driveways.

"What do you think about that?" Canfield asked, pointing to a driveway ahead that disappeared into a thicket of trees, indicating the residence wasn't near the road.

"It's a risk," Brooke responded, "but we're running out of daylight."

Canfield pulled into the driveway, and Brooke began to realize the residence hadn't been tended to since before the apocalypse. The lawn, along with a number of weeds, had grown to knee-high length. Several posted signs were hanging on trees, the dilapidated fence, and even the house itself when the two-story structure came into view.

Weathered, gray asphalt siding lined the exterior walls of the house, indicating it hadn't been tended to in quite some time, possibly due to financial hardships by the owners. Some of the shingles were chipped, even missing in some spots, long overdue for a makeover that never happened. Isolated from civilization, it appeared mostly intact with no foundation issues, or broken windows.

"Is it structurally sound?" Canfield wondered aloud.

"We're about to find out."

Over time, the pair learned to travel light, because they were in and out of vehicles, sometimes walking several miles until they located fuel, or a suitable ride. Sometimes they found changes of clothing, and often hoped to find houses with blankets, or the means to start a fire. Traveling light, and having to walk too often to carry items in bulk, the couple didn't pack extras beyond food, water, and weapons. Thus far, cold overnights hadn't been a major issue, but winter was on the horizon and they remained in the upper portion of the country.

Exiting the vehicle hesitantly, both studied the old house, and Brooke wondered if it was lost due to tax reasons. She hoped for an empty interior, because houses with clutter often attracted other problems, like rodents, insects, and travelers searching for a place to settle. She didn't hear any noises, except for leaves rustling from the breeze, and a few crickets. Looking to Canfield, she drew a pistol from her side, and he took hold of his modified bat.

Each of them looked around their respective sides of the house's exterior, seeing no danger lurking. Overgrown shrubs obscured some of their view, but they didn't hear sounds of the undead anywhere nearby. Quietly stepping up the concrete stairs to the front porch, Canfield looked to the front door, receiving a nod from Brooke before turning the doorknob. It swung inward, and Brooke took aim with the her sidearm, barely able to see inside as dusk surrounded the area. She stepped inside first, finding a fireplace in the living room, and a house mostly devoid of belongings.

"Looks promising," she said, just above a whisper.

Both of them cleared the downstairs, room by room, and then the upstairs, never getting too far from their fellow traveler. Once Brooke stated that she felt secure staying there all night, Canfield fetched their belongings from their most recent car. He waited until dark, using some wood he found nearby to start a fire in the fireplace, because doing so before dusk put a target on them. Nefarious people would attempt to steal belongings if they thought travelers weren't expecting trouble, or they were easy targets.

Only two boxes of items remained in the house, and they contained random trinkets and a homemade quilt which Canfield laid atop the floor in front of the fireplace.

"Are you trying to drop a hint?" Brooke asked suspiciously, realizing they hadn't made love in over a week.

In response, Canfield held the bottle of hard alcohol by its neck and waved it back and forth in a ringing bell motion with a smirk.

"Do we even have cups?" Brooke groaned.

"We don't need cups, darlin'," Canfield replied. "Let's pop this bad boy open and see where the evening goes."

***

Less than an hour later, the two were lying atop the quilt, the bottle beside them more than half empty. Brooke stared at the stained ceiling above, feeling Canfield's warmth on her right side. Both kept weapons nearby in case someone discovered their location and barged into the house, but she actually felt a bit more relaxed than usual.

Part of the time they spent setting up their accommodations, and the other half securing the house's access points. Once they started sharing the bottle of spirits, they talked about the days ahead, and what they missed most about living normal lives.

"Tell me about your childhood again," Brooke finally said after a few minutes of silence.

"Why?" Canfield questioned. "You've heard this several times now."

She paused.

"Because it sounds so much better than mine."

Canfield looked to the fire before turning his attention to the ceiling as well. Growing up in Texas, he had loving parents, two siblings, and every chance to do what he wanted in life. Brooke sensed his reluctance to talk about his past once again, not because he hated to, but because he felt genuinely connected to her.

"Let's save that for another day," he said. "I want to hear your story. Your real story."

She had given him fragments of a fictitious backstory previously, but by now, he knew much of her previous life with him had been a scripted affair.

Brooke rolled over to face Canfield, running her fingers through his beard. He stared directly into her eyes with concern, as though he knew the story wasn't going to be gumdrops and fairy dust with a happy ending.

"I was born in Missouri," Brooke began, her eyes shifting between Canfield and the floor. "Unlike you, I was an only child to parents who were barely middle-class much of the time. Mom worked as a secretary at a local elementary school, and my father was a welder who claimed to have struggles finding work, but had plenty of time to frequent the local tavern."

Now Canfield appeared slightly uncomfortable, having an idea of where the story might be going, but he remained close to Brooke, even taking her hand.

"To this day, I don't know if my father was upset that he didn't have a son, or just a miserable son-of-a-bitch. My grandparents on both sides were non-existent for all intents and purposes, so they were no help. My father would come home drunk, and take out his frustrations on my mother. She took the abuse to protect me, but there were times when I found her holding a gun when she thought I was asleep. I wonder if she thought about ending her own life, or his, but she never got to make that choice."

"How old were you?" Canfield asked, his expression filled with awe.

"Six."

Canfield shook his head, looking at the quilt momentarily before returning his gaze to Brooke.

"One night he beat her, and threw her against a wall. I know now that it killed her instantly, but in his drunken stupor, he didn't know any better, so he wandered off to bed. For what seemed like an eternity, I tried to wake my mother, her eyes wide-open and staring at me. I didn't understand death, John. I kept thinking she would wake up and tell me everything was alright like she always did."

Brooke sniffled, and a tear formed in the corner of one eye. She went to wipe away the teardrop with her free hand, but Canfield gently clasped her fingers before they touched her face.

"You don't have to be a rock all the time, you know," he said with empathy before caressing her palm with his thumb and slowly releasing her hand.

"Unfortunately, I have to now, more than ever."

"It's me. You don't have to put up walls."

"You shouldn't judge me until you hear the rest of the story."

"I'm all ears."

Brooke touched his face once more, and the tear traveled freely down her cheek. She hadn't opened up about these events in her life before, and her insides felt as though they were being churned in a blender from nerves, and having to relive the experience.

"I finally realized my mother was gone, and I contemplated a future without her. My parents never consciously taught me how to use a gun, but I studied them when they shot the revolver on weekends. One time I found my mother cleaning a revolver, and she told me to never point it at any living thing, because shooting anything meant killing it. Strangely, I knew exactly what, and who, she meant with that statement, and I studied movies, and watched them shoot when they thought I was reading, or watching a video. All because I shared my mom's fears, and I wanted to know how to protect us."

Giving a light sigh, Brooke recalled the night in vivid detail. A mix of deep sadness over the loss of her mother stuck with her, while any feelings of her father died that same evening.

"When you were six, did you ever consider killing one of your parents?"

"I can't say I did," Canfield answered sympathetically.

"It's not something I took lightly, but the thought stayed with me until that night. John, I had never fired a gun before that night, but when I saw him sleeping off his latest binge, I went into their bedroom, found the gun in a dresser drawer, yes, a dresser drawer, and took it out. I didn't feel the least bit scared as I pointed the gun at him. If anything, I felt numb. I wanted him to wake up, to see it coming, but he wouldn't, and I'm not sure he would've had his senses about him anyway."

Canfield's face expressed deep sorrow, having never known the extent of Brooke's true childhood. She knew him to be a good father, even keeping an otherwise useless wallet because it held photographs of his children. Although his cell phone lost its charge a few days prior, he kept it for the same reason, hoping to come across a charger so he could access the images trapped in its technological confines.

"Like I said, I hadn't fired a gun before," Brooke continued. "So, I walked to the side of the bed, pointed the gun at his skull, and pulled the trigger so close that it couldn't miss. I remember the sound of the gun scaring me enough that I dropped it on the bed. For hours, maybe more than a day, I curled up in the bathtub until someone called the cops to have them check on us. It didn't take a rocket scientist to figure out what transpired, and because of my age, I entered the foster system."

"No one could take you in?" Canfield questioned.

"My grandparents were distant on both sides, and I didn't really have any close aunts or uncles. They tried therapy with me, but it didn't help much, because I had very little to say. I wasn't allowed to talk much at home when my father was around, and that stuck with me. Months passed, and I watched other kids go into foster homes, and no one seemed to want me. I figured I was going to be a ward of the state forever when an older man and his wife took me in."

"Older?"

"Close to fifty. Not exactly the age where people are looking to start a family."

"Is this one of those stories where they steal the kid from the orphanage and turn them into a killing machine for the government?"

Brooke grinned, removing her hand from his and running it down his beard before lightly clasping his throat. Canfield appeared apprehensive, and she removed her hand, giving him a smile to indicate she was fooling around.

"He worked for the CIA," she informed him. "I can't say the people who eventually adopted me showered me with love, but they cared, and they kept me on the straight and narrow. Thomas, my foster dad, took me to work sometimes, and I grew intrigued by the work he did. He didn't see gray when it came to the law. Everything was black and white, right or wrong. I like to think he was proud of me the day I said I was going to apply to the CIA, but he wasn't one to wear his feelings on his sleeve."

"How did you end up doing the deep cover stuff?"

"I showed a knack for it early on. Having a detachment from emotion most of the time comes in handy when your entire life becomes a lie."

"Was everything between us a lie?" Canfield asked cautiously, as though he wasn't sure he wanted to know the answer.

"At first," Brooke answered, causing him to deflect his gaze momentarily. She turned his head back to her gently. "If it makes you feel better, I chose you out of a dozen or so bachelors and divorcees."

Canfield didn't look entirely certain of himself, as though he pondered why she picked his life to weave in and out of regularly.

"Was it my striking good looks?" he asked, trying to disrupt the awkward tension.

"I never dated a jock before," Brooke confessed. "Maybe I wanted to be the cheerleader."

Canfield snickered, breaking into a controlled laugh.

"That's me. The dumb jock."

"You're not the least bit dumb," Brooke informed him truthfully. "It's one of the things I've come to love about you."

"There's more than one?" Canfield asked playfully, beginning to run one of his fingers around her waistline.

"There are a couple. Now, are we going to get down to making out in front of the fireplace, or what?"

"Shit," Canfield said, a thought suddenly crossing his mind.

"What?"

"I don't have protection."

Brooke knew he didn't mean firearms, or his baseball bat.

"That could be a problem."

"Not really. I was a pull-out guy for years because my wife was Catholic."

"Refresh my memory on how that's relevant to our predicament."

"Well, strict Catholics don't believe in using protection during sex, so the alternative is constantly having babies, or pulling out before, well, you know."

"Wait," Brooke said, putting any sexual activities on hold. "Doesn't the Roman Catholic Church also have a strict policy about divorce?"

"They do, but I think the ex was out to emancipate me."

"Emasculate, John. Emasculate."

"Sorry. Whatever. I was just letting you know I'm well-versed in keeping my partners from getting pregnant when the condoms run out."

"Partners?" Brooke asked with an arched eyebrow.

"You know how we jocks are," Canfield answered with a mischievous smirk. "I never cheated on you, if that's what you're worried about."

"I know you didn't," Brooke said, pressing her forefinger against his lips, openly making him feel even less secure.

Canfield drew a deep, cautious breath.

"I'm going to be honest," he said. "You terrify me in so many ways, but I'm like that praying mantis who knows he might get his head bitten off after the deed is done."

"Does that mean you're having trouble getting it up?" Brooke asked, reaching for his pants, and finding the answer immediately.

"No," he said. "I'll confess that I'm rather aroused by the whole thing."

Brooke gave him a lengthy kiss as the fire crackled behind them.

"Then let's get down to it," she said. "Because tomorrow, we face some real danger for the first time."

Canfield's eyes widened a bit, and Brooke initiated their night of passion as darkness surrounded their temporary quarters.

Chapter 19

Two days had passed since Mike Mullins arrived with Hewitt at Naval Station Norfolk, finding the arrangement intact, and very little red tape when it came to being allowed inside. He hadn't stepped foot on a military base since his Army days, thankfully, but the situation looked like a far cry from the tight ship his supervisors ran. In order to keep the military men and women able to carry out their duties, civilians worked menial jobs to earn their keep at the base, or the restored city of Norfolk. From what he gathered, the civilians were related to military personnel, or essential workers, like doctors, electricians, and folks who knew how to keep the local grid working.

He never saw Hewitt again once they whisked the man away to test his blood and hopefully begin drawing samples to develop a vaccine, or a cure. Mullins felt a bit surprised he didn't see Hewitt, because the military took him immediately to draw his blood for testing. Apparently, Mullins didn't possess blood capable of combatting the undead infection, but they followed through with their agreement, testing for cancer, and even running additional tests during his first day there.

Although short of five-star accommodations, the apartment they set Mullins up with for two days held amenities that nature and abandoned houses lacked. They spared a soldier to watch over him, because they didn't trust a stranger in their town, or on the base. Private Thompson appeared a bit green to Mullins, and the former cop questioned whether they found the young man and enlisted him *after* the apocalypse began. Thompson accompanied him wherever Mullins ventured, and even grew to trust his assignment after they swapped a few military stories.

Currently, he sat inside an examination room, waiting for the doctor to bring news to him about his test results. He hadn't spoken to a physician directly since arriving at the base, but they apparently knew about his case, because they drew a second round of blood, and had some questions to ask through their staff members. He didn't assume he was being ignored, but he understood that current military personnel on the base took precedence over a stranger.

Since they did not require him to don a gown, he figured this meeting would yield results only, with no further testing.

A double knock came at the door, and it opened a few seconds later to reveal a woman with black hair wearing camouflage scrubs. She held a chart with some paperwork attached, walking past Mullins to don a pair of blue exam gloves after setting the chart on the sink momentarily.

"More tests?" Mullins inquired, swallowing hard after speaking.

"No tests," the doctor answered. "I'm Sheila Mendez, and I requested your case."

Mullins could see she was a major in the Army based on the emblems on her uniform. She appeared old enough to have seen quite a bit during her career, though he wasn't sure if Dr. Mendez became a doctor before, or during, her time in the military.

"I'm not even sure why I put these on," she said, staring at the exam gloves. "I don't like delivering bad news to anyone, even outsiders."

"If it's any comfort, Major, I didn't expect good news. My body hasn't felt right for a few weeks now."

"Normally, I would offer some words of comfort, and options, but I'm afraid the latter isn't feasible in this circumstance. Michael, I'm afraid your cancer has returned, and based on your status, or lack thereof, we can't treat it here."

"What about the clinic down the road?" Mullins joked.

Although it required a moment for her to catch his meaning, Sheila smiled at the comment.

"I'm glad you have a sense of humor about it," she said.

"I've been through it before, Major. How long do I have?"

"Wow," Sheila said dryly. "Getting right to it, are we?"

"Well, my bucket list changed significantly last summer, but there are a few things I'd like to finish before my number is up."

Sheila set the medical chart down, leaning against the sink and folding her arms.

"Now I feel kinda bad."

"I'm guessing this isn't the best news."

"I'm so sorry."

"For what?" Mullins asked, assuming his assumptions proved true during the test results.

"I had your results yesterday, but I wanted to give you an extra night in the lap of luxury before we cut you loose."

Mullins chuckled.

"The food was a welcome change, but the apartment lacked a breathtaking view. Still, I appreciate the sentiment."

Sheila pulled up a wheeled stool, taking a seat beside Mullins and looking him in the eyes.

"Look, our expert told me the scans show the cancer is in the bone just above your right knee, and spreading. What did you have before?"

"Colon cancer. I had part of my colon removed."

"Under normal circumstances, what you have could be combated with chemo, or radiation, mostly likely. I would tell you that amputating your leg might save you this time, but they found other spots in your chest."

"This just gets better and better," Mullins said, cupping his face with his hands before sliding them downward to his lap.

Because he assumed such news was coming, he didn't feel shock, or numbness. He simply wondered about the amount of time he possessed before he couldn't fend off the dead, or the cancer claimed him.

"Because I don't have a baseline, it's really hard to tell you how long you'll retain your strength and mobility before-"

"Before I die," Mullins finished as Sheila hesitated.

Both sat in silence a few seconds.

"I realize you can't help me, but do you have the means to do chemo or radiation here? Or anywhere?"

"We do, but it's limited. Retrieving machines and medicine hasn't been a top priority when there are so many mouths to feed."

"Overall, how are things here?"

Sheila paused a moment, and a thoughtful look crossed her face.

"Between you and me, they've sent out a number of patrols to search for supplies, and sometimes they don't come back. I don't think the dead get them. I think they choose not to return. The latest patrols tend to have married men and women who have something to return to. Dangling a carrot, if you will."

Mullins knew food and shelter were the two things the military could offer its employees, and without either one, they might choose to take their chances, and their families, into the untamed wilderness beyond Norfolk.

He started to hop off the exam table, but Sheila held up a finger.

"Give me a minute before you take off," she said.

After exiting the room, she returned with a white paper bag, already folded over along the top, and handed it to him.

"There are a few goodies in there for you when things start getting tough."

"Like a cyanide pill?" Mullins half-joked.

"No. Things that will help with the pain, and some supplements. We put some paperwork in there, so you know what each medication is for."

"We?"

"A few members of the staff are sympathetic to your plight. Some of us have lost family to cancer before all of this."

"I appreciate it," Mullins said, cautiously stepping down from the exam table and its foot pad.

"If you hurry, you might be able to catch up with your friend," Sheila added.

"My friend?"

Mullins momentarily wondered if someone else from Maplewood had shown up. His only true friend was down in South Carolina, last he knew, and Brad Weir had no reason to leave the warmer, safer climate.

"The guy you brought here," Sheila elaborated.

Mullins shot her a look of complete exasperation and horror.

"You let him *go*?"

"His blood didn't prove a match for the antibody like we were told, so we didn't have any reason to keep him."

"How could his blood not match?" Mullins asked, his mind overwhelmed at the horrific possibilities that accompanied Hewitt and his freedom.

"He was cut with a sword, like we were told, but our guess is the sword tip didn't have infected blood on it when it cut Mr. Hewitt. It was an honest mistake, but we already had your bloodwork done, so there wasn't any sense in denying you the results."

"*That's* not what I'm upset about," Mullins stammered. "Hewitt is a mass murderer. A serial killer. And your people let him walk out the front gate?"

"Our hands were tied," Sheila said, though her expression indicated she didn't know the extent of Hewitt's misdeeds. "We can't take third party information as gospel and hold him prisoner. And he's just another mouth to feed who can't aid our cause. That's how the brass look at things around here. Very cut and dried."

Out of habit, Mullins checked around him to make certain he wasn't forgetting anything, because he certainly needed to get moving. He wasn't certain where Hewitt might head first, but the man likely wanted revenge for what occurred in the Adirondacks with Metzger and his in-laws. Mullins hadn't decided to blindfold Hewitt when they left Maplewood, because he never expected the man to leave the military base. As calculated as Hewitt was, he likely knew exactly which way to go, and he certainly knew about the tunnel bridge.

"Fuck," Mullins muttered.

"I'm sorry," Sheila reiterated.

"Not as sorry as Hewitt's next victims will be," Mullins said. "I've got to figure out where he's going first, and try and stop him."

Mullins walked past the physician to the door, stopping short to turn around.

"I appreciate you shooting straight with me, Doc."

"Just wish I had better news for you, Mr. Mullins. Take care."

"Thanks. You, too."

***

When Kevin Gebbert departed the community of Maplewood, he risked more than just his well-being in an attempt to better the village. Although he worked to earn his keep, he didn't feel as though many of the residents respected him. His attempts to garner the attention of Luke Johnson failed utterly, because the man seemed more intent on being a father than finding a new love. They spoke at length about Luke's partner from New York, and Luke stated that Gebbert reminded him of his younger self.

Considering only a handful of gay men likely resided in Virginia, and those at the Navy base were probably in the closet, Gebbert decided he needed to make himself useful and lower the population at Maplewood. His interest in being Luke's partner paled compared to the need Gebbert felt to feel useful in the community. He knew Robert McAllister wasn't keen on strangers joining their group, but he accepted Sutton's faction because they offered skills and food. Harboring a wanted Navy officer, who could help provide relief to thousands of worried people, no less, placed their community in danger. Once already, visitors from the military paid them a visit in search of their missing lieutenant commander.

McAllister wasn't in a position to personally report the Navy man's location since he never left the village. He wasn't going to ask others to carry out his dirty work, either, because he hated showing weakness. He didn't like strangers, because he didn't like opposition to his power, or the laws he created to keep the community intact.

After some careful deliberation, Gebbert decided to make the move and ask for forgiveness instead of permission.

He packed some food, a roll of toilet paper, bottles of water, a knife, and a map of the area before sneaking out of the gated community during early morning hours the day after Bryce Metzger and his family replaced the other newcomers. An uneven balance of workload had left the village in need of supplies, with only a select few hunting and gathering outside the walls. Although some of the new arrivals brought skills with them, Gebbert viewed them as more mouths to feed.

Deep down, he supposed he resented Luke for choosing fatherhood over a relationship, providing excuses that Gebbert didn't embrace.

"I'm not immature," he muttered as he reached the entrance to the main tunnel bridge that led to the military base.

He stopped short of the entrance, amazed at his luck during the past few days. He only spied the undead from far distances a few times, and never encountered one up close. Now, however, standing at the mouth of the tunnel bridge, which looked more like a foreboding cave entrance, he swallowed hard. He saw lights inside, but they flickered, and he knew the undead, the military, or worse, marauders, might lurk within the lengthy tunnel.

What took less than a few minutes to cover in a vehicle likely required close to an hour on foot. With no other mode of transportation available, he sucked in a deep breath and entered the tunnel, attempting to remain quiet.

A steady, loud dripping sound reached his ears the moment he stepped inside, and he surmised the sound came from farther down the underwater roadway. Until his eyes adjusted to the darkness, Gebbert took hesitant steps, looking in every direction for hidden dangers. Ahead of him, lights continually flickered as though he had entered a haunted house attraction.

Attempting to steady his breathing, Gebbert sucked in a few deep breaths and released them slowly. Eerie silence surrounded him as he made his way through the manmade cavern, hoping to find daylight on the other side soon. As though passing through a paper towel tube, wind could be heard near the entrance of the tunnel bridge, but soon the heavy sound of sloshing water from above replaced the noise, providing Gebbert little comfort.

Only a few abandoned vehicles remained within the underwater bridge, but each one held the potential to conceal evildoers. He stayed along the opposite wall, prepared to run if anyone emerged each time he passed a car, truck, or van. Possibly a quarter of the way through the claustrophobic roadway, he spotted a gray van parked along the outer lane of the opposite side, so he hugged the wall farthest from it, waiting to see if any danger emerged from behind the vehicle.

His heart skipped a beat when someone stood after using the vehicle for cover. Gebbert immediately knew this person wasn't hiding from him, or anyone, because he towered over the smaller man. He knew the stranger by name and reputation, having no idea why Hewitt wasn't at the military base under constant supervision.

"Well, what have we here?" Hewitt asked, stepping slowly, methodically toward the Maplewood resident.

"I don't want any trouble," Gebbert stammered quickly.

"You're heading in the direction most people avoid," Hewitt noted, his face a neutral blank slate.

"I'm looking for shelter," Gebbert lied.

"No, you're not. I recognize your voice from the village."

Gebbert knew Hewitt was locked up during his entire stay at Maplewood, so encounters with other people were brief at best. A few people likely brought him food, or stopped to make certain he wasn't attempting an escape.

"I'd like to know where that village is," Hewitt said, a sinister smirk forming along his lips.

He had read Gebbert's hesitation as confirmation that his instincts proved correct, and now the smaller man knew he needed to run, because he would be tortured, or dead, otherwise.

Breaking into a sprint, he headed in the direction of the base, hoping assistance might meet him halfway, like soldiers, or fellow travelers. He heard Hewitt begin to chase after him, but the footsteps quickly fell off, as though Hewitt knew he couldn't catch the wiry young man who excelled in running. During his high school years, Gebbert came close to qualifying for state finals a few times in middle-distance events.

After nearly a minute of sprinting away from the dangerous man, Gebbert drew to a stop, daring to turn around and stare back at Hewitt, suspecting the man couldn't catch him. He quickly realized that Hewitt had stalked him by jogging, cutting the distance between them to half of what it might have been if the killer remained perfectly still. Gebbert knew he could run off like a gazelle once again, putting half a mile between them in no time, but he noticed too late that Hewitt held a pistol in his right hand. He raised it and fired, creating an echo throughout the tunnel as Gebbert felt a shell pierce the left side of his abdomen.

Now, Hewitt simply walked aggressively towards his target as Gebbert ran his left hand along his stomach, feeling the warm blood ooze out from the wound. It stung, as though a hot poker were jabbed into his guts and left there to fester. Before he could assess his wound and determine if the round went through him, or he could possibly run to safety, Hewitt's powerful hands wrapped around his throat, squeezing tightly. Feeling his supply of oxygen cut off, Gebbert began to fight, clawing and scratching at Hewitt's forearms before reaching for the man's eyes when he realized his efforts were futile.

Hewitt threw him to the ground instead of crushing his windpipe, or inflicting further damage. Gebbert recoiled, trying to decide which course of action to attempt next, like a cornered animal with little hope of escape.

"I don't need to know where your village is," Hewitt growled. "I already have a pretty good idea, considering where we are, and how long it took to get here."

"You don't have to kill me," Gebbert almost pleaded, terror growing within him as the bullet wound continued to leak blood. "I can get what you want."

"What do you think I want?" Hewitt inquired, his eyes gazing coldly at his prey.

"Food? Shelter?"

"I want some good old-fashioned revenge," Hewitt admitted, his words slow and decisive. "The only question is where I begin."

"What makes you so hateful?" Gebbert questioned, partly to stall for time.

"This world simply allowed me to be myself," Hewitt replied, pulling a knife from a sheath on his right side. "Killing you outright is too easy. I need you to be part of my next plan."

He pulled a pouch from his side, unzipping it before dipping the knife inside. When he pulled the blade free, it appeared to be dripping some sort of fluid. Gebbert couldn't tell for certain, but the liquid appeared crimson in nature, and thick, as though it might be coagulated blood. In his mind, he knew he couldn't escape, but he needed to try.

Before he could even stand and regain his footing, Hewitt grabbed hold of his left arm, pulling him close before plunging the knife into the bullet wound. Although the blade entered only a few inches, the pain was excruciating, particularly when Hewitt wiggled it side to side slightly, as though further toying with Gebbert. Now Gebbert groaned in pain, doubling over and falling to the ground as Hewitt released his grip and extracted the knife.

Hewitt knelt down before him, continuing to hold the blade, now dripping with Gebbert's blood as well.

"I may have lied when I said I didn't know where to start," Hewitt admitted, waving the blade back and forth to terrorize Gebbert all the more. "The truth is I know exactly where I'm going to start. Everyone who crossed me is going to pay eventually, and you're going to help me."

"I'll never help you," Gebbert sputtered, beginning to feel light-headed from the wound and internal bleeding.

"You already have," Hewitt said confidently, causing Gebbert to wonder if he somehow slipped with his words. "When you die, you're going to help me complete my plan in the most glorious way possible."

"No," Gebbert muttered, knowing only a miracle could save him from the injury.

Even if he received help for the wound, if the blood was contaminated blood from the undead, which he suspected it was, no amount of assistance could save him.

Without another word, Hewitt walked in the direction of Maplewood, and Gebbert contemplated what just happened. With the wound nearly doubled in size, he didn't like his chances of making it to the military base for medical assistance. Even if he did, he doubted the military doctors would help a civilian. He suspected blood from the undead was Hewitt's added ingredient on the knife blade, and if so, Gebbert didn't have a chance either way. As an agonizing sensation throbbed along the wound, and for a moment, he dropped to his knees and began to sob, feeling like a failure in every sense of the word.

Chapter 20

Three Days Later

Like his companions, Metzger grew weary of travel on the road because after the truck they used to leave the deadly bunker ran out of fuel, they found themselves walking.

Occasionally, in the middle of nowhere, they located a vehicle that took them several miles down the road before they ran out of fuel all over again. Most of the airports in New Mexico were located in the northern half of the state, or the southern half, with a few dotting the eastern border in the middle. Timmons chose to avoid an international airport north of them for a smaller airport called Sierra Blanca Regional Airport, south of the bunker where they failed to locate Nadeau.

Metzger and Jillian walked ahead of the others along a highway that hadn't been frequented since the previous summer. By his best estimate, they were within a few miles of the airport Timmons selected from the handful of choices. A burning question remained in the back of his mind, created by a few discussions with people he considered friends. He decided to tread lightly when asking his girlfriend about the possibility of her being pregnant.

"I need to ask you something," he said, feeling safely distanced from Timmons and Brooke, who appeared to be talking strategy.

Behind them, Sutton and Gracine appeared to be holding their own discussion.

"What is it?" Jillian asked in return.

"If the world ever gets back to normal, well, some sense of normal, do you ever wonder what our lives will be like?"

Jillian walked along in thought momentarily.

"I guess I've pictured a farmhouse with a fireplace and some critters in the yard. Maybe even some wild flowers and vegetables nearby. I'm not sure we'll ever get back to having home movies and emails again."

She looked to him before speaking again.

"What's your idea of a peaceful ever after?"

"It's hard to imagine a life where the military isn't hunting me down. I suppose I like the idea of riding a motorcycle again without having to dodge the dead. After living in the Adirondacks, I know we have the supplies out there to live with most of the creature comforts we had."

"You didn't exactly answer my question."

Metzger took Jillian by the hand as they continued to walk.

"I don't want to live alone, if that's what you're asking. Once the world is halfway safe, it would be awesome to find a patch of land near some loved ones and maybe raise a family of our own someday."

"So, I'm in this future?" Jillian asked as though slightly surprised.

"Do you think this is some kind of fling on my end?" Metzger questioned. "We've been through a lot together. I love everything about you."

An uncertain look crossed his girlfriend's face.

"What is it?" he asked.

"I'm still not sure I deserve you after some of the things I did in my hometown last year."

"We've *all* done things, Jillian."

"But the nightmares haven't stopped since the day I left."

"That means you still have a conscience," Metzger said. "You're still a good person."

Jillian looked ahead momentarily, and both of them expected to see the airport come into view any second.

"I'm not sure it's as simple as good and bad when we're fighting to survive each day."

"It's no different than when settlers came to this country. They worked, hunted, and traveled by foot, or by horse. I don't consider the military to be evil. I'm not sure I understand their methods, but they have their reasons for wanting me and Bryce."

"They have survival in mind, too," Jillian surmised.

Metzger squeezed her hand lightly, letting Jillian know he supported her. In truth, she had become a half that completed him, because she continued to write her journals, documenting the horrors they witnessed along the way. He wondered if she jotted down the worst parts about the experiences at South Hill.

"People like Hewitt are still the evil in this world," Metzger stated quietly. "People who murder indiscriminately, thinking only of themselves, are the biggest threat we face."

Noticing his feet were a bit sore from walking so much, Metzger hoped they located the airport soon. Signs along the road, a few miles back, indicated they weren't far from their destination. Even so, Metzger sensed his feet would grow useless without some rest, or more comfortable footwear. He currently wore some hybrid tennis shoes with brown coloration, indicating they were also workwear. Possibly half a size too small, they made his feet feel like trash slowly being compacted.

Although their backpacks grew lighter during their travels, the flip side was the fact that their rations grew fewer, and they hadn't stumbled across many accessible buildings along the way. Most of the structures they found were off the highway, not appearing promising. Brooke urged the group to continue moving forward, stating they would find supplies at locations along the way. Her words hadn't rung true, and Metzger hoped they could find a suitable aircraft at the airport, because he wanted to see what answers Wyoming held.

"The people who killed Juan weren't any better," Jillian said, reinforcing Metzger's statement about evil people.

"That's why you shouldn't lose any sleep over what you did to them."

At long last, the fence surrounding the airport came into view, and the group felt a collective tingle of excitement. Timmons appeared to notice something before the others did, because he jogged forward, the cowboy boots he'd worn the past few days, clopping atop the pavement.

"What is it?" Jillian asked him.

"No, no, no," the pilot muttered, still staring straight ahead as he walked with a quickened pace, brushing past Metzger and Jillian.

Metzger stared beyond the fence, seeing a mammoth plane out of place within the small, regional airport. Obscured in part by a hangar, the plane didn't appear to be perfectly upright, as though it crashed during an attempted landing.

When the group collectively reached the fence, they found dozens of undead staggering around the grounds, or standing still, waiting for something to gain their attention. From what Metzger could tell, an airliner of some sort crashed along the edge of the runway, taking out several of the hangars with its mammoth wings. At least half of the large aircraft appeared charred, and Metzger questioned what kind of issue caused the crash.

"This isn't the first time we've seen something like this," Sutton commented as he took Metzger's side.

"No," Metzger replied almost absently, his mind taking him back to the airliner crashed in a waterway near Sutton's family camp.

"Unfortunately, this may be worse for us," Jillian commented. "Most of those hangars look flattened."

"They *are* flattened," Timmons said, turning to the group with anguish in his eyes. "We may have come all this way for nothing."

Now the undead began to take notice of the interlopers just outside of their reach as they approached the fence. Measuring in square miles, the airport wasn't going to be easy to enter, and as of yet, they hadn't spotted any breaks in the mesh wire fence.

"We have to find a way in there," Gracine said, drawing close to the fence, even as the undead staggered toward the group from the other side.

"Then we follow the road," Metzger said, knowing every airport connected to a road. "Maybe we'll get lucky and find a hole in the fence."

Considering the group hadn't stepped far off the highway to examine the fence in the first place, they were back on pace momentarily. Within a few minutes, they came across a disabled car, halfway in one lane, and halfway off the road, dangerously close to the ditch. Sutton deviated from the others long enough to give the vehicle a quick examination, both inside and out. He returned to the group with a grim expression.

"It's on empty," he reported. "No gas can, and nothing we can use."

As they walked, the undead inside the fence began to follow, attracting more zombies to their collective. Metzger considered dealing with them by stabbing them through the mesh wire, but if the airport turned out to be useless to them, the group would expend energy for no reason.

Metzger hoped they found at least one intact aircraft on the grounds, and ample fuel from a pump, or other planes. Traveling on the highways and county roads hadn't proven kind to the group, and Nadeau's people succeeded in keeping them from reaching their next destination, giving their lives in the process.

Drawing closer to the main portion of the airport, the group began to see what transpired weeks or months before they stepped foot in New Mexico. An airliner had likely attempted a landing at the airport, either overrunning the runway, or experiencing technical difficulties. The left side of the large jet faced the group, part of its side blackened from fire.

"What the hell happened?" Metzger asked Timmons as they walked along the fence line, their entourage in tow on the other side.

"Your guess is good as mine," the pilot replied. "I can't tell if it happened early in the apocalypse, or months later."

When the group made their way to the main gate, they found it wide-open, either jammed on purpose, or stuck in the open position when the power died. Unfortunately, the dead took notice of the lack of barriers, and began stumbling out of the airport property, hoping to fill their stomachs.

"Well, this just got a lot worse," Gracine muttered.

"I'm done being patient," Timmons said angrily, pulling his sidearm from the holster along his right hip before opening fire on the undead who crossed the sliding gate's threshold.

He struck two of them in the forehead before everyone else could even pull their own weapons. Timmons typically dealt with the undead out of necessity, but the idea of getting out of New Mexico lit a fire beneath him and brought out his aggressive side.

A quick tally by Metzger indicated about two dozen undead crowded the main gate, waiting their turn. He suspected quite a few more scoured the grounds in search of an easy meal, but for the time being, the group could manage this batch. He pulled his sword from its sheath, prepared to step forward and eliminate a few of them.

After making certain he wasn't going to accidentally get shot by a friend, he sliced into the skulls of a few undead, downing them as gunfire rang out from either side of him. His friends made short work of the new adversaries, clearing a path for everyone to step through the open gate, and over the bodies. His ears rang momentarily from the lack of hearing protection, reminding him of the other reason he hated using firearms on the undead.

Once they stepped into the main portion of the airport, with one runway readily visible, they discovered only one hangar remained intact after whatever accident caused the airliner to crash.

"That thing skidded along here," Timmons noted when they drew closer to it. "I bet the front landing gear was trashed."

"What about the fire?" Jillian questioned.

"Must've been inside," the pilot answered. "I don't see blistering on the exterior. Makes me wonder what happened in there."

Walking around the downed airliner took several minutes, but no one found any indication that any passengers or crew managed to escape. Every door appeared intact, and though a few windows along the side were missing, no person could fit through them. From within, they heard the sounds of the dead, and Metzger wondered why so many dead still scouted the property if they hadn't come from this particular aircraft.

"Just asking for the sake of practicality," Sutton said, "but why are we examining this thing? Learning what happened to it doesn't help our situation in the least."

"If it's not a burned-out wreck, and there aren't hundreds of dead inside, we might find supplies," Metzger answered. "We just need a safe access point to make that assessment."

Jillian kept looking up, since the nose of the plane rested on the ground. Portions of its metal were sheered as though a planer had shaved off a few layers. Her eyes moved along the fuselage, studying details while searching for an opening of some kind. She stopped and stared at one particular area, and when Metzger glanced upward, he spied two of the porthole windows missing. Likely jarred loose from damage incurred during the crash, they provided an opportunity to glance inside, but they were dangerously high off the ground. A mammoth wing led directly to one of them, but at a steep angle, meaning walking on the wing wouldn't prove easy.

"How the hell do we get up there?" he questioned aloud.

"I'll look for a ladder," Sutton said, understanding the importance of what they found.

Timmons walked around the airliner, a despondent look on his face as he studied the flattened hangars.

"It's not all lost," Metzger said.

"One hangar doesn't necessarily mean we find a suitable aircraft," Timmons muttered.

"It doesn't mean that we don't, either. Take Brooke and go have a look."

Brooke stepped forward, appearing as ready to move along with their journey as the pilot.

"I'll keep an eye on him," she promised.

A few minutes after the pair departed to check on the one intact hangar, Sutton emerged from a nearby shed carrying a standard step ladder. After a few attempts of safe placement against the wing, he found an area where the ladder rested without sliding. Gracine stepped forward, prepared to head up for a look through the window.

"I can do it," Sutton said.

Gracine eyeballed him from head to toe.

"Your big ass would slide down that wing like a kid on a playground slide."

"I'm sensitive about my big ass, you know," Sutton countered, though not serious by his demeanor.

"Does someone have a flashlight?" Gracine asked, thinking ahead to the darkened interior of the plane.

Metzger fetched a reliable flashlight from his backpack, tossing it to Gracine who caught it cleanly before heading up the ladder. Sutton footed the bottom to keep it from moving, watching her with concern as she ascended to the wing. He put a hand up to support her, accidentally cupping her butt and causing her to look down with a mix of surprise and admonishment.

"Sorry," he said quickly.

Gracine made her way up the ladder, carefully stepping onto the aluminum surface, finding the wing a bit slick at first. Without the benefit of a railing, or something to grab, she walked up a slight incline to the open window, greeted by a throaty hiss. A member of the undead reached for her through the small opening. Drawing a knife from her side, Gracine managed to maneuver the weapon through the window, stabbing the charred nuisance in the skull. From the ground, Metzger felt reasonably certain he heard at least one other groan from within the downed aircraft.

Gracine dropped to her knees beside the opening and switched on the flashlight, shining it inside.

"Oh, Lord," she mumbled.

"What is it?" Sutton asked.

"They're all burned to a crisp in there," she reported. "Whatever caught fire went through the entire plane. There's nothing useful in there."

"How many had turned?" Metzger questioned, his curiosity eating at him.

"Only a few," Gracine reported. "What's odd is that only half of them are wearing seat belts."

Metzger wondered if a few of the passengers were already contaminated when they boarded, and created some havoc by attacking other passengers during the flight. He envisioned chaos and panic during the last minutes of the flight as people carried out desperate, perhaps foolish, measures to rid themselves of unknown threat.

"This probably happened early in the apocalypse," he said to Jillian, who nodded in agreement. "They probably didn't know what they were dealing with."

Gracine carefully returned to the ladder and climbed down before continuing her story.

"Almost everyone was burned to a crisp, and the few undead could barely raise their arms. It stunk like burnt hotdogs, but worse."

"How does a fire start *inside* a plane?" Metzger questioned, wondering if one of his fellow travelers possessed a notion.

"Maybe they found some dead and tried to deal with it," Sutton suggested.

"What?" Jillian asked. "With a flamethrower?"

"Airliners have oxygen," Metzger said. "It could've been anything. Even sabotage."

"The rest of this place is going to be hard to scavenge," Gracine noted. "Especially with everything being as flat as pancakes."

Sutton addressed Metzger.

"Your boy is on a bad string of luck. First, he picks the wrong bad guy hideout, and then he leads us to the one airport with nothing useful."

"This isn't the time for your conspiracy shit, Colby," Metzger said with a stern tone, sending a warning. "Scott has risked as much as any of us."

"Sorry," Sutton said. "Guess I'm just frustrated."

"Ain't we all," Gracine commented.

A few minutes later, Timmons and Brooke returned from the distant hangar, and Metzger knew from their expressions the news wasn't going to be good.

"We found two planes," Timmons reported. "Both were dismantled, and I think they were waiting on parts."

"What now?" Jillian asked, looking to Metzger, as did everyone else.

"We need to check the other hangars," Timmons said before Metzger could muster a response. "If there's any chance we find an intact plane under the rubble, it's worth a try."

"Agreed," Metzger said. "If we don't find *something*, we're going to be on foot for a while."

Not far from them, the village of Ruidoso might provide a vehicle and some supplies. When they passed through the small town the first time, they located a vehicle that appeared to have sufficient fuel, but stranded them halfway to the airport when something in the motor blew. Metzger wondered if they might have better luck backtracking to the town before heading to the next airport.

He also questioned how long his family would remain safe in Maplewood.

***

Bryce Metzger hadn't particularly enjoyed his stay in the community of Maplewood. He felt on-edge more often than not, because he felt certain that McAllister's paranoia regarding the visitors in his neighborhood kept them from being welcome with open arms. On this particular afternoon he walked with Luke Johnson, catching up on gossip and other local news. Both men walked the interior perimeter of the gated community, being careful what they said because it seemed someone was always within earshot.

"I'm worried because Kevin disappeared around the time Mullins took that prisoner guy to the base," Luke confided in the Navy officer as they strolled. "What worries me more, is no one around here seems to give a shit."

"Does he go on supply runs?" Bryce inquired.

Luke scoffed aloud.

"He hardly ever leaves these walls. I have concerns he did something stupid."

"Like what?" Bryce asked, genuinely perplexed because he didn't have much background about the community or its residents.

Luke had brought up several topics the past few days, including Gebbert, but he hadn't mentioned many details. It seemed like everyone wanted a turn speaking to the new guests, so no conversations lasted very long. Most people asked them about their adventures on the road, taking turns picking their brains when they weren't pretending to ignore them simply to please McAllister.

"I think he had thoughts of turning you in," Luke admitted. "He hinted about it several times, and I wonder if he followed Mullins to the base."

"Well, fuck," Bryce muttered, knowing such a move placed his family in danger of being scooped up by the military.

"If he left, it would be ill-advised," Luke added. "He has no experience out there."

"But the dead are mostly cleared between here and the base," Bryce noted. "If he hoofed it, the trip would take a few days, but he'd probably make it safely."

"It's been more than a few days, and no one's come knocking at our gates."

"It just feels like there's a target on my back most of the time."

"I understand. Just know you've got an ally in me. I owe your brother more than you'll ever know for keeping me and my girl alive."

"Speaking of which, how did your daughter come to be yours, if you don't mind me asking?"

Luke chuckled, understanding how Samantha didn't resemble him in the least, right down to the color of his skin.

"Her parents were killed early on when the apocalypse struck our city," he explained. "My partner and I were holing up, minding our own business, when that little one showed up on our front doorstep."

"She's lucky to have you."

"It's actually the other way around," Luke admitted. "I needed a purpose after Albert was killed by the dead."

"Sorry to hear that," Bryce said with empathy.

"I think we've all suffered losses. I still find it hard to believe we share a Buffalo connection."

Bryce grinned.

"I'm ashamed to admit I didn't get home nearly as much as I should have after I joined the Navy."

"I know Dan was crushed when we found out about your parents, but the rest of us felt it, too. He risked so much to find out what happened to them."

"So did all of you," Bryce gave credit where it was due. "None of you had to assist him, but I'm thankful you did."

"Dan has this way of making us feel safe," Luke said. "It's almost like he was born for this, it comes so naturally to him."

Before their conversation could continue, a commotion emerged near the front gate as the two sentries on guard spotted something outside the walls and began calling out for backup. Bryce and Luke joined several people who emerged from their houses to check on the situation, reaching the gate within a minute.

Despite the two guards trying to prevent him from looking beyond the gate, Bryce brushed past them, peering beyond the iron bars.

"It's Mullins," he said, finding the man approaching the community in reasonably good condition.

Hearing the words, one of the sentries appeared to remember the man from his brief stay in the community. He opened the gate doors without waiting for permission, or McAllister's blessing. Mullins nodded his thanks to the guard as he walked inside, seeing more residents emerge from their assigned houses.

"Did you get your answers?" Bryce asked immediately.

"I did," Mullins replied. "We can talk about that later. Right now, we have a bigger problem."

"What's that?" Luke asked.

"The military released Hewitt."

"They did *what?*" Bryce questioned as his eyes widened with surprise.

"It turns out he doesn't have what you and your brother do," Mullins relayed to the two men, "so they weren't about to provide food and lodging."

"I'm confused," Bryce said. "I saw my brother cut him with contaminated blood on that sword."

"The tip of that sword may not have had the blood on it," Mullins explained. "They tested Hewitt, and he doesn't have any immunity."

"Fuck," Bryce muttered. "That maniac could be anywhere. When did they release him?"

"The day before they cut me loose."

"And when was that?"

"Three or four days ago."

Exasperated, Bryce walked away from the others, trying to collect his thoughts.

"If he had that kind of head start, maybe he slinked off somewhere," Luke surmised.

"Or to the Adirondacks," Bryce reasoned. "Who knows what he has in mind, but he's going to want revenge."

Luke appeared deep in thought momentarily before he asked Mullins a question.

"Did you happen to see Kevin Gebbert on your way back?"

"I didn't see one living soul," Mullins replied, shaking his head negatively. "Not even the military."

Giving a sigh, Luke couldn't mask his concern, even if Gebbert wasn't the most popular person in the community.

"We have to warn McAllister," Bryce determined aloud. "Even if it means he blames me, or our friends, we can't have these folks oblivious to the danger he poses."

"How can we be certain he's coming here?" Mullins questioned. "Even for me, finding my way back here wasn't easy."

Bryce suspected Hewitt calculated any number of moves that benefitted him and brought harm to those who wronged him. If the man wanted to find his way back, he would in time.

"There aren't many places like this once you're west of the Hampton Roads," Bryce deduced. "He's probably coming here, and it's only a matter of time before he locates the community."

"That's not good," Luke stated flatly.

"No," Bryce agreed. "It's not."

Unfortunately, several residents overheard their discussion, and Bryce wasn't sure which of them would tell McAllister first. If the unofficial mayor felt threatened before, this new revelation would certainly infuriate him. Bryce debated whether to take his family and leave immediately, or stick it out and await the consequences. He imagined McAllister would save himself future headaches by turning the family over to the military, but Bryce decided he wanted to stick around to help inform, and possibly defend, the community from whatever Hewitt planned for the residents.

Misfortune seemed to follow their entire group to Maplewood, and now the residents were placed directly in the line of fire if Hewitt chose to pick them off a few at a time when they went out for supplies. He murdered more than a few dozen people in central New York simply because they threatened to dwindle his food and supplies. Someone who killed so indiscriminately, so selfishly, wouldn't hesitate to kill again. Bryce couldn't pretend to know the man's motivations, but he suspected Hewitt hadn't begun an attack on the populace *only* because he wanted to scope out the village first.

Once he knew their routines, and any direct threats to him, Hewitt would attack at will if he had indeed remained in Virginia.

When the group appeared ready to disperse, Mullins looked to Bryce.

"What's wrong?" the fugitive military man asked.

"When I said I didn't see anyone on the way back here, that wasn't exactly true," Mullins confessed.

"Why didn't you say anything before?"

"What I have is for your ears only," Mullins said, pulling a slightly tattered piece of paper from his pants pocket. "It's possible we have other trouble coming this way."

Chapter 21

Bryce didn't wrestle with the decision to tell McAllister about the potential danger for very long, and within the hour, the leader of Maplewood knew. It turned out he knew even before Bryce informed him, which made the decision that much better in the Navy officer's mind. Although displeased, McAllister didn't take immediate action, and actually left most of the community running in its typical fashion.

Before daylight broke the following morning, Bryce heard a knock at the door of the house where he and his family were staying. Already up and dressed, Bryce walked downstairs to answer the door, finding only McAllister on the other side. He immediately figured he and the other newcomers were about to be ousted at best, turned over to the military at worst.

"Have you received word from your brother?" the unofficial mayor asked.

"A few days ago," Bryce answered. "They were unsuccessful in New Mexico."

"Unsuccessful?"

Bryce treaded carefully while formulating his answer, because he didn't want McAllister worrying that every turn presented a trap in the apocalypse, though it felt that way sometimes.

"The bunker there was abandoned," he said, telling a partial truth.

McAllister nodded, though he didn't look certain he was being told everything he wanted to know.

"Father Paul has approached me about taking a group out for fishing and hunting as our fresh food supply is getting low. He knows the truth, and he's willing to risk his well-being to go out there anyway."

"And you think I should go with him, because indirectly, I'm the reason we're all in danger."

"Something like that, yes."

"I agree," Bryce said immediately. "I only ask that you protect my family while I'm out there."

"That, we can do. Without creating a panic, I've beefed up security around here, and we're going to have a community meeting tonight."

Bryce drew a deep breath, wondering what the tone of the meeting would be.

"I can promise you this," he said. "If I see Hewitt out there, I won't hesitate to do what needs to be done."

"I would expect nothing less."

Father Paul had approached the house, though he remained several paces behind McAllister, as though trying to avoid the appearance of eavesdropping.

"I could use a few extra hands for fishing," Father Paul informed McAllister. "We could probably double our haul, and Sister Rosa already volunteered."

McAllister stared at the priest momentarily while he weighed the options. Bryce wondered if he considered the Catholics a flight risk, but said nothing.

"Take her with you," McAllister finally said. "And take Samuel. It's about time to see if he can be integrated into the population."

Samuel Brown had been virtually imprisoned since pursuing Timmons with a shotgun, and isolated with only occasional visits from those who brought him meals, or chatted with him momentarily. Bryce wasn't quite certain why the man was treated like a pariah when he technically did nothing wrong. His wife blatantly attempted to cheat on him, and Timmons was nearly collateral damage.

Bryce thought McAllister sounded almost calculating and robotic in his assessment of Brown and the situation as a whole. When McAllister left a moment later, Bryce looked to the priest with a knowing smirk, and Father Paul appeared to understand that neither of them were McAllister's biggest fans.

"Give me a minute, Padre," Bryce requested before heading inside to speak with Isabella.

Both she and Nathan remained in bed, so he knelt down beside her and lightly kissed her forehead, waking her.

"Where are you heading this time?" she asked quietly to avoid waking Nathan.

"Doing some gathering with Father Paul," he answered. "We should only be a few hours, but keep Nathan close."

"Worried about Hewitt?"

"I'm worried about us staying here," Bryce admitted. "Keep a close watch on everyone."

"Always do."

"That's why I love you," he said, kissing her cheek before heading out of the room, prepared to start his day.

***

Using one of the two vehicles parked inside the community, the foursome spent the first five minutes in awkward silence as Bryce sat in the back of the sedan beside Father Paul while Sister Rosa drove. Apparently deciding someone needed to break the silence, the priest addressed Samuel Brown as they headed for a nearby pond.

"Samuel, have you been doing alright?"

"I wouldn't call how I've been treated 'alright,' Father."

"How do you mean?"

"I've been locked up and treated like a criminal after my wife strayed on me."

"Samuel, you *did* go after a man with a shotgun."

Brown contemplated his answer momentarily.

"Karen broke biblical law, Father. Does that not supersede all other laws?"

"We're all subject to God's word, my son. I'm personally glad you didn't break one of his commandments that fateful night, or we would've had a much worse situation on our hands."

"I've had some time to think on it, Father," Brown said from the front seat without turning around. "I blame Karen, not the stranger she lured into our bed. In part, I blame myself for not being the man Karen wants me to be."

Father Paul reached forward, placing a compassionate hand on Brown's shoulder.

"My son, don't go changing who you are to satisfy anyone else. God loves you just the way you are."

"Truth be told, I'm just glad to be out of that house, and out of Maplewood for a little bit. I was going stir crazy."

"For what it's worth, I'm sorry we brought trouble to your doorstep," Bryce said.

"I don't blame any of you," Brown replied, sounding somewhat defeated. "McAllister plays favorites, and I'm definitely not *that*."

When they reached the pond, Bryce was impressed by the area because it offered a few old docks, several large trees for shade, and the path used to drive from the road to the nearby field remained smooth. Most everything else around them looked overgrown, and he could tell mosquitos would certainly be a problem later in the year. Stealing a glance at the pond, he noticed tiny air bubbles along the surface, and a few minor splashes, indicating fish were active below.

Bryce waited until everyone began unloading fishing poles and tackle from the trunk before asking the question that weighed on his mind.

"I get the impression a lot of you aren't happy with McAllister's leadership, so why stay? Or why not replace him?"

"He has support," Brown answered, openly unafraid of additional consequences. He likely trusted the two Catholics in his presence, and probably didn't consider Bryce the type to blab. "His leadership is built on promises of protection from what's out there. Only a few of us step beyond the walls to do the real work, and if a few of us don't make it back, he won't lose much sleep. We aren't his golden residents."

"Is that true?" Bryce asked, looking to the sister and the priest.

Neither answered with words, but their deflecting glances and uncomfortable postures indicated they agreed with Brown.

"He's not necessarily an evil man," Brown conceded, "but he rules by instilling fear, and keeping just enough residents on his side."

"Politics," Bryce muttered.

"Exactly."

After a few minutes, each of them had cast their lines, using worms caught by the children within the community in recent days. Father Paul made mention that they brought a few manmade lures, but a few had been lost before winter the previous year, and they couldn't afford to lose many more.

Possibly done on purpose, Father Paul and Sister Rosa left Bryce fishing beside Brown, as though knowing the two men needed to speak.

"Look, I'm truly sorry about what happened when we arrived," Bryce said.

"What's done is done," Brown said calmly. "Things weren't great in my marriage before you arrived. The apocalypse might have saved me from divorce, or at least some tough life lessons."

Within a few minutes, Brown tugged at his line when he felt resistance from the opposite end. He likely snared a fish as he began reeling at a fevered pace, showing some fishing prowess.

"Done this before?" Bryce inquired.

"Yeah," Brown answered with a bit of strain in his voice as he continued to battle whatever took the bait.

A moment later, Brown pulled the fish from the surface, eyeing it with some admiration. Bryce appreciated the size of the fish, placing it around fifteen inches in length. It might save a handful of people in the village from rations, or the same old canned goods for an evening. Glistening in the sun that finally peered through some clouds, the fish continued to struggle as Brown held it up for a closer examination. Its distinctive olive-green coloring along the upper half shimmered in the sunlight, and the bass's strength soon faded just before Brown dropped it into a five-gallon bucket.

"I married into money," Brown said, looking directly at Bryce. "My wife has always ruled the roost, but recently she's taken things beyond treating me like the hired help."

"There had to be happier times," Bryce said, thinking about the sacrifices Isabella made being a military wife.

"There were," Brown admitted. "I grew up working on farms, including one her folks owned, and she was fascinated with that life. None of her flings could ride a horse, or fish, or use a firearm for more than shooting at paper plates. So, against the wishes of her parents, she eventually married me."

"I'll bet family gatherings were a joy."

"They didn't exactly put out the welcome mat," Brown said, preparing his line for the next cast. With ease, he hooked a worm, and used a professional-looking technique to cast the line into the pond for another round.

"How dangerous is this Hewitt guy everyone keeps talking about?" Brown asked once the hook pierced the surface and plunged downward.

"The worst," Bryce answered. "He's killed at least two dozen we know about, and twice we thought we were free of him."

"How does a man wipe out that many people himself?"

"It's a game to him. He wants all of the supplies for himself, so he picks off a village one or two at a time until he claims everything inside."

"A village like Maplewood?" Brown asked with concern written on his face.

"He's targeted less organized camps in the past," Bryce answered. "That's not to say he wouldn't attack your people to get back at me and my brother."

"Sounds like we might be finding out sooner than later if he's got something in store," Brown noted.

Such thoughts had already crossed Bryce's mind, but he also knew if Hewitt got within range of a firearm, the lieutenant commander wouldn't hesitate to fire every round into the man's torso and skull.

He cast his own line, feeling a bit more uneasy about the return trip to Maplewood.

***

After locating two vehicles in Ruidoso that worked, and possessed ample fuel reserves, the group headed east to the next airport Timmons considered their best bet. The van ran out of fuel after only twenty minutes due to a faulty fuel gauge, and after they all climbed into a car not meant to hold six adults, and luggage, they traveled less than fifteen minutes before smoke billowed from the engine compartment.

After that, the group walked along the highway toward the next destination, wallowing in their misfortune. When dusk drew near, they began looking for some shelter for the evening, traveling light, and spotting only occasional undead adversaries. All of this transpired the previous day, and as Sutton awoke just before dawn, he found Gracine beside him in the bed of a motel room. Although the roadside motel wasn't anything fancy, with remnants of a pool behind it, dust covering virtually every piece of furniture, and not one scrap of food, it did provide shelter.

Metzger and Jillian took one of the fourteen available rooms, and Gracine and Sutton took another, because they both knew they needed to talk out a few of their issues. Both discovered they were too tired to talk, and ended up falling asleep after securing the room against the undead and potential invaders.

"You awake?" Sutton asked, knowing dawn was coming soon.

"You know I am," Gracine answered.

Despite there being two beds in the room, they shared a queen-size bed, though they did so platonically upon Gracine's request.

Sutton draped his arm around her to test the waters of their relationship. She hesitated a few seconds before brushing it off and rolling over, facing away from him.

"I was a fool," Sutton said, spouting his confession before he even consciously knew what he was doing. "And I was hurting."

"You can't just turn us off and on like a light switch," Gracine said softly. "I wanted to be something more to you, and you shoved me away like you do everyone else."

"I lost my son," Sutton said, his voice more neutral than he intended. "I wasn't in a good place."

"I tried to be there for you," Gracine said, rolling over so their faces were mere inches apart. "There are times where I feel like I've known you since childhood, and others where it feels like we met yesterday. You've got to decide what you want from life, whatever life is these days."

Sutton exhaled through his nose.

"I want us to give it a try. A real try."

"I'm with Reggie."

"Fuck Reggie." Sutton paused. "Figuratively."

Gracine grinned, placing her index finger across Sutton's lips.

"I promised him I would wait. I'm not one to go back on my word."

"How long do you think he'll wait for you? A day? Maybe two?"

"Now you're just reverting to Mean Colby."

"More like Realist Colby," he countered.

Gracine felt warm beside him, and the thin blankets they found in various hotel rooms, and just off the main lobby, did little to keep him from freezing when the overnight temperatures dipped drastically. Sharing body heat helped them ward off the near freezing temperatures. Sutton fought off the beginning stages of an erection, thinking of any and everything else to keep his instincts from taking over.

"What's the matter?" Gracine inquired, being coy as her hands rubbed along his torso, heading south from there.

"Don't you be teasing me," Sutton insisted, his voice just above a low growl.

"Reggie already thinks we're fucking, Colby."

"Then let's justify his suspicions," Sutton said, reaching for the button-up shirt Gracine had worn so she didn't have to sleep in the nude.

She clasped his hands, keeping them at bay.

"We both know Reggie is just a placeholder," Sutton said, not content to cease his attempts at winning Gracine.

"You're awful sure of yourself, Colby."

"I know I was stupid for putting this off for so long."

"Now I'm forbidden fruit, and you just can't stand it."

Sutton freed his hands and glided them from the sides of her torso downward. Gracine didn't fight him this time, and he felt certain she was about to let him consummate the relationship they both desired for months. Gracine finally gave in, leaning in to kiss him deeply, letting down all barriers as Sutton wondered where his wallet might be. Strangely, he continued to carry it, with a sealed condom inside, for just such an occasion.

He began unbuttoning her shirt as they both breathed heavily, and Gracine moaned in anticipation of finally being a couple. As Sutton reached the final button, however, a knock came to their door, followed by Metzger's voice.

"It's dawn," he said from the other side of the door. "We need to get moving."

Instantly, the moment died between Sutton and Gracine, and slowly, both began reaching for their warmer clothing to face the cooler elements outside.

Neither could bring themselves to words, because they both knew what nearly happened, and what such an act meant for their relationship going forward. Now, they weren't exactly sure where they stood, because more danger surely awaited them in Wyoming, and a return home to Reggie Mitchell, and Maplewood, if they survived that.

A nagging feeling that something horrific would happen in Wyoming weighed on Sutton's mind, and he knew he couldn't protect everyone at all times.

Nadeau wasn't going to be easy prey, and he wondered if Brooke truly knew what she was doing based on her knocking over a few safehouses. Sitting on the edge of the bed after putting on some pants, he began tying the tactical boots he had worn since joining the Maplewood collective.

He questioned if everything that led up to this moment was worthwhile, and if they would actually receive the answers they wanted. More importantly, would those answers protect their loved ones going forward?

Chapter 22

Mid-September, The Previous Year

"How do we play this?" Canfield asked nervously from the driver's seat of the current car he and Brooke were taking into Elkton, Kentucky.

"We play it like we're supposed to be here, John," Brooke answered, feeling unusually calm, despite the danger of interacting with a Nadeau loyalist.

She wanted answers to the difficult questions, like why these people followed Nadeau, how they were compensated, and what paths led her to the man who caused the world so much trouble.

"We have to fake it until we make it," Brooke said, knowing the sheet gave little information beyond the safehouse coordinates.

"That doesn't sound reassuring," Canfield noted.

"Look, there probably isn't a VIP list, or reservations for this kind of thing. If he asks, you're Rupert Clarke and I'm your girlfriend."

"Ugh," Canfield groaned. "That name makes me sound like some dignitary from England."

"Well, the man was an asshole who knew the world was ending, if that helps you get into character."

"I can be an asshole," Canfield conceded.

"I'm aware."

"Hey," Canfield said, feigning emotional hurt as their car reached the edge of town. He quickly recovered to ask a question. "How do we know where these coordinates lead?"

"I just know it's somewhere in this town," Brooke said, deciding their journey wouldn't take much longer because downtown was comprised of only a handful of paved streets.

She spotted a downtown strip with several stores, pointing for Canfield to drive in that direction. Brooke hardly expected a welcome wagon when they located the building, and any contact was likely going to act as a sentry, not giving away his or her spot to random strangers. Brooke stared at the sheet of paper in her hand, knowing it was the only thing that might buy her an audience with Nadeau's lacky.

Only a few cars remained within town limits, and Brooke grew concerned that no one survived to eliminate the half dozen undead wandering the streets. No signs of anyone living presented themselves to the couple safely tucked inside their vehicle. Almost immediately, the dead took notice of movement and sound, targeting the car as they staggered after it.

"Let's try those buildings over there," Brooke said, pointing to three brick buildings, all painted slightly different variations of brown, representing local businesses less than two months prior.

"They have two levels," Canfield noticed aloud. "Better vantage point."

"You're getting the hang of this."

Brooke had noticed some churches in town, but people would still go to a church to pray for forgiveness, or an end to the hell surrounding them. She knew if she were a watchdog, she would want a vantage point, and the ability to hear and see everything around her. Each of the buildings also provided ample space for living quarters, and access to the main drag, and beyond, in case a need to flee arose.

"If someone is here, they've already spotted us," Brooke said as Canfield parked the car in front of the trio of adjoining brick buildings.

"We have to take out the dead heads," Canfield said. "Don't want them sneaking up on us."

"Agreed."

When they emerged from the car, both of them set to eliminating the nearby undead. Canfield used his bat more effectively than ever, and Brooke opted to use a knife, despite having to stand dangerously close to their predatory adversaries. Her boyfriend had adapted quickly to using the bat in various portions of their skulls for easy kill shots. Where her doubts lingered, however, was in his ability to be fierce against the living. As a coach, Canfield fought valiantly for his players, getting ejected sometimes, and occasionally cussing out umpires to fire up the team. Brooke needed that kind of spirit backing her, not because she required protection, but because the people they were about to face weren't merciful. If Canfield didn't believe in her, or her mission, his lack of focus might get them killed.

Blood in liquid and coagulated forms flew through the air, and both she and Canfield stood tall a few minutes later, their clothes barely stained by the red substance as they had learned to avoid getting blood on themselves for safety reasons.

Brooke stared upward at the brick buildings, hoping to spot someone looking through a window at them, but she saw no one step aside to hide, or a curtain whisked to one side. She began to wonder if Elkton was a wasted stop, but she possessed no other leads, and they had literally just stepped foot in the small town.

"Let's try the doors," she said, opting for the front door to the middle building while Canfield tried opening the front door to her left.

Both found their doors locked, which Brooke actually found promising. She walked toward the building to her right, which had painted red bricks, almost the color of blood. Formerly a drug store, this building already had the front door kicked in, allowing her to take a few steps inside. Brooke found the store heavily looted, and only a few knickknacks randomly strewn across the floor, like paper products and holiday items.

"Someone's been through here," Canfield noted, his voice trailing off as he spoke the words.

"I doubt this place had much to begin with," Brooke added.

Brooke walked through the store, looking for access to the upstairs, because each of the three brick business buildings had second stories that appeared to be residential. She didn't find an access to the upstairs from within the store, which meant the apartments to each building likely had staircases around the back. She picked up a doll from the shelf, staring at it momentarily, wishing her childhood provided her with a bit more innocence.

And toys. She felt as though she had been trained for government work from the moment she joined her foster family.

Canfield walked over to her, beginning to reach for her arm, but Brooke snapped out of her brief trance and collected herself.

"We need to go around back."

A few minutes later, they found a staircase along the back of each brick building.

"We shouldn't separate," Canfield said, clearly worried about Brooke falling victim to some kind of trap.

"This won't take long," she said before ascending the first set of stairs to find the door unlocked.

A quick look inside revealed a ransacked apartment with items strewn across the floors in multiple rooms. There wasn't enough room inside to reside beyond the mess, and Brooke knew any surviving sentry wouldn't leave the door unlocked at any given time. People in Nadeau's network were carefully chosen, and they wouldn't betray his trust.

She brushed past Canfield, who had come up the stairs in case she found trouble, heading to the next apartment while surveying her surroundings. No other dead wandered through the area, and considering the size of the town, Brooke didn't feel surprised. In the recesses of her mind, she began to doubt she would find Nadeau's contact, leaving her to a life of escorting Canfield to Texas with no other objectives. She didn't know a life without orders, or directions, and the thought of simply settling down at some makeshift camp to survive as long as possible nauseated her. Coasting along while the maniac who decimated the world continued to live ate away at her. Brooke couldn't believe that no one from *any* government knew what Nadeau had planned before his chemicals started a lethal chain of events.

"This is going to be it," Canfield said as they approached the middle stairway, leading Brooke to think he was being falsely optimistic.

After ascending the stairwell, Canfield took the initiative and reached for the doorknob, surprised when the door flung inward before them. Both he and

Brooke were confronted by a shotgun, and a young man with an angry countenance behind it.

Two distinctive scars lined his face, one on either side, and he possessed a beard that could be termed a week of stubble. His head appeared evenly buzzed along every side, and Brooke noticed yet another lengthy scar along the right side. Not at all what she expected, this man appeared to be in his early twenties, and certainly not battle tested before the apocalypse. As Canfield took a step back, she confidently held her ground, prepared to play the part until she hit a snag.

"Rupert Clarke, and guest," she said, motioning toward Canfield, then herself.

Now the man gave them a puzzled stare in return.

"We just got in from Indiana."

Appearing skeptical, the man motioned for them to wait a moment and slammed the door shut.

"That isn't reassuring," Canfield mumbled.

"He's probably checking a roster, John."

"How the hell could a network this big exist?"

Brooke shrugged, giving him a look that indicated they should keep quiet.

When the door opened a second time, the man held the shotgun in one hand, and a paper list in the other.

"You don't look like a Rupert," he commented, aiming the shotgun downward this time as he studied Canfield from head to toe.

"I go by John these days," Canfield said without missing a beat. "My parents liked British spy movies back in the day."

Now the stranger provided a glance that didn't divulge his thoughts in the least. Brooke couldn't see much of the apartment behind the man, and her curiosity grew about what kind of accommodations Nadeau's followers were given. Perhaps they chose their own specific hiding spots, or the man placed them before he unleashed his chemicals on the masses that fateful, late summer day.

Canfield started to push forward, thinking they were in the clear, but the man held up his free hand, still clutching the shotgun.

"Not so fast, partner," he said. "Password."

"Password?" Brooke asked, unable to contain all of her surprise, thinking they were about to be exposed as frauds and possibly murdered.

Blocking the door, the man remained deadpan serious another few seconds before finally cracking a smile.

"I'm just fucking with you. Come on in."

Canfield looked at Brooke warily, as though he still didn't trust the sentry. Truth be told, she didn't either. She felt as though the man might be stalling, though she doubted help was anywhere nearby. Regardless of his intentions, she intended to remain vigilant and scope out his quarters the best she could. Canfield tightened his grip on the bat, as though ready to swing away at the first sign of trouble, but Brooke gently put her palm atop his closest hand.

She stepped inside first, finding the apartment rather spacious, and far neater than she originally envisioned. The first room she passed appeared to be furnished as though designed to be an office space with filing cabinets, a computer, and some other electronics. Brooke immediately questioned if the underlings possessed means other than sat phones to communicate with Nadeau, and possibly alternative power sources that kept the lights on.

In addition to the office, a stocked kitchenette provided a place to cook and eat, and a bedroom with neatly-tucked sheets and a blanket had a feeling of home with some posters, books, and even a record player. Brooke noticed a second bedroom farther down the hall with the lights off and a bunkbed barely visible. Their host stopped in the kitchenette, pulling some paperwork from his back pocket before looking at his guests.

"I was kidding about the password," he said, "but something still bothers me about you two."

"What's that?" Canfield asked without tightening his grip on the bat this time.

"The fact that you said 'and guest' without saying your own name," the sentry answered, looking stonily at Brooke.

Her mind raced for an explanation about how she worded the phrase, but the sentry appeared to be done with any pleasantries.

Canfield reacted first, thrusting the business-end of his bat upward as the man went to raise the shotgun in Brooke's direction. A shot fired into the ceiling as the man yowled in pain with nails and spikes immediately penetrating the underside of his right hand. Canfield didn't pry the bat loose before he charged the man, pinning the shotgun barrel away from any of them, and shoving the man against the wall. Now Brooke drew her semi-automatic to back him up, taking aim at the man who couldn't budge the larger Canfield to free himself.

Brooke expected the sentry to react to the bat lodged in the bottom of his hand in horror because fresh blood from the undead created red cobwebs between the nails and other sharp objects *before* piercing his flesh. Perhaps the pain shooting through his hand kept him distracted, and not thinking about anything beyond that moment, but Brooke questioned why he wasn't in sheer terror at the notion of a slow death that led to reanimation.

"Keep him subdued," she told Canfield, who continued to press the man against the wall.

"Subdued?"

"Yeah. Tie him up, or knock him out."

Now the man really began to struggle, but Canfield quickly grew irritated and as Brooke walked down the hall. She heard what sounded like a punch, followed by a thud. She assumed Canfield followed through with her request, and if not, the gun in her hand would definitely put the sentry on the ground. She heard the sound of Canfield's voice behind her, reassuring her that he was a capable ally during her pursuit of information.

"He's going to wake up eventually."

"Only if we let him," Brooke answered. "We may not need him for answers if he was careless and left information lying around."

"I'm not a murderer," Canfield said, raising his voice as he took a step down the hallway.

"John, you're going to have to reinvent yourself, or we aren't going to make it far."

She stopped, turning to face him.

"Killing the dead is one thing," he said, "but I don't want murder on my conscience."

"Fine. I'll take care of it when the time comes."

He gave her a look of complete loss, like he didn't know her any longer, or ever, and she supposed that stemmed from her own actions.

"Just tie him up and help me look for information," Brooke said. "We'll cross the other bridge when we reach it."

Canfield didn't appear content with the impending task of dealing with the sentry, but he began searching for the means to keep the man subdued. In the meantime, Brooke began rifling through every piece of furniture that might contain paperwork. She chose to save the electronic devices for last, because they were likely password protected, and their owner wasn't any help at the moment.

Locating some zip ties in a nearby drawer, Canfield secured the sentry's hands behind his back. Instead of helping search for answers, however, he approached Brooke, which hindered her search.

"I'm not sure I can do this," he said.

"Do what?" Brooke asked, lifting her eyes from some documents inside a filing cabinet.

"*This.* You keep pushing forward like some kind of robot, letting nothing slow you down. These are living people you're talking about exterminating once you have what you need."

"Those were living people in Indiana, too, John. They were sick. They were dying because of what people like this asshole did. Maybe you haven't lost enough people in your life to feel the impact, but there are *millions* out there who won't see their family members ever again."

"I'm aware of that."

"Are you? I thought we cleared this hurdle already, but we can't leave anyone alive to warn Nadeau that people are tracking him down."

Canfield didn't appear content, but he seemed to accept the cold nature of Brooke's mission.

"I'll see if I can tackle the computer and the tablet," he said.

Nearly half an hour passed and Brooke hadn't located any paperwork that indicated what the sentry would tell visitors about their next phase of the journey to find Nadeau and his apocalyptic utopia. She walked out of one of the spare rooms, finding Canfield lounging on a chair with his feet propped atop an ottoman that matched the chair. He held the tablet, casually flicking his finger along the screen.

"I thought you said the tablet and the computer were password protected."

"The computer still is, but I used our friend's fingerprint to access this thing," Canfield reported. "I'm checking the files to see if there's anything useful in here."

Brooke started to ask for the tablet, but she decided that trusting Canfield to look for information might mend some of their recent issues. She couldn't ask for his assistance only to undermine him at every turn, as though he wasn't capable of carrying out everyday tasks. Canfield used tablets constantly in the baseball world, and he knew how to dig around their files. She decided to crack the computer, because it provided their last chance at locating information before she resorted to torture.

She spent a few minutes bypassing the password by starting the computer in safe mode and using some tricks the government taught her to bypass the computer's security. Brooke had just reached the main screen, feeling a tingle in her spine as she anticipated finding answers. Her fingers reached for the keyboard as Canfield filled the room's doorway with his cagy grin, holding the tablet.

"What?" she inquired neutrally, anticipating a roundabout sex inquiry.

"Jackpot."

Brooke virtually jumped from her seat and took his side, seeing where he had located a folder containing three documents inside that appeared to be snapped with the tablet's camera option.

"Someone didn't read the documents and destroy them as instructed," she said as she zoomed in on one of the photos.

Within five minutes she knew the next portion of their journey, and exactly what the man was supposed to tell approved visitors to the safehouse. She still didn't know a few other details that weighed on the back of her mind. Because the sentry was awake, and sitting upright, she decided to inquire about her concerns before deciding his fate.

"I can't believe you didn't destroy the documents," Brooke said to him, holding the tablet up so he could see that they bypassed his weak security measures.

"There's too much to remember," the sentry confessed almost casually. "And you two are the fourth and fifth people I've seen this entire time."

Brooke took a seat on the ground in front of him, looking him in the eye.

"One thing has bothered me this entire time," she confessed. "Nadeau had to recruit all of you before he killed off most of the planet. How did he contact you, and why did no one alert the government before the bombs went off?"

"In your narrow view of the world, I'm sure you think we were all sheep who fell for some lies, or got brainwashed with promises of riches and survival, but the truth is we were the ones looking for someone like him to lead us into the future."

"What kind of future is *this*?" Brooke inquired with a hardened tone.

"One without pollution, or overpopulation, or the extinction of another animal species every single day. Politicians can say what they want about global warming, or climate change, but *we, people*, are the cause of our own demise."

"So, you're a tree hugger," Canfield stated stonily.

"I'm a realist. The few times people have been trapped inside for a week or two when pandemics or a weather crisis kept them there, we saw ponds clear up, oceans turn blue, and air quality improve tenfold. Earth needed us to push the reset button."

"And Nadeau recruited like-minded people like you?" Brooke asked.

Now the sentry scoffed.

"Hundreds of us, probably thousands, wanted to see this done a long time ago. We hid in the shadows, powerless because we didn't have the finances, or the numbers to pull off any plan of significance. Nadeau simply provided us with the means to make a change."

"There's no way in hell a network like that could remain secret," Canfield grumbled.

"How long were you supposed to remain posted here?" Brooke inquired.

"Until the first day of April, next year," the sentry answered.

Brooke decided he would readily answer questions, so long as they didn't compromise his overall objective and loyalty to Nadeau. She suspected Nadeau communicated with them, using backdoor web access, and providing them with assignments, but never major details in case one of them wanted to alert the authorities. Based on the fact that no one ever came forward made her wonder if they were all loyal to the end.

"Do you know where Nadeau is hiding?" Brooke finally asked, already suspecting the truth based on what she found.

"Lady, I doubt *any* of us know where he really is. He isn't stupid, and he couldn't take any chances that some of us weren't government moles."

"He's just about outlived his usefulness," Canfield said, obviously changing his mind about violence against the living in the short time they conversed with the sentry.

"Do you have kids?" the sentry asked Canfield, looking directly at him.

"Yes."

"It's conceivable that within their lifetime, this planet might have been uninhabitable. If your kids survived, at least they have a clean world to look forward to."

Canfield took a step forward, but Brooke intercepted him, realizing how little was required for him to take her side on the matter. Even so, she needed the sentry to answer several more questions before she took Canfield to their next destination.

"I need a minute, John," she said quietly, leaning in close to his right ear.

Canfield said nothing, opting to do an about-face and exit the apartment through the sole doorway.

"I don't care about your politics, or your view of how mankind has brought our planet to the brink of extinction," she said, turning her attention to the sentry, who remained seated on the floor. "I want to know if you're in communication with others like you, and what password I need to know going forward."

Now the man provided a knowing smile, because he wasn't going to answer her questions, and they both knew it.

"I'm dead no matter how this goes," he said. "We accomplished what needed to be done, and there's no way I'm selling out the people who helped me."

"Answers are the only thing that can keep you living from this point forward. Otherwise, I won't have a choice but to end you."

"Let me save you the trouble."

Brooke heard a clicking sound from within the man's mouth, and she immediately knew he had taken measures to end his own life. She suspected some form of cyanide pill, which sounded old-school comparatively, but apparently still worked, because the man began foaming at the mouth slightly and convulsing as he slumped to the floor. His face struck hard, and his eyes remained wide-open.

She didn't attempt to stop the process, or save him, because she knew nothing could be done under current circumstances to keep him alive.

"Fuck," she muttered, feeling as though extremely little was accomplished after coming such a long way.

If future encounters went much the same, she would never find Nadeau.

Brooke spent a few minutes collecting the necessary items for the next portion of their journey. She crossed the threshold, closed the door behind her, and found Canfield taking out his pent-up frustrations on a few undead who dared cross paths with him in the streets below. He couldn't hit a ball well enough to make a major league roster, but the man knew how to cave in skulls with a baseball bat. She approached him, eyeing the two shattered, bloody skulls near his feet from the brief skirmish.

"The nerve of that dickhead," Canfield muttered, speaking of the sentry. "I would've liked to have done this to him."

"You're too late for that."

Canfield provided a quizzical stare, as though inquiring whether Brooke ended the man's life so quickly.

"I thought you had more questions for him."

"Turns out he didn't feel much like answering. He used a pill to kill himself."

"That's a shame," Canfield said without a shred of remorse. "Where to next?"

"Well, we're definitely heading south to reunite you with your family. Let's find some fuel and I'll read these documents. I think there were several options."

"Options can mean dead-ends."

"It's the risk we run, John. This whole thing might be for nothing."

"You act as though you have a personal stake in this," Canfield noted. "I'm not sure you'll ever find what you're looking for, even if you find Nadeau."

Brooke wondered if the risks involved with completing her task outweighed the possibility of finding a long-term survival solution momentarily. She reminded herself that Nadeau might have other attacks planned, and that locating him might provide them with a solution to ending their undead problem. Perhaps the science involved with creating them also meant providing a vaccine to his allies who remained in the field.

"He's dangerous, John," she told her boyfriend. "I may be one of the few people left who know the details of what he's done."

"Who's to say he doesn't swallow some pill when you reach him? If these people are fanatics, he may be from the same mold."

"It's bad enough having to look over our shoulders for the infected, and survivors who mean us harm," Brooke reasoned aloud, "but I want him eliminated so we don't have yet another worry looming over us."

Canfield gave an easy sigh, touching her chin gently.

"Then let's get some fuel and head in a southerly direction."

Chapter 23

As a commander in the United States Navy, Mark Dascher expected to follow an array of different orders without question, but the latest request from his superiors baffled him somewhat. Standing in the middle of a road west of Naval Station Norfolk, Dascher possessed a backpack with some rations, a knife, and a 9mm Ruger with a few extra magazines. He wore civilian clothing, and carried nothing with him to indicate he worked for the government. A map remained folded and pocketed within the backpack, and the only piece of technology he possessed was clutched in his right hand.

"This is fucking stupid," he muttered, not liking the assignment one bit.

For one, it opposed his moral code in two ways. His second argument could be that the military possessed men and women far more capable of carrying out this assignment in the wilderness. Trained to work and live on a ship, Dascher felt completely out of his element, particularly since the day explosions rocked the entire world and brought about the apocalypse.

Unfortunately, the commander was tasked with following Mike Mullins from the military base to wherever the man called home. The military deduced that Mullins knew the Metzger brothers, and almost assuredly Hewitt provided information about them and everyone associated with them. Hewitt probably provided such facts to secure shelter and food going forward, but instead the military kicked him loose. From what little Dascher knew, Hewitt wouldn't hesitate to kill anyone who threatened his food supply, which included the two men the military desperately wanted to locate.

Mullins left on foot, which left the military no viable options to track him without being spotted. Mullins likely knew about their tracking devices, and based on the fact he had stopped several times, changed directions, and moved slowly, the man apparently suspected they would follow him. Because of this, the leaders provided Dascher with a civilian vehicle, namely a black Honda Civic with some dents and a cracked windshield. Fortunately, the base mechanics made certain it ran like a top before releasing it to him, but Dascher couldn't simply drive around searching for Mullins.

For that, he used the drone in his right hand, occasionally sending it skyward to do a thermal search for his quarry. A brief crash course from an Army corporal didn't make him an expert by any means, because he struggled to fly the device accurately. He lamented the fact that they hadn't sent someone else on this particular assignment, but Dascher proved their perfect choice because he knew Bryce Metzger on sight, and this provided him with a backup cover story.

Dascher's crash course was given during the day Mullins stayed at the base, and them keeping him overnight was by design. The commander recalled saying goodbye to his wife and two children, knowing a realistic chance existed that they might not see him again. With Hewitt already released, and the everyday dangers wandering the roads beyond Norfolk, Dascher wasn't sure what to expect. Because his assignment equated to being an undercover cop, he couldn't carry a radio, or have any kind of security detail lingering behind. Liberated and vulnerable at the same time, his thoughts wandered to his son and daughter, who couldn't understand why their father was leaving them for an undisclosed amount of time.

His wife knew his mission wasn't something he could talk about, and she stated that it wasn't fair for the new military regime to send him on something dangerous. Dascher always put on a tough front for his ship personnel, but he couldn't hide the hint of fear in his eyes from his better half. Based on the fact that he wore civilian clothing, and couldn't take any military items with him, she suspected the brass asked him to carry out an assignment outside of his comfort zone.

She wasn't wrong.

Dascher pulled out the remote that controlled the drone. About the size of a cell phone, it allowed him to control everything through a flat touchscreen. Programmed to search for heat signatures within a grid, it required him to provide a direction before it did most of the work. He could override the autopilot feature, and switch the thermal detection to infrared or standard, but he worried that he might not remember how to get it back to the mode he wanted.

Provided with a few spare batteries and some chargers adapted to vehicles, which were readily available beyond the military base, Dascher figured anyone who spotted him would suspect him of being in the military based on the advanced nature of the drone. Dascher wondered if the brass somehow set him up, as though he might be bait to lure Bryce Metzger out of hiding.

Now on solid land, halfway through the Hampton Roads region, Dascher didn't have to worry about bridges, or the sounds of water impairing his hearing. Hampton Roads was comprised of several towns, bodies of water, and the military base, providing tourism and a thriving business district as recently as the previous summer. In the open world, survivors wanted the ability to see and hear everything around them at all times, which made Dascher thankful the incoming tide didn't reach his ears to drown out other sounds.

Standing at the edge of town, near one of the exits, Dascher saw a gas station and several buildings on either side of the street that once housed businesses. Setting the drone down on the concrete, he powered up the controller and sent the device skyward. He let it fly about forty feet overhead, knowing if he kept it too close to the ground that the noise might attract any nearby undead. Thus far, the commander encountered only one threat without a heartbeat and he managed to dodge it easily, walking briskly enough to avoid further contact.

Currently, his car sat several blocks behind him, close enough to use at a moment's notice, but far enough that anyone who saw him walking didn't assume he possessed a car and belongings.

Dascher looked up, barely able to see the drone hovering above him. He glanced at the controller's screen, his eyes looking at the numbers in the corners first, to ensure the drone was running properly and possessed ample battery life. Next, he cycled from the regular camera view to thermal, seeing the screen change in contrast. He saw a yellow figure shaped like a human being against a background of blue and green colors. Dascher believed the figure was him, and he went to maneuver the drone forward to begin scouring the streets of Suffolk when his eyes noticed a second light-colored figure on the screen.

He whirled around, seeing a tall figure standing beside a building, staring a hole through him. His body immediately felt tingly from nerves, because he knew he might be minutes from dying. Details eluded the commander because sunlight and shadows where the man stood forced Dascher to squint. Knowing in an instant that Adam Hewitt meant him harm, Dascher returned his eyes to the drone's controller screen just long enough to push the button for the drone to return to its original position. Glancing up again, he didn't see Hewitt in plain sight any longer, but a look at the controller still indicated a second thermal form nearby.

"Shit," Dascher muttered as the drone dropped down near him, descending too slowly for his taste.

He snagged the drone by its safe underside before it was able to softly touch down, prepared to make haste in a safe direction. Although he didn't particularly value the drone over his own life, Dascher dared not return to the base without the device, if he survived this encounter. With his heart already racing, and his breaths coming nervously, the commander realized he couldn't go back the way he came, because Hewitt effectively blocked his path by standing behind the building extremely close to the road.

Holding the drone in one hand, and the controller in the other, Dascher backed away from where he spied Hewitt, prepared to run if necessary. Rumors of the man's ruthlessness, raw power, and quickness spread through the base upon his arrival because military personnel had little else to do except gossip during their downtime. He considered stuffing both components into his pack and reaching for the sidearm, but Dascher dared not avert his eyes from the buildings and road again.

Fully capable of defending himself in most situations, the Navy commander wouldn't tangle with a man who murdered two dozen people over a long winter. Returning to his family remained his top priority, and with no means to contact the base, he definitely couldn't count on backup. Surveying the area around him quickly, and finding it clear, he stuffed the drone and the remote into the backpack and fumbled for the gun inside a slip pocket. Dascher quickly grew frustrated that he couldn't pull it cleanly from the pack, and as he continued to backpedal towards the safety of town, he failed to notice someone taking a position behind him until he bumped into that person.

Falling to the ground, out of defensive prowess for a few precious seconds to secure the firearm, Dascher pulled the pistol from the bag and aimed it upward at the man silhouetted by the sun.

"Come with me if you want to live," the man said, offering an open hand, but holding a firearm in the other.

Shifting his head to one side, Dascher was able to see the face of Mike Mullins, which beat the alternative of confronting Hewitt. Mullins didn't aim the pistol his way, but kept the firearm in a ready position.

"Shit," the commander muttered, allowing Mullins to help him to his feet.

***

Mullins led Dascher a few blocks away, careful that Hewitt wasn't able to track them. He purposely took a winding path from the military base because he suspected they might send someone to follow him. Despite being a former Army man, Mullins didn't trust the current state of the military, because no one he met during his travels trusted them.

"I'm giving you one chance to give me straight answers," Mullins informed the man he hadn't seen previously. "I know you've been tailing me since I left the base."

"I could be a deserter," the man countered.

"Not likely with the way you conduct yourself out here. You'd have to be looking to get yourself killed."

Now the man gave a long sigh as he stared into the street momentarily. He likely contemplated being truthful with Mullins versus taking his chances against Hewitt.

"My name is Mark Dascher, and I'm a commander in the Navy," the man admitted. "You're not entirely wrong about why I'm out here."

"Some clarification would be nice."

Dascher gave a sigh, sitting on the floor of the hardware store with no front window that the duo settled on for safety. Any tools useful for dispatching the undead were long gone, leaving boxes of nails, canned lubricants, and furnace filters behind, among other less useful items. Dust covered the floor and countertops, and Mullins knew much of it came from skin cells that fell from the dead, or their victims.

A frenzy hit the store at some point, because several sets of footprints disturbed the dust along the floor, and most of the pegboards were hastily stripped of their hooks and items. Some of the items lined the floor, and some were gone altogether, leaving only their plastic and cardboard packaging behind.

Mullins cleared a wooden countertop with a swipe of his arm, sending dust, and various small packages of nails and multi-tip screwdrivers to the ground. He hopped up on the sturdy checkout counter and located a reasonably comfortable position with which to converse with the Navy man.

"I was Bryce Metzger's commanding officer," Dascher revealed.

"And who better to send to locate Bryce," Mullins surmised.

Mullins believed Dascher was indeed part of the military because he remained well-groomed with a cleanly shaved face and a haircut. He also appeared fit and fed, certainly not the type who barely survived, going town to town looking for supplies. On two occasions, Mullins detected a noise overhead while walking, and suspected that someone might be following him, so he deviated his walking pattern several times until he could detect who was tracking him.

"I suppose they thought I was the ideal person to locate Bryce. None of this was my idea. I didn't ask to follow you through the village of the dead."

"So, they asked you to follow me?"

"They thought you were our best shot at finding Bryce, and they didn't want to waste time interrogating you, or send out a whole squad."

Mullins shifted his seated position slightly, finding his hands covered in dust from clasping the countertop.

"You're being awfully forward with this information, Commander."

"I don't want to be out here. I also have a lot of respect for Bryce, so I don't want to sell him out."

"But he can bring a life-saving vaccine to everyone on your base."

"A base that's already safe from the undead threat," Dascher noted. "There's also another reason."

Now Mullins gave the man his full attention.

"I was summoned to meet with the general in charge of our base, and the military on the eastern side of the country," Dascher began. "While I was waiting outside his office, I was told he was on an important call. I didn't think much of it, and everything sounded muffled through the door, but the general kept raising his voice. So, when the lieutenant who serves as his secretary left for a bathroom break, I couldn't resist the temptation to look at the phone and see which line was lit up."

Mullins gave a grin, knowing most military men and women never contemplated such outright betrayals of trust.

"I know what you're thinking," Dascher remarked, shaking his head. "The seed of distrust was planted before this meeting with the general. The upper echelon has their secret meetings, which I'm not privy to, and they appease us by keeping our families safe and feeding us, but they have an agenda. And they still take orders from politicians we never lay eyes on."

"I haven't witnessed much reason to trust them," Mullins revealed.

"No," Dascher said, disappointment showing in his eyes. "All this time I believed in my heart of hearts that my people were searching for Nadeau to bring him to justice, and perhaps find a way to solve our problems. Instead, I overheard a conversation that shook me to my core."

Mullins witnessed a mix of frustration, fury, and fear cross the Navy officer's face as his entire body shook a moment.

"They know," the commander finally stammered. "They *know*."

"Know what?"

"The powers that be are in touch with Nadeau. They have some kind of brokered treaty with him."

"You heard them say this?" Mullins asked, unable to disguise his surprise at the statement.

"McCall, the general in charge, was speaking directly with Nadeau so far as I could tell. I pressed the button on that phone and the gist of it was the military won't pursue Nadeau so long as he doesn't provoke them with more attacks."

"That sounds like a stall tactic on Nadeau's part, if ever I heard one."

"That's what I thought," Dascher said. "And for all I know, they may have people tracking Nadeau as they play along."

"Either way," Mullins thought aloud, "Bryce Metzger may be the answer to their prayers."

"I don't see how Nadeau gets anywhere near the base with his chemicals."

"He may not have to. The particles float through the air, and with the right wind direction, he need only get near the city of Norfolk to infect enough people to begin a chain reaction."

Dascher's head drooped as he realized the true nature of being stuck between a rock and a hard place. He couldn't necessarily trust his employers, and Nadeau could very well finish what he started when the opportunity presented itself.

"I can't lead you to Bryce," Mullins finally said. "I won't. His people took me in, and I wouldn't betray his trust."

Dascher nodded in understanding.

"I'm not asking you to."

He dug through his pack momentarily to pull out a pad of paper and a black ink pen. He spent a moment jotting down three sets of numbers before tearing off the top sheet and handing the scrap paper to Mullins.

"What's this?"

"The number to my satellite phone aboard my ship," Dascher answered. "I usually have it on me. Bryce should have it if he decides to return to the fold, or in case he needs help."

"I'm not sure he has a phone," Mullins answered, though he knew the lieutenant commander possessed a functioning sat phone.

"He has one," Dascher answered. "If he's anything like his brother, he's prepared and has one."

"How do you know Dan has one?"

"Because Dan called the general and gave him a piece of his mind recently. That guy has brass balls."

"What do you mean?" Mullins inquired, furrowing his eyebrows.

"He told McCall he was going to do his job for him and locate Nadeau. I'm pretty sure that's what intensified things around the base recently."

"You seem to know a lot about the general and his dealings," Mullins stated, questioning how a commander became privy to seemingly private conversations.

Dascher grinned.

"One of my fellow officers heard the general blowing off steam about how he'd get back at Dan Metzger and make both brothers pay. I heard he called Dan some choice words in the process."

Mullins felt inclined to believe the Navy commander. If he wasn't legitimate, Dascher possessed some incredible acting skills. Knowing that the military wanted to use him to find Bryce, and that Hewitt remained in the area, he knew he would have to exercise even more caution returning to Maplewood.

As both men attempted to stand, they disturbed dust all around them, finding a thin layer on their hands, and particles floating in the air.

"I have to get back to them," Mullins informed the officer. "Hewitt being out here endangers all of us."

"You can't just leave me," Dascher said, openly fearful of stepping outside alone. "I have a family to get back to, and that maniac would just as soon kill me than look at me."

"You'll be okay if you keep your gun in the open. He doesn't tend to carry weapons."

"I heard what you told our people about him, and I'm not willing to leave that to chance. My car is less than a mile down the road. If I can get to it, I'll return to the base and you won't see me again."

"What will you tell them when you don't have any leads?"

"That I ran into Hewitt, and that it's their fault for letting him live."

"Indeed it is," Mullins muttered.

He contemplated his options momentarily, knowing he needed to circle around the area for a while anyway, hoping to shake Hewitt off his trail. With his recent prognosis, Mullins wasn't worried about his own well-being. If the commander made some attempt to force him back to the base, Mullins would retaliate without fear of death. He wanted to warn the others at Maplewood about Hewitt, but they remained vigilant enough to watch for all outsiders anyway.

"Fine," he agreed. "Lead the way."

Mullins knew that Hewitt wouldn't dare attack them in the middle of the street, so he planned to walk in plain sight with Dascher. Personally, he wouldn't hesitate to shoot Hewitt between the eyes if the opportunity presented itself. As he stepped out of the building with the commander, trailing dust behind them, Mullins actually hoped Hewitt made a bold move in the open. The former cop would certainly sleep better at night knowing the sociopath was among the dead.

Chapter 24

Three days after his return to Maplewood, Mullins found himself out with Karen Brown and two other residents of the secluded community. Concerns about Hewitt discovering their location weighed on his mind, but he wanted to do his part for the people housing him, particularly after Bryce Metzger brought him up to speed about McAllister and the man's irritation over the new residents switching in and out.

Fortunately, McAllister didn't have the means to remove anyone from his village, short of using his own armed residents to act as bouncers. Unless he possessed a method of contacting the military and reporting Bryce Metzger, a fugitive in their eyes, the new residents would remain.

Mullins understood that food and supplies only went so far, hence him standing beside the nearby pond with three people he barely knew. Karen Brown and her husband had yet to reconcile, though she made it a point to chide him before departing the village. Samuel Brown had regained his freedom after a brief period of incarceration. His wife called him a coward for not leaving Maplewood to fish and hunt with them, but Mullins viewed the man's decision as peace of mind to avoid additional confrontations with her.

After all, *she* attempted to cheat on *him*.

Although he hadn't spent much time in the village recently, Mullins felt as though most people sided with Samuel, despite McAllister punishing him and not her. Brown had a right to be upset at his wife, though his decision to wield a shotgun likely caused his brief imprisonment.

A recent addition to the community's supplies included portable radios that allowed them to communicate with people in the village while on the road. Karen possessed one of these radios, though she had yet to use it after an initial test a few miles away from Maplewood. A charging bank allowed them to keep the radio batteries charged within the walls of Maplewood, powered by a small solar panel capable of running a few plug-in items.

"We going to catch some fish, or what?" Karen asked as they unpacked the gear at the edge of the pond.

"Will fishing it this much deplete the pond?" Mullins asked, not very familiar with the pond, or finishing in general.

"It was stocked annually," Karen replied. "Should give us a few good years of eats. Enough to get us by until things get back to normal."

"They're never going back to normal," Jon Koger lamented as he examined the hook at the end of his fishing pole.

"Not if the military just stays put on their bases," Matt Davison added. "We've only seen those fuckers twice this entire time."

"That might be for the best," Mullins noted aloud.

Koger and Davison were younger members of the Maplewood collective, eager, yet naïve about some of the apocalypse occurrences outside of their walls.

Jon Koger stood a little over six feet in height, proving himself very capable as a former wilderness expert and tour guide from the state of Washington. Misfortune struck when he got one of the last commercial flights ever to Virginia, only to find his family missing or deceased when he visited their homes. Before he made formal plans for his future, Koger was discovered by a few members of the village and invited to stay with them. A thick young man with broad shoulders and a dark beard that almost looked like an illustration because it was so full, Koger commanded respect within the Maplewood walls without having to ask for it.

As for Davison, he worked as a corrections officer at Sussex 1 State Prison, not far from the community. Despite the struggles for people to find shaving accessories in the new world, Davison managed to keep his face free of facial hair daily.

His wife knew Nancy McAllister from church, and a previous workplace, and her dying words were for Davison to take refuge in the community after an offer from Nancy. Shellshocked after his wife was bitten by the infected, Davison briefly considered taking a journey to Oklahoma where some of his cousins lived, but news on the television always appeared bleak. He spent the day after the infectious bite with his wife, slowly watching her wither away until she reanimated with pale, frightening eyes. His opportunities after her passing numbered very low, and making it to his family would be extremely difficult.

Virtually hopeless.

He decided to communicate with Nancy before making any life-altering decisions, and she invited him into the fold. Davison toured the community while events still unfolded everywhere in the world. People were still dying, joining the undead, and fighting for their lives, and here he was looking at Maplewood as though shopping for his next apartment. He decided to stay, because phones, mass media, and virtually every way of gaining information about the outside world suddenly failed.

An unfortunate aspect of living in a small community where hardly anyone stepped beyond its walls was that everyone knew everything about everyone else. Backstories didn't stay secret for very long once people talked to one another, and about the only person capable of keeping information to himself was Father Paul due to obligations that mirrored speaking to a doctor or psychologist.

"We have other ponds to fish besides this one," Koger said, drawing a nod from Mullins. "They're further away, though."

Each of them readied their poles momentarily.

"I heard the trip to the base didn't go well," Karen said, addressing Mullins after casting her line.

"That's one way of putting it."

"What's this about them letting some homicidal maniac loose?" Davison inquired.

"Well, he was a bargaining chip for some information. The information was more bad news, and they set him free to boot."

"They don't give a rat's ass about our problems," Koger chimed in. "The only time we see them is when they're looking for someone."

"Deserters?" Mullins asked, knowing better.

"They usually don't say much," Karen said, causing Mullins to wonder if she knew more than she let on, because Bryce Metzger's immunity to the plague wasn't exactly a secret.

Within a few minutes, the group caught their first few bass, and as the fish were placed inside a bucket, Mullins thought he heard something odd in the distance. He quit slowly reeling his line to devote his conscious mind entirely to listening, but no other sounds reached his eardrums.

"What's wrong?" Davison asked, still reeling his own line in hopes of catching a second fish.

"Thought I heard something," Mullins answered. "Must be the wind playing tricks."

"We going to do any hunting while we're out here?" Koger asked Karen, openly preferring the tactics of hunting wild game to angling.

"Only if the fishing goes south," she answered. "So far, it's looking like Maplewood is going to have a good fish stew tomorrow."

Mullins reeled in the remainder of his line after receiving only one or two nibbles for his efforts. Neither tug on the line was strong enough to warrant yanking the pole straight back in hopes of snagging a fish. He checked his bait, finding it in place, and cast the line once again with bait and sinker, into the water ahead. The others used a variety of methods, including a bobber, trying to catch some of the smaller fish breeds within the pond.

His fingers maintained a gentle touch on the reel handle, about to begin drawing the line into the reel once again, but another noise reached his ears. The hairs on his neck stood up, because he felt certain he heard the throaty growls of the undead up the hill, closer to where the group parked the older, purple, four-door Saturn they drove from the community.

One glance indicated the others heard the same noises, and in unison they carefully set down their poles and Mullins led the way up the hill, keeping crouched the entire walk. When he reached the top, Mullins stared out beyond their parked vehicle, eyes wide as they spotted a danger beyond anything he had encountered since the apocalypse began.

"Holy fucking shit," Karen muttered.

"You said it."

***

After days of running into poor luck, Metzger and his comrades finally came across a plane capable of carrying six of them, supplied with adequate fuel already. A lack of transportation on the road, coupled with missing, or bad planes from various hangars, left the group stranded several times. In addition to searching for vehicles and aircraft, the group took a few short detours to scour small towns in New Mexico for food and supplies as they began to run out of virtually everything except ammunition.

"We're getting close," Timmons said with Brooke seated beside him in the front of the Cessna 206 the group located near the northern tip of New Mexico.

Despite cloudy skies that threatened rain that morning, the group encountered partly cloudy skies shortly after takeoff. All six members of the group had camped out at the airport overnight to ensure nothing harmed the Cessna. One positive aspect about their time in New Mexico proved to be the lack of living and dead threats. It appeared as though the climate didn't appeal to many survivors, possibly due to the lack of natural resources and urban areas to raid. Metzger personally found little reason to return to the state if he survived whatever awaited them in Wyoming.

"Any idea what we're looking for?" Timmons asked Brooke specifically when a glance below the plane revealed nothing to him.

Metzger didn't love the look of the plane with its white body and garish yellow stripe from front to back on either side. The wings were positioned above the windows, allowing everyone a look below their position at any given time. Only Timmons and Brooke wore headsets, and the roar from the single propeller's engine forced everyone else to yell if they wanted to converse. Extra headsets were found during their search for the best plane to use, but no functioning adapter boxes were located to utilize the headsets.

For his part, Metzger had grown reasonably adept at reading lips when the group was flying.

"I'm going by coordinates," Brooke answered. "It could be within a village, or just a small outhouse in the middle of a field for all I know."

Brooke spoke of the bunker entrance, and Metzger knew from recent experience that they didn't want anyone spotting them in the air. Metzger hoped to locate the bunker entrance from afar, land safely, and formulate the final phases of his plan. He already knew where he wanted everyone positioned, in theory, while he and Brooke acted like a happy couple seeking sanctuary after doing their part of Nadeau's grand plan.

From across the small aisle, Jillian took his hand and they interlocked fingers. He looked at her, his concern not showing, because Metzger learned almost from the onset that anyone's time could be up on any given day.

"I don't love the idea of you being the one to do this," she confessed, raising her voice as she leaned toward him.

"Someone has to," he replied. "I've been gearing up for this day since I learned about my parents."

"I was worried the first time, and after that turned out the way it did, I'm more concerned this time. What if it's another trap?"

Metzger shook his head negatively.

"I don't think so. Let's hope we can fool Nadeau and his people, or this will all be for nothing."

"How do you suppose your brother is handling the Maplewood residents?" Sutton asked, cutting into their conversation.

"I'm sure he's keeping an eye on McAllister. Part of me wishes you'd taken over the town so my brother didn't have any worries."

"He chose the easy way for a change," Gracine stated. "He even gave up his precious box truck to gain us access."

Jillian turned her attention to Sutton.

"You never gave up the box truck for us," she said, keeping a straight face, giving Sutton a hard time before finally grinning.

"Maybe I didn't consider you guys worth it," he said, playing his part with an equally serious, stony expression.

His friends knew better, because he didn't particularly love the residents at Maplewood.

For what felt like the dozenth time since leaving the ground, Metzger checked his short sword and sidearm, finding them ready beside him. His sword rested within a sheath contained by loops along the side of the pack. The pack itself held some ammunition for the .357 pistol his father gave to him some years earlier. He felt fortunate to still possess both weapons after watching some of his travel companions switch firearms to match whatever ammunition they found more plentiful, or because they lost their weapons in the field, battling the undead.

"You won't need those," Sutton assured him with a sly grin. "Not so long as I have this."

Metzger turned in his seat just enough to see his friend pat the sniper rifle he brought along from Maplewood. It possessed a scope capable of switching between several modes, which provided him with an advantage in any kind of terrain or weather conditions.

"Assuming we make it inside the bunker, that won't be much good."

"Not for you, but I might find some worthwhile targets outside."

"Colby," Metzger warned, his voice turning a bit stern.

"Just kidding. You know I wouldn't endanger you, or the chance to get Nadeau."

"I keep wondering if this place will be like a fortress, or real discreet," Jillian said, a concerned expression crossing her face.

"I still can't believe the government sold him a bunker," Gracine said with a chastising tone.

"Have you met our government?" Timmons chimed in. "I've been to half a dozen of these places toting senators and cabinet members for tours and their meet and greets."

"And what do they look like from the outside?" Metzger inquired.

"They're all different. There are some with no visible entrances. At least not until you get close, and sometimes that's too late."

Sutton grumbled.

"You're painting a bleak picture."

"Well, our guy has invited guests coming," Timmons added. "I doubt there's a moat or man-eating lions guarding the place."

Metzger didn't feel comforted by any of the words spoken. He felt nerves tingling throughout his body, not from fear, but rather anticipation of *finally* seeing what the endgame might be.

"When we get there, I need to ask an important favor from you," Metzger said to Jillian, keeping his volume at a level only she could hear.

Jillian tilted her head to one side and gave him a look.

The look.

She knew exactly what he was about to ask, because he always intended to keep her out of danger.

"You can't keep sidelining me," she said.

"That's not my intention," he replied. "This time."

"I know I'm not entering the facility with you, but you can't keep me miles away from the action."

Metzger leaned in closer.

"Colby has a sniper rifle. Gracine is going to be at his side. I need you to stay with the plane, and with Scott."

"Why is that important?" Jillian asked, wanting specifics.

"It's important because Brooke and I could die inside that place. I need you to keep him safe and make sure no one fucks with this plane. If something happens, the four of you need to get out of this place and let someone know where Nadeau is located."

"I don't think the captain would let us leave without you, Dan."

"Damn skippy I wouldn't," Timmons shouted without turning around.

"I thought old people were supposed to have worse hearing," Gracine noted, surprised like everyone else that the Navy captain could hear them over the Cessna's engine.

"Girlfriend, you and your man aren't that far behind me in years," Timmons added, again keeping his eyes on the task at hand as he mimicked Gracine's occasional tone.

Gracine chuckled, and Metzger realized he would miss lighter times like this if anything tragic happened to any of them. Strangely, Gracine didn't object to Sutton being called her man, and Metzger had taken notice that the pair spent quite a bit of time together. Timmons and Brooke appeared chummy away from the plane when the group traveled. Although the captain didn't say much about his discussions with her, Metzger sensed nothing of a sexual nature occurred between them. Brooke appeared emotionally detached most of the time, and almost broken at others, as though something ended badly for her. She seldom spoke about her past, at all, but Metzger began to think something traumatic shook her to the core during her travels.

"You better not let anything happen to you in there," Jillian warned Metzger warmly, keeping her voice lower this time. "The captain isn't going to let us leave until we see you again."

"I know."

Metzger had survived some miraculous encounters since the previous summer, but he wasn't bulletproof, and he felt certain Nadeau's layers of security might see through their potential ruse. He looked out the window, finding what looked like grassy knolls as far as the eye could see. Thus far, the group had flown near mountain ranges, forests of naked trees, and wide-open fields as they were currently. Occasionally, snowy patches fought spring temperatures, mostly along the tree lines. Metzger remembered New York spring seasons embattled by winter snow that lingered, stacked in short, snowplowed mountains beside every road.

A mammoth barn appeared below them, along with several large cabins that broke up the discolored grass. Possibly a working ranch before the world fell apart, the land displayed no signs of people or animals. Timmons had maintained a high altitude, making it difficult to see much detail on the land below.

Metzger hadn't heard much discussion about whether they were close as Brooke held a sheet of paper with coordinates and Timmons occasionally checked it against their current position.

"We're close," the pilot finally announced about two minutes later.

Brooke craned her neck to the captain's left side to look at the ground, and Metzger noticed something along the ground that broke up the mix of tan and green grasses. Timmons intentionally kept them at a higher altitude, and Metzger now looked out his window with cautious optimism, seeing a few light-colored buildings with dark green roofs sitting perfectly aligned with one another. As Timmons banked their plane in the direction of the buildings for a better look, most of the passengers noticed a total of five buildings. Four of the structures appeared to be houses, creating a perfect square pattern over a reasonably sizable distance. The fifth, centered in the middle of the sprawling field, and the other four buildings, looked taller to Metzger, with the same green roof and beige siding.

"That's it," Metzger muttered, feeling certain the structures were built purposefully, and likely before the apocalypse occurred.

Nadeau didn't leave anything to chance, which left Metzger feeling pessimistic about successfully pulling off a ruse. He hoped Brooke knew what she was doing, and took the lead when it came to getting them past whatever security force loomed in, or near, the five buildings.

Although Metzger couldn't hear the exact words from Timmons, he knew the captain was asking Brooke about ideas where to land so they could approach the compound with minimal risk. Feeling a bit sick to his stomach from nerves, Metzger clutched his pack once more, wondering if this would be his last day among the living.

Chapter 25

Mullins stared in disbelief with his three companions as they saw a group of undead in the distance. By no means an ordinary cluster of zombies, which often numbered around a dozen at most around towns or landmarks, this group could be heard almost a mile away. Mullins lost count almost as soon as he started, because dust from the nearby fields obscured his view, and the sheer number of staggering corpses caused his mind to numb temporarily.

"There have to be hundreds of those things," Koger said, absently stroking his beard as he stared straight ahead.

"They're heading for the village," Karen stated.

In all his travels, Mullins had never spotted a group even remotely close to the size of this one. Typically, the dead remained scattered, distracted by whatever occupied their attention for a minute or two. Something very bright, or very loud, caught their attention and kept them moving toward the unsuspecting Maplewood community.

"You have to warn the others," he told Karen, who looked at him with bewilderment until he nodded at the radio clipped to her belt.

"Oh," she said, snapping out of her trance and grabbing the radio.

She tried for several minutes to reach someone at the community with no replies. While she did so, Mullins studied the horde before him, hearing their collective groans and throaty emissions as they staggered along. Fortunately, the collective remained approximately half a mile from the pond, and they were just beginning to cross the perpendicular line where the pond was located. Davison aimed his right ear toward the group, apparently trying to listen for something specific.

"What is it?" Mullins inquired.

"I could swear I hear music," Davison reported, causing the others to believe the former corrections officer's ears were failing him due to workplace hearing loss.

Mullins took a careful listen, and all four of the Maplewood residents remained out of sight, just below the bank leading to the pond where the undead couldn't spot them. The likelihood of being noticed half a mile away felt unlikely to Mullins, but he didn't want to take any chances. Mullins thought for perhaps one or two seconds he heard rock music over the stampede before him, but he couldn't be certain.

"Have you ever tested the radio signal before?" Mullins asked Karen.

"Of course we have. There's never been any trouble."

"No one's probably listening for it back home," Koger said, shaking his head. "We have to get back there and warn them."

"That's not a good idea," Mullins stated. "Even if we beat the undead to the village, the residents wouldn't have much extra time to prepare, and we'd be stuck inside with them. And don't they have lookouts in the towers?"

"They do," Koger noted.

"Now you're being a coward!" Karen shouted at a lower volume toward Mullins.

"I'm being pragmatic," Mullins countered. "If everyone in Maplewood is trapped inside, who's going to be left to lure these things away, or sneak up from behind and kill them? Our best bet is to reach them by radio and stay in reserve. Something, or *someone*, is leading the undead straight to Maplewood."

Davison stared directly at him, as though Mullins caused all of their problems.

"You could've shot that guy in the head and ended all of our problems."

Mullins looked a bit surprised that him taking Hewitt to the base was public knowledge to virtually everyone in the community.

"Word travels fast," Davison assured him.

"So it would seem. And, yes, I probably should have ended Hewitt, because taking him to the base did no good for anyone."

A few seconds passed before Koger spoke.

"Are we just going to stand here debating this? We have to get home."

"If Hewitt is leading the undead to Maplewood, he could just as easily turn them on us," Mullins retorted. "Maplewood has gates, and it will keep them out long enough for us to formulate a plan."

"We have two firearms and maybe a few dozen rounds," Karen said. "Hardly enough to deal with that."

"We don't need to shoot them," Mullins said. "We can lead them away from the community just like something is leading them there now."

"It could be someone else wanting our supplies," Davison thought aloud, obviously stunned by the turn of events, simply spouting whatever came to mind.

"It doesn't matter who it is," Karen said, on the cusp of yelling. "We need to take action."

Her left arm, fingers spread apart, aimed and shook at the ambling herd, the expression on her face showing desperation.

Mullins remained perfectly calm, having dealt with dangerous situations before.

"We need to assess what's in front of us, gather our weapons, and keep trying to communicate with the community. If all of us get trapped inside, who the *fuck* is going to help us or kill these things? I'm not being a pussy here, folks. We *are* the rescue team, like it or not."

While the other three let his words sink in, Mullins conducted some mental math, feeling certain each person at Maplewood would have to kill a minimum of twenty undead to neutralize the threat. His estimate felt low, and he doubted the weapons and ammunition supply inside the community could outlast such numbers.

Luring them away with a vehicle seemed like a much better idea, but first, he needed to know exactly what they were up against.

"If someone is leading the dead to the village, and it looks as though they are, we need to neutralize that threat before we deal with the dead. Kind of like cutting the head off a snake."

Karen looked to him, before her gaze fell to their companions, and at first Mullins thought he was going to be left behind and labeled a coward as they drove off to save the village with virtually no plan. Instead, her countenance softened, and she realized Mullins thought more rationally than most, because he had dealt with the undead.

And some very dastardly people among the living.

"Alright," she said before putting the radio up to her mouth. "We stay and hope that someone at the base can hear us."

***

Timmons landed the Cessna several miles away from the camp the group had spotted from the air. He descended far enough away that the plane might not be seen by anyone surrounding the bunker, and taxied the aircraft towards the five buildings once the plane was safely on the ground. In such a vast expanse, no towns or villages existed to resupply, or steal a vehicle, so everything needed to be done on foot.

As though sculpted for their needs, the landscape proved smooth and forgiving for the aircraft, and Timmons found a few trails that made the rolling journey easier. He brought the Cessna to a stop approximately two miles from the coordinates and everyone stepped from the plane to stretch their legs. Plenty of daylight remained, meaning they needed to get to their positions while they could still see the area clearly.

"You be careful down there," Jillian said to Metzger once he grabbed his pack of weapons and a few supplies.

"You, too," he replied. "And keep the captain safe. "Don't let him get any boneheaded ideas about coming down there."

Metzger's words 'down there' were figurative and literal, because the area surrounding the five buildings appeared to have some elevation from what they saw in the air. Sutton and Gracine would be able to set up on one side of the overlook and peer down as Metzger and Brooke made their way around the structures, searching for any sentries, or the means to enter the bunker. Possibly manmade, the area where the structures stood appeared to be a small valley centered in the otherwise flat landscape.

"Colby has my back if anything goes wrong," Metzger assured his girlfriend.

"I know, but if you make it inside, none of us can help you. And I still feel as though Brooke is holding back about something."

Standing far enough away from everyone so their words couldn't be heard, Metzger and Jillian kept their voices low just the same.

"Mullins trusted her, and he seems like a good judge of character. I'll have more time to talk to her and decide if it's safe before we reach the bunker."

"You be careful," Jillian said before giving him a lengthy kiss that nearly kept him from breathing.

Timmons had approached without them noticing, and their lips parted when he cleared his throat from a few feet away.

"Can I break in?" he inquired, drawing sheepish smiles from both of them.

"All yours," Jillian said, slowly backing away as her fingers dropped away from Metzger's light grip.

"You don't have to say it," Metzger said once Jillian was out of earshot.

"I'm just going to wish you luck," the pilot said. "If you make it inside, I'd say you're home free."

"Why's that?"

"Well, if they're going to shoot you, they'd do it outside so they don't make a mess."

"It's probably a good thing you didn't make admiral, because pep talks aren't very inspiring," Metzger noted.

Timmons attempted a grin, but it fell short.

"Look, I'm worried about you, but I know you can take care of yourself. And if this is another false alarm or trap like the last place, get the fuck out of there."

"Yes, sir," Metzger replied, giving a very loose salute.

A glance to his right let him know Jillian and Gracine were sharing a moment. He knew they had gone through a horrific ordeal with Dark Lady's people that he couldn't fully understand. Jillian wasn't entirely forthcoming about the events that transpired the previous fall, but Metzger didn't pry. Everyone had lost people in the apocalypse, but Jillian found hope when she learned her father was alive, simply to have him ripped from her life within hours.

"I need you to promise me something," Metzger said adamantly to the man he admired like a father figure.

"Name it."

"If you even think things are going south, load whoever you can and get out of here."

Timmons didn't look entirely certain about committing to the request. Metzger reached into his pack and took out the sat phone he had kept with him religiously. He powered it up and handed it to his friend, looking him in the eye.

"I'll call, I'll signal, if I'm able. If something happens to me, I don't want collateral damage."

"Understood," Timmons said, eyeing the phone momentarily. "But you need to survive this. And you need to bring him to justice."

Metzger scoffed.

"Hell, this might just be another maze in the Nadeau funhouse."

"Yeah. Well, that last false alarm looked pretty deadly, so watch your back."

"Always."

Metzger offered his hand for shaking, but Timmons pulled him into a hug, patting his back and not letting go for a few seconds. Once he did, the pilot simply offered a quick nod and turned around so Metzger could depart with his three traveling companions. Jillian's eyes appeared misty, but she didn't say a word as everyone turned to head for the compound. She simply provided Metzger with a wave goodbye by curling her fingers in and out a few times as she held up her right hand.

As he walked away, Metzger questioned how he and his friends had managed to locate Nadeau, with help from a single government agent, while the military hadn't come close. He began to question how much effort, or resources, they put forth, as though Nadeau possessed no value to them. To Metzger, it seemed they were content to track *him* and his brother for means to manufacture a cure, rather than search for the source of the apocalypse.

He currently put his faith in Brooke, and he hated relying on people he barely knew for help. The lives of his four friends along for the ride also depended on her, and he hoped he hadn't made a grave error trusting her so implicitly. Metzger didn't believe his desire to locate Nadeau had overridden his sense of self-preservation, or concern for his friends. He looked back to Timmons and Jillian one last time, hoping he saw them again as they both watched, attempting to be strong for him.

***

Mere minutes passed before Timmons and Jillian wondered how their allies were doing, now that they were beyond their sight.

Jillian paced the area around the plane, unable to simply sit around and ponder how the man she loved might die a horrible death at the hands of a man who already killed millions.

"How can you stay so calm?" she questioned Timmons, who was lying on the Cessna's wing, his back and head resting against the plane's body.

In an unusual show of serenity and intellectualism, Timmons held a book that appeared to be a history book of some sort, based on the dust jacket coloration. Jillian thought she saw a military ship, and possibly several planes in the artwork that consisted of three colors.

"Fretting and walking in circles doesn't help anyone," Timmons replied, flipping the book down, across his chest as he looked at her.

"Metzger is like a son to you," she noted. "Why are you not chomping at the bit to know what's happening?"

Timmons cocked his head to one side, providing a mildly irritated expression.

"Why do you think I'm reading? When was last time you saw me do this? I'm trying to distract myself."

"I don't have a book," Jillian stated, "and I don't have anything to keep me occupied."

"Sorry about your luck."

Jillian paced again momentarily, deciding she needed to expend her nervous energy somehow.

"Talk to me," she said to the pilot.

"About what?" Timmons questioned, acting perturbed that he couldn't get back to reading.

"Anything. Something to keep my mind off this."

Timmons paused a few seconds before his lips formed a mischievous grin.

"Fine," he said. "Tell me what happened to you when you went home last fall."

Jillian hesitated, wondering why he would bring up such a painful time in her life.

"You know what happened. I lost my father."

"Not that," Timmons said seriously. "The other thing."

"Other thing?" Jillian questioned, legitimately not knowing what Timmons wanted her to say.

"The woman who fucked with you," Timmons said. "The one you killed."

Jillian shook her head. She had barely told Metzger much about the incident beyond what happened to her father, and the fact that they dealt with Dark Lady and her group.

"They're all dead," Jillian said. "Why trudge up the past?"

"Because something about them, about her, still haunts you. You won't tell Dan, but maybe you can tell me."

"I don't think so," Jillian said, quickly dismissing the idea. "And how do you know about any of this anyway?"

Timmons stared at her momentarily with grave concern.

"Dan worries about you," he answered. "He doesn't tell me everything, but he knows something happened to you over there. He's pretty certain you haven't told him the whole story."

"And suddenly you're qualified to be my shrink?"

"Consider me a confidant, Jillian. I won't go running to Dan and tell him anything. Assuming we all make it through this."

Jillian heard his words, prompting her to test the pilot's loyalty, which she already knew was unnecessary.

"If Dan gets in trouble, we're disobeying his wishes, right?"

"You know I'm willing to go down with whatever ship Dan is on, but if anything happened to you, he'd murder me." Timmons paused to contemplate his next words momentarily. "That being said, of course we'd go after him if we *knew* he was in trouble."

Jillian debated whether to tell Timmons about the constant guilt she felt for her merciless actions against the woman known as Dark Lady. Purposely using the undead as a weapon to murder the woman bothered her, mainly because Dark Lady kept returning to her in dreams and taunting Jillian, saying Jillian would never be free of her.

"I'm not going to talk about it," she finally decided aloud.

"That's fine," Timmons said, almost indifferent for a moment. "You're going to have to confront it at some point, or it'll haunt you forever."

"What if I don't know how to confront it?"

"Sometimes we try and make up for our mistakes with good deeds, Jillian."

"Does that work?"

"Sometimes."

"And when it doesn't?"

"You learn to live with it. This woman cost you something. I'm not sure why you feel guilty at all."

"It isn't guilt per se," Jillian admitted. "This woman had a, well, a presence. Her voice, her appearance, just sticks with a person. Almost like a feeling you can't shake."

Timmons appeared thoughtful momentarily.

"Maybe you're worried you'll end up like her."

Jillian scoffed, though the thought had crossed her mind more than once before.

"Maybe we should talk about something else," she suggested.

"Like what?"

"I think it's time you tell me about your past. Your younger days, if you will."

"This isn't about my kid, is it?"

"No," Jillian said, though Metzger had made brief mention of the autistic son Timmons couldn't rescue when the apocalypse began.

As Jillian took a seat on the ground near the plane, they both realized they used Metzger as a sounding board at times. Because all of life's previous luxuries were ripped away, survivors were left with little else except talk and rudimentary means to pass the time when they weren't hunting, gathering, or battling the dead.

"We spent the whole winter with Isabella's folks and every single time we brought up your past, you changed the subject, or found some reason to leave the room. What gives, Scott?"

"Nothing special," Timmons said nonchalantly. "Are you expecting some kind of patriotic inspiration tale? Or maybe I followed in the family tradition by joining the military?"

"Quit stalling and tell me, flyboy."

Timmons chuckled, sitting more upright against the plane. After landing, he changed into his cowboy boots and put on his leather jacket because it wasn't particularly warm in Wyoming.

"My father was a major in the Marine Corps," Timmons began. "He wasn't always a major, but whatever rank he was at the time, I was expected to know and respect it. Mom tended to mellow him out just enough to keep him from berating us all the time."

"Us?"

"I had a sister. And, no, I don't know how she fared after Nadeau blew up the world. We didn't keep in touch like most siblings do, especially after I left home."

"Left home?"

"You sure are pushy," Timmons said, drawing a smile from Jillian as she almost forgot about Metzger and the danger ahead momentarily.

Almost.

"My father was strict," the captain said, looking as though some memories pained him momentarily. "I had to shave twice a day when I reached adolescence, I was expected to make good grades in school, and of course there were chores. Life was always about his next promotion, and we moved every couple years. Technically, I'm a Californian by birth, but I've lived in North Carolina, Virginia, and Georgia. We were also overseas for a few years, which inspired me, in part, to become a pilot as I got to see pilots in action over there."

"What else inspired you?"

"We had an uncle we got to visit a couple times during my youth. He owned a plane, strictly for-profit, and he took me up a few times while he was shooting pictures, or spraying pesticides on crops. Those chemicals probably caused cancer, but it's water under the bridge these days."

"What did your dad think of you joining the military?"

"That's the funny thing," Timmons said, smiling reflectively. "I graduated high school and there was never much discussion about my future. My mother would always prod, and I knew she was the go-between for me and my father. College was never mentioned, and I'm not sure what my father thought I was going to amount to, because I was a bit of a free spirit. He wanted me to set an example for my sister, and I did. Just not in front of him."

Jillian thought of her own sister, killed early in the apocalypse, realizing how they all lost contact with family and friends, or lost them altogether.

"In secret, I talked to recruiters, and they steered me in the right direction. When I called my parents, I never gave them details. I told them I was making ends meet, and never spoke about being in the service until I entered Officer Candidate School. My dad played it cool, of course, and I think he was relieved I hadn't become a bum, and probably proud that I joined the military. He never really said much about my chosen occupation. I wished he would have called me a pussy for not joining the Marines, or said he admired that I chose to fly like his brother, but he never really indicated his feelings one way or the other."

"What about your mom?"

"Mom was proud. So was my sister. I think we all shared a bond because none of us knew what Dad was thinking. Ever."

"How did you feel about your dad once you made the grade?"

"I never really got to find out where things would've gone," Timmons said, looking slightly morose about whatever thought crossed his mind. "My parents died in a car crash when I first started flying. They were visiting my mom's sister in South Dakota for Thanksgiving. My sister was graduated and visiting a friend that year, so she didn't go with them. The police said my dad couldn't stop the car due to ice on the road, and a snowplow t-boned them. It flipped the car three times."

Timmons hesitated, and Jillian didn't want to push. Telling the story hurt him emotionally, and there was a possibility he had never relayed the events of that day to another soul, short of family members.

"A lot of my life doesn't have closure," Timmons finally said after a moment of collecting himself. "I never made peace with my father, I wasn't a great father in my own right, and I've never felt like my military service helped a lot of folks. When Dan came along, at first, he was just a civilian who wanted something to pass the time. I didn't think much of it, but I found out about his importance to the brass and I didn't much care about their wants or needs. I saw the opportunity to do the right thing for a good person when Isabella approached me."

"You've talked about him being worth protecting at all costs," Jillian said, thinking back to the pilot's words. "Why do you believe in him so much?"

"Because he's a better man than anyone I've followed in my career," Timmons answered without hesitation. "He's articulate, intelligent, and capable of defending all of us. Dan is everything all of us should want in a leader, and I think he's beginning to accept that role."

Jillian contemplated something momentarily before looking at the captain.

"If he's so important, why are we sitting here instead of backing him up?"

"Because we trust in his decisions, dearie," Timmons answered. "And because he told us to stay here."

Timmons now assumed a relaxed position on the Cessna's wing and folded his arms contently. She supposed if Metzger's surrogate father trusted him that much, she could as well.

"I need to ask you something, now that I've revealed all," Timmons said.

"Shoot."

"Are you with child?"

Jillian wasn't certain she heard the question clearly for a moment, but she quickly realized exactly what her eardrums absorbed.

"Just so we're clear, you're asking if I'm pregnant?"

Timmons provided a shrug as though they had been discussing the weather instead of the creation of human life.

"Why would you ask that?"

Again, Timmons shrugged, unable to look her directly in the eyes.

"Does Dan think I might be?" Jillian pushed.

Now the pilot hesitated momentarily before answering.

"He might."

Now Jillian realized why Metzger, and possibly a few others, had acted differently around her recently. It also explained why her boyfriend insisted she stay behind with Timmons, rather than stage closer to the action.

"Damn it, Scott," she said just above a whisper. "I'm not."

Timmons looked away and nodded slowly.

"Why would anyone think that?"

"Couple things you said. Couple things you did."

Thinking back, Jillian realized she had acted differently in recent days and weeks, but she had experienced a number of flashbacks about her hometown, and the thought of mortality bothered her a bit more.

"We've been careful, Scott," she stated quietly, feeling a need to clear the air. "The *last* thing I want during all of this is a pregnancy."

"I would hope so." Timmons paused a few seconds. "Because I'm not ready to be a surrogate grandfather."

Jillian chuckled.

"You'd be good at it."

"I'm not so sure."

"When she's old enough, you can teach her to fly."

"No chance of it being a boy?" Timmons asked playfully.

"Zero."

"Will I be assigned diaper duty?"

"Possibly. But Dan and I will teach her how to shoot."

"I can do that, too, you know."

Jillian tilted her head to one side, her countenance skeptical.

"I miss sometimes to make the rest of you look better. And my shooting is a *lot* better than you think."

"We live in a world where ammunition is scarce, Scott, so I know you don't miss on purpose. And your accuracy has gotten marginally better."

Timmons scoffed at her words.

"I can't be a cool grandpa if I just teach the kid how to fly."

"Then you'd better come up with some other skills. You don't strike me as a hunter. Master chef perhaps?"

"No."

"Expert camper?"

"Well, I had training in boot camp."

"Doesn't count. Experience in the medical field?"

"You know I don't."

"Botany experience?"

Timmons furrowed his eyebrows.

"How practical is that nowadays?"

"It's a skill that might make a comeback."

Before either spoke another word, they heard a sound in the distance, possibly miles away in the tranquility of the Wyoming landscape. Jillian thought it sounded familiar, but couldn't quite place it, wondering if another plane was preparing for takeoff or landing. She looked to Timmons, who clearly recognized the sound as a concerned expression crossed his face and he swung his feet off the Cessna's wing in case the noise drew closer.

"Motorcycle," he stated, hopping off the plane to prepare for a possible encounter.

Chapter 26

Throughout the morning, and into the early afternoon, the community of Maplewood remained quiet as people carried out their daily chores. Bryce Metzger felt a bit guilty, because he didn't really have an assigned chore, yet he remained under the protection of his hosts, eating their food and feeling somewhat like a trapped animal. He couldn't be certain the military wouldn't find him, or that one of the hard-working people around him wouldn't find a way to alert General McCall to his location.

He now knew that his former supervisor left the base to search for him, and though Mullins tended to believe Dascher's story, Bryce couldn't be certain. As a former cop, Mullins possessed solid instincts, but Bryce knew desperate times led people to carry out desperate acts. Dascher wasn't the type to leave the safety of Naval Station Norfolk unless under orders, or offered some kind of favor in return.

Bryce and Dascher respected one another well enough, but each of them had a family, and their different personalities kept them from being colleagues who grabbed beers after hours. Unfortunately for Bryce, Dascher was keenly observant, and capable of tactically deducing solutions to virtually any problem. He likely knew the approximate location of Maplewood, and where to find at least one Metzger brother for the military brass.

"Penny for your thoughts," Luke Johnson said, approaching Bryce as most of the village residents went about their chores.

"I'm thinking it's not safe for me and my family to stay here much longer," Bryce answered, knowing Luke could be trusted.

"You can't let what Mike said get to you."

"The hell I can't. If they manage to locate me, or Dan, they're going to haul us to that base until they derive a cure."

"I'm not trying to play devil's advocate here, but how much worse is that than wandering across highways and scavenging for food? Eventually, they're going to make their serum, and they'll be done with you."

Bryce scoffed.

"Except now they're pissed because we're evading them."

"They left you for dead, Bryce. You have a right to some trust issues."

Taking up a stroll, the two men headed toward the front gate.

"Any word about your friend?" Bryce inquired.

"Kevin? No. Something tells me he did something stupid."

Bryce caught the meaning, and it wasn't the first time someone suggested Kevin left the safety of Maplewood's walls to strike a deal with the military.

"If Mullins ran into Hewitt, then it's likely Kevin did as well," Luke surmised aloud. "And if that's the case, you and your family are *much* safer staying here."

"It might be safer for us to take our chances out there," Bryce said. "But I can't leave my brother hanging. He's expecting us to be here when they get back."

"Don't you both have working phones?"

"We do," Bryce answered, feeling confident telling his brother's ally the truth. "I guess I just don't have anywhere in mind to take my family at the moment. Most of our family homes and getaways are compromised, and I don't have the means to travel efficiently at the moment."

"Having the kids makes a world of difference."

"That it does," Bryce agreed.

Luke glanced at the porch of the house they passed, seeing something that caught his attention. He looked around, as though trying to track someone down, before finally approaching the porch and snatching a radio from the railing where it sat quietly.

"I don't know why we even assign these to people because they always wander off," Luke said, openly irritated, though Bryce figured the residents got busy doing their chores.

He didn't recall the radios being assigned to specific people, and he wasn't certain he'd laid eyes on a radio before today.

"How do you keep the batteries charged?"

"We have a small solar panel we use only for high-priority items," Luke answered. "The battery bank for the radios is one of those things. I guess one of the salvage groups found the radios and batteries at some remote fire station."

Flipping the radio over a few times, Luke made a face that displayed his obvious displeasure with some of his neighbors.

"The battery ran dead."

"You're up in arms over these radios."

"We have people out there scavenging and hunting," Luke retorted. "And Hewitt is out there."

"Point taken," Bryce agreed.

Luke walked to a nearby house where the solar panel rested atop a sturdy porch railing to catch as many rays from the sun as possible. Set atop a nearby table meant for the outdoors, a battery bank charged extra batteries while two cell phones received charges as well.

"Why those?" Bryce inquired.

"We still use them to tell the date and time," Luke answered. "Sometimes we take them in the field to take pictures of areas we scout to point out hazards, or potential loot."

Luke removed the old battery and placed it into the charging bank, slapping a fresh battery into the backside of the radio. He turned the knob on top, and the device immediately blared to life with a frustrated, bordering on panicked voice coming through.

"Would someone from Moon Base come in?" the sound of Karen Brown's voice came over the speaker.

Bryce assumed the group referred to Maplewood in such a way to keep marauders from knowing exactly where to locate them.

"This is Moon Base," Luke replied after pushing the button to talk.

"Thank God! You have a situation heading your way, and it's at least two-hundred strong."

Luke took the meaning and looked at Bryce with more than simple concern.

"Is this threat living or dead?"

"It's dead, but it's a herd. It appears they're being led directly there."

"Clear," Luke said. "I'll warn the others and make preparations."

"You won't have time to clear everyone out," Karen warned. "They'll be there in less than thirty minutes. Arm everyone, and prepare for the worst."

"Understood. I'll keep this radio on me in case you can give us updates."

Luke clipped the radio along the outside of his belt and began marching in one particular direction without a word to Bryce.

"Where are we going?" the Navy officer decided to ask, having to quicken his pace to keep up with Luke, who was already calling the names of people they passed, rallying the troops.

"Everyone, follow me to the armory," Luke said once half a dozen people had heeded his call, curious why he was asking for their assistance in such a hurried fashion.

"What's wrong?" one of them asked.

"We're about to be attacked," he answered, determined to meet the threat head-on.

***

Several states away, Metzger walked with Brooke, having left Sutton and Gracine almost half a mile back. The pair planned on finding a vantage point overlooking the compound, to carry out surveillance of the area and protect Metzger and Brooke during the final phase of their journey. Like Timmons and Jillian, they heard the sound of a motorcycle, though they never laid eyes on one.

"Are you nervous?" Brooke asked as they trod along the ground just recently freed from the prison of winter.

"I worry about never seeing my family again," Metzger admitted. "So many things could go wrong with this plan. But, for some reason, I'm more concerned that I'll never get the answers to the questions I've had since last August."

Metzger and Brooke had gone over their plan several times, knowing they needed to pretend to be a couple to sell their cover and get inside the bunker. Brooke couldn't provide details, because she indicated each safehouse she and her boyfriend visited was slightly different than the last. She made no guarantees for the safety of Metzger, or his friends, because she had nearly died several times already.

"We're close to the point of no return," she indicated to Metzger. "You could still walk away, then fly away, with your friends and let me do this on my own."

"I really can't do that," Metzger said, though he appreciated the offer. "He's the reason my parents are dead, discarded in a pile of the dead behind some building like they were trash. Nadeau may not have ordered such a thing directly, but his people were behind it."

"I'm surprised you can follow through with this, with so much to live for," Brooke noted as the grass crunched beneath their feet.

Snow and leaves never remained stationary in Wyoming, because the winds constantly blew them somewhere else. A high school friend who moved there for work once told Metzger that when they met for lunch just outside of Buffalo a few years prior. Cold temperatures, however, only left in brief spurts, including an abbreviated summer. Growing up in New York, Metzger saw gorgeous fall leaves in rural areas, but the wide-open plains of Wyoming matched the beauty of any other place he had visited, even in the spring.

"I'm not sure I could do this if they didn't support me," Metzger admitted.

"How serious are you and Jillian?" Brooke dared to ask without anyone around to eavesdrop.

Only the wind made any noise around them, and it hadn't let up since they began the long walk. Metzger felt his face getting sore from windburn, and his notion that his cold-weather clothing was suitable didn't seem so certain now.

"I suppose you're asking if the end of the world made us more compatible?"

"Just making conversation."

"I think the age barrier might have been an issue before," Metzger admitted. "Social conformity and whatnot. Being a teacher, I probably couldn't have dated someone barely older than a high school senior and not heard about it from everyone if my life."

"But?"

"But Jillian is cute, witty, and she's intelligent. Did you know that she records our journeys to create a historical log?"

"Really?" Brooke stated more than asked, her surprise evident.

"She says no one else is doing it, with everyone just struggling to survive."

"History always has two sides," Brooke said, looking straight into the wind as they walked.

"I hope we're on the right side," Metzger said after a moment of contemplation. "How could we not be?"

"Well, we assume we are because we're good people, but we don't know everything. You're following orders from a government that could have an agenda, and I'm following a gut instinct that could get all of us killed."

"The evidence points to Nadeau. A mountain of it."

"While that may be true, he didn't personally drive every truck to those factories and city monuments. You know as well as anyone there's a network in place."

"What are you saying?"

"I'm saying that cutting the head off the snake, whether we get answers or not, probably isn't going to help anyone's situation. I'm holding out hope that Nadeau already has some kind of vaccine made for him and his people so we can protect the remainder of the living from this virus, or whatever it is."

Metzger noticed some tree stumps around them, indicating someone downed some of the foliage within the past few years. He suspected Nadeau created the buildings surrounding the bunker purposefully while he planned the deaths of millions. Metzger questioned if the man's plan went off with the intended results, or the chemicals exceeded his expectations, leaving fewer people alive to track him and question his motives.

"Did you leave Jillian with the captain because you're more worried about her or him?"

"We give Scott a lot of shit about his gun skills, but he's actually fairly proficient with a firearm," Metzger admitted. "I didn't want Jillian in the fray if this goes bad, but I don't think either one of them would leave me behind. There's no need for all of us to go down with the ship if Nadeau finds out you and I are imposters."

"At first, I had trouble believing that Nadeau set up some kind of utopia for his loyal followers, but only after losing the most important thing I had left, I got what I considered confirmation."

"I assume you're talking about John."

Brooke turned to him with a grin that quickly faded at thoughts of her ordeal.

"You haven't talked much about him," Metzger noted. "Did you love him?"

Hesitating momentarily, Brooke appeared to mentally frame her words before speaking.

"At first, John was my means to an end, because he helped keep my cover intact. I was masquerading as a reporter, but I needed to travel. A man involved in professional sports, who was somewhat recently divorced, provided just what I needed."

Metzger listened, though he stared ahead to ensure no one surprised them with an ambush as the five structures began to materialize. He suspected some armed guards would intercept them at some point, because even bunkers that once belonged to the government possessed weaknesses that might be exploited by determined intruders.

"We traveled, and I kept a low profile for the most part. The agency assigned me to monitor a few of Nadeau's trusted friends just before the apocalypse hit. John was horrified when he realized I had killed them, and the truth about my job. He looked so betrayed, and it took the end of the world for him to accept the truth. Later, there were times when I wondered what would have happened to him if he wasn't with me in Indiana."

"I feel as though you have a guess."

"He would have tried to get to Texas from Chicago, or New York, and he wouldn't have survived. It took him a while to get used to dealing with the dead, and I'm not sure he ever adapted to what motivates the living these days. To answer your question, I grew to love him at the end. John was faithful, caring, and he desperately wanted to see his family again. There came a time where he could have finished the journey to Texas without me and made it, but he stuck by me because he cared whether I survived *this* journey."

"I'm guessing John wasn't sold on finding Nadeau and avenging the millions murdered by him?"

"Not so much. He had the complete family package waiting for him in his home state. His parents owned a place where they could live off the land for years."

Metzger shrugged lightly.

"I can relate to that notion after this past winter."

He hesitated, wondering if enough time remained for an answer to his next query.

"You've told us a little bit leading up to the end," he stated, "but you never said what happened to John."

Brooke gave him a look that combined personal pain and a need to confront that dark time in her life once and for all.

"I think we have just enough time," she said, prepared to tell all before the two of them confronted an uncertain future.

Chapter 27

Brooke and Canfield visited three more active Nadeau safe havens as they headed south in the general direction of Texas from the autumn season until the winter months. Several other visits yielded mixed results because there weren't sentries left to interrogate. One, in Alabama, turned out to be abandoned after they searched the town of Jackson, finally locating the makeshift apartment and finding no paperwork. Another, in Oklahoma, still had a guard posted inside, but a bite to the man's arm made him a member of the undead army.

Unfortunately, the sentries kept most of their information memorized, so there wasn't documentation lying around to assist Brooke with her search. Even the three living guards they encountered provided very little assistance, because one fought to the bitter end, nearly shooting a crouched Canfield until Brooke shot him. That particular man had seen them coming, and decided they were trouble, opening up fire from above on the pair in the street. Canfield dove behind some trash totes, while Brooke found a dumpster that provided more protection and returned fire. Her fourth shot caught the sentry just above the heart, and he bled out before revealing anything to the adventurers. Brooke never knew if he was trigger happy, simply shooting at anything that came near him, or he was forewarned that Brooke might be coming for him. Being alone, in isolation, could easily have driven him to some form of insanity after nearly five months.

Fortunately for Brooke, Canfield began to find his groove in the apocalypse, not only bashing the skulls of the undead with modified baseball bats, but occasionally he discovered amusing ways to put them down. Sometimes, he would toss a baseball into the air, only to swing like he might when conducting batting practice. With high velocity behind them, they often shattered a zombie's skull, effectively destroying the brain and killing them for good.

He discovered that throwing larger stones often worked much the same, so when they encountered a single zombie, or two, Canfield experimented sometimes. Brooke let him have a little fun without judgment because he nearly died on a few separate occasions.

During their travels, his beard grew rather bushy until they located a battery-operated hair trimmer in an old flea market. Brooke suggested he trim his facial hair if he wanted to continue having relations with her. He managed to get both his hair, and beard, close to a pre-apocalypse style, using a bathroom mirror in a random house they borrowed for an evening.

In another instance, Brooke and Canfield managed to subdue the guardian of the apartment rather easily, but the man wasn't talking, or being cooperative. When Brooke informed her boyfriend that torture would be necessary, Canfield decided he didn't have the stomach to watch. He stepped outside with a pack of his belongings, only to find himself confronted with two young men that followed the couple from a distance, hoping to jump them for weapons or supplies.

Forced to defend himself without assistance from an occupied Brooke, Canfield tried reaching the two youngsters with logic, even using his coaching techniques, but they were desperate to survive. Because they didn't have any firearms, Canfield used a baseball bat rather than a bladed weapon, attempting to subdue them without leaving them battered or crippled. He got in a few good strikes before they teamed up like hyenas, both tackling him at once, attempting to pry the bat from his hands. Knowing no help was coming, Canfield's instincts reached a higher gear, and he managed to use his size advantage to throw the younger men aside just long enough to regain his footing.

One of them pulled a small knife from his pocket, and the other a short section of steel pipe from the back of his blue jeans, showing Canfield they weren't entirely defenseless.

"Come on, boys," he said. "You really don't want to do this."

"Then give us your supplies," one of them said.

"The missus would kill me," Canfield answered, falsely indicating he and Brooke were wed.

"Your goods, or your lives," the second young man said, forcing Canfield to realize his life indeed hung in the balance.

Overhead, the overcast skies had gotten darker, and rain began to spit on the three men as they squared off just outside the safe haven apartment. Canfield set down his pack and switched out the fresh baseball bat for one enhanced with nails and metal shards attached with industrial adhesive. Now, the young man with the knife looked with wide eyes, seeing the dangerous weapon up close.

"Come on, Tommy," the second one said. "It's two of us."

"That thing has blood and guts on it," the first one said. "If that thing touches us, we get infected."

"He has to hit us first."

Now the rain picked up, becoming light showers from just a spattering of raindrops.

"I'm out," the first man said, pocketing his knife and walking away from the situation without another word.

"Just follow him," Canfield said, on the verge of pleading with the second potential attacker.

"I haven't eaten in days," the man stated with a pained sneer.

"This is a fucking town," Canfield said, exasperated. "Go pillage for food like the rest of us."

"I tried, but you and your woman kept beating us to the good stuff."

"What the fuck?" Canfield asked, holding the bat out to his side. "We haven't touched this town, and we didn't take every last supply from the others. There's something wrong with you for stalking us like this."

Canfield didn't get to continue his conversation with the unreasonable younger man, because a steel pipe was swung at his skull.

No part of the weapon connected with the former baseball player, and Canfield gave him one more free swing before unleashing the longer bat. Although the younger man ducked the first swing, Canfield caught him on the backswing, tearing at the sweatshirt his adversary wore. Apparently knowing how close he came to having zombie blood and guts mingled with his own blood, the young man appeared to rethink his choice momentarily. He might have left the altercation altogether, but his friend returned, unseen by Canfield, from a side alley.

Catching a brief glance from the second man to his friend, Canfield dodged a knife thrust at him and defensively swung the enhanced bat, catching the man in the side of the neck. When he tried freeing the modified weapon, Canfield ended up tearing off significant flesh from the man's neck, even catching an artery as he did so.

As the man yelped and retreated from the battle to tend to his wound, Canfield focused on his initial attacker, fully prepared to stand his ground and end the skirmish. He didn't want to fight the living, but his moral compass told him these two couldn't be allowed to bring harm to other survivors. Perhaps they hoped to confront Brooke instead, which would have ended worse for them when they couldn't use her as a hostage or double-team her. She possessed little use for talking to strangers when a fight was impending, and now Canfield understood why.

Now the other man appeared nervous as he held the lead pipe before him, his hand shaking it nervously. He began to understand the time for peaceful negotiations with Canfield had passed, and their ill-conceived idea to follow the couple through several Mississippi towns backfired. Brooke and Canfield ended up doubling back to find this particular safe haven, leaving ample supplies and food to scavenge in some of the other settlements.

Canfield barely waited two seconds before going on the attack, swinging furiously at the younger man. Barely able to duck and dodge the first two swings, the man couldn't avoid the third swing that planted the prickly portion of the bat in his left hamstring, drawing blood immediately. The man attempted to hobble away, but Canfield pursued him like a predatory cat, yanking the weapon painfully from the man's leg before he swept the man off his feet with his own foot.

When the first man attempted to intervene, making the mistake of removing his hand, and the pressure it provided along his neck, blood began to spurt even before Canfield swung the bat. It connected with the man's skull, making a squishy *thuck* sound upon impact. He fell to the ground like a sack of potatoes, possibly dead at this point, but he pulled Canfield downward, because the bat's spikes remained stuck inside flesh and bone.

Left with the choice to either flee and leaving his dying friend, or confront Canfield in highly risky combat, the second man decided to attack during the second or two it required Canfield to pry his baseball bat from the dented skull. Taking a calculated swing, the man missed a ducking Canfield's head with the steel pipe, but caught the former coach along the back and arm along the right side. Knowing he couldn't let the pain slow his response, because any second could be his last, Canfield swung the bat in a longer loop than necessary, catching his adversary off-guard. The modified weapon grazed the man along the torso, cutting through the sweatshirt and shirt beneath, drawing blood for the first time.

"No," the man muttered, looking down at the wound, giving Canfield another precious second in which to thrust the thicker end of the bat at the man's chest, knocking him to the ground.

In a purely defensive move, the man swung the pipe at Canfield's knee, but the former professional athlete avoided contact by pulling his leg back. Simultaneously, he gripped the bat with both hands and prepared for a swing that his adversary couldn't possibly block or avoid without the bat injuring at least part of his body.

Striking the man in the nearest shoulder, Canfield ensured the lead pipe would no longer be in play as it dropped from the man's trembling hand. Nerve damage set in immediately, leaving him virtually defenseless, but Canfield had come to a realization that the living simply couldn't be trusted at first glance. As the man attempted to sit up, possibly to flee, Canfield kicked him flat to the ground, already bringing the bat around for a final swing as it descended quickly, striking the man in the side of his head when he tried to turn away from the attack. Canfield watched momentarily as the body of the man convulsed, eyes bulging in their sockets from the cranial pressure. Only a few seconds passed before Canfield felt uncertain about whether the man was suffering, or not, and the bat came down a second time to finish the job. This time, brain matter, flesh, and blood created a red, pink, and white swirl atop the pavement as though someone had thrown a large strawberry pie on the ground.

Canfield did not observe his deed like some deranged murderer, but rather a man contemplating the impact of taking human life after being raised in a Christian family, and living a reasonably wholesome existence. Brooke knew this, and she could virtually read his mind as she stared through the scope of the rifle she kept aimed in his direction. She never would have let any harm come to her boyfriend, though she felt a wave of relief that he dealt with an adversarial situation the correct, and only, way possible.

She observed him taking a knife to the other man's skull, just to ensure he didn't turn undead from his wounds, and pulled the rifle back, stepping inside before he turned and saw her. Inside, the subdued guardian of the safehouse required some motivation to provide information, and Canfield needed some time to collect his thoughts.

"Back to work," she said under her breath, prepared to gather information for the next location in their national tour of Nadeau safehouses.

***

By the middle of January, the couple neared what Brooke hoped would be their last stop before finally locating Nadeau's compound. She had a feeling she would never learn the truth unless she convinced someone she was a survivor and loyal follower of the man. Each of the previous sentries died needlessly in a shootout, found a way to kill themselves during the interrogation process, or died before Brooke and Canfield arrived.

Canfield grew weary of the process, particularly after killing the two young men in Mississippi. He never spoke at length about the incident, and Brooke saw a brooding darkness that ate at him, and she hated that the only joy left in his life resided in Texas. He showed little interest in furthering their relationship, and grew more despondent until she promised him the next stop, in Arkansas, would be their last before she escorted him to Texas.

Drawing close to their destination of Charleston, Arkansas, the couple decided to look for shelter approximately ten miles from the small town. Dangerously close to dusk, they discovered a row of houses south of Interstate 40 that appeared to be devoid of life.

And the dead.

When they drew closer with their current vehicle, a recent Kia hybrid car, both began looking at the row of houses in the neighborhood as though looking to buy. Brooke sat in the passenger seat, letting her boyfriend take a turn at driving after they switched off once they syphoned some fuel. Similar thoughts ran through both of their minds momentarily about a life beyond simply surviving and existing. When their eyes met, however, both realized daydreaming didn't help their situation as their gazes quickly drifted in other directions.

For the first time during their journey, Brooke seriously contemplated going on without Canfield, and she wondered if she could handle it. Naturally, she could take care of herself, but without his funny quips, his loyalty, and an uncanny selflessness in bed, Canfield made himself invaluable. She chastised her thoughts, positive she was simply being selfish, but Brooke genuinely wanted to continue life with him. She began to question if the journey was worth finding Nadeau, and decided if this next safe haven didn't pan out with solid information, she would accompany him to Texas and stay if his family permitted it.

In a world where people felt less inhibited without rules and regulations, people sometimes let their worst traits bubble to the surface. Canfield actually became more attune to Brooke's needs, both surviving on the streets, and in bed where he never behaved aggressively unless Brooke requested him to.

She continued to study their surroundings. Houses in the area ranged from ranch style to two-story residences with mammoth garages. A number of them displayed front doors already kicked in, and Brooke considered those safer because looters would likely have come and gone rather quickly. A house with a secured door possibly meant people chose to live there and make a go of it for a while. Such people might still be there, or be deceased inside. The latter meant the house would reek of death and defecation, and possibly present a danger to people walking into the dark abode.

"What do you think of that one?" Brooke asked of a house set farther back from the road.

She couldn't tell if the front door was slightly ajar, or closed, but if they cleared it, no one traveling in the night would spot it.

"Let's try it," Canfield said with no enthusiasm in his voice.

Due to the house being near the edge of the woods, it appeared almost completely engulfed by darkness when they pulled down the driveway. Only a silhouette of the house remained as they pulled up beside it, and Brooke indeed noticed the front door slightly ajar. Stepping from the passenger seat, she pulled a sidearm with a flashlight attachment mounted on the underside, switching the light on as she lightly tapped the door inward with her right foot.

She spotted a small debris field along the living room floor immediately consisting of potato chip bags, empty soft drink bottles, and random candy wrappers. Nothing appeared fresh to her, and she headed straight inside, letting Canfield choose if he wanted to follow, or wait at the door. He chose to remain at the door, because he didn't have a flashlight, and he had learned not to be protective with Brooke too often. In a small setting such as this, he might bump into her, which he knew irritated her to no end.

Brooke made short work of checking the kitchen, two bedrooms, and single bathroom, finding very few personal belongings left inside. She wasn't sure if a family left for another area when the apocalypse began, or if scavengers grabbed what clothes and supplies were left inside the house since the previous summer.

"It's clear," she informed Canfield when she returned to the front door.

"No basement?"

"I didn't see a door for one," she answered, thinking that she hadn't checked the attached garage for an access point. "This way," she added before heading for the door to the garage, smacking it with a fist a few times.

When nothing sounded in return, she opened the door, shining the light inside, finding a Harley-Davidson motorcycle along one wall and several gas cans atop a workbench. Other tools and equipment were randomly lying around, as though the owners of the house left rather suddenly, choosing to take only the essentials.

"Not a bad haul," Canfield commented. "Especially if those containers actually have gas."

After they checked the house, and the garage, for useful items, the couple found several large candles stowed away in a closet. After setting them in the bedroom and using the book of matches they had toted through several towns, they illuminated the room before stripping down and hopping into bed. Long gone were the days when they fretted about clean sheets or sleeping bags when they found new locales.

"Ready for tomorrow?" Brooke asked, initiating the conversation when Canfield turned away as though ready for sleep.

"As I'll ever be."

She wanted to tell him that tomorrow was their last stop, short of finding a miracle in the form of Nadeau's location. Brooke decided such information could wait, because their journey wasn't guided by the stars, or a handler that Brooke hadn't conversed with in over a month. They traveled solely on her desire to use what little information she found to guide her to the next possible viable source.

She remembered her last message from Taylor being extremely grim, and Brooke hoped for a more favorable, certain future in her own journey.

GOVERNMENT AND INFRASTRUCTURE CRUMBLING.
COMMUNICATIONS SKETCHY.
OUT OF SUPPLIES.
EVACUATING TOMORROW TO A POSSIBLE SAFEHOUSE.
GODSPEED, BROOKE.

In her mind, Brooke imagined most of the handlers left soon after the dead began walking to locate loved ones. Perhaps some of their agents in the field met horrible ends, ending their government obligation. If that occurred, their job was basically rendered purposeless, leaving them little reason to stay since each handler typically dealt with only one or two field agents.

"What's wrong?" Canfield asked, catching her in momentary thought.

"Nothing," she answered, deflecting instinctively before reconsidering. "That's not true. I was thinking how I haven't heard from Taylor since that last cryptic message."

By now Canfield knew almost everything about her undercover work, including the name of her gender-neutral handler. Brooke had never truly pictured Taylor, simply because he could be a nerdy, overweight computer guy, or a struggling mother of two. Although the latter seemed highly implausible, Brooke supposed anything was possible.

"You can't give up hope," Canfield said, draping an arm across the blanket covering her otherwise nude body.

"I'm surprised to hear you say that," she said, finally turning to face him.

"Why?"

"After the incident in Mississippi, you've been keeping to yourself a lot more. Kind of depressed."

Canfield shifted his glance away from her momentarily.

"I'm coming to terms with it all," he admitted when he looked her in the eyes. "I'd do anything to protect my family, and now, that includes you."

Brooke wanted to tell him so badly how she had committed to him in her mind. She was ready to forego government work and live with him once the following day proved to be yet another dead-end. Canfield appeared content to simply share bodily warmth, but Brooke decided to reward him for being such a faithful companion. She ran her hand up and down his stomach to his torso, several times, feeling body hair he didn't always have as a player and, later, as a coach. For some odd reason, he tended to shave his body for swimming and workouts in the gym, saying he felt more comfortable that way. Brooke assumed he wanted to look more attractive to other women before he landed her as a steady relationship.

"Take me," she whispered in his closest ear as though she might be heard by adjoining neighbors.

His eyes widened, as though alarmed, instead of his typical excited mannerism.

"What's wrong?" she asked.

"I don't have any protection," he said. "We left those bags behind the last time we changed cars."

"They fit in your wallet, John," she said, trying to keep from using a chastising tone and ruining the mood.

"I know, I know. Look, we can—"

"Don't worry about it," she said, cutting him off mid-sentence. "You're an expert pull-out guy, right?"

"Well, yeah," he answered hesitantly.

"Then we're good."

During the past two days, the couple hadn't eaten extremely well, attempting to ration their food and water until they came across another decent cache. For nearly ten minutes, their bodies intertwined, sweating because the brisk winters they both experienced in previous years hadn't touched Mississippi this winter. Typically keeping her guard up, even during intercourse, Brooke let her guard down, trying to put herself in the moment because she had already decided tomorrow was her last day as a diligent employee for a government that clearly no longer existed.

When Canfield finished, either due to fatigue, or forgetfulness brought on by an insufficient diet, he didn't pull out immediately. Instead, he began to relax out of habit, like he might while wearing a condom, prepared to settle beside her.

Canfield quickly realized the fact that he had started to ejaculate while still inside Brooke. He didn't say anything right away, but the way he pulled back quickly, accompanied by the concerned expression he wore, indicated he wasn't at his sharpest.

"Sorry," he said. "Had a split-second lapse there."

"I think we'll be okay," she said, knowing he caught the lapse in judgment quickly.

She felt confident she still possessed some day-after pills to make certain no pregnancy occurred, because a woman could ill-afford to carry a baby to term in the apocalypse.

"Tomorrow is *it*," she informed Canfield after lying still a minute or two.

"'It?'"

"I'm not asking anymore of you after tomorrow," Brooke elaborated. "We're going to get you home to Texas."

Canfield looked at her with concern.

"You can't do this on your own."

"Let's just see how tomorrow goes," she said, not wanting to make any promises she couldn't keep.

"Hang on," Canfield said, touching her on the shoulder before reaching to the side of the bed and unzipping his pack to pull something from it.

"What's this?" she asked when he handed her a folded piece of paper.

"A map to where my family is holed up in Texas. I drew it up a few nights back, just in case something happened to me."

"Why?"

"I wanted you to have somewhere safe to go," he answered, scrunching his face with a hint of surprise that she didn't already deduce his intentions. "If anything happens to me, and you don't want to go, please destroy it. I don't want the wrong people showing up at their doorstep."

"You got it," she said softly with assurance. "I appreciate you looking out for me."

Now the grin ran from Canfield's face to a serious, if not somewhat despondent look.

"Truth be told, I never expected to make it this far," he admitted. "You were trained for this. I was just a jock who blew out too many body parts when he was young."

"You're selling yourself a little short."

"I'm not sure I am. I've been damn lucky to have you by my side, even before the world ended."

Brooke looked him in the eyes before giving him a gentle kiss on the forehead.

"I'm glad you've had my back these past few months."

With that, she turned to face the nightstand, blew out the candles, and questioned if her next stop would prove any more fruitful than the previous dead-ends.

Chapter 28

Exercising more caution than their previous stops, Canfield and Brooke parked at the town limits of Charleston, Arkansas, and walked into the small town, staying close to the buildings along the main drag. Brooke had noticed a rinse and repeat methodology regarding the safehouses and their locations. Almost all of them existed in reasonably small towns with a primary main drag that harbored at least one or two buildings with a second level. Such buildings provided adequate living space, and a vantage point to see allies or enemies approaching.

Buildings in the historical business district appeared to be two stories, but none of them had windows upstairs. Brooke began to doubt the possibility of the safehouse being located inside any of them. Finally, adjoining a GMC car dealership, they spotted a two-story brick building that might have been an office building for the business, or a separately-owned apartment building that happened to be historically preserved.

Canfield scanned the dealership first as they walked past, staying within a foot or two of the building because the glare-resistant windows didn't allow much of a view inside during daylight hours. He stopped momentarily, seeing a few showroom vehicles parked inside, and little else except desks, computers, and a few dead roaming the floors as unwitting sentries. A face smacked against the glass directly in front of Canfield, startling him enough that he jumped back. Brooke smirked as she touched his shoulder, because the zombie spied him before he noticed it approaching from the side.

"Obviously, he can see through this glass better than I can," Canfield muttered.

When they reached the adjoining building, Brooke tried the front door, finding it locked. She peered inside, seeing very little, as though it was abandoned before the apocalypse. A sign upstairs indicated the space was for rent, so she pointed upward without a word, letting Canfield know she intended to check the rear for access.

He followed her lead, and in the back, she found an access door to the bottom only. She tugged on it, finding it locked. Most buildings were already broken into, or the windows were shattered. This building appeared intact, possibly because of the thick glass, or because it appeared to offer nothing to the scavenger, or weary traveler looking for somewhere to sleep.

"Well, smashing a window, or kicking in a door doesn't exactly seem like the stealthy approach," Brooke said, turning to Canfield.

"I've got an idea," he replied, looking upward. "Hop on my shoulders."

Brooke gave a quick shrug before scaling him like a human ladder. Canfield was able to stand erect, allowing her to clasp the decorative edge above her and take a look through one of the windows. Inside, the apartment appeared as devoid of objects as the ground level.

"That's not it," she said once her feet touched the pavement again.

"There were some buildings on the other side of the business district that looked promising."

Brooke recalled seeing a courthouse and a school down the road, among other buildings. Such locations weren't the norm in her experience, but the town felt similar to others the couple had visited. She knew the safehouse would be highly visible, and those buildings were definitely along the main drag.

"If they're in one of those buildings, they've likely seen us," Brooke indicated aloud.

"They didn't exactly roll out the red carpet."

"Do they ever?"

After experiencing instances where the sentries were either gone or deceased, Brooke no longer created expectations. She wondered if the sentries memorized addresses specifically for the next location, which might explain why she and Canfield always had to hunt and peck for the safehouses. Answers never came easily, or clearly, and she felt as though little information had been unearthed during the process.

Much like the other towns that housed Nadeau's underlings, Charleston had little to no undead roaming the streets. Some remained inside secured buildings, as Canfield witnessed, but they didn't walk the streets and pose a danger to newcomers or whatever sentry guarded this area.

"Any chance it's the school?" Canfield asked once he and Brooke began backtracking the way they came down the center of Main Street.

"Doubtful," she answered. "It's safe, but they want high ground, or a vantage point of people coming from every direction."

Now making their second trek down the main drag, the couple knew their presence was known to any living person inside a building. They hadn't seen any prying eyes on their first walk through the city, but they had remained close to the structures and sidewalks. Both of them wore their heads on a swivel as they basically walked down the middle of the abandoned town, seeing no activity anywhere around them.

A cloudy sky loomed overhead, though rainy weather didn't appear to be coming their way. Brooke simply wanted to find the sentry, likely learn nothing from the visit, and live a life with Canfield in Texas, away from the undead and government work. Brooke never pictured herself as the domestic type, always learning to use technology, fight, or pretend to be someone she wasn't for her occupation. A few weeks prior, she wouldn't have dreamed of giving up the search, but traveling to each safehouse felt like running in circles. She began to wonder if Nadeau purposely mislead his own people, or they were clever enough to provide false clues on paper, or verbally, when tortured.

Momentarily, the wind picked up, swaying trees and nearby shrubs, looking eerie along a thruway that once teemed with life. Such scenes harkened back to the days when a power outage overtook whatever town Brooke lived in at the time, giving her a slight sense of helplessness because power dictated so much of her modern life.

Thunderstorms came and went, bringing damage and the loss of lights and communication with them. She felt stuck in that weird, transitional time, particularly now that she possessed no contact and no connection with anyone outside of her line of sight. At this point, Brooke wasn't even certain who to contact if she discovered vital information, or located Nadeau. Taylor had informed her of a few government centers that remained open, initially, but even those likely dwindled and closed as people left their posts. She knew at least some of the military bases remained open, particularly in San Diego and Norfolk, but their leadership would have to get creative to feed and shelter thousands.

When the courthouse came into view, Canfield eyed it up and down, seeing its potential as a safehouse. It possessed two levels, each containing large windows that added to its architectural charm. Along the bottom of the brick structure, windows that looked to be enlarged slats indicated a basement area. While basements were often secure, acting as panic rooms, this one could likely be accessed by breaking one of the windows. A few were covered with wood panels, indicating they were broken, and someone took the time to cover them.

"All that glass," Canfield thought aloud, openly wondering how the building remained mostly unmolested.

"Someone's been protecting it," Brooke said as they stepped directly in front of it. "Time to find out who."

Canfield started to walk away from her, ready to check the back of the building so no one escaped while Brooke checked the front. She grabbed his wrist, indicating she didn't want him to go solo this time. Had he wanted, Canfield could have broken free from her grip and done as he pleased, but over the nearly five months they had traveled together, he learned to trust her instincts.

"Let's just try the front door first," she suggested.

Both of them approached the door, and when Brooke tried pulling on one of the double entry door handles, she found the door locked, then the other.

"So much for that," she muttered.

Taking the initiative, she led the way toward the left side of the courthouse. Canfield immediately took her side as they crossed paths with a woman who appeared to be in her late twenties. Her pants were urban camo, a mix of gray, black, and white, with a charcoal shirt that appeared very much in contrast with her red hair and freckles that didn't disappear with adolescence. Her unkempt hair didn't quite reach her shoulders, and she had an air of survival about her, as though she might be Nadeau's contact person.

"It's not safe out here," she said immediately, looking beyond them at the vacant street the pair had just traversed to arrive at the courthouse.

"Not safe?" Canfield asked, stealing a glance behind him that indicated no danger.

"Do you live here?" Brooke inquired, wanting to initiate a conversation about Nadeau if possible.

"I do, but you can't be standing in the open like this," the woman insisted, her eyes indicating she spoke a grave truth.

She motioned with her right hand for them to follow her, and quickly.

Now Canfield appeared concerned, and Brooke took a step to follow the woman around the large building. Her boyfriend started to say something as they decided to exercise caution.

"Hey, we should-"

Canfield didn't finish his statement as blood spurted from the left side of his neck, and the sound of a gunshot from down the street followed. Someone with a high-powered rifle had just shot the man who dedicated his life to keeping Brooke safe. His knees buckled, and Brooke helped him to the ground as a second shot rang out, the bullet missing where her skull had been by mere inches.

"We have to get out of sight!" the woman insisted, grabbing Canfield's left arm as Brooke grabbed the right and they quickly pulled him to the side of the courthouse.

Safely out of any gun sites, Brooke turned her attention to Canfield, who was trying to speak with the side of his neck bleeding profusely. She initially put a finger across his lips, indicating for him not to speak while she applied pressure directly to the wound with her free hand.

"Tet, tet," he repeated twice, stammering.

"Don't say anything," Brooke told him, keeping two fingers directly on the wound until the woman ripped off a sleeve from her shirt, handing it over.

"Texas," he finally said after battling his own body to speak.

"Yes," Brooke said quickly as Canfield reached up, attempting to help her put pressure on the wound, but she gently shoved his hand aside. "We're going to Texas as soon as we get you sewed up."

Canfield's eyes began to roll back slightly, and he fought to stay in the moment.

"No," he finally said firmly, beginning to accept his fate. "You."

Brooke felt her heart plummet at the thought of traveling to Texas, much less living there, without him by her side. She fought to keep her emotions at bay, because she needed to make every effort to save Canfield, and a complete stranger remained beside both of them.

At best, the round nicked an artery, and at worst, obliterated the vessel that carried blood, and life, through her boyfriend's body. The latter couldn't be survived in any conditions, but a less severe cut might be cauterized, even stitched, if the bleeding could be subsided for a few minutes.

Canfield focused on Brooke at first, wanting to say something he considered extremely important. His eyes soon began to lose focus, however, and he entered what Brooke considered a death trance as shock set in. Blood immediately soaked the cloth when she pressed it against his neck, feeling the warm substance in his beard, and running through her fingers. The coppery odor reached her nostrils, and Brooke felt repulsed by the smell of blood after having become immune to it during her travels.

"John, stay with me," she pleaded, realizing she didn't want to go on without him.

A tear rolled down her cheek as they pressed the cloth against his neck and held his hand, internally praying that somehow, he could be saved. A thousand regrets ran through her mind at once, the worst being the decision to visit this town instead of heading straight to Texas to keep her boyfriend safe. His children would never see their father again, and his family would wonder the remainder of their lives what became of the man who left the Lone Star State to pursue a full career in the world of professional baseball.

Brooke glanced at the stranger, and the woman continued to remain by their side, indicating she wasn't a direct threat, and she *had* attempted to warn them. She quickly returned her attention to Canfield, who fought to live. A small pool of blood formed beneath his neck, indicating mere minutes remained until he expired, unless the two women could stop the bleeding.

***

"We're getting close," Metzger said, feeling bad about interrupting Brooke's tale of woe.

"I noticed," she said. "There isn't much left to tell anyway."

After a few steps and some awkward silence, Metzger spoke again.

"I'm assuming things didn't go well in Arkansas?"

"You assume correctly. We couldn't save John."

Brooke walked a few more steps, remaining silent as she looked skyward.

"I did manage to locate solid information while I was there, which is what led me your way in Virginia."

"How were you so sure these locations were legit when so many others didn't pan out?"

Brooke grunted slightly with a smirk, shaking her head.

"I guess you could say I changed tactics slightly."

Metzger wasn't sure what she meant, and he didn't want to press her for information when they were about to be intercepted by Nadeau's security people at any moment.

"I was caught between heading to San Diego, or heading northeast to Norfolk," Brooke said as they continued walking. "I decided on the East Coast, mainly because of familiarity, but also because I knew Norfolk had a solid operation still online. I hadn't heard as much about San Diego."

"Oh, they're still operating," Metzger said as an almost bitter afterthought.

Brooke absorbed his words, giving a nod that indicated she now knew San Diego was up and running for the military.

"Before I did anything, I decided to return John to his family," she informed Metzger. "The man died because of me, and his family deserved to know the truth."

She looked skyward once again, as though searching for the correct words.

Or the strength to speak them.

"And to give him a proper burial."

"I'm sorry," Metzger offered, seeing how it truly pained her to move on without Canfield. "How did dealing with his family go?"

"Oh, they were surprisingly understanding, and appreciative," she answered, still looking up, and not making eye contact with Metzger, as though it pained her to speak about the journey.

Metzger understood the long-term impact of losing loved ones in the apocalypse. Surprisingly, as he drew closer to possibly confronting Nadeau, his blood no longer boiled with anger. Perhaps the letdowns from the past several months changed his perspective, and he didn't expect to ever meet the man. Metzger had also accepted that other villainous men murdered his parents, and Nadeau simply put them in power positions to carry out such heinous acts.

He realized Brooke was tough and independent, hating to show her vulnerable side to anyone. It paid to act tough in the apocalypse, and Metzger knew *being* tough was far more advantageous. They now walked on flat ground, with the five buildings directly ahead of them in the distance. Metzger anticipated contact with Nadeau's people at any moment, likely leading to a shakedown where the security people would make certain he and Brooke were authentic followers and not troublemakers, or people searching for a bunker.

"The trip south wasn't easy," Brooke admitted, finally looking at Metzger. "You can't just hop on a motorcycle, or turn tail from a hairy situation when you have cargo with you."

"Cargo, huh?" Metzger asked skeptically of her wording, raising an eyebrow.

"You know what I mean," she said on the cusp of hostility.

Metzger fully understood, and he wondered why Brooke refused to show emotion around him, or his group, when she admitted to being tender with Canfield in the months following the dynamics of their relationship changed. Part of him wished he could have met her boyfriend, but Metzger hated tragic endings, and in the back of his mind he knew some of his friends were destined to die in front of him. He couldn't protect everyone, but he hoped to find some answers that might help build a better future.

"I need a second," Brooke said, deviating from their path momentarily to stop by a small tree that stood a head taller than her, and hadn't been removed by the locals.

Metzger watched her dig into her bag momentarily and pull out a gray sweatshirt, which she quickly pulled over her head after removing the winter jacket she was wearing. He was about to ask why she would opt to don a thinner piece of clothing, particularly with cold and wind all around them, but she took a step back and put her hand up to her mouth. Metzger started to take a step toward her, but she put a defiant hand up before she vomited near the tree. Brooke quickly cupped her mouth before wiping any excess vomitus.

"I'm sorry," she said, returning to his side a few seconds later.

"Sorry for what?"

"I don't know what caused that," she stated. "Maybe something I ate."

"We haven't eaten *much* lately," Metzger said. "That could be part of the problem."

Brooke simply gave him a glance that made him feel he wasn't far from the truth. A picture of health, Brooke wasn't one to suddenly grow ill, and she certainly hadn't been bitten. Very few undead roamed the plains of Wyoming, particularly in areas where cattle and horses outnumbered humans prior to the apocalypse.

"Just remember to let me do the talking," Brooke reminded him before he could inquire about her health.

Metzger assumed she did so to keep him from following up his initial inquiry.

In the distance, the sound of a motorcycle rumbled, and he saw two men appear in the center of the makeshift town and walk toward them. Both wore casual clothing, and one held what appeared to be an automatic, or semi-automatic rifle of some kind. He looked to Brooke, who was still adjusting her sweatshirt and digging through her pack for something.

"We're about to receive our welcome wagon," he said.

"I noticed," she said, pulling out a few sheets of paper.

Metzger wondered if they were like the golden tickets in the Willy Wonka stories, granting them access to the otherwise sealed and secretive bunker. They appeared official, and along one side, he noticed a shimmer, possibly a fancy watermark, or a holographic stamp of some kind.

On a collision course with the two men, and no turning back at this point, Metzger fought the urge to clutch the revolver currently holstered along his right side. His sword remained sheathed in the backpack he wore, and he had mastered clutching it and using the bladed weapon in an instant the past few months. He felt as though his acting was subpar, but his allies told him he did fine when lying with a straight face. At this moment, he hoped their words weren't simply flattery to make him feel better.

"You seem to have come a long way," the man on the left spoke first when the four drew within a few feet of one another.

Both men appeared clean-shaven, and healthy in both color and fitness. They didn't lack for exercise, or food, from what Metzger could determine.

"We're here for sanctuary," Brooke said, handing over the two sheets of paper that Metzger hadn't read.

Scrutinizing the paperwork for only a few seconds, the man on the right handed both sheets back to Brooke.

"Come with us."

Playing the part, Metzger barely gave Brooke a glance before they stepped forward, ready to see what awaited them inside the bunker.

Chapter 29

Within minutes of the radio traffic, the entire community of Maplewood buzzed with anxiety, confusion, and uncertainty, which Bryce considered a horrible combination. He watched as Luke took charge of the situation, ordering citizens to unlock the armory and arm themselves with guns, blades, and whatever they could find. Sean Sutton stepped outside with Buster, and the canine immediately growled upon sniffing the air, indicating the undead couldn't be very far away.

Luke began handing out weapons to the residents at first, getting some of them armed. He shoved a semi-automatic pistol in Bryce's hand, staring beyond the Navy man toward the locked gate.

"How many people do we have outside the walls?" he asked a woman he obviously knew from his time in the community.

"Four fishing at the pond, and another two searching some rural houses."

"We need to secure the gate, and make certain we have means of escape," Luke stated more to himself than the woman.

"What can I do to help?" Sean asked Luke, Buster at his side, and openly irritated by the scent of the dead.

"See if you can get a vehicle or two a safe distance from the village. Maybe a couple hundred yards. We need means of escape from this place aside from the front gate."

Sean pondered the request momentarily.

"We have a few vehicles inside the gates."

"Bigger," Luke said. "Something that can get more than a handful of us out of here at once."

Sean nodded.

"I might have an idea," the young man said before taking his leave with Buster.

"What can I do?" Bryce asked.

Before Luke could answer, Robert McAllister appeared before them with a bewildered look on his face.

"What in God's name is going on?" he demanded.

"Our fishing party reported a large group of undead heading straight for the village," Luke answered. "Possibly a couple hundred of them."

McAllister looked downward momentarily, the wheels of his mind attempting to grasp what the influx of zombies meant.

"We can't withstand that number," he stammered after a few seconds.

Taking a nervous look around, he spotted his people arming themselves without his orders.

"We can, and we will," Luke assured him.

"Somehow, this is your fault," McAllister said, directing newfound anger at Bryce. "Ever since your people arrived here, it's been nothing but trouble."

"Robert, there's time for that later," Luke said. "Can you and Nancy get the children and the elderly to a safe spot?"

McAllister calmed down slightly, his mind switching gears with a task at hand.

"We can gather them and bring them to the armory. There's a panic room area behind the weapons."

"Good," Luke said, keeping his calm. "I've been talking to our fishing group, and they're keeping me informed about what's coming. We'll be ready."

McAllister nodded, and departed to locate his wife to start rounding up anyone within the walls incapable of using a weapon, or helping with the impending battle.

"You handled that well," Bryce said directly to Luke.

"Robert requires a delicate touch," Luke responded. "He likes to be in charge, so I let him think this is what he wanted by giving him an important task."

Luke keyed the radio, trying to reach their residents stranded outside of Maplewood.

"Karen, are you there?"

"We're here," her voice answered.

"How much time do we have before they're at our doorstep?"

"Half an hour, tops."

Luke looked to Bryce.

"I think we need more people out there. We may need a distraction."

"That's a dangerous proposition. I thought you just sent Sutton's kid to work on that."

"I didn't tell him to *stay* out there. If we get surrounded, and we can't get out later, it would be nice to have a way to lure the dead away from the walls, or attack them from another direction."

"Can't argue with that," Bryce stated.

In his mind, Bryce was already contemplating the idea of calling the military, namely his former supervisor, and surrendering himself to them in exchange for clearing the undead away from the village. He decided to keep that notion on the back burner, because the present was not the time to make phone calls when the community was about to be under siege.

Taking a moment to look at everyone around him bustling with nervous energy, Bryce saw the village pull together. McAllister and his wife called for the children while going from one house to the next, searching for anyone incapable of fending off the undead. Others continued to check the gates, or look for their own loved ones, and a few approached Luke to ask him how they could assist.

Two such people were Father Paul and Sister Rosa, who carried their weapons of choice with them. Bryce hadn't interacted with the pair very much, but the community appeared to enjoy having them present. He knew they fought the undead particularly well, but also provided a comfort to the residents as religious centerpieces, helping the community cope with the new world around them.

"What can we do?" Father Paul inquired with a determined expression.

"Find Sean Sutton," Luke said without delay. "We need an emergency means of exiting the village if we get surrounded and can't fend off the dead. Sean is getting us an escape vehicle, so I need safe means for people to exit Maplewood. Maybe a zipline of some sort from one of the rooftops."

"We'll see what we can find," Father Paul assured him, nodding at Rosa before the pair departed.

"A zipline?" Bryce questioned.

"If the dead surround every wall, we won't have a conventional exit left, short of tunneling beneath them."

Luke began walking, checking that everyone was armed as he made his way through the increasing crowd of residents. Bryce heard murmurs from their mouths, most concerned about a virtual army of the undead heading their way, some blaming the newcomers, and a few scared for their lives. He also heard Robert and Nancy McAllister calling for everyone to bring the children to the armory, personally hoping the dead never breached the walls.

"What's going on?" Isabella asked him after managing to squeeze through some residents to reach her husband.

"The group outside the walls reported a horde of the undead heading directly for us."

"Wouldn't they just pass on by if we kept quiet?"

"It sounds like they're being led here on purpose," Bryce answered.

"But who would-"

Isabella reached a conclusion before even finishing her sentence.

"Hewitt," she said with a shake of her head, anger visibly rising within her body. "But how would he know where to find us?"

"He's determined, and he hates us," Bryce replied. "I'm sure we're all he's thought about since the military released him."

A thought suddenly occurred to the lieutenant commander.

"Where's Nathan?"

"He's with McAllister and the other kids. When I heard we were being invaded, I got him to safety."

Bryce wanted to tell his wife to stay back and protect the children, mainly to keep her safe, but virtually every capable adult in the community was armed with a firearm, spear, or some blunt tool. Isabella would never concede to hiding in a panic room, or taking a backseat to everyone else while they risked their lives for their homes. If they were ever going to fit in as new residents, Bryce, Luke, and everyone else from his brother's group would need to prove their worth.

"Has anyone actually seen the undead?" Bryce questioned Luke when he and his wife caught up to the self-appointed protector of Maplewood.

"Only the folks at the pond. Maybe Sean, or our Catholic duo will spot them outside the walls."

"Is anyone on watch in the towers?" Isabella asked.

"We had them come down to grab some better rifles with scopes. I'll send them back in a few minutes."

Everyone nearby appeared to be checking their weapons, or loading them, determined looks scrawled on their faces. Bryce checked the pistol he was given, and Isabella inspected her shotgun, requiring no instruction as she helped defend the place her parents called home in the Adirondacks. One might have thought a band of marauders was heading their way, but in truth killing the undead wouldn't prove troublesome, assuming the walls held. If they somehow breached the brick walls, or the gate, weapons would not be enough to stop the onslaught when the dead stumbled through whatever opening they created.

"God help us all if that happens," Bryce said under his breath.

***

Sean Sutton looked frantically for an appropriate vehicle in the makeshift parking lot about a quarter of a mile from the community. A few vehicles were kept up close for emergency purposes, but they were mostly smaller vehicles, better on gas and used for scavenging runs, or transportation. His heart raced at the thought of being a potential salvation for the village. He wasn't sure what vehicle might prove best, but his eyes kept going to an old RV, and the short, blue bus beside it.

A converted school bus, the blue vehicle later served a Baptist church, offering rides to older patrons and children whose parents couldn't make it to church during a given week. Sean figured the bus could transport more residents, should the situation grow dire, and it also offered some height in which to escape the undead, both inside, and on top.

"Come here," he called softly to Buster after reluctantly taking the canine outside the walls with him.

Buster obliged, wagging his tail as he followed Sean to the blue bus. Pushing the door open, Sean gave a cursory exam inside for any trespassers as the makeshift parking lot certainly wasn't secured or guarded. Every seat on the bus appeared vacant, a few even showing light coatings of dust because the bus hadn't been driven in a few weeks.

Each vehicle remained unlocked, and each had a certain hiding spot for the keys. From what he knew, the villagers decided early on to leave all motor vehicles close to the empty mark in fuel. Fortunately, the bus didn't have to travel far for the time being, but if it did, their fuel reserves weren't too far away. Despite McAllister's reservations about newcomers, the other residents took to the recent batch of guests, openly telling them everyday information because they assumed no one would ever want to leave the safe haven.

Buster entered the bus for a quick look, but he turned his head toward the outside within a few seconds, as though detecting something nearby.

"What is it, boy?"

Buster growled, indicating whatever drew closer wasn't friendly.

Armed only with a handgun, and its limited number of rounds, Sean stepped from the bus with the gun in a ready position and Buster brushing past him.

Buster immediately started barking and standing his ground as a member of the undead weaved between a few nearby vehicles toward the movement it spied. Sean took aim with the sidearm, hesitating to shoot and draw more danger his way. Buster turned and growled fiercely in the opposite direction, and Sean spun around to find two more walking corpses heading his way. One of them displayed an open fracture in her right arm, just below the shoulder, and the other, a husky man with months of decay, wore blue coveralls covered in dried blood.

Considering that Maplewood residents weren't typically allowed to walk around with bladed weapons, Sean saw little choice except to begin shooting the undead that seemingly appeared from nowhere. He began taking aim at the skull above the coveralls when a blur came from one side, disabling the zombie before Sean could pull the trigger.

He watched with a bit of surprise at the quickness of Sister Rosa as she pulled her weapon from the skull of the zombie, letting it drop to the ground. In virtually the same motion, she turned and used one of its sharpened edges to stab the other threat through the eyeball, stopping it mid-growl. It had begun to grope at her, but its arms dropped harmlessly to its side, like some movie robot suddenly disabled or powered down. She retracted the crucifix weapon once again, looking directly at Sean before speaking.

"Don't shoot it," she said with her Spanish accent, referring to the last of the undead creeping up behind him, which he had momentarily forgotten about.

She brushed past him, giving it the same treatment as the other two, negating the threat in a timely manner.

"Why are you here?" Sean questioned, trying not to sound defensive.

"Father Paul is looking for rope, or a cable. We're going to try and make an emergency zipline to one of the taller vehicles."

"This one should run," he said, thumbing toward the bus. "I was about to start it after I cleared the area. Buster kept growling, so I stepped out here to see what was coming."

"We're running out of time," Rosa said, urging him to start the bus. "Once the dead make it to our gates, there won't be any leaving."

"Hop in," Sean said, about to find the keys and start the bus.

"No. I'm more use out here."

"Don't get yourself locked out," Sean said, openly concerned for the religious woman.

"Say a prayer for any dead I find out here. Their souls will be put to rest."

Sean gave a quick smile before returning to the bus with Buster, quickly locating the keys behind the driver's seat, taped near the bottom where it appeared duct tape was used to patch a hole. He put them in the ignition, elated when the bus roared to life without a single hiccup. He closed the door and began driving in the direction of Maplewood, uncertain about where to park the vehicle. Father Paul would likely provide him with that information if and when he found the materials for a zipline, or some sort of ladder.

Fortunately, the designated parking lot was actually an area with a large concrete pad, but no building on the property. Perhaps a stop for long-haul drivers, or a parking lot for a church or retailer that no longer existed, the solid surface provided ample space for the vehicles to remain a safe distance from one another. Sean found no trouble navigating the bus out of its spot, and in the direction of Maplewood, eyeing Rosa along the right side. She intermittently walked and jogged as she searched for additional undead in the area.

Time wasn't on his side, and Sean didn't possess efficient means to communicate with anyone inside the community walls. He would have to draw close to Maplewood and speak with someone inside, hoping they could locate Father

Paul for him. With luck, the priest discovered something useful for exiting the village if the need arose.

***

Father Paul didn't particularly like the fact that his counterpart had gone outside the walls without him, and thoughts of her safety continued to distract him from his search. Two small sheds within the community held odds and ends, along with tools, plastic tarps, and items essential to repairing the houses.

He didn't hold out much optimism about locating a rope, chain, or anything else that might help the residents escape in a pinch. While every other resident sharpened blades, loaded firearms, or kept watch beyond their gates, Father Paul felt somewhat useless searching for a potential escape route. He wasn't an accomplished fighter, but he performed well against the undead. His weapon of choice kept him safe by offering several deadly sharp ends with which to permanently disable any zombie.

Moving several boards and boxes aside, the priest went straight to work, searching up and down the walls for items hanging on hooks, or anything that might provide a pathway over the walls. Had the community been old enough, a metal tower used to hold a television antenna might have proven perfect, but the community was built when satellite dishes and digital cable became the norm. Maplewood's two guard towers were constructed near the front gate, possibly to intimidate, but the front gate was about to become the *worst* place to exit the village. He felt as though he could be of more use preparing for the impending battle instead of searching for scraps the community might not even possess.

"Any luck?" Luke asked, poking his head inside the shed in passing.

"Not yet," Father Paul answered. "Just got started."

"Keep at it. Having a way out could mean the difference between life and death for some of these folks."

"You got it."

Although he spoke the words, the priest didn't feel very inspired. He decided to quit being conservative, setting items neatly aside, because cleanliness wasn't a top priority at the moment. Becoming more like a rodent searching for food or nesting materials, he dug through each box, and searched each corner thoroughly until he discovered a possible answer to his prayer. From one of the last boxes, he pulled out a coiled bundle of nylon rope. Still in store packaging, the print on the cardboard sleeve indicated it was one-hundred feet in length.

"Thank God," he said under his breath before stepping out of the shed, hearing the first panicked shouts of his fellow residents.

"There they are!"

"Who's driving that car?"

"Why would anyone do that?"

More comments and questions hovered in the air, and he began to realize someone indeed purposely led the undead directly to their sanctuary.

"What is it?" he asked Luke when he took the man's side near the front gate.

"Someone's been driving that car, and blaring the music, to bring them straight here."

Father Paul could see the car through the gate, but it remained barely more than a speck, several hundred yards away.

"Do we have a sharpshooter?" he inquired.

"Our best shot went with Dan Metzger. I can check on that while you find Sean Sutton and get that rope rigged up."

"On it," the priest promised, clutching the rope and heading for the opposite side of the village where he found Sean Sutton already standing on the other side of the wall.

Most of the wall was solid brick, but every ten feet, for decorative purposes, wrought iron bars that matched the front gate occupied less than two feet of width. Father Paul and Sean met face to face at one such space.

"I've got a bus," Sean reported. "How much rope do you have?"

"A hundred feet."

"That won't get us very far across this wall."

"Better than nothing," Father Paul said with a shrug.

He looked up to the two-story house directly behind him. A chimney hugged one side of the house, along the roof, providing an anchor point. The rope could be wrapped around the chimney and tied into a knot. He tossed one end of the rope over the fence to Sean after ripping it from the packaging.

"I'll try and figure out the distance," Sean said, taking the rope with him several feet before dropping it on the ground so he could drive the bus closer.

Taking a look up to the chimney, Father Paul knew he needed a ladder. He started walking briskly toward the storage sheds, hoping his allies outside the wall were faring better. His thoughts also dwelled on what Metzger and the others were trying to accomplish in the Midwest. Although he expected nothing different, the apocalypse had a knack for bringing new problems on a daily basis.

Chapter 30

Luke stood beside his designated sniper at the front gate, watching the horde grow closer as a slow-moving Buick Regal headed in the general direction of the sole entrance. He wished he had used Sean Sutton as a sniper, believing the young man likely possessed some of his father's talents for shooting firearms. He couldn't change the past, and now he stood beside a young woman named Sara, who grew up on a working farm, and spent some time in the military. Granted, she wasn't a professional sniper, but she knew firearms, and proper shooting techniques.

"See anything?" he asked her as she peered through the magnification scope mounted to the Remington 700 she had aimed at the car.

"There's no one in the car," she reported. "Either they've been ducked down this entire time, or they somehow rigged the gas pedal."

Luke cussed under his breath, not letting the others see his frustration.

Sara took a moment to look away from the rifle, to him, as though asking what to do next. She kept her strawberry blonde hair just short of her shoulders, and she looked older than her twenty-something years.

"Can you disable the car?" Luke asked after a few seconds of deliberation.

"I think it's close enough. It's a matter of hitting the engine block."

Luke exhaled through his nose.

"Do it."

He motioned for everyone to stay down, and stay quiet, as Sara took aim at the car's grill. A few seconds passed before she fired, causing a small plume of steam to emerge from one side of the hood. Still, the car traveled in the direction of Maplewood, and Luke knew he bought the village mere minutes, perhaps half an hour, if Sara crippled the vehicle. He waited a few seconds, but the car refused to slow, despite its initial wound on full display.

"One more shot," he said calmly, seeing that the undead remained focused on the car, and not the least bit distracted by the echoes of gunfire.

He turned away before Sara even shot the next round, determined to see where Father Paul had gotten with his portion of securing an emergency escape route. Several people spoke to Luke, questioning where he was going at such a crucial time as the dead drew near.

"I'll be right back," he assured them with volume enough that all could hear. "No one fires another shot until I return."

Everyone exchanged glances and shrugs, and he heard Sara's shot, followed by a few of his fellow residents giving muffled cheers, as though it struck home. Luke focused his attention on the back of the village, finding Father Paul perilously atop the pitched roof, tying the last of a knot that secured his side of the rope around the chimney. He looked down, spying Luke, and provided an affirmative nod that the job was complete.

"Thank you," Luke said before staring out the wrought iron break in the otherwise brick wall, seeing Sean Sutton busy at work securing the opposite end of the rope to the emergency exit window atop the bus.

Luke suspected Sean had knocked out the window to provide a solid anchor point for the line, because vehicular safety measures weren't very important in the apocalypse.

Assured they had the backup measure in place, he briskly walked to the front gate, seeing the undead ambling closer, despite the car continuing to blare music. He questioned why they didn't encircle the car, instead focusing on the village ahead of them. Luke couldn't imagine they heard or saw anything from that distance that enticed their primitive brains.

"Can I borrow that a second?" he asked Sara before she handed him the rifle.

Taking a look through the scope, he tried to decipher anything unusual in the large group as most of the several hundred meanderers walked toward Maplewood. He saw one zombie in particular turned around as though walking against the flow, but the zombie in question righted itself slowly, rotating to join the others, ignoring the music and the Buick completely. Every other zombie around it tended to follow the crowd, rather than direct their attention to the typical distraction.

"Somehow, someone is herding them this way," Luke muttered, drawing the attention of several residents around him.

"What do we do?" one of them asked.

"We wait until they get close enough to see their pale eyes, then we attack. They can only be killed by shooting or stabbing them in the skulls. We cannot afford to waste ammo by shooting too early."

Tense minutes passed as the audible growls, hisses, and random croaks grew closer, openly terrifying some of the residents who hadn't dealt with the undead at close range.

"Hold your ground," Luke said firmly. "The walls will hold long enough for us to take them down one at a time."

Bryce approached him with Isabella at his side. Both held firearms, openly ready to assist the residents however possible.

"We have those decorative spaces in the walls," Bryce noted. "Do you want us to cover some of those?"

"Yes," Luke said. "I need some volunteers to help cover the openings once the dead arrive."

Several heads nodded, and all of them knew the decorative areas with wrought iron weren't necessarily a weakness in the wall. Enough weight against them for long enough might cause them to buckle eventually, but they provided an opportunity to stop more of the undead in a variety of areas.

Bryce and Isabella departed for one of the openings and in less than a few seconds, the murmurs began.

"They're probably trying to leave."

"This is all their fault."

Luke put a stop to the contagious hatred before it could grow.

"These are *my* people," he said. "If you don't trust them, then you shouldn't be trusting me."

Everyone suddenly grew silent as guilty eyes looked anywhere except his direction.

"And another thing, there's always going to be someone out there who wants what we have. We're always going to be looking over our shoulders, and it isn't anyone's fault. We need to stick together right now, and going forward, or there'll be a lot fewer of us living here."

Within minutes, the dead drew closer to the walls of Maplewood, as though something inside acted as a beacon. No one panicked, or made noise enough to lure them closer, so Luke stared through the front gate, wondering what, aside from the disabled car, brought them to his current residence.

***

Sean Sutton tied the line securely along the top of the bus, able to tie a knot just inside the emergency window. He returned to the same area where he and Father Paul had communicated earlier, hoping to find the priest once again. Buster remained by his side, though openly agitated by the undead drawing closer to the gated community.

"Father?" Sean called as loudly as he dared. "Are you there?"

A few seconds passed with no response, and he was about to begin walking along one side of the village toward the front, but the priest finally arrived, hastily walking to the wrought iron opening.

"Sorry," the priest said. "Had to climb down from that roof."

"I need to get inside," Sean said.

Father Paul looked to the wall, likely thinking the younger man could simply climb and jump over, but he looked to Buster and understood the dilemma.

"The dead are getting close," Father Paul said. "But I think we have enough time to get the gates open and let you both inside."

He hesitated before heading for the front.

"Did you see Rosa out there?"

"We did. She cleared a path for us."

"She hasn't come back," the priest said with obvious concern. "Meet me up front and I'll get you both inside."

Father Paul navigated through the buildings in the village, making one quick stop along the way to grab a spare radio near the armory. After briefly testing its battery life, he clipped the device along the small of his back. He arrived at the front gate in time to see dozens of zombies closing in on the people of Maplewood. They remained quiet and poised, and he wasn't sure who to approach about opening the front gates with so many residents already aiming out of the decorative bars. He finally saw Luke taking charge of the situation, and rushed up to the blond-haired man.

"I need the front gate open to let Sean Sutton and Buster inside," the priest said without hesitation. "We got the emergency escape in place."

Luke nodded, a show of relief washing across his face that contingencies were in place.

"Unlock the gate," he said to the man standing closest to the clasp that kept the swinging gates in place, receiving only a cursory glance before the man did as he asked. "When Sean and his dog get here, let them inside and secure the gates immediately."

Now the man gave a nod, and clearly the community began to rally together, knowing they needed to stand as one against the invasion heading directly for them.

Father Paul leaned close, so only Luke could hear his words.

"Sister Rosa is still out there."

Luke looked at him with a conflicted stare.

"We can't risk looking for her."

"I'm not asking you to."

"Don't you risk yourself, Father."

"It's what we do," Father Paul said, giving him a reassuring grin. "I promise we'll do some good for you out there once I locate her."

"I know you will," Luke said, openly concerned about such a risk. "Watch your back."

From out of nowhere, a small truck headed toward the front gate, and everyone collectively gasped, wondering if an enemy meant to ram the gate to compromise it. Somehow the truck had weaved through the undead horde, and several people recognized the vehicle as one of their own. Even so, they weren't certain who was behind the wheel until the truck stopped about twenty feet short of the gate and two members of the village stepped from the vehicle and dashed for the gate. Residents recognized them as the other two gatherers who had left that morning before the four unfortunate souls who went fishing.

When Sean Sutton arrived with Buster at the front gate, the gate was opened to let him, Buster, and the two Maplewood residents inside. Before anyone could intervene, the priest slipped past everyone, and the open gate, into the dangerous beyond.

"Father!" Sean called out, but the priest never looked back as he skirted toward one side of the village, carrying the religious symbol he'd forged into a weapon months ago.

"Lock the gate," Luke ordered the man who had opened it.

"What is he thinking?" Sean asked somewhat heatedly.

"He's going to find Rosa, and they're going to take the fight to the undead out there."

Sean stared out the front gate momentarily as the dead drew closer. They barely paid attention to Father Paul as he departed, and Luke studied the horde momentarily, finally seeing something out of place. Nearly a head taller than some of the undead, a man with varying patches of skin and fur staggered in pace with them, occasionally turning subtly to make certain none of the flock turned away before walking directly for the front gates of Maplewood. He looked like a human calico with the various colors of skin and fur attached to his body, and Luke thought back to a certain man who wore the same things to blend in with the dead.

His attention temporarily diverted to the front of the undead pack, and he noticed several in the front row, tied together by ropes along their wrists. A protective barrier of sorts, they were almost assured to lead the remaining dead forward. Luke felt numb when he saw one particular member of the undead leading the way.

"Kevin," he muttered, seeing his fellow resident in a minor state of decay, snarling and growling like the other undead around him.

Luke flushed with anger, and although he was never directly wronged by Hewitt until now, he wanted the man dead for bringing grave danger to his doorstep, and murdering Kevin Gebbert. Likely looking like a madman, he raised the pistol he held in his right hand, took aim at the skull of Hewitt from nearly a hundred feet away, and shouted.

"You motherfucker!"

He pulled the trigger before Hewitt could possibly duck, but his aim missed low, because a member of the undead unwittingly stepped in front of the bullet and fell in a heap. Now alerted to the fact that the Maplewood community knew of his presence, Hewitt ducked down slightly and made his way through the crowd in the opposite direction.

"Can you see him?" Luke asked almost frantically.

"See who?" Sean asked.

"Hewitt. That was Hewitt out there leading these things our way."

As the remainder of the undead closed in on the village, there was no chance of slipping out to pursue Hewitt, even if Luke wanted to. He felt the radio pressing against his side where he had clipped it, and he knew he needed to contact the Maplewood residents at the pond. With luck, they could track Hewitt, and possibly even take him down if an opportunity presented itself.

"Wait until they're at the gates," he told his fellow residents, standing beside him. "Wait until you can't possibly miss, and aim for their skulls."

***

Father Paul managed to elude most of the undead when he darted to the side of Maplewood, hoping to find Sister Rosa sooner than later. He knew full well about her ability to take care of herself against the undead, but she sometimes took on too much. They worked better as a team, using two sets of eyes and ears to defend one another while bashing skulls of their adversaries.

Two members of the undead wouldn't stop following him, so the priest paused to deal with them, using the sharpened edges of the modified crucifix that once stood beside the altar of his church. Typically, he used the weapon more like a sword, particularly a fencing sword where he could jab, but the cross-guards on the weapon could also pierce flesh and bone because they were sharpened. Currently, he used both hands to thrust the weapon into the soil, allowing it to stand like it would have in his church, and waited for his adversaries to approach. They did so, growling and lurching toward him until they drew close enough for him to palm each of them along the side of their skulls. They snapped at him, so he carefully thrust their heads into the sharpened ends of his weapon, ending them instantly.

"I always wanted to do a cool kill," he said, examining his work momentarily, until he realized he needed to remove them from the makeshift skewers and somehow clean the portion of the weapon he normally held. "Yuck."

He shook them free of the sharpened edges until they dropped onto the ground. Tearing the shirt off one of the zombies, he cleaned the weapon, and began to realize he didn't have much time to waste. Plucking the crucifix from the ground, he prepared to resume his search when the radio tucked along his back came to life.

"Karen? Are you there?" Luke's voice sounded over the device.

"We're here. What's your status?"

"The dead are here, and we'll be surrounded in minutes. Look, Hewitt led them here, and I took a shot at him and missed. I think he's heading back towards you."

"Understood."

"Be careful. Do *not* approach him."

Father Paul listened for a reply, but none came. Any number of reasons might explain why, but he suddenly questioned whether to aid the four residents stuck outside the walls, and end the larger threat in Hewitt. The majority of Maplewood citizens remained behind sturdy walls, and Luke seemed to have them prepared.

Father Paul's thoughts were interrupted by the slurpy sounds of something eating nearby. Cautiously stepping over to investigate, Father Paul found a zombie on its knees, feeding on something lying motionless on the ground. Fresh blood covered its hands, and for a fearful moment, he sucked in a breath, praying Sister Rosa hadn't somehow fallen victim to one of the hundreds of threats lingering nearby.

He slowly circled the woman wearing her Sunday best dress, now tattered and stained, sloppily chowing down on some hapless animal that might have already been injured or trapped. Now dead, the furry critter remained perfectly still, and Father Paul breathed a sigh of relief. Taking a quick look behind him, to ensure no additional undead had followed him, he raised his weapon to finish off the female zombie when a sharp weapon jabbed it in the head as he turned around.

Startled, he jumped half a step back to see Sister Rosa had done him a favor by stabbing it in the side of the head with her religious weapon.

"Good to see you, Sister," he said, catching his breath.

"Likewise. I thought you would be inside with the others."

"I came looking for you. Figured we could be more help out here, thinning their numbers, but something else came up."

Sister Rosa provided a confused expression.

"It turns out Hewitt was leading the dead straight to Maplewood," Father Paul explained. "The four people who were fishing are going to try and stop him."

"Not if we get to him first."

"My thoughts exactly."

"Where do we look for him?"

Father Paul had already considered the possibility that Hewitt watched them for a period of time before gathering the dead.

"I think he might have been staying in that cabin where we store extra supplies," the priest revealed his thoughts.

"It would make sense. Do you think he's heading there?"

"They reported him heading that way. We should split up, and run along either side of the dead so we can take some out along the way. We'll meet at the cabin and see if he's there."

Sister Rosa nodded, and chose the side closer to where they already stood. Father Paul had to double back to get to the other side of Maplewood, along the back side. He suspected Sister Rosa planned to take out her fair share of the undead along the way, wishing to keep him safer by making him go the less treacherous route.

Giving a sigh, he started jogging around the gated village, thankful his cardio had improved since taking up residence in Maplewood. He hoped they could find Hewitt before the sinister man brought harm to more random strangers.

Chapter 31

Mike Mullins stared intently from the pond area after most of the undead had passed. The fishing group had received the message about Hewitt heading their way, and he didn't want the man to know members of Maplewood were already outside the village walls. If they were able to catch him by surprise, they could put a bullet in his brain and begin picking off the nearby straggling undead.

"Why are we still hiding down here?" Karen Brown asked beside him. "We could get in our car and start searching for him?"

"We have the element of surprise," Mullins answered. "Maplewood is well over a mile away and he'd hear us coming and take cover. It's going to take him a while to walk here."

Davison and Koger peered over the edge of the grass at the damage done to the field ahead by the hundreds of undead that crossed.

"They trampled everything," Davison muttered.

About twenty undead continued to linger in the area, and the fishing party wasn't heavily armed. They possessed knives, and a few firearms, but nothing to pick off zombies, or Hewitt, from a safe distance.

"What if we split up?" Koger suggested.

"That sounds like the worst possible idea," Mullins said flatly.

"Hear me out. Two of us take the car, so we can search for him, and two of us go on foot to start taking these things out. It would give us two search parties."

"It would also leave us at a disadvantage," Mullins noted. "Hewitt isn't a normal human being. And we only have one radio. We could easily get separated with no way to locate one another."

"Then maybe we all take the car," Karen thought aloud. "You said it yourself. Hewitt can't walk here very quickly, so we're bound to intercept him if we head for Maplewood. There aren't many places a man his size can hide."

"We could run his ass over," Koger said.

Mullins wanted to play it safer than his colleagues, because he didn't believe they understood the danger that an angry and determined Hewitt posed. He supposed the idea of being together in a vehicle beat separating into two pairs that Hewitt could pick off through sneak attacks. Part of Mullins wanted to help the people of Maplewood first, and form a lynch mob to locate Hewitt once everyone was safe and the army of the undead was truly dead.

Taking a cursory glance around them, the four saw no immediate danger, so they ran for the car, leaving their fishing gear behind. One member of the undead, wearing undiscernible clothes caked in dried mud and dust, drew close enough to Davison that he used his survival knife, stabbing it in the side of the skull. Mullins wasn't even certain the zombie had laid eyes on the former corrections officer, but Davison appeared pumped up, as though he had just scored a touchdown in a nationally-televised football game.

When they reached the car, Karen made certain to assume the driver's seat, giving Mullins a look before they all hopped inside. Her brief, penetrating glare appeared to indicate she didn't fully trust him.

Or his judgment.

He felt like the only sane person in his party at the moment, and now he was going after Hewitt with no recourse.

Despite outnumbering Hewitt four to one, Mullins didn't like their chances if they didn't spot the man before he took notice of the car. Mullins considered retreat a viable option if Karen drove them straight into a trap. If they had taken the time to down some of the undead and paste their skin atop their clothes with coagulated blood, the four could have moved more naturally through the dead and watched for Hewitt.

Although doomed by cancer, Mullins didn't want to die on this particular day. As the car traveled toward Maplewood, he kept monitoring the area from the back seat, where he had gotten last pick of seating. He hoped the battle at Maplewood didn't bring about any casualties, but he wasn't sure how long the gates could last against pushing and shoving beings that never tired.

***

Bryce and Isabella had taken turns, working well together at stabbing the undead who groped at them through the wrought iron area between brick wall sections. Although he fought to keep from getting distracted, Bryce couldn't help but wonder if he should call his former boss in the Navy to bring assistance. He wasn't certain he could trust Mark Dascher, but Bryce didn't want to see anyone in Maplewood die because of his presence.

Whether Hewitt thought Bryce, his brother, or any of the others were present, didn't much matter. He intended to send a message to the Metzger brothers that he hadn't forgiven, or forgotten, any of their encounters in the Adirondacks, or his forced captivity in Virginia. Perhaps he intended to turn the residents of Maplewood against them, and to some extent he succeeded, whether he planned it or not.

"What's the matter?" Isabella asked as he stabbed a zombie pressed against the wrought iron squarely in the right eyeball.

He dared not speak his thoughts, because he knew she would tell him none of this was his fault, and they could fight their way out of it.

"Nothing," he finally said dismissively, jabbing the next zombie in line squarely in the right temple.

It fell against the wrought iron decorative trim, adding to the small stack forming in their area. Undeterred, the remaining undead stepped on their fallen brethren, beginning to stomp them into the ground where they formed bloody blobs. Bryce heard some panicked cries from other areas of the village, hoping no one received a bite, or got dragged off by the never-ending stream of attackers.

"You're worried this is somehow your fault," Isabella said, half-correct in her assessment.

"*We* brought Hewitt here," Bryce retorted. "How can it *not* be our fault?"

"There's no way any of us could've known Hewitt wasn't immune and this wouldn't backfire."

Bryce certainly didn't blame his brother. His brother stood up to Hewitt, which is something no one else dared try. Virtually everyone else who crossed the man wound up dead, often put on public display for the sinister man to warn others about crossing him.

"Focus up," Isabella warned him as she thrust her knife forward, taking down another zombie that clamored over its permanently deceased kind. "We're going to get through this."

Bryce waited for another member of the undead to stick its head up to the wrought iron trim, growling at them threateningly, before he rammed his blade upward from the base of its chin. It ceased making any noise the second the blade penetrated its brain, falling silent as it fell to the ground.

"How many of these things are there?" he lamented.

"Enough to keep us busy for a while."

Bryce felt the sat phone in his right front pocket, and he questioned whether he needed to call Dascher. If his former boss hadn't been truthful, calling the Navy commander might result in Bryce sentencing himself to Naval Station Norfolk as a guinea pig. Even worse, he would likely face charges as a deserter, even though his own people left him for dead in his home state.

He always felt somewhat guilty about not allowing the military to use his blood, like they had his brother's, but Bryce knew how the government treated objects they *needed*. While they considered him a necessity, he wasn't entirely certain how they would treat his family the second time around, or if they would use Isabella and Nathan as leverage against him.

Regardless of what he decided, Bryce needed to help in the fight against the undead until there was some kind of break, or the dead broke off their bombardment of the front gate and any other small opening they located.

Looking down, he saw blood speckles across the clay-colored shirt he wore. It reminded him of the numerous deaths he had witnessed since returning from sea on the *USS Ross* the previous year. He and his fellow sailors were shocked at what they saw, after hearing horrific stories across the news, and from family members. Access to the outside world remained restricted on a military vessel, and the sailors couldn't believe what they heard.

He decided he wanted to see just how grave their situation appeared at Maplewood, so he looked to Isabella, who openly knew he wasn't acting himself.

"I need to check something," he stated. "Can you handle this for a few minutes?"

"I've been handling most of it anyway," she replied. "They're starting to stack up, so do what you need to do and come back."

Bryce nodded, walking toward the front of the community where he saw most of the inhabitants busily fending off the undead. Without being noticed, he reached the house closest to the front gate and stepped inside, wasting little time taking the stairs to the second floor where he found a bedroom facing toward the front gate.

"No," Bryce muttered to himself as his eyes remained fixated on the scene ahead.

Almost as far as he could see, the undead lined the ground, forming a large, giant mass of darkness that began to encircle the community. Behind them, a mostly sunny sky illuminated the gloomy circumstance, informing Bryce that hundreds of zombies had followed Hewitt to the village. He didn't hold out much hope that the few stragglers outside the walls could help thin the undead numbers, or locate Hewitt, so he exhaled through his nose and reached for the satellite phone in his pocket.

***

"Dear Lord," Davison said beside Mullins as their car drew closer to the undead mob surrounding the Maplewood.

Strangely, the place all four people inside the car called home was barely visible at the edge of the horde ahead of them.

"He could be anywhere," Koger muttered, since they hadn't located Hewitt.

"Where would he go?" Karen asked. "He's probably been spying on us since the military booted him."

Mullins attempted to think of any landmarks near the community, and though several towns weren't incredibly far away, they weren't places conveniently reached by walking.

"Are there any isolated houses near the village?" he questioned aloud. "He's probably on foot to avoid detection, and he's not going to walk farther than he has to."

Everyone thought of the surrounding area momentarily while Karen steered the car to the right, away from most of the undead awkwardly attracted to Maplewood.

"The cabin?" Koger finally said slowly, as though uncertain it might appeal to Hewitt.

Karen looked at him with a growing smile on her face that frightened Mullins. He worried they would head to this place, pedal to the metal, and alert Hewitt so he could prepare to defend himself before they laid eyes on him.

Even worse, numerous undead began to peel away from the Maplewood scene because they couldn't get close enough to hear or see activity, so a car going by provided them with a new distraction. Karen wasn't driving very fast now, as the cabin was located nearby, and the undead appeared to keep up with them. Dealing with Hewitt, or dozens of undead, could be a deadly prospect, and both simultaneously felt like certain death.

"What do we have for weapons?" Mullins questioned.

"Each of us has a knife," Koger replied. "And we've got the two pistols."

"The second we step from this car, we're going to be surrounded by the dead," Mullins stated. "If we can't shoot Hewitt and get the fuck out of there, we're going to get devoured. And I can promise you, Hewitt isn't stupid enough to make himself a target."

"What are you saying?" Karen asked. "Sounds like you're getting scared again."

"I'm being cautious. Killing Hewitt is only worthwhile if the four of us don't get killed. The people of Maplewood are going to need our help."

"He's got a point," Davison conceded. "We've only got a few dozen rounds, and using the guns will only draw the dead straight to us."

Karen's faced reddened at this point.

"We're killing him, and that's the end of it."

Other than passing a message along to the Navy officer and his friends, Mullins couldn't think of a single, sane reason he opted to return to Maplewood. Karen Brown was about to drive them straight into the arms of Hewitt, and even though he felt above average when it came to shooting, or defending himself, he didn't feel confident.

More undead peeled away from the Maplewood allure, following their car instead. Mullins felt certain Hewitt had already spotted them, and he wished Karen would drive faster toward the cabin. If their adversary already knew they were coming for him, adding a few dozen undead to the mix wasn't going to increase their odds of taking him down.

All four people in the car kept looking in every direction for anyone that stood out from the typical undead staggering around the area. Walking without any rhythm to their steps, the undead were typically easy to decipher from living people, but Mullins knew Hewitt stood taller than most survivors. They passed trees along some uneven terrain, as Karen didn't stick to the road at all times, and encountered several small hills.

Mullins grew uneasy around the trees and hills, feeling certain Hewitt had already seen them and plotted his next move.

He considered the possibility that they beat Hewitt to the area, if he was indeed heading for the cabin, which also allowed their adversary to spot them first. His thoughts proved incorrect when he spotted a tall individual lumbering between the trees ahead of the car. To Mullins, the sight reminded him of the Bigfoot images and blurry videos he saw as a student, and he wondered if Hewitt intended to reenact those memories with his odd sense of humor.

"That's him," Koger said, pointing in the direction. "Isn't it?"

"Yes," Mullins confirmed. "He's heading straight for the cabin."

"He's familiar with it," Davison thought aloud. "He has to know we're here."

"He does," Mullins said. "He's daring us to come for him."

For the first time, Karen had little to say, because she realized Hewitt was frightening, and dangerous, as he walked directly toward the cabin without so much as a glance their way.

"What exactly do you store in there?" Mullins questions as they watched Hewitt open the front door and step inside as though he owned the place.

"Mostly furniture and extra clothing," Koger answered. "No food or weapons."

"Anything that Maplewood can't afford to lose?"

All eyes turned to Mullins as Karen stopped the car.

"Going inside is a suicide mission," Mullins said, making his point. "It's going to be dark, and we don't know which corner or closet he's hiding in. I say we set the building on fire and make him come to us."

Everyone sat silently in their seats a moment, and Mullins questioned whether they possessed the means to adequately smoke Hewitt from the building.

"We have a gas can," Karen thought aloud. "And I'm pretty sure we have a flare or two tucked in the trunk somewhere."

Once Karen pulled within walking distance of the cabin, where their footsteps wouldn't be easily heard, everyone quietly exited the car and left their doors slightly ajar to avoid the risk of slamming them. Unfortunately, the undead didn't adhere to their planned assault on Hewitt, because they immediately headed for the four living souls they had been following for a quarter mile.

"Make this quick," Mullins said to Karen just above a whisper as he drew his knife. "We can keep them off you long enough to pour the gas."

Giving a nod, she pulled the gas can from the trunk, reached for one of the flares and the flare gun, pocketing the two latter items. She took quick, but cautious steps toward the cabin, trying to keep from being heard as her three companions silently took down the nearby undead with knives to the head. Karen kept one of the two firearms on her, and Koger possessed the other. Under normal circumstances, any of them knew how to use a firearm proficiently, but Mullins had been trained as a cop to squeeze the trigger under duress.

Mullins downed a zombie in his proximity with a knife into its deteriorating skull, glancing to see Karen beginning to pour gasoline around the cabin. He began to think they had chance to eliminate Hewitt with minimal risks to themselves when something unexpected flipped the script, and the former cop felt certain they were all doomed.

When the front door suddenly opened, he attempted to alert Koger, so the man had a realistic chance of firing a shot at Hewitt. Instead of a mammoth target walking through the threshold, however, a riot shield, like the kind used by police and jailers, emerged to protect the man behind it. Hewitt remained crouched, and didn't necessarily need to, because he struck like a viper, first knocking Karen to the ground by using the shield as a weapon that he easily swung with one arm. Mullins saw her eyes open wide with fear before the tactical device struck her squarely in the face, likely reducing her cheek and cranium bones into particles.

Her head struck the side of the cabin, and even before her already limp body fell to the ground, Hewitt made certain to strike her right temple again with his knee as she plummeted toward the grass. Keeping the shield between him and his remaining three adversaries, Hewitt stepped forward, taking aim at Koger next.

"Surround him," Mullins shouted to Davison, who only had a knife to defend himself, with more undead closing in by the second. "He can't shield all sides."

Even as the three men attempted to encircle Hewitt, Mullins didn't like their chances. Bullets couldn't penetrate the riot shield, and Hewitt certainly wouldn't willingly let all three men take jabs or shots at him. Mullins detected the stench of rotted flesh and dried blood emitting from their adversary, and he knew Hewitt had skinned undead corpses to use their components to blend in with them.

Prepared to make his final stand against the man who truly embodied selfishness and evil, Mullins hoped for the sake of Maplewood that one of them landed a killing blow.

Chapter 32

"What the hell are we going to do?" Timmons asked Jillian as they sat inside the plane, continuing to hear the occasional motorcycle in the distance.

Possibly from the unsettling noise of rumbling engines in the distance, or the fact that his surrogate son was in potential danger, the pilot appeared uneasy.

Jillian didn't feel particularly fearful about a single motorcycle rider, but if the plane was spotted, and one of the people guarding the perimeter of the bunker called for backup, they might have an issue.

"We're only hearing one bike at a time," she reasoned aloud. "They haven't spotted the plane, or they would've investigated."

"Clearly they saw us from the air."

"Not necessarily. They might do routine patrols."

Timmons didn't appear convinced.

"Look," Jillian said, trying to settle the pilot's nerves. "We'll do whatever it takes to make sure we're available for Dan when he needs us. If that means taking out a biker, we take out a biker."

"That's another thing. How the hell are we supposed to know if Dan is in trouble?"

"He knows what he's doing, Scott. And Brooke is very capable."

"We're taking her word on that. She hasn't done a whole lot to impress me, except lead us into a deathtrap."

"And here I thought you two were being chummy since you keep pairing up."

"By default," Timmons scoffed. "I was trying to learn more about her, but she's pretty tight-lipped about her past."

Jillian harbored her own doubts about Brooke's information, and her motivations, but Mullins and Metzger both trusted her enough to follow her lead.

She felt a bit surprised no one had located the plane, since open plains and very little cover surrounded their makeshift landing strip. Because of this, she felt reasonably confident the motorcycle person, or people, hadn't been specifically looking for a plane. Perhaps they were riding along trails, conducting routine patrols of the area, or on the hunt for something else.

"I'm going to admit, I still don't know why the risk is worth it to Dan," Timmons said.

"He needs closure," Jillian said. "You weren't there when he learned about how his parents died. He was a wreck for a while."

"He's risking a lot to come all the way out here on a gamble. And what if this doesn't pan out? What's next? Do we go looking for more Nadeau flunkies?"

"I don't have the answer to that," Jillian responded. "But I know Dan isn't going to move on completely until he finds some answers. You know he wants to help people."

"He *was* helping people at the Navy base."

"What exactly does that mean?"

"His blood could have provided a cure. A vaccine. Something to combat this infection."

"He was a prisoner, Scott. He doesn't deserve that."

"It wasn't that bad, Jillian. He was protected, safe, and well-fed."

"And he was under the belief that his brother was a walking corpse. A lie your bosses kept him believing while they milked his blood."

Both of them sat silently a few seconds, enjoying the temporary silence with no heavy winds, or motorcycle engines growling in the distance.

"If Isabella hadn't learned the truth, we'd all be in different places now," Jillian reminded him. "Except you."

If her words struck a nerve, Timmons didn't show it. He simply stared at the tan grass in its winter dormant state.

"I'm sorry," Timmons said, shaking his head. "I'm just lashing out because I'm nervous."

Jillian wasn't certain her boyfriend's mentor regretted all of his words. Timmons didn't like being out of his comfort zone, but it wasn't like him to question Metzger's motivations. Perhaps something along their journey had skewed his view of Metzger's overall objective, or he felt more threatened in the middle of nowhere. What disturbed her most was his sudden apology, because he made it readily apparent some of these topics were on his mind since going AWOL from the military.

She felt he spoke at least some previously suppressed truth, because his life at Naval Station Norfolk was excellent by apocalypse standards. He could have turned in Metzger and Isabella for planning an escape from the base, but he went along, basically making himself a criminal in the eyes of the military that housed him.

"Dan is going to be alright," she said, trying to reassure Timmons by taking the high road instead of arguing with him. "We need to stay right here until he's ready to fly out."

Timmons nodded without saying a word, which left her questioning his mindset even more. A motorcycle roared in the distance, and both gave a cursory glance in that direction without any remnants of fear. Both had decided whatever came their way, they would deal with it when the time came.

***

"They're inside," Sutton reported to Gracine as he looked through the scope of the rifle until Metzger and Brooke disappeared from view.

At that point, he looked to her, and both exchanged concerned stares.

"I feel so helpless," Gracine confessed, wishing they all could have gone with Metzger to the bunker.

Knowing bunkers only opened from the inside if one didn't possess the passcode, the group needed to use their one plausible cover story to get inside. Brooke possessed the insight and knowledge to get them past the guards. Metzger provided extra muscle, and a yearning to learn the truth about Nadeau's motivations, and whether or not a cure already existed.

Like their allies at the plane, they both heard motorcycles in the distance at regular intervals. Sutton reported that he saw very little through the scope of his rifle, indicating the one motorcycle he saw depart from the compound emerged from between two of the outbuildings. Gracine questioned how anyone could withstand riding a motorcycle without numerous layers of clothes. Winter certainly hadn't released its grip in Wyoming, despite the springtime month of April arriving a week or two earlier. She didn't personally feel prepared for the elements, despite wearing a few warm layers, gloves, and an exterior jacket she packed for the cold desert overnights.

"If we make it through this, where do you and I stand?" she decided to ask, since they remained completely alone atop the hilly area above the compound.

"Focus," Sutton said, obviously trying to avoid topics that dealt with emotions.

"I think we've avoided this for long enough, Colby."

Gracine mostly made small talk with Sutton during their recent travels, but she felt ready to learn his state of mind regarding their relationship. Emotionally anorexic after the death of his younger son for months, Sutton distanced himself from virtually everyone and everything important in his life. He forgot all about former family destinations, and sacrificed his prized box truck to gain his son and friends access to Maplewood. Gracine then moved on with Reggie Mitchell after he pursued her in Maplewood, and soon enough she moved in with him.

During one of their last layovers, Gracine thought she and Sutton had made a breakthrough, only to get interrupted. Sutton basically hit the reset button on talks of their relationship, or their near physical connection, the following morning.

Sutton rolled to one side, surveying the level ground around them to ensure none of the guards had discovered their whereabouts before speaking.

"You're committed," he said. "Are you willing to break that bond?"

"I'm here, am I not?" Gracine retorted, raising an irritated eyebrow.

"Are you here to help Dan, or here because you want to be with me?"

"We've been through this already," Gracine said, growing tired of him shoving her away emotionally. "If we survive this, I'll break things off with Reggie. If I do that, *no more* games."

Sutton exhaled heavily through his nose, the wheels of his mind churning.

Gracine's insides felt like a twisted knot, because she fully expected him to rebuke her advances once and for all. She decided she couldn't let that happen without getting one last statement in defense of their somewhat rocky relationship.

"Look," she began, "we saved each other that day we met. I never for one second thought I was going to fall for this stereotypical redneck, or his dog, but it happened."

She drew a smirk and a snicker from Sutton after her redneck comment, but she continued with some momentum.

"You've been hurt, losing Jacob, and your old campground before him. This world has a way of taking everything from us, but maybe we can make something good out of the hand we're dealt. And if it doesn't work, we can always walk away."

She looked him in his unblinking eyes, trying to read his expression, which now remained stoic and neutral as he breathed in through his nose.

"It's all I can ask," Gracine finished, leaving the decision up to him.

Sutton took another glance around, prudent as could be about their safety, saying nothing for a few seconds.

"I'm in," he said, being a man of few words once again, causing Gracine's heart to pound in her chest as she heard exactly what she wanted to.

"You mean it?"

"I don't say things I don't mean. If we get through this, you and I need to give it a try."

"Even if we're no longer welcome at Maplewood?"

"Even if."

Once again, the sound of a motorcycle upshifting reached their ears, and Sutton looked through his scope for a few seconds.

"Another one is leaving the area," he reported. "Something has them stirred up."

"Probably something we did. Or they don't believe Dan and Brooke came alone."

"Why would they? It's unlikely anyone would walk this far."

"Guess we didn't think of that," Gracine conceded, though she knew finding a vehicle to make Metzger's arrival with Brooke more plausible might have taken hours, or another day.

Both she and Sutton sensed danger near them at the same time, and as they turned around, they found a man, silhouetted by the sun, approaching them with a pistol in his left hand, and a shotgun in his right. He was already close enough to use either weapon on them, and she knew Sutton would want to fight, rather than surrender, so she clasped his nearby arm to keep him from pulling a weapon.

"Don't even think about it," the approaching man said in a gravelly voice, pointing the weapons directly at them.

He appeared to be wearing gear for riding a motorcycle, which included a thick, black leather jacket, and chaps over his blue jeans. The glaring sun behind him made it difficult for Gracine to pick out details, but his head appeared shaved, and his sunglasses were perched atop his head so he could have a better look at the intruders.

"What are you two doing out here?" the man inquired, not moving the guns an inch away from them.

"Looking for lodging," Gracine answered, not giving Sutton a chance to escalate the situation.

"This is a private residence," the man said, not budging. "And most people use binoculars instead of a rifle scope."

"You can never be too careful," Gracine retorted. "Is this *your* place?"

She asked, trying to discern whether this man worked directly for Nadeau, or the group had fallen into another, different trap. She guessed him at slightly under fifty years in age, which wasn't typical for Nadeau's zealots.

"I'll ask the questions here," the man said, and Gracine began to question if he was loyal to Nadeau, or found motivation in some different form. "What are you really doing here?"

Gracine knew they couldn't answer the question honestly, or they placed Metzger and Brooke in danger before they even learned anything inside the facility. She watched as Sutton rolled over, covertly pulling his sidearm from his stomach area and letting it lie on the ground beneath his back in case he found the opportunity to use it.

"We're here seeking a man named Nadeau for sanctuary," Gracine said, leaving everyone else in their group out of the picture.

"Nadeau?" the man questioned with furrowed eyebrows, his confusion obvious despite his details being shadowed with the sun behind him.

"You're guarding someone," Sutton said, finally speaking up. "We know it's him."

"The person we're guarding is important," the biker said. "Once my fellow peacekeepers arrive, we'll get answers out of you two."

"Peacekeepers?" Gracine questioned. "Is that what you call yourselves?"

"No. We call ourselves the Five Horsemen of the Apocalypse. Five Horsemen for short."

"Why?" Gracine wondered aloud.

Before answering, the man grumbled, as though growing irritated with them asking questions in return.

"Because there are five of us. And it *is* the end of days."

"Tell us who you're guarding," Sutton said, growing irritated with idle conversation, and having firearms pointed directly at him.

"A very important politician," the man answered, not lowering the guns.

Now Gracine and Sutton exchanged perplexed expressions.

"*One* politician?" Sutton questioned. "Out here? That's bullshit."

"Think what you will. I don't give a shit."

When the sound of a motorcycle engine in the distance sounded as though it drew closer, both Gracine and Sutton questioned whether to act, or take their chances with additional bikers. Gracine couldn't imagine why Nadeau would have such a setup protecting him, but she didn't want to find herself in a worse scenario.

She saw little choice, however, because even Sutton couldn't outdraw a gun already trained on him. As the sun became obscured by some clouds, she began to read the weathered face of the man before them, seeing he meant business. Perhaps he once served in the military, but he wasn't a ruthless killer because he hadn't shot them outright. His hazel eyes locked on them as the sound of a motorcycle drew closer.

"Don't even think about it," the man said, causing Gracine to look at Sutton, who had begun slowly reaching his hand behind him.

"No," Gracine whispered, not wanting to see him killed over wounded pride.

Everything that transpired over the next few seconds caused a whirlwind in Gracine's mind. The roar of an incoming motorcycle was soon replaced by the armed man screaming at Sutton as he dropped the pistol to clutch the shotgun with both hands. Sutton, being his stubborn self, refused to be anyone's hostage. Gracine saw his hand clutch the pistol along his back, knowing he would never get to fire the gun. To his credit, the biker gave Sutton every possible inkling of time to change his mind, but as Sutton's forearm began to emerge from behind him, gun in hand, the biker fired the shotgun directly at Sutton's stomach.

Screaming as she turned away from the impending horror, Gracine felt something brush along her back, imagining it was part, or pieces, or her boyfriend.

***

Father Paul fought his way around the gated community, weaving between trees and the undead on his way to the cabin. He knew the way there, as he accompanied residents during several trips to drop off, or retrieve items from the crude building. He actually had the inside track to the cabin once he got to the other side of Maplewood. If Sister Rosa got blocked by the undead, or they began to follow her, she would have to take a longer, looping route to the cabin.

His weapon wasn't light enough to be used on the run, so occasionally he would stop long enough to deal with a threat so too many zombies didn't start tracking him. He kept up a steady jog, but cardio exercise wasn't his forte, so stopping allowed him to catch his breath while he disposed of a few primal adversaries.

Occasional screams of panic, or close calls, caused the priest to turn around with concern for his fellow Maplewood residents. He couldn't help them as much by returning to the village as he could by helping eliminate Hewitt. He knew the Bible told him that pursuing another human being for the sole purpose of killing them wasn't morally right, though he recalled numerous wars being fought in those ancient stories, and God often chose sides based on His chosen.

Deciding to press onward, Father Paul stopped when a small group of five zombies impeded his path. He dared not let too many follow him, because these stragglers had already broken off from the pack, or didn't have enough stimulation to keep them interested in Maplewood. Taking up his weapon, he carefully handled the hilt, stabbing one squarely in the forehead before retracting the sharpened edge. He jabbed at the next closest adversary, a woman dressed in sweatpants and some kind of Japanimation cartoon tee. He caught her in the temple, which reached the brain in the process, causing her to drop before he could pull the modified crucifix away.

With three members of the undead closing in, the priest struggled to pull his weapon free. To buy a few seconds, he kicked one of them back, allowing him to spy an opportunity lying on the ground. He picked up a rock slightly larger than a softball and rammed it into the forehead of the next closest zombie. It didn't fall, but instead began groping and biting at him. He began striking it several times in the face while grabbing it by its greasy and matted hair until it grew quiet and limp.

Finally able to pluck his weapon free from the fallen zombie, he jabbed at the next attacker's forehead, careful to stab and retract in one motion so his weapon didn't abandon him again. It worked, and he used both hands to turn the opposite end of the weapon toward his grasp. Remaining careful not to handle the coagulated blood on the pointed end, he grasped the center of the lengthy piece of metal, closer to the hilt. He waited for the last pair of undead to draw close to him, and used the pointed ends of the hilt to jab each of them in the sides of their skulls, by swinging the weapon left, then right, to strike both of them down.

He tore the shirt from one of the downed undead, cleaning all three sharp tips of his weapon before continuing. Much of the time, he kept stoppers of rubber, or cork, on the ends to keep anyone from getting cut by the weapon in Maplewood. His primary concern at the moment centered around him accidentally cutting his hands and infecting himself. Had he been better prepared, he would have brought some sort of work gloves to protect his skin.

His mind wandered briefly to Sister Rosa as he picked up a jogging pace once again. Often, they worked as a team, garnering kills against the undead while protecting one another. He didn't want her to arrive first, attempting to take on Hewitt alone. By the same token, he didn't like his own chances of facing the mass murderer without assistance. He had already decided if he needed to die to bring down the monster who brought hundreds of undead to Maplewood, Father Paul was ready to meet his maker.

More undead staggered ahead of him in every direction, and he began to wonder how many of them never reached the walls of Maplewood. Thankful his fellow residents faced less danger, he attempted to duck and weave around the nearby zombies, his concern growing for Sister Rosa and the four residents who first spotted the horde.

Wishing he carried more than his crucifix weapon and a knife sheathed at his side, Father Paul felt some relief that he wore a protective jacket over his shirt and collar. Some form of nylon, the plain, beige jacket worked in the warmer weather because it wasn't insulated, but the material provided some protection against bites. It also kept him from getting scratches and cuts when ducking through shrubs and trees to avoid the undead.

Now farther from Maplewood, the sounds of chaos began to deaden, leaving the small wooded area eerily quiet. Nature dared not make a sound with so many undead around, and the zombies typically made noise only when they spotted something that looked eatable. Sticking to his wooded surroundings, Father Paul finally found little danger around him. He felt his body relax a bit as he slowed to a walk to catch his breath momentarily.

For some unbeknownst reason, a memory entered his head of him during his teenage years, sitting at dinner with his parents. His father, a farmer with religious convictions, provided him with a proverb because he hadn't begun looking for a summer job.

"Idle hands are the devil's workshop, son," he said.

His father explained that being idle, or bored, led to nothing except mischief and laziness. Back then, it prompted a young Paul McNulty to deliver newspapers on his bike all summer. Now, although the words didn't *exactly* describe his current motivation, they made him feel as though he could be doing more to reach the cabin sooner.

Picking up his pace, the priest kept looking around, hoping for a sign that Sister Rosa navigated the infested Virginia landscape to catch up. Perhaps she was ahead of him, closing in on Hewitt, which spurned him to return to a jog, despite him laboring to catch his breath. Daily walks helped very little with his cardiovascular conditioning when he needed to travel a mile with deadly obstacles.

Drawing his knife, he picked up the pace, jabbing a few undead in the sides of their skulls as he scurried past them, assuring few of them followed in his wake.

Venturing outside the walls of Maplewood helped him adapt to surviving against the undead the past eight plus months. Jogging closer to the edge of the small woods, Father Paul saw daylight ahead of him, and silhouetted in the light, he felt positive he saw the devil, complete with horns, pitchfork, and a pointed tail. Slightly apprehensive, thinking perhaps Hewitt had a flair for being eccentric, he held his knife close to his chest, and as he drew closer, he found a member of the undead. Parts of the illusion stemmed from shrubs and tree branches, but he felt the odd vision provided him with a warning of what lie ahead. He held up his arm, giving the zombie a quick puncture to the head, silencing it as a growl began emanating from its throat.

When he emerged from the grove, he found quite a sight ahead of him. He saw the car the four adventurers took to go fishing, because he had used the same vehicle himself several times. It appeared intact, with the trunk open, so he approached, and discovered a truly horrific sight when he drew parallel to the vehicle.

Several undead staggered around the area, but centered in the turmoil ahead of him, he saw Hewitt standing with a riot shield planted in the ground beside him. Covered in various skins and blood smears, the man was breathing heavy, as though he had just survived an ordeal. On the ground beside him, a fresh corpse continued to bleed out from the neck, which was against the shield, because the device had been used to decapitate one of the men on the expedition. Still throwing several dying twitches, the victim had likely been murdered just before Father Paul emerged from the woods.

He walked closer, without fear, carrying his weapon as he sheathed the knife. His blood boiled from anger, as his face flushed, and he fought to maintain his composure so he didn't die needlessly. One wrong move against Hewitt meant the end for many an adversary, and he knew a collected mind was his best chance of besting the man.

Or at least surviving.

Behind Hewitt, Karen Brown lie motionless against the cabin as the odor of gasoline reached the priest's nostrils. Her face looked bashed, so red that someone might have thrown a strawberry pie into her face and no one would know the difference. While she wouldn't have won any popularity contests in the village, she deserved better than a brutal death at the hands of a sociopath. Despite their differences, her husband Samuel would likely be devastated if she was indeed dead.

In the distance he saw another motionless body that appeared to be Matt Davison, the former corrections officer. A man who could take care of himself, he was somehow bested by Hewitt, and the priest could detect no rise and fall of his chest to indicate he was still breathing. Father Paul continued to walk closer, and although Hewitt had yet to acknowledge him, the sinister being knew of his presence.

A few steps closer brought the final victim into view as Father Paul spied Mike Mullins struggling to prop himself up, blood emerging from his mouth. He had either been stabbed, shot, or had his insides brutalized so badly that his internal organs bled. He appeared completely unaware of his surroundings, as though in shock. Silently, the priest prayed for the souls of Mullins and the other three Maplewood residents, because they were almost certainly departing the physical world. Either way, he was now alone against the man who cared not who he confronted. Both Hewitt and Father Paul were tired, and winded, making the fight a bit more even.

"You are the epitome of evil, my son," Father Paul said, causing Hewitt to look at him with curiosity as the priest removed his jacket, revealing his black shirt and clerical collar.

Hewitt stared momentarily, internally deciding something.

"Even I have limits, Father," he finally said. "I have no interest in murdering a man of the cloth."

"Like you murdered my fellow citizens? People I live with, Mr. Hewitt?" Father Paul paused a few seconds for effect. "People I care greatly about."

"There's really no need for this," Hewitt assured him. "Your death wouldn't mean a thing to me. Go back to your people and comfort them, as they'll be suffering and dying."

"No," Father Paul said firmly. "You and I have unfinished business."

Hewitt scoffed, his fingers tapping the riot shield before him before he took it up, simply staring at the priest. Father Paul angled the modified crucifix to an attack position, prepared to begin the fight without his reliable companion. He hoped she wasn't harmed, but he needed to focus on the task at hand.

"Why would you throw away your life so recklessly?" Hewitt questioned.

Father Paul further assumed his attack stance, his face stern and determined as he put one shoulder forward.

"A shepherd must protect his flock."

Chapter 33

A simple code gained access to the bunker for the guards, though Metzger and Brooke were shielded from seeing the combination by the second man. When the door opened with a theatrical hiss and sigh, one of the men motioned for the visitors to go first. Metzger stepped inside, finding it dimmer than he imagined, with only the occasional inset light along the walls to guide them, like generator lights that kicked on when the power went out.

As his eyes adjusted, and he walked forward, Metzger realized they were high above the living quarters of the bunker. Space wasn't wasted as the stairwell ahead descended to another platform where they walked another ten to fifteen steps before descending again. A cursory glance down from the second platform indicated they were just short of a few hundred feet above their objective.

"No elevator?" he inquired.

"The boss doesn't like using the energy reserves," one of the guards answered.

"Makes sense," Brooke noted.

Metzger began to realize they were likely about to meet Nadeau for real. Brooke's paperwork proved legitimate, and he couldn't imagine the guards letting them inside, much less near their boss, if something seemed amiss.

A little more than halfway down, Metzger noticed some doors along the walkways between sets of stairs. He theorized that various bedrooms and common areas occupied much of the bunker space. No one wanted to live in a bunker, but seeing it was a long-term commitment, any resident would want some space, things to occupy their time, and amenities they enjoyed on the surface.

Powering the bunker didn't appear to be an issue, and as they drew closer to the bottom of the facility, Metzger had counted a dozen doors on the levels above him. Along the bottom, the bunker branched out with several hallways in various directions. Although the bunker felt and looked incredibly sturdy, Metzger noticed how drab the place appeared. No attempt was made to give it color, or any personality, as though it were run by a military installation.

"Where is everyone?" Brooke questioned the two men.

"There aren't many of us here," one answered.

"I thought this was supposed to be a sanctuary."

"It's a destination. One of many."

Now Metzger felt disheartened. Had they simply come all this way for nothing? Was this yet another depot, just larger in size and scale?

"So, what's next?" Brooke asked.

"We're close," the second man answered. "You'll see."

Metzger let his eyes wander, and he was amazed how large the facility was, particularly because it didn't appear recently built. If he had to guess, he might have placed it in the 1960s or 1970s through casual observation of architecture and building techniques over the years. He saw a kitchen, what he would call a game room with various arcade and family games on tables, and a room of relaxation, complete with sofas, chairs, a large television, and huge speakers. Metzger began to think someone important set up this bunker with modern equipment before the apocalypse hit, *knowing* the future.

He possessed little doubt that a government bunker would have supplies, food, and some creature comforts, but this appeared as though someone planned to live here long-term.

Several more rooms awaited them down the corridor, but their armed guards took them to a small room that seemed like a foyer, or coat room by size comparison. Once all four were inside, the men didn't threaten them, or draw their guns, but they appeared very stern about their impending request.

"We need you to leave your weapons and packs here," the first one stated, and his tone indicated the matter wasn't up for debate.

Brooke set down the pistol and knife she possessed, making certain the two men made note of her compliance, before she unshouldered the pack she carried and plopped it on the small, stainless steel table inside the room. Metzger removed his backpack, which also carried the short sword he carried with him. He placed his father's .357 Magnum on the table as well, not thrilled about being separated from his belongings.

At this point, Metzger felt reasonably certain they were going to meet someone important. If not Nadeau, then one of his lieutenants or trusted loyalists. Metzger knew he couldn't keep following leads if Nadeau's labyrinth never led to anything concrete. Brooke chose to check every lead available to her, and it cost her the one relationship she had left in the world. If the person they were about to meet wasn't Nadeau, he felt certain they would both be lost, without answers, and the mastermind of the apocalypse would remain free.

Taking an extra moment of precaution, the two men patted both Metzger and Brooke down, ensuring they hadn't concealed additional weapons.

Neither had, and the men appeared content to move to the next phase of the tour.

"You arrived with everything in order," the second man said, "but we can never be too careful. We've only had a few visitors, and some people have changed their tune about what the boss stands for."

Metzger struggled to hide his surprise, because he legitimately believed they were about to meet Nadeau for the first time. A glance toward Brooke didn't tell him her thoughts, because she appeared determined, perhaps even angry about something. He dared not ask, because he couldn't risk blowing their cover, assuming it was even intact at this point.

Now the two men guided them to a room in the last wing that the pair hadn't yet visited. A few rooms branched off to the side, but the main area, octagonal in shape, housed furniture, a large stereo system, two mammoth televisions, a fully-stocked bar, and even a day bed off to one side. Five of the eight walls held floor to ceiling bookshelves, and Metzger couldn't find a spot to stuff an additional book along any of the shelves. Two oscillating fans occupied opposite ends of the room, though neither ran at the moment. Again, every item in the room appeared expensive, and new, as though the main occupant of the bunker planned to be here ahead of time.

At the opposite end of the room, a man sat in a chair with his back to them. Metzger could only see that the man had a full head of brown hair, and he appeared to be reading a book. Surely the guards had alerted the man that he had company, and almost assuredly this staged scene was part of an elaborate act put on for Metzger and Brooke.

"We brought you company, boss," one of the men said, prompting the man to put down his book after initially acting surprised.

When he turned around, Metzger recognized the face immediately. Although Jean Pierre Nadeau wasn't the most famous, or wealthy person in the world before the world collapsed, he was in the top ten financially. Had he made more of a splash in the controversial sense, more worldly citizens might have known him, but he wasn't married, and didn't make an ass of himself on social media. Being Canadian, he kept a low profile as well, despite many of his investments being located in the United States.

"Welcome," he said with a smile. "I can only assume you've traveled a long way to find refuge."

Despite living in solitude, the man maintained his handsome features, complete with flawless skin and a haircut that appeared professionally trimmed. Nadeau maintained his color, and looked fit, as though he found time to work out between his plans to dismantle the planet. He wore clothing suited to his old lifestyle with color, soft materials, and fashion sense allotted to models and the wealthy.

"We served you for months before making our way here," Brooke said, and Metzger questioned whether she wanted to get into a conversation that might bring up details.

Details neither of them were prepared to reveal, because they hadn't lived in service of Nadeau.

"You didn't serve me," Nadeau said, his smile beginning to fade. "You served the cause. The greater good."

Metzger fought to maintain a neutral expression. Part of him wanted Brooke to signal him to turn around and attack the two guards with the hope they could neutralize them and have their way with Nadeau.

"But you didn't serve me at all," Nadeau said after a few seconds, his expression turning downright sour and vengeful.

He pulled a pistol from the arm of the sofa where he had been sitting, aimed it at Brooke, and pulled the trigger before Metzger could even react and jump in the way. The round struck her in the lower right abdomen, and she hunched over as blood began spewing from the wound. She looked up at Nadeau with shock in her eyes, as though she fully expected her plan, and everything she had worked for the past eight months, to reach her endgame.

"I know all about your orders to monitor my activities, and bring me down, Miss Palacio," Nadeau said as Metzger went to aid her. "Don't, Mr. Metzger," Nadeau added, loosely aiming the gun in his direction. "I'm very cross with you for murdering Mr. Clarke. He was a loyal friend, and an asset to the operation."

"You bastard!" she spat with as much energy as she possessed, taking a step toward him before the two guards intercepted her.

She pressed both hands against her wound, attempting to stop the bleeding on her own.

Now Nadeau addressed his two henchmen.

"Take her to one of the holding rooms. Leave her there to bleed out, and make sure she doesn't escape."

Each of the men cupped Brooke by an armpit, and she didn't appear in much condition to fight with a bullet lodged in her body. She struggled to breathe, and kept moaning from the pain as they dragged her back the way they had come.

"You needn't return," Nadeau called to them.

He focused his attention on Metzger before continuing.

"We have much to discuss, Dan," Nadeau said, holding the firearm, but not aiming it at Metzger. "May I call you 'Dan'?"

"You're the one with the gun," Metzger noted, implying the wealthy man could do as he pleased.

"Let's have a seat," Nadeau said, motioning for Metzger to sit in one of the chairs as he returned to his sofa.

"Does the same fate await me?" Metzger questioned, referring to the cold-blooded act Nadeau had just committed.

"I certainly hope not," Nadeau answered. "Miss Palacio was aiming to bring me down this entire time. I doubt half of what she told you was true, because her entire career, and life, were about deception."

Metzger shook his head negatively.

"You disagree?" Nadeau asked.

"I'm not sure you're good at reading people."

"That may be true," Nadeau conceded with a smirk. "I'll admit I don't like most people. It's people that brought our planet to the brink of extinction."

"Is that why you did what you did?"

"We'll get to that," Nadeau answered earnestly. "I've learned some things about you, Dan. I know that you blame me for the death of your parents. Fair enough. I also know that you and your brother possess an immunity to the concoction I whipped up to lower the world population."

Metzger said nothing, but his curious expression gave him away.

"I have people out there," Nadeau said. "Even after the world transformed, *especially* after the world transformed, I was able to recruit people. You'd be surprised what people will do if you promise them supplies and meals. Even the military your brother works for isn't safe from my prying eyes. The politicians think they've placated me, but they don't know that I'm stalling for time."

Metzger grew concerned with each fact that Nadeau revealed to him. Being pragmatic, Nadeau wasn't going to unveil his entire evil plan and let his guest walk away to potentially inform the military, and anyone that would listen. Nadeau spoke very eloquently, though his personality seemed a bit awkward, as though he bordered on the spectrum of autism and didn't function well in public settings. Most people with wealth thought far too highly of themselves and projected confidence, and Nadeau simply spoke a linear tone of what he considered facts.

"Surely, you're not planning a second attack," Metzger stated, unable to mask his revulsion at such an idea.

"I have plans," Nadeau revealed. "The first wave didn't accomplish everything I'd hoped for."

Now Metzger scoffed, his thoughts venturing to Brooke, and her suffering, instead of his potential death.

"How much is enough?"

"As long as there is a threat to this planet, my work isn't finished."

"I'm not sure I understand all of this."

"We have so much to talk about, Dan. Can I offer you some food? A beverage?"

"I'm good," Metzger answered, unenthused about sustenance after watching one of his allies being shot like a rabid dog. "What, exactly, do we have to talk about?"

Nadeau put his arm across the top of the sofa, propping one leg up on the other, getting comfortable. In his right hand, he still held the firearm, though he didn't bother pointing it directly at Metzger.

"Your story resonates with me," Nadeau revealed, being honest so far as Metzger could tell. "You sought me out because you blame me for the death of your parents."

"I can't argue that. They'd be alive today, if not for you."

"Life doesn't come with guarantees, Dan. Any number of things could have killed your parents, or you, if I never set off those bombs."

"Something tells me you didn't personally deliver any bombs."

Nadeau gave a thin smirk.

"You'd be surprised how dirty my hands got. I had followers, but I didn't have *that* many. When you own a trusted company that's made hundreds of deliveries, guards get complacent and don't check beyond the surface of the trucks and pallets you bring them. I relied heavily on human error, and they didn't disappoint."

"That day," Metzger said foggily, his mind returning to the previous summer. "I remember it like 9/11, only it was so much worse."

"I'm sorry you went through that, Dan," Nadeau said without any inflection in his voice.

"Are you? I remember my neighbors attacking one another. Attacking *me*."

Nadeau nodded, possibly trying to put himself in someone else's shoes for a change.

"I'm glad you survived," Nadeau said. "And I'm glad you made it here."

"Do you plan to use me as a guinea pig like the government?"

"No," Nadeau answered, openly dismissing the notion. "I don't need you for that. My team developed a cure for the infection before we even released it."

Metzger shook his head, unable to fathom the words as they entered his ears. Now he knew one of the answers he so desperately wanted to hear from the beginning. He thought back to the losses he endured along the way, starting with Albert in New York, and now Brooke, with several in between.

"As we sit here, your brother and the residents of Maplewood are fighting for their lives."

Metzger grew angry at the words, shifting slightly in his seat.

"Not at my doing," Nadeau added, sensing his agitation. "A horde of the undead are at their gates, likely led there by an old enemy of yours."

"How could you possibly know this?" Metzger asked, unable to hide his awe at the web Nadeau weaved.

"I have eyes and ears everywhere. Military bases, cities and towns, and even overseas. There's more to be done in other countries."

Metzger recalled that Canada fared little better than the United States, so Nadeau's operation certainly didn't show favoritism.

"What is your endgame?" Metzger asked, genuinely confused, yet curious. "You've already wiped out virtually everyone on the planet."

"So long as governments have power, and their military, a threat remains."

"What threat?"

"To our planet, of course."

"I still don't understand."

"Then allow this to be the part of the story where the hated villain reveals the entire scope of his evil plan to the protagonist. I won't hold anything back. You deserve to hear the truth, and I'll answer any questions you have."

Metzger felt for the first time that Nadeau really didn't intend to kill him. He wasn't certain why the man held him in any special regard, because he didn't possess any usefulness to the billionaire mastermind like he did the military.

"Why would you do that? I'm no one special."

"*Because* of that. You aren't a cop, or a trained assassin. You risked life and limb to find me, so the least I can do is give you the answers you're wanting. We having nothing but time, and I confess I don't get much company these days."

Metzger's mind returned to Brooke, wondering if she could escape her predicament long enough to assist him, or if her injury would indeed going to end her life. He also worried about his allies around the compound, and his brother, stuck in Maplewood, dealing with Hewitt. Metzger couldn't help any of them until he found a way out of the bunker. Accomplishing that meant playing along with Nadeau until an opportunity presented itself.

"Fine," Metzger said, playing along. "I want to hear everything. But first, I think I'll take you up on your earlier offer. I could use a drink. Preferably something with a kick."

Nadeau grinned, giving a friendly nod.

"One double coming up."

End Volume 4.

www.ingramcontent.com/pod-product-compliance
Lightning Source LLC
Chambersburg PA
CBHW060427310726

48977CB00001B/79